Innocence Lost

Book 1 of the Bootleggers' Chronicles series

Sherilyn Decter

Innocence Lost is a work of historical fiction in which the author has occasionally taken artistic liberties for the sake of the narrative and to provide a sense of authenticity. Names, characters, organizations, places, events, dialogue, and incidents are either products of the author's imagination or are used fictitiously.

Print ISBN: 978-1-9990014-0-7
EPub ISBN: 978-1-9990014-1-4

Edited by: Marie Beswick-Arthur www.mariebeswickarthur.com
Cover Design by: JDSmith Designs www.jdsmith-design.com

Innocence Lost

SHERILYN DECTER

Chapter 1

Philadelphia has not yet lost its soul. It's still the early days of Prohibition. Sure, you can see the rot around the edges beginning to creep in, but people, for the most part, are enjoying the thrill of being lawbreakers. The times; they're dangerous, but not yet deadly. Bootleggers are still the boys from down the street, and hooch still has a bit of quality control to it. Hell, the most dangerous thing about the Twenties, so far at least, is hemlines. Those short skirts are trouble.

You can smack your lips at the scandal of it all. Everyone has a bit of an outlaw in them, don't they? Many of the good people of Philadelphia are secretly thrilled to be able to thumb their noses at a senseless bit of government regulation imposed by morons in Washington. It's a buzz to sneak out to the local speakeasy, get in with a secret password, and tip back a refreshing swig of illegal booze.

Ah yes, that inevitable illegal booze. Stashed in old warehouses; some of them are by the river, some close to the tracks, all hidden from view. Brick carcasses of abandoned enterprise, those warehouses now bustle with new business. Risky business. Bootlegging.

Inspector Frank Geyer leans against the brick wall inside one such warehouse. Shrouded by shadow, he is a dapper old gent, his walking stick resting beside him. The high shirt collar, heavy woollen suit, and thick moustache over a neatly trimmed beard paint him from a different generation.

The slow draw off his cigar provides fuel for his dark thoughts. Frank doesn't see the glamour that his fellow Philadelphians seem to be enjoying; the comfortable danger, the shaking off of the heavy burden of the recent Great War. He's been trained to recognize crime when he sees it, regardless of the cheap dress it wears. Like a bloodhound, his heightened senses catch that faint whiff of decay.

'Death is nothing. But to live defeated and inglorious is to die daily.' Perhaps Napoleon was right. Certainly, 'inglorious' is a good description of Philadelphia these days. But have the bootleggers and corruption managed to defeat her? Have we lost the fight so easily? Have I been reduced to this: an old man standing idly by? Maybe Philly isn't the only one defeated.

Dark thoughts, indeed.

Melancholy, even philosophical, Frank draws in warmth from his cigar as he watches a dozen young men load large, wooden casks onto the flatbeds of three trucks. They appear too nattily dressed for the work they are doing. They joke, familiar with each other and with the task at hand, eager to get the trucks loaded and the deliveries made—there will be money in their pockets tonight.

Two men cradle tommy guns and guard the operation. Their feet are solid on the dirt floor. They speak quietly around the cigarettes that dangle from their mouths.

Moonlight through murky windows boosts the weak lighting under which the young men labor. Two wooden garage doors, slightly ajar at one end of the warehouse, expose the frozen ground of February and invite its chill inside. Winter keeps the dust down.

Crates and barrels line the walls, several rows deep. Open rafters store boards, hoses, tarps, ladders, and the other paraphernalia common to buildings of its type. Off to one side are tables covered with tubes and funnels, used sticky pots of glue, and stacks of paper labels. Boxes of empty glassware are stacked around the operation.

He'd been taken too soon, but Frank's sense of duty rejects the imposed boundaries he now labors under. Continuing his thoughtful watch, he muses on the developments during the past four years since Prohibition was enacted. The menace of the bootleggers is expanding. Criminals have grown in power and influence. They've been a plague on his city. He concedes, though, that the arrival of Colonel Smedley Butler as Director of Public Safety has finally got the police making more of an effort to crack down on the bootleggers, moonshiners, and rum-runners. Hopefully, Butler will attack corruption with the same zeal.

The media has dubbed Colonel Butler 'the Fighting Quaker'. Because of his own training, Frank admires the cut of the man. With Butler's military background in the Marines, he's bringing new tactics and discipline to the task. And as an outsider, he adds the appearance of integrity to the process, something that has eluded previous crackdown efforts.

Frank knows the colonel hasn't been on the job for long, so they will have wait and see if his changes stick. While Colonel Butler has been closing more speakeasies and gin joints in his first two weeks than had been accomplished the whole of last year, there are judges on the take who are as busy flipping the padlocks back open on them just as fast.

Back in my day, the cops were the heroes who caught the villains and brought them to justice. People respected the law. Those were better days. The front line is faltering. Am I the only one that sees it?

Despite his cynicism, Frank sees potential in the new director.

Butler, now there's a man of action. A man you can look up to. All I'm good for is standing watch. Napoleon Bonaparte was right, death is indeed nothing. There are worse things. I was born to serve and protect. An old sheepdog standing between his flock and the wolves. But I'm not even that anymore, am I?

S

Frank's thoughts are interrupted. In a far back corner, he can see three small boys have pushed open one of the high windows on the wall. From their waving arms and pointing fingers, the group appears divided about climbing through or staying outside to watch. A convenient ladder leaning against the wall decides it. They scramble down.

The trio are caught up in their own world of adventure, but thankfully are aware enough of the danger to be taking care not to be seen. Bundled in overcoats, the earflaps of their woollen caps meeting their tightly wrapped scarves, they creep behind boxes and crates, always staying in the shadows, out of sight. Frank begins to move in their direction, but is distracted by the workers near the trucks.

"How much more time we got left, Gus?" shouts one of the workers.

"Lots. Twenty minutes. Maybe more," Gus answers. "We'll be outta here in plenty of time before they come in. And Porter, when you're shooting, watch the windows this time, okay? I don't want to have to go up there and fix another one."

"Cutting it pretty fine, ain't they? Maybe they could come early and help us load these barrels? They get heavier every time," Porter says.

"Less complaining and more lifting. We got a schedule to keep," a man with a clipboard hollers back.

There's a lot of activity in and around the warehouse tonight. When Frank arrived, he saw a squad of Philadelphia police outside, enjoying a smoke while waiting for the signal. And now these young boys are here. Frank knows what's ahead. This warehouse is no place for children, especially tonight. Even if he can get close to them, they'll not hear a thing he says. He curses inwardly at his powerlessness to help them. Hopefully the boys will leave before the police begin their supposed raid.

* * * *

"Hey Jimmy, isn't that your uncle?" The medium-sized boy whispers to the boy in the lead.

"Yeah, Uncle Charlie. He's been working with Mickey for a while. Ma says the money's good, 'though my auntie worries," answers Jimmy.

"My pop worked for Mickey before he got sent up, and my brother Ernie quit school last week to join up with Mickey's crew. He's a runner," the medium boy brags in a low voice. "And if I'm lucky, he says I can be a runner next year, when I'm bigger."

"You're lucky, Oskar. That'd be a swell job," whispers Jimmy. "Hey, Tommy, wouldn't that be swell?"

The smallest boy nods, eyes wide. Plenty of young boys can imagine nothing finer than being part of Mickey Duffy's gang. Tommy cranes his body to try and see around his two friends. "Do you think we'll see Mickey tonight?"

A worker stretches then arches his back, working out the kinks.

"*Shhh.* Get down, you guys," whispers Jimmy.

"We should scram. It's way past dark and Ma's going to skin me if I'm late again," says Oskar.

"Mine, too." Tommy echoes the concern. He nudges Oskar. "Hey, isn't that one of those new tommy guns?" he says, pointing to one of the guards.

Oskar punches Tommy's arm. "Named after you, I suppose?"

Tommy shoves him back.

"Come on you *idgits*, cut it out. They'll hear you," whispers Jimmy. "We got front row seats. Don't wreck it."

"Think there's going to be any action tonight? I'd love to see those choppers lit," Tommy whispers. "They call 'em Chicago Typewriters in the newspapers, on account of the noise. And they can shoot nine-hundred rounds a minute. Nine hundred. That's twenty rounds every three seconds. Can you believe it?"

Oskar rolls his eyes. "I can't believe you did all that math."

Jimmy shushes his friends.

"I didn't say nuthin." Oskar complains in a soft voice.

A hand grabs Jimmy's shoulder. "You lads shouldn't be here. Get on home with ya now," a policeman whispers.

Surprised, Jimmy yelps and bumps against a crate.

"Hey, who's there?" shouts one of the workmen. Instantly, the crew pull handguns from shoulder holsters. The men with the tommy guns swing around and turn in the direction of the noise.

Two uniformed policemen appear at the door, raising their guns and shouting orders.

"Philadelphia police. Drop your guns."

"Drop your guns or we shoot."

"Ah crap, it's way too soon," says the policeman who's with the boys.

The bootleggers' guards swing back and open fire, tommy guns spraying bullets at the walls above the door. Police at the door return fire, their shots aimed above the workers' heads.

At the gunfire, the boys attempt to scatter. The policeman lunges, grabbing two of the boys—one in each hand. He pulls them behind wooden boxes for cover.

Workmen swing into the cabs of loaded trucks. They rev the engines while remaining workmen rush to try to load the last few barrels onto a remaining truck. They won't dare leave all the beer unloaded; more concerned about their boss's reaction than a handful of Philadelphia police.

* * * *

With the first shot, Frank scans the warehouse urgently. *The children. Where are they?* He heaves a sigh of relief to see the shadow of a policeman standing beside the crates the boys had been behind.

None of the gunfire is doing any damage. Frank's not surprised that the bullets fly high and wide. *Another sham raid for the statistics and tomorrow's headlines. Another bunch of police on the take. Oh, my brothers.*

Frank had hoped for more than just a show. He takes his walking stick and strolls toward the warehouse doors. Along the way, he checks that the boys are still well-hidden, protected. *They'll be safe now that the copper is with them.*

The drama unfolds around him. Bullets fly as he moves through the chaos without a ripple. He leaves it behind and heads into the crisp, winter night.

The three loaded trucks tear past Frank, careening out of the warehouse. They cross the yard at breakneck speed. Men cling to the sides of the truck beds, shooting over the heads of the police. Police cars give chase, lights flashing and sirens wailing. Frank continues his steady pace, unnoticed.

* * * *

The bullets stop flying after the trucks and bootleggers pull out of the garage. The policeman with the boys waves his arms, trying to get the attention of his fellow officers. "Hey, there are some kids here." He's ignored by the other policemen who are now creating mayhem in the warehouse. Shouting, yelling, smashing. The adrenaline of the gunfight still pumping. And, of course, stealing. The order was to get rid of the booze after the raid, but they didn't say how.

As soon as the officer lets go, Jimmy and Tommy bolt.

Hiding from the policeman, they reach the ground and crouch behind a bench seat that's been pulled out of a car and left leaning against the wall. They hear strikes of axes followed by wooden barrels cracking, and the shattering of glass bottles filled with whiskey. Tommy covers his ears. The sweet smell of beer floods the warehouse.

"Come on. Let's get outta here," says Jimmy.

"Where's Oskar?" asks Tommy.

"He got a head start. Lucky he didn't get caught. Probably waiting for us outside." Jimmy nudges Tommy. "Come on, we gotta go."

Tommy peers out from around the edge of the car seat. He looks back at the open window and across the floor to the open door. "The window's too far away and they'll catch us for sure when we go up the ladder. I say we try for the door."

Jimmy pokes his head out from behind the bench seat, gauges the distance and the risk, and nods. "Okay. Let's go."

Head down, Tommy tries to keep the remaining crates and barrels between himself and the cops. He races across the open space toward the warehouse door. An officer shouts, "Hey, stop."

Other voices follow. "It's some kids." "I told you so." "What the hell?" "Grab them."

Tommy's arms and legs pump, his breath loud in his ears. More shouting. All he can see is the open door. He stumbles, regains his balance, and keeps going. Feet pound close behind.

"We're almost there," Jimmy shouts.

Tommy makes for the front gates, aiming for a parked car to use as cover.

When he turns to check on his friend, Jimmy slams into him. "Don't slow down. Go. Go." Jimmy shoves him hard in the direction of the street corner.

Tommy gasps for breath, one hand on the parked car and the other on Jimmy's shoulder.

Jimmy grabs his hand and tugs Tommy toward the corner. "Come on, Tommy. Let's get out of here. There's cops all over the place. We'll be in so much trouble if they nab us. They'll turn us in for sure."

"But where's Oskar?"

"You're so slow, he's probably home by now. Come on, move." Jimmy takes off down the dark street.

Tommy follows Jimmy into an alley. Their running footsteps echo on the quiet streets, the sounds at the warehouse fading as they move away from the raid, away from the violence and chaos of what Philly is becoming. The boys sprint for the safety of home.

Chapter 2

Close to the waterfront with its docks, mills, factories, breweries, and tanneries; the Northern Liberties district in Philadelphia is a mecca for immigrants. They're looking for work and wanting to set down new roots in the fertile soil of America. The streets are teeming with newcomers: Irish, Germans, central-European Jews, Poles, Lithuanians, Russians, Latvians, Ukrainians, Hungarians, Slovaks. It's a gregarious, global stew: different languages reverberate, cooking smells of regional dishes fill the air, different cultures and religious observances are practiced cheek and jowl.

Running along the far edge of this delicious fusion is Marshall Street, the commercial center of this vibrant and diverse neighborhood. Making their way home from school for lunch, Jimmy and Tommy bob along in the current of the street's commotion. The smells make their noses twitch and their stomachs growl: heady yeast aromas from the rye and pumpernickel breads baking, garlic and spices from the pickle barrels, the smells from the cigar-chomping men carrying hot corned beefs dripping fat high in the air from the kitchen to the cart, and the fish—oh, the stink of the fish.

A rare treat in February, the midday sun brings warmth to the bustling commercial neighborhood. Trollies clang their bells and roll along tracks running through the center of the busy street. Passengers onboard lean their faces against the sun-warmed windows. A steady stream of cars and horse-drawn delivery wagons are part of the flow. Winter coats are unbuttoned some, hats pushed back to take advantage of the bright day. Even the towering wooden poles, strung with electrical and telephone wires, appear less frosty.

Everyone jostles for space. Loud, male voices warn or greet over honking horns. Many merchants have lowered their awnings to shade the window displays. Others have put their merchandise on the sidewalk, hoping to attract passersby. The pushcarts are on the street, merchants and customers haggling. Pedestrians weave around each other, hurrying about their business. It's a different city than the one last night—not a tommy gun in sight.

Tommy and Jimmy pick up their pace. Growing boys are always hungry, and the insistent demands of their growling stomachs keep them moving past the distractions. Eventually, they turn the corner onto the residential street where they live. The uniformity and calmness is a stark contrast to the hubbub behind.

The boys walk through a neighborhood built to accommodate Philadelphia's rapidly expanding growth. The houses are thrown together overnight, speed over craftsmanship. Narrow, brick rowhouses line the sidewalk, each dwelling identical except for the color surrounding the window sashes. Between every two units, a short flight of stairs rises to a shared, wooden veranda where housewives shake mats and young children often play.

Along the sidewalk, a parade of newly planted trees with thin bare branches wait for spring. They've been planted with the long-term vision of becoming stately shade trees. Their roots are taking hold as an unconscious symbol of a more established future for the people living inside houses where the smell of plaster and wallpaper paste still linger.

As they trudge along, Tommy looks sideways at Jimmy. "Did you see Oskar today?"

"No, you?"

"Nope." Tommy kicks a stone along the sidewalk.

"Maybe we should go to his house after school," says Jimmy. "I bet you he didn't study for this morning's test, so he's pretending to be sick."

"That's probably it," says Tommy, nodding. "Got home too late to study."

"He better not tell his Ma where we wuz at."

"That was pretty wild last night."

Jimmy grins at Tommy. "I'll say. Did you see how fast they pulled out of the warehouse? I thought those barrels of beer were going to roll right off the trucks. And the cops were no match for the tommy guns." Jimmy pretends to fire the machine gun. "*Rat-a-tat-tat, rat-a-tat-tat!*"

Tommy copies him. "*Rat-a-tat-tat.*" The boys dart around, chasing each other with their imaginary guns. "Do you think that cop is going to rat us out to our folks?" Tommy asks.

"Nah, how'd he even know who we are? We never told him our names," Jimmy says, and grabs hold of Tommy's arm. "Just make sure you don't tell. We'll all be in real big trouble if anybody finds out."

Tommy nods at him solemnly. He's no rat.

Jimmy spits in his hand and shoves it at Tommy. "Swear you won't tell."

Tommy grabs it tight. "You neither."

A sacred ritual cemented with wet spit.

Tommy grins. "Holy cow, I didn't think I could run so fast."

"Ha, you weren't so fast." Jimmy gives his friend a shove.

"Faster than you. You run like your sister," says Tommy and takes off. Jimmy gives chase, easily beating him to the corner. He waits for Tommy and they continue, heads close, recreating stories from last night's adventure.

*****

Further along the street, inside one of those brick rowhouses, Tommy's mother, Peggy, goes through the mail that has just landed with an ominous thud in the front hall.

She winces in shame that the postman would have seen the familiar "Past Due" notice stamped in red ink on the front of the grocery store envelope. Unless circumstances change soon, there will be another envelope next week, and the week after. She didn't think the tightening in her chest could get worse, but she was proved wrong with the next envelope. A letter from her mother.

Her mother's regular letters always have the same theme: *Come home. Your living in Philadelphia is an embarrassment to your family. The neighbors wonder why you're not with us now that you and your son are alone.*

While her mother rarely phrases it quite so plainly, Peggy can read between the lines and knows the judgemental message will still be there. *It just isn't done in polite circles, a young woman living alone, even if she is a widow. And the boy—he needs a strong man to look up to; a man like your father.*

Her mother's rigid, hidebound approach to the world is from an earlier time when women were merely adornments of their husbands, dependent for security and a place in society. And that place was well-defined, with no exceptions. Society would gleefully tear you apart if you stepped away from the narrow path prescribed a lady, which is exactly what Peggy had done when she'd run off with Jack.

In her mother's day, women abided by rigid expectations. Peggy wishes her mother were more modern, but recognizes the futility of her wish.

Mother's attitudes are as rigid as her posture. What does she know about my circumstances and what my life is like? There are a lot more women on their own raising kids than that old relic will ever admit. At least two war widows on this street, and they're managing. And what about the women whose men are in jail? Heck, there're probably as many families without a man at home as not.

She squares her shoulders, rehashing old arguments. *Mother is off her nut if she thinks I want my son anywhere near Father. If it wasn't for him, Jack would still be alive. Hell can freeze over before I share a roof with that man.*

Peggy stomps toward the kitchen, clutching the envelopes tightly.

Although she's still a young woman, time and fate have scoured away much of Peggy's youthfulness. The shock of losing Jack, the crushing burden of never having enough money, the strain of raising Tommy on her own, and the relentless anxiety about the future have dulled sparkling eyes and carved deep worry lines into her forehead. Bouncing ringlets have been squeezed into a practical knot at the nape of her neck, and traitorous threads of gray are starting to appear. She'll go gray early, like many of the women in her family. Today, Jack would be hard-pressed to find the carefree scamp of a girl he had married seven years ago.

Peggy pulls her threadbare cardigan tighter. The last four years following Jack's death have been difficult. They'd had only three years together before he died. She'd been a coy sweetheart, a young bride, a young mother, and then suddenly a young widow, but grief and hard times have taken their toll.

What she wouldn't do to see Jack's smile. He was always in good spirits; nothing ever got him down. But if she's being honest, he's not in her thoughts as much as he should be. There are many days when worry and exhaustion drive everything but the harsh day-to-day reality from her mind. Thank goodness for Tommy, who's the spitting image of Jack.

And thank goodness she has the house. She and Jack had jumped at the first house they could afford, especially with the baby on the way. They hadn't thought about the false economy of what a cheap purchase price might actually cost them. The ongoing maintenance and repairs on their cut-rate house—albeit a large house—were ruining her now. And they certainly hadn't thought that it would be just her left holding the bills. Thank goodness she owns it free and clear; one more bill would be the end of her.

Peggy throws the envelopes onto the kitchen table. She won't complain too loudly, though. As bad as it is, it could be worse. There are a lot of widows who have to live crowded together in much smaller places. The four bedrooms upstairs give her some options. As does the small room Jack and the neighbors had tacked onto the back of the porch off the kitchen. They had originally planned to use it for newly landed immigrants passing through; now the rent from it will put food on the table. The idea of a bit of rent money coming in and Peggy can almost see daylight.

Kitchens are often described as the heart of the home, and Peggy's is no different. There are no modern conveniences; she relies on the wooden icebox and a wood-fired stove. Her dishes are neatly tucked away in a glass-fronted cabinet that stands next to a wall-hung porcelain sink. On the other side of the sink is the kitchen's work-horse,

20

the wooden Hoosier cabinet with its flour-bin sifter, and various drawers and nooks and crannies for storing kitchen staples.

The letter from her mother lies on the top of the pile of offending mail. *I need a cup of strong coffee before I can tackle it.* Glancing at the clock, she realizes that Tommy will soon be home from school, looking for his lunch. The thought reminds her again of the near-empty icebox and the outstanding bill from Howard, the grocer. *What am I going to do? What happens if he stops letting me buy my groceries on account? Who knew young boys could eat so much?*

She'll water down the soup, again, after she's read her mother's letter. There's just enough in the pot for one last cup of coffee. *That will have to do.*

Peggy settles into one of the three mismatched wooden chairs at the kitchen table. She sips a little of the steaming coffee, then picks up the letter. She knows exactly how it will begin: a name her mother intentionally uses to erase life with Jack, and to ignore the present. Jack always called her Peggy.

> *Dearest Margaret,*
> *Your father is extremely disappointed in you.*
>
> *We were shocked when we saw the advertisement you had placed in The Inquirer. In my day, a respectable woman was only mentioned in the newspaper three times: at birth, when she married, and in her funeral notice. She certainly didn't take out an advertisement, looking for boarders.*
>
> *You have no idea the comments I had to endure from Mrs. Galbraith at the Garden Club. I really must insist that you stop this nonsense immediately and return home. A*

21

*daughter's duty is to her parents. It's our responsibility to
see to your security. Think of your reputation, Margaret.*

*Your father and I have tickets to the theater for
Thursday. We will call around prior to the performance to
discuss the matter further.*
Until then,
Your loving mother.

There it is again, grating along her already raw nerves. *Margaret.
Mother does it just to annoy me. Disappointed in you. When isn't she?
Think of your reputation.* Peggy snorts. *Reputations don't put groceries
on the table, reputations don't feed hungry, growing boys, which are
much more pressing concerns than the opinion of Mrs. Galbraith, thank
you very much.*

Peggy's toe starts to tap as the hand holding the letter curls into a
fist. *Loving mother? Controlling, yes; rigid, yes; but loving? Ha! She's
always been more concerned with the opinions of that stupid Garden
Club than how I feel.*

The letter is tossed away as the front door bangs open. Tommy
charges down the hall. "Ma, I'm home," he shouts. He bounds into the
kitchen. "What's for lunch?" Tommy sheds his outer coat. Underneath,
he has on a shirt and tie, argyle vest, and a jacket that's a bit too small.
Knickers and knitted socks complete the outfit. Tommy often complains
that winter is one long, prickly woollen itch.

Peggy grimaces. "Tommy, a boy with good manners says 'Mother'.
You are not one of those foreign boys from down the street. And there
is no yelling inside this house, young man. You know better. Now, go
hang your coat and wash up. I'll get your soup and bread."

Tommy tosses his coat onto the hook by the back door and heads over to the sink. He turns the tap, but all that happens is an ominous gurgle. He looks at his mother, alarmed.

"Not again. That's the second time this month," Peggy mutters under her breath. *Where am I going to find the money for another plumber?* "It's all right Tommy, just wipe your hands on the dish towel. Come sit, I'll get your soup."

Hunched over his bowl, Tommy devours his soup and bread, chattering on about his day. Peggy continues to twist the handle on the sink faucet, busy reconciling the diminishing household budget for the month against this latest crisis. *Maybe I can pick up a few more shirts to mend from the Bright and Clean Laundry. It'll be spring soon, and warmer...*

"And I wish I could run as fast as Jimmy. Oh yeah, and Oskar wasn't at school today."

... so I can maybe cut back on the coal order?

"Mother, did you hear me? Oskar wasn't at school today."

"Oh, is he sick?" she asks, listening with only half an ear.

"We had a test today and he missed it."

Peggy's head snaps up. "And how did you do on the test? You know you're going to need top grades, young man, if you're going to get into Boys' Central High School in a few years."

Tommy kicks at the table leg. "I don't wanna go to that stupid school. Nobody else has to go."

Peggy gives Tommy a stern look. Then she catches a glimpse of the clock and hurries to grab his coat. "Tommy, the time. Off with you now. And bring home that test tonight so we can look it over after dinner." She hands him his coat and pecks his head.

"And don't slam the..." The front door slams. She carries his empty soup bowl to the sink, turns the tap, and the pipes rattle. Still no water.

Chapter 3

What am I going to do now? The house isn't that old, but it's falling apart. The cupboards are bare. The plumbing barely works. Tommy's clothes are all too small. I'm so tired of trying to make ends meet. It's not supposed to be this hard.

Peggy sits, elbows on the table, and rests her chin in her hands. This is definitely not the life she bargained for when she ran off and married the dashing Jack Barnes. That girl had rushed starry-eyed down a road of romance and adventure and into his rebel arms. He was so handsome: tall, strong, a wicked grin, bright blue eyes. It was thrilling to work side by side with him. To be caught up not only in Jack, but in the work he was doing: fighting for workers' rights, passing out handbills, late nights at this very table writing letters to politicians, signing up new members at the rallies. Passionate times.

During the Great War, America had needed men like Jack to build the mighty warships. Thousands of men had been hired at Hog Island Shipyards, working 'round the clock to make sure America and its military had the ships they needed to win the war. And when that glorious day finally happened, there was no further need for battleships. Thousands of welders like Jack were laid off overnight. Other trades too, and on down the line of suppliers and others dependent on the shipyards. All turned out on the street.

Jack and the rest of them had been so proud of the work they did to fight the Huns, and then to be discarded so abruptly. But Jack and those in the labor movement would make sure that they didn't go quietly, that they would get the respect they deserved. After he and his pals had been let go, Jack had joined the fight for their rights, Peggy at his side. That had caused a bit of a stir; she was the daughter of Hog Island's chief accountant, the second in command—the man who controlled the purse strings at the shipyard. Peggy's parents were adamant she should have been home in their parlor pouring tea, not waving placards and shouting demands for fair treatment.

And that's not all she and Jack had been up to. Passionate times, indeed. A baby.

That rebel spark still flickers, not completely stamped out by reality. *Now I shake my fists for other reasons. A single mother has other foes to battle.* No longer the carefree girl; these days, she's a widow, a single mother of a hungry son, estranged from her family, isolated in a neighborhood of foreigners—people she chooses not to mix with. They're just not her kind of people.

The pressure from her mother rests alongside the opportunity to walk away from hard times by considering Howard's marriage proposal. The lesser of two evils? As the owner of his own grocery store, he would be a good provider. He's also kind. Tommy likes him. But he's twenty years older than her, and a walking example of the effects of a generous diet.

People married for love, not security. People like Jack and Peggy married out of pure passion. No, she couldn't marry someone like Howard after being wed to someone like Jack.

Peggy knows she is out of options. Death benefits from the union had run out the year after Jack was killed, and the small amount of money she is able to make taking in piecework for the laundry isn't enough to fill the icebox, let alone repair the plumbing. Jack's parents aren't able to help much anymore, being in tight financial circumstances themselves. She's sold everything she could bear to part with, and there is absolutely no way she'll humble herself and crawl back to live under her father's roof again. Penniless she might be, but she still owns this house.

Peggy is good at maintaining the façade of coping, during the day, in front of Tommy. But the dark hours during the night, tossing and turning in her bed, are a different matter. Daytime is all about the mountain of chores that need to be done. Nighttime brings anxiety; tomorrow lurks at night. What new hardships and calamities will the future bring?

The house is always full of worry. In her darkest moments, Peggy worries that she is letting Jack down and failing as a mother. She's concerned that she's not giving Tommy a secure childhood. She frets about having no money. Peggy imagines a row of gremlins perching on the end of her bed, each squawking a different tune. *Is he getting enough to eat? Will you be able to afford to send him to Boys' Central? What if he wants to learn to play the piano? Sure, he's never wanted to play the piano, but what if he did?* Those three-in-the-morning gremlins are large, ugly, and persistent.

A black cloud hovers over Peggy at her kitchen table as she stares at the taps. Backed into a corner, she has considered selling the house, but this house, shoddily constructed as it was, is the place where she and Jack had built their dreams. Though they had such a brief time together, there are still memories: the laughter when he got wet paint on his nose redoing the trim in the living room; the time she burnt the chicken when his parents came for dinner; Tommy had been born here and taken his first steps into Jack's outstretched arms.

Despite hard feelings her father and the role he may have played in Jack's death, Peggy is her father's daughter. She understands the differences between assets and revenue, liabilities and expenses. Her house is her only asset. The money from the sale would need to be spent on rent and would eventually run out, leaving her penniless again. Selling the house might buy her time, but it isn't a long-term solution to her problems any more than marrying the grocer is.

She rereads her mother's comments about the advertisement. Peggy is glad she placed a newspaper ad for lodgers. Desperate times call for desperate measures; there are precious few options open for a woman on her own. She may be backed into a corner, but she is going to come out fighting.

And, of course, there's the added benefit of her mother shuddering when Peggy becomes an official landlady. How old do you get before you stop enjoying tweaking your mother's nose?

Peggy considerers phoning the plumber for a return trip, but she remembers he has also sent a past due notice. She drums her fingers against the tabletop, plotting. She could postpone buying a new shirt and jacket for Tommy, which would help a bit. She could also get the butcher to give her soup bones again. Those savings might pay off the existing plumbing bill. Then she could ask the plumber to come again, on credit. *Around and around we go, like the carousel at the fair.*

Judgement glares at her in the form of her mother's letter. *There's no way I'll ask her for help. And I'm not selling my house. And I'm certainly not going to marry Howard.* She knows independence and financial security rides on the success of this afternoon's interviews with potential lodgers.

Chapter 4

What forces a single mother of a young child to become a business woman? To open her home to strangers? Money? Security? Stubbornness? Pride? Or is it an inner drive, perhaps not even acknowledged, to enter the world of commerce? Setting up shop as a landlady. For Peggy, it is all of those and more.

In the 1920s, women are becoming resourceful, discovering new confidence. Peggy's plans exceed her address. It scares her and excites her. Without her vision and ingenuity, it would be easy to drift back to the privileged life she had run from. She is caught between the proverbial rock and hard place, her mother being the Rock of Gibraltar.

The parade begins promptly at two. Peggy meets each potential lodger in her living room, its formality setting the proper tone.

Peggy loves this room. It is cool and serene, with as much elegance as she and Jack could afford. From the gold-striped Empire couch that her mother had grudgingly given her, to the mantle with its shiny brass carriage clock that sits beside the framed photo of she and Jack on their wedding day, the living room is a showpiece for Peggy's aspirations. The fact that the furniture is strategically placed over the worn spots of a threadbare Aubusson rug is something she deliberately pushes from her mind.

Peggy sits stiffly. Throughout the afternoon, she has been conscious of not letting her spine touch the back of the chair. It was the way she was raised. It's important to her that the applicants understand what kind of house they might be living in, and the expectations she will have of any occupant.

To make ends meet, she needs three lodgers, but most of the applicants she's interviewed are too coarse or too loud. Worse, one leered in a manner suggesting he'd want more than room and board in the arrangement.

She rejects a trolley car driver, two mill workers, and a pastor. She's accepted a bookkeeper and a teacher; good influences on Tommy, not to mention their steady income providing on-time rent payments. *Two down, one to go. One last chance to get this right. My kingdom for another schoolteacher.*

The last applicant is a young police officer. There is a scrubbed earnestness in his sharply pressed uniform; a sense of pride in the way he holds his cap. Yet, Peggy hesitates, considering whether it's wise to open her home to someone in the thick of the violence and mayhem that's developing in the city. Her mother has always warned her about inviting trouble to her door. *Oh, why couldn't you have been an English teacher, Mr. Policeman?*

She taps the handful of reference letters he's handed her. "Constable Kelly, your people are Irish, are they?"

"Yes, Mrs. Barnes. And please, call me Joe." Usually a confident young man, Joe is feeling awkward sitting in front of this stiff woman in her stiff living room.

Determined to remain a disciplined interviewer, Peggy looks at him over the top of the papers. "Oh, I don't think so. Please continue, Constable Kelly," she says, emphasising his title and name with a clipped tone.

"Yes, ma'am. We're originally from Kilkenny. Me family has always worked the coal mines there. But then me mam and da' came to Ardmore, back in '95, I think it was. I was born and raised in Ardmore. That's a little ways up on the Main Line, ma'am. Me da' works in the

Smedley-Mehl Coal and Lumberyard there. I guess you could say we've always been in coal." Joe turns his police cap in his hands.

"And your duties as a policeman. Do you often come into contact with criminals, Constable Kelly?" Peggy asks.

Joe's laughter echoes around the room. "Well ma'am, it's kind of hard to be a policeman and not come in contact with criminals." He chuckles again, but stops when he sees she hasn't intended it as a joke.

I've already got an accountant and a math teacher. Do I need a police officer? Is that wise? Maybe if I wait to put out another advertisement, there might be a geography teacher in the next batch. Sheesh, what am I thinking? I can't wait.

Joe takes a deep breath and tries again. "I'm honored to have been chosen to be part of Enforcement Unit Number One with the Philadelphia Police. Colonel Butler handpicked me himself, ma'am. We both believe strongly in upholding the law. He says that laws are what civilize us and that he aims to enforce the laws, even if it tears him apart. He said that to a newspaper reporter. Did you happen to read it?"

Joe leans forward, a missionary full of enthusiasm for his subject.

"Colonel Butler says, if we don't have laws, that we can't have a civil society. And ma'am, I'd say right now, in Philadelphia, that's pretty much true. With people not respecting and obeying the laws, we don't rightly have a civilized society. At least, that's what the colonel says. And it all starts out harmlessly enough. I mean, who doesn't like to have a swig of beer every now and then?"

"Constable Kelly, let me assure you that this is a dry household," says Peggy, her hands folded primly in her lap.

"Of course, ma'am, I'd expect nothing less from such a fine, upstanding lady like yourself. But like I was saying, it starts out with a beer. If you're already breaking the law to enjoy the beer, it's not that hard to have another. And if you have more than one or two illegal beers, and are feeling full of yourself, then maybe you'll go over to that fellow who's been annoying you and punch him right in the nose. And before you know it, there are blotto drunks brawling in the street, speakeasies, and professional skirts standing on every corner."

"Oh my, Constable Kelly."

"Sorry ma'am, I forget me-self and me good manners, spending so much time with the lads and all. Coppers can be a rough lot, you know. Living here would be good for me, I think. It will remind me of why I'm working with Colonel Butler."

Peggy hears a lot of Jack's passion in Joe Kelly's words. Jack wasn't a teacher or an accountant, and Jack was decent, driven, committed. Jack was her everything. "And are you comfortable with the rent, Constable?"

"Well, it is a bit of a stretch, ma'am, what with me having to give them pols, I mean them politicians at City Hall, their due. It works out to one day a month from me pay to keep this job. But don't get me wrong. I love being a cop, and Colonel Butler is a fine man. It's a privilege to work with him. So, yes ma'am, I will pay the rent. Every month."

"I've been reading about Colonel Butler's exploits. The newspaper's photo shows him striking quite the figure, with a scarlet cape and all that gold braid. He seems to be pretty determined to rid our city of the bootleggers and speakeasies."

"He is very determined. And successful, too. Did you know that Philadelphia had twelve-hundred saloons at the beginning of the year and we've already managed to close almost a thousand of them?

Although I guess some of them was joints closed more than once, but still, a grand number. The colonel has only been on the job a couple of weeks. We've been working day and night at it. You know, ma'am, I was in his office when he hired me for the First, and he has two Medals of Honor, a Distinguished Service Cross, and a bunch more medals I don't even know the name of. He's a real war hero. The most decorated Marine in America, they say."

Peggy sees the hero-worship shining in his eyes. "Certainly commendable, but it all may be a bit more... more *active* than I was looking for in a lodger. I have an impressionable young son. I'm not sure exposure to all that front line action would be a good thing."

Joe looks crestfallen. "I understand, ma'am. I do. It's just I'm sleeping on me pal's couch, and there are a lot of us in the house. I'd been hoping to find a place a bit more quiet, the kind of place that me mam would like. She's not happy with me living here in the city. She'd rather I went back to Ardmore and work the coal with me da'."

Peggy weighs the looming plumbing bill against the consequences of adjusting her strict criteria that she was relying on to protect her from any risks. But there was something about the young policeman. *It's important to keep to high standards, but then, Jack hadn't worn a suit and tie every day.*

Peggy says, "I suppose it would be like me doing my part to make our city safe again." *This whole boarding-house effort is a risk. What's one more? In for a penny, in for a pound.*

Peggy taps the edges of the papers against her knee, aligning them neatly.

"All right. I'm pleased to say that you can stay here, Constable Kelly, but on probation only, mind. Three months and then we'll evaluate whether the arrangement is working out." She rises and reaches to shake Joe's hand. "I'll accept a deposit now, and your rooms are ready if you want to bring your things around first thing in the morning. I expect that, unless you're working a shift at the police station, you'll be sitting at my dinner table tomorrow at seven sharp."

"Yes, ma'am."

"And when you arrive in the morning, please have the rest of the first month's rent with you."

"Yes, ma'am, and thank you, ma'am."

Joe is still smiling and nodding when the front door bangs open and Tommy, all noise and action, roars into the house. He comes to an abrupt halt when he spies the policeman in the living room with his mother. He turns and tries to make a hasty retreat down the hall.

Peggy calls after him. "Tommy dear, please come in and meet Constable Kelly."

His slow, small steps are not missed on his mother.

"Now," says Peggy.

Tommy takes two more steps into the room. Peggy goes over and leads him to where Joe is standing. His shoulders remain hunched.

"Constable Kelly, this is my son, Tommy."

"Tommy, this is Constable Kelly. He's going to be staying with us as a lodger."

Joe extends his hand. "Hello, Tommy. It's a pleasure to meet you. I'm looking forward to living here."

Tommy's shoulders relax. "Oh, I get it now. Staying with us. You're going to be one of Mother's lodgers." Tommy focuses on the constable's badge that Joe has pinned to his chest. "That's swell. Nice to meet you, sir."

Joe keeps a firm hold on his hand. "Nice to meet you, too. Say, you must be, what, six?"

"Almost seven, sir."

"Big enough, eh? You and I should have a chat about the neighborhood, young man. I'm sure you'd be able to fill me in on all kinds of things."

"Umm, yes sir."

"Soon, now. All right?"

"Yes, sir," says Tommy, backing out the door.

"Young boys tend to see and hear things adults may not notice," Joe says.

"I'm sure that you're right, Constable. However, I should tell you that my son does not spend much time with the neighborhood children because of his school homework. He's very clever and hoping to go to Boys' Central High School in a few years," says Peggy.

Peggy does a quick calculation the moment Joe is out the door. She'll put the teacher in the room beside her bedroom at the front of the house; the young policeman can take the room at the top of the stairs next to Tommy's; the accountant had seemed eager to get the tiny room off the kitchen. With the policeman's hours, she had a moment's doubt about the room assignment, but a policeman closest to Tommy felt right.

With three lodgers and their first months' rent payments, she'll be able to pay the outstanding plumbing bill, and put some money on account at the grocer. She hurries to pull on her hat and gloves. She'll go over to Howard's grocery store to use his phone and call the plumber for tomorrow morning, and while she's there she'll get a chop for Tommy's supper.

Mother and Father will be furious when I see them Thursday, but I'll have a cake to serve, and water to make coffee. With a satisfied smile, Peggy busily makes a mental list of groceries and other items she needs to buy now that she has an income.

Chapter 5

Peggy's mattress hasn't felt this comfortable for years. She stretches, a grin on her face. For the first time in ages, it feels like the curtains have been flung open and sunshine is pouring through the windows. What a difference a day makes. From desperation to landlady in less than twenty-four hours. It is exhilarating to face all comers and emerge victorious.

And that good feeling carries through the day. "Don't slam the—," Peggy laughs over Tommy's energy, and celebrates her own, enjoying washing the dishes in hot, sudsy water. *There is something so very satisfying about cleanliness and order.*

She drains the water and starts to dry the dishes in the rack next to the sink. *Whatever was wrong with the taps can't be that hard to fix... it only took him a few minutes, for goodness sake. All that money, but at least the water is running again.* Peggy has a satisfied smile as she puts the cutlery away.

The plumber had almost not come this morning, not until she had promised to have the money from the previous bill ready for him before he started the work. And she had had to promise to pay him for today's job before he left. *Those days are behind me, now that I'm a landlady.*

With the rent money, she'd also been able to put a little down at the grocery store, as well. Howard had been flustered when she handed him the funds to put on her account, and how he'd hemmed and hawed about accepting it. Fortunately, he'd not mentioned the proposal. And neither had she. She wasn't going to be beholden to anyone if she could help it. Feeling flush, she'd indulged and bought a small bag of sweets for Tommy.

The tapping at the back door is so light she mistakes it for her own sounds of putting dishes away. Peggy rarely gets visitors; none of her foreign neighbors mix with her, or she with them. She'd envied Jack's innate ability to mix with all people. The tenants had moved in this morning before they headed off to work, but all have keys. The plumber had come and gone. Perhaps he'd forgotten something? And, if this was her mother, she'd use the front door.

Peggy dries her hands on the dish towel and opens the door to a short, round woman, her head wrapped in a floral scarf. "Yes, can I help you?"

The woman twists the ends of the headscarf. "Missus Barnes, sorry to bother, but my boy, Oskar, he no home last night or night before. You see him?"

"Oh, Mrs. Leszek, isn't it?" *The Pole from down the street. Tommy's friend's mother.* "I'm sorry, but I haven't. Perhaps Oskar is at school?" Peggy blocks the doorway.

"No Missus, I go there first thing," says Mrs. Leszek.

"Well, I don't know where he is. I'll ask Tommy when he gets home from school."

Mrs. Leszek steps onto the threshold, preventing Peggy from shutting the door. "Maybe, Missus, you could help me look for Oskar? Please?"

Peggy pushes against the door, preventing her neighbor from further entry. Her mother has trained her not to mix. She's made a point of not getting to know her neighbors too well. But this woman needs assistance. The angel on her shoulder pulls one way, the devil the other; Peggy's emotions swing between the two.

She remembers the Leszek family now. Mr. Leszek is in jail—bootlegging or fighting—and with a brood of children at home, it can't be easy for Mrs. Leszek. Haunted by knowing that Jack would dive in and help, Peggy continues to struggle against the urge. *If I say yes this time, there will be a steady stream of 'them' at my back door, looking for something.*

"I'm so sorry Mrs. Leszek, but I'm very busy this afternoon. Maybe your own people can help you? I will talk to Tommy and let you know what he says. Now, I really must get back to my work." The door, and Peggy's resolve not to be involved, is stronger than the woman who is blocking it.

The dish towel is returned to the oven door handle. *I'm sure her boy's out there somewhere getting into trouble, just like his brothers and their father. These people are different than we are. Tommy's too much like his father—a friend to all. I'll talk to him after school. Tommy needs to know this Oskar is going to be a bad influence on him, what with not coming home at night.*

Peggy tidies up in an effort to not think about Jack and how disappointed he'd be by her behavior. Now Jack, he had loved sitting on the back porch with the neighbors, a bottle of vodka and a plate of pickles resting on the step. Together, the men had hung clotheslines, repaired roofs, tinkered with cars, and complained about the Phillies ball team. Jack had even convinced her that he could build an extension off the kitchen to help house immigrants looking for work. She'd allowed it—a compromise so as not to have a stranger in one of the bedrooms upstairs. But, he died before it was even used.

In the rest of their neighborhood, people would be in and out of each other's kitchens like they were their own. And Jack was one of those people. He'd gently tease her when she hung back from going to the potlucks, and when she made excuses for not sitting at neighbors' kitchen tables. He never understood that she had little in common with these foreign women and no interest at all in getting to know them better. The way she'd been raised was not the way he'd grown up.

Peggy rationalizes Mrs. Leszek's concern by telling herself that someone will help. Someone from her family's church, a friend of the jailbird husband, one of their own. *It's not my problem, Jack. Really, it's not my problem. This is what happens with bad influences. I've raised our boy properly. He'll have to stop hanging out with those kind of people. That'll keep him out of trouble. You can trust me, Jack. I'll keep Tommy safe.*

Thinking about Oskar Leszek gets her thinking about who would help her, heaven forbid something should happen to Tommy. Who would she ask for help? She knows none of her neighbors and she's sure her family wouldn't help. Peggy supposes she could ask Howard or, if her lodgers stay, she could ask them. *Thank goodness* I *don't have to worry about that.*

Peggy puts her hands on her hips and surveys her orderly kitchen. Apples shine in a bowl on the table, a trussed chicken in a roaster sits on top of the icebox, celery and onions are piled on the counter, and a bag of flour sits beside the canisters. "Now," she says to the heart of her home, "on to act two of 'The Landlady Serves Dinner'."

Busy at the counter, Peggy can feel the shadow of the back door behind her. *Jack opened that door to everyone. Maybe I'll mention Oskar to Constable Kelly at suppe*r.

Chapter 6

A satisfying afternoon of chopping, stirring, seasoning, and taste-testing, and supper is ready; despite the lingering guilt over Mrs. Leszek's situation. Standing in the doorway between the kitchen and dining room, Peggy surveys two of the new lodgers gathered at her dining room table. She savors the moment. With a contented smile, she smooths her dress over her hips. *No apron for me tonight. I'm the landlady.*

Peggy loves the dining room. It reminds her of childhood dinners cooked by staff. She recalls carefree afternoons, new clothes, and indulgences that provided a soft place to fall—until she fell hard for Jack.

The dining room suite had been a wedding gift from her grandmother, who never held Peggy's impetuousness against her. Peggy adored her for it. To her, the dining room suite's elegant Federal style implied a certain place in the world. She loved Jack and all he stood for; yet attempted to replicate that which she missed from her own childhood home. Jack used to tease her about it, his *Principessa*.

She and Jack had wallpapered the walls above the wainscoting, and painted all the woodwork a bright white to match the living room. At some point, she hopes to find a carpet to go under the table, but for now, the hardwood floors gleam.

A blue and white Spode soup tureen holds pride of place on the marble-topped sideboard. The tureen had also belonged to her grandmother and was part of the china dish set that she had left Peggy in her will. When Tommy was a toddler, he had broken the china ladle. Jack had glued it back together so that, with the tureen's lid on, the set looked perfect.

Peggy gracefully perches on the chair her lodger, Mr. Mansfield, holds out for her. She admires the table with its starched white cloth and blue and white dishes. The elegance of the Spode is a talisman for her, a symbol of where she'd come from, and a nod to better days ahead. She's sure there isn't a nicer set of china in any of the houses along her street.

The smile of her other lodger, Mr. Smith, suggests an air of occasion; their first dinner all together. Almost all together. Peggy taps her foot. Tommy is extremely late from school. He is only just washing his hands in the kitchen. Constable Kelly sent word that he will be detained, and asked that she put a plate in the oven for him. Peggy sharply snaps open her napkin and lays it across her lap.

What do boys that age get up to? Tommy and Constable Kelly's tardiness sets a bad example to the other lodgers, and is disrespectful of all my hard work putting together a delicious dinner for them.

When Tommy finally sits, his fidgeting causes Peggy to excuse herself and Tommy from the table before she's even introduced him.

In the privacy of the kitchen, she says to her son, "I need you to understand that taking in lodgers is necessary, Tommy. And I expect that you'll be courteous to our guests. We're running a business now, and I need you to behave." She hands him another jug of gravy and picks up the bowl of cranberry sauce she had forgotten.

Tommy's mouth is watering as he carries the gravy to the table. His stomach gurgles with delicious anticipation. It's been ages since they've had this kind of food. By the time he's in the dining room, his smile is the widest she's seen in a long time. "Save room for dessert," whispers Peggy, "I made apple crumble, and there's cream to go with it."

"Mr. Mansfield, Mr. Smith, this is my son, Tommy. Tommy, this is Mr. Mansfield and Mr. Smith, who will be living with us for a bit. Mr. Mansfield is a teacher at the Boys' Central High School. Tommy has aspirations of attending Boys' Central when he's older."

Peggy settles back comfortably into her chair at the head of the table. "I believe you mentioned that mathematics is your area, Mr. Mansfield?"

"Ah yes, Mrs. Barnes. I've taught mathematics at Boys' for ten years now." He accepts the bowl of mashed and sweetened turnips from Peggy.

Tommy glances up from his plate, rolling his eyes when his mother looks away. But that disagreeable fate is a long time in the future, and the plate of roast chicken is in front of him now. His smile returns quickly.

"And, Mr. Smith also has a background in figures. He's an accounting clerk. What firm did you say you're with, Mr. Smith? My father was an accountant with Hog Island Shipyards. He's retired now."

"I was with Lybrand, Ross, and Montgomery for a few years, but now I'm out on my own."

"Mrs. Barnes, I see we have one empty spot at the table. Who might our third lodger be?" asks Mr. Mansfield.

"Constable Joseph Kelly is with the Philadelphia police. Unfortunately, he has been detained this evening and won't be joining us for dinner. You'll have a chance to meet the constable at breakfast tomorrow."

Mr. Smith's knife and fork slip from his hands and clatter against his plate. "A police officer, Mrs. Barnes? Is that wise? With all the violence on the streets? Perhaps someone less notorious would have been more prudent?"

"Why Mr. Smith, I think that having Constable Kelly in residence will enhance our safety, not detract from it."

Eugene Smith, his face flushed, gapes at Peggy. She lifts her chin and returns the stare. Eugene takes a breath and looks at his plate.

"I'm sure you know best, Mrs. Barnes," he says.

After dinner, Tommy helps clear the table while Peggy fills the sink with sudsy water. They stand side by side, Peggy washing and Tommy drying. The first dinner was behind her; not quite as awkward as she'd feared. Even though, the anxiety of having outsiders in her home had made the dinner conversation stiff and formal.

Jack would have welcomed everyone with open arms. By the end of dinner, they would have all been fast friends. But I am not Jack. I am... Oh heavens, I am my mother. No, I won't let that happen. Tomorrow will be more relaxed. It will become normal to have three men at the table.

"Mother, I'm waiting for another plate. You stopped washing."

"Oh, right. By the way, Oskar's mother came by today. She said Oskar hasn't come home the past few nights. I told her I'd ask you if you'd seen him. Have you, Tommy?"

"No, Mother." He hoped she couldn't hear his heartbeat. "Jimmy and me worked on our homework last night and Oskar wasn't there." He looks at his mother sideways.

"Jimmy and I."

44

"That's right. It's what I said."

"Jimmy and I, not Jimmy and me."

"We were. Jimmy and I were doing our homework."

"Tommy, you've been wiping the same plate for ages. There're lots more to be dried." Peggy passes him a new one. "Oskar's mother asked me to help look for him. I said I was too busy. Can you see me trooping around the neighborhood? And with the lodgers and my new responsibilities, I am too busy."

"But Mother, maybe you could help. Oskar's one of my best friends. I told you, yesterday, he wasn't at school, and he wasn't there today either." Tommy pauses, staring at the plate. "It's not my fault he's not at home, but maybe we should help look."

Peggy doesn't reply, her hands in the sink.

"Well, I'm going to help, even if you won't," he says. Tommy puts the plate in the cupboard and folds his arms.

"Goodness, Tommy." Peggy is shocked to hear her son talk back to her like this. *No, this Oskar and his family are definitely not a good influence on my son.* "Look, young man, I'm not sure I like your attitude. There will be plenty of people looking for the boy, including the police. I'm going to mention it to Constable Kelly myself when he comes home. But we should let the authorities and his family look after this. It's best not to get involved."

Tommy scowls at his mother, the dishes forgotten. "What if he's hurt, Mother? What if he needs help? What if something bad happened?"

Peggy takes a breath and gets her bearings. Behind his scowl, she can see the worry in his eyes. She goes over and brushes some hair off his forehead, and puts a hand on his shoulder. "What's all this then? Hurt? Needing help? Why would you say that? I'm sure he'll turn up having been with his brother, up to no good no doubt. And when he does return, I don't want you playing with him anymore. He's from a wild family, and his father's in jail. He is not a suitable playmate for you, Tommy."

Tommy shrugs off her hand and throws his dish towel on the table. "That's not fair, Mother. Oskar is my best pal. You never do anything for my friends. Other mothers give us cookies and I get to play over at their houses all the time, but you never let them come here. I think you're mean. Mean to me and my friends." His lip is trembling and tears threaten to spill over.

Peggy is rattled by his outburst. "That's enough of that, Tommy. I think you have homework to do in your room, young man. Now march." Peggy nudges him out of the kitchen. *It's a good thing that there are some proper gentlemen living in the house now. He needs a good role model.*

Tommy pouts, kicking the doorframe on his way out. "Tommy," Peggy warns.

"Yes, Mother."

Peggy is staring after Tommy when there's a frantic pounding on the back door. Mrs. Leszek is standing on the porch. She's been crying. "Mrs. Leszek. Is it Oskar?"

"No Missus, Oskar no home yet. Does Tommy see Oskar?"

"No, I asked Tommy and he hasn't seen your boy, and doesn't know where he is."

46

"Maybe I ask Tommy?"

"No, I'm sorry but that's not possible. He's gone upstairs to do his homework. Goodnight now, Mrs. Leszek." Her uneasiness over the altercation with Tommy transfers to the woman on her porch. *I need her to leave before Tommy knows she's been here again.*

"Missus, we search tomorrow morning, first thing. I ask you again to help. Please?"

Peggy imagines her mother lecturing on separation, position, and 'those people'. *But this is so important to Tommy; Oskar is a good friend, apparently. What would Jack think?* Peggy hunches her shoulders against this reproachful chorus. It seemed that there would be no getting out of it. *Enough already.*

"I'm not sure I can help canvass the neighborhood," Peggy says with chilly dignity.

She hears Tommy groan behind her. Through clenched teeth she says, "I can help make coffee and sandwiches for the searchers. I will have Tommy drop them off at your house in the morning." *There, that ought to keep everyone happy.*

"Thank you, Missus. That is good. Thank you."

Tommy rushes into the kitchen as Peggy closes the back door. He wraps his arms around his mother. "Thank you, Mother. I can help you make the sandwiches in the morning before I go to school."

Peggy hugs him back. "Well, I'm glad that Oskar is your friend, because you'll be sacrificing the leftover chicken for the cause. Now, off to your room, young man. Future students of Boys' Central need good

SHERILYN DECTER

study habits. Especially when there's a teacher from there living in the house."

Peggy listens to Tommy scamper up the stairs. She surveys the tidy kitchen and turns off the light. Tommy is happy. Jack would be proud.

Chapter 7

Tommy's stomach churns as he knocks on the back door of Oskar's house. True to his word, he'd gotten up early to help make sandwiches. And he'd raided the newly filled cookie jar, stuffing a dozen oatmeal cookies into a paper bag—for the good of the cause. A large pot of coffee had been added to the wooden box.

He's not used to lying to his mother. And he's pretty sure something horrible has happened to Oskar. He really doesn't feel well. Wonders if he'll throw up. *Why didn't Oskar come home that night? Maybe he took off with his brother or uncle? Maybe Mickey Duffy decided that he was old enough to start working for the crew? But if all that were true, wouldn't he still be home to eat and sleep?* Nope, as far as Tommy can tell, something is really wrong.

Tommy knocks again, trying to balance the box. He chews on his lip and focuses on his shoes. Just as he decides he'll leave the box, the door swings open to reveal a burly, bald man. "Yeah kid, whatcha want?"

"My mother sent sandwiches and stuff for the searchers."

Oskar's mother's kitchen is crowded with people, but Tommy cannot see Mrs. Leszek.

"Put it on the table, kid."

Several women stand by the sink, their gray, worried faces staring out the window. Oskar's baby brother has been plopped on a blanket on the floor, banging a wooden spoon on an overturned tin. Next to him, a toddler chews on a toy car. At the kitchen table a trio of men are finishing bread and jam, and mugs of coffee. Smoke from a saucer of lit cigarettes curls toward the ceiling. Tommy recognizes Oskar's oldest brother, Ernie. He'd been at the warehouse. If Ernie's here and looking worried, then that for sure means that Oskar isn't with Mickey's crew. Tommy swallows hard. *Yup, something bad.*

They stand as Tommy lowers the box of food. Ernie reaches in and grabs a cookie from the bag. "Thanks," he says.

Coats are gathered as the men share plans for the search. "We're off now. We're gonna try down by the tracks again, and talk to the yard bulls. Maybe they saw something."

"He really coulda jumped a train. Tryin' to get to see his old man."
"He might be in another state by now."
"I'm sure he's okay. You know kids."
"Keep up the prayers."
"Say, did anybody check the docks out on Hog Island? Maybe he went down to the water?"

One of the women by the sink stifles a sob. The bald man goes to her and rubs her back. He makes soothing sounds and speaks to her softly in Polish, then he leaves. The kid on the floor whacks the baby. The baby wails. A woman takes away the wooden spoon, scoops up the baby and parks it on her hip.

Tommy stands in the middle of it all, shoulders hunched and his hands stuffed deep in the pockets of his pants. He looks to the women, hopeful for direction.

The woman with the baby picks up a forgotten cigarette. She takes a long drag, then butts it out in the saucer. She begins unpacking the box with her free hand. "You're the Barnes kid, right?" Tommy nods. "I knew your father. He was a good man. Thank your mother for us."

"Have you found anything yet?" Tommy dare not ask in more than a whisper in case he shouts out that Oskar was at the warehouse.

"Nothing yet. But we keep looking."

Mrs. Leszek drifts into the kitchen, swollen face and red eyes. Her hair hangs loosely down her back. She looks like a drowning victim. Tommy swallows, alarmed by the intensity of her grief. Adults are supposed to be calm and in control. Oskar's mother looks like she could fall apart at any minute. He realizes she is in her nightgown and not wearing a housecoat. He hardly has time to blush or turn away before she is surrounded by a group of women who guide her to the table.

"Come sit, Alicja," they croon.

"*Mo'j kochany synku*. My dear son," she cries. Polish flies back and forth and Tommy feels like an intruder. He keeps his hands in his pockets. He's anxious to get going, but his feet are unsure whether he should.

Alicja Leszek sees Tommy and her hand shoos away the women. "You Tommy, yes? Oskar's friend? You see Oskar?"

"Yes, ma'am. I'm Tommy. No ma'am, I haven't seen Oskar. I don't know where he is." He returns his gaze to his shoes.

"Here boy, you come here."

Alicja reaches out and grabs him by the arm. "You good boy. You go find Oskar. You know where he is. Tell him come home."

Tommy's alarmed. Does she know? Mothers always know stuff. Maybe he should have told his own Ma about being out with Oskar. *But she'd go nuts. No, they'll find him and I won't have to get into trouble.*

Tommy tries to pull his arm away, but she has an iron grip on it. "You tell him come home," she repeats, her voice rising and dancing to the edge of hysteria. She starts the sobbing again. "Oh, Oskar. Oh, Oskar."

"Yes, ma'am. Goodbye, ma'am." Tommy pulls away. It is only when he's outside that he lets out a breath he hadn't realized he'd been holding. He follows the path around the side of the house and kicks a broken toy car out of the way.

Tommy hurries off, his shoulders hunched against the blows of his guilty conscience. He's worried about Oskar, really worried now. The drama in the kitchen has jarred loose the small voice in his head. Responsibility. Duty. And there's also a whisper of disappointment. Tommy has a flashback of riding on the strong shoulders of a young, wild man. The air is laced with that energy. *Oskar will be proud I haven't told anyone about the warehouse. He'll think its swell Jimmy didn't squeal either. But, we have to do something. I need to talk to Jimmy and we need to go look around the warehouse. We need to find Oskar.*

* * * *

"Nope, not a chance. No way I'm going back there." Jimmy says as he runs a stick along a picket fence on their way to school. Tommy has told him about the box of food, the crowded house, the search party, and about promising to help look for Oskar.

"But what if Oskar needs us, Jimmy? Who's going to look for him at the warehouse? Nobody but us even knows we were there."

"And that's the way we want to keep it, chump. Oskar wouldn't rat on us, and we can't rat on him. Besides, the cops were there. He got out and he's prob'ley mixed up with something in his family." Jimmy whacks the stick against the fence. The stick breaks in two.

"I think we should tell. I think we should say we were at that warehouse," Tommy says.

"No way. Uh-uh," Jimmy says, shaking his head. "You gonna' rat me out? You know the kind of trouble we'd be in if our folks find out. Is that what you want?" Jimmy glares at Tommy.

"No. But what about Oskar?"

Jimmy uses pieces of his stick to mimic a pair of hand guns. "They got guns, Tommy. No way I'm gonna get shot at again."

"Chicken, *bawk! bawk! bawk!*" Tommy runs around Jimmy, flapping his arms.

Jimmy pretends to shoot at him with both sticks, but Tommy keeps flying. *"Bawk! Bawk! Bawk!"*

"No way. I'm not a chicken. Come 'ere, you." Jimmy lunges at Tommy, pushing him to the ground. Wild punches fly between them. Jimmy connects with Tommy's nose. The blood makes them stop. Jimmy hands Tommy a dirty handkerchief from his jacket pocket. Tommy tries wiping, but it doesn't stop bleeding.

"Here, gimme that. This is how you do it." Jimmy clamps the handkerchief over the bridge of Tommy's nose. "There, just like my pa showed me."

"Chicken," Tommy says, snuffling into the handkerchief.

"Am not."

"Are too." Tommy sits and dabs at his nose. Jimmy taps his sticks together. Eventually, Tommy pulls off the handkerchief and rubs his hand under his nose to make sure it's stopped bleeding. He returns the bloodied rag to Jimmy, who crams it into his pocket again.

"Come on, then," Tommy says, standing and reaching for his friend. "Oskar's counting on us. Let's go look in the windows, at least. Maybe we'll see something."

Jimmy brushes the dirt and grass off his pants. "Okay, fine. We'll meet up after school and go look. But if I get shot at, I'm gonna really punch your lights out."

Chapter 8

Prohibition has been slowly buffing away Philadelphia's veneer of civility and lawfulness. In the wild, predators rule. In a city, in a country without the harness of laws, predators emerge. Prohibition has created an opportunity for those entrepreneurs who can see a need, and are comfortable with the methods to meet that need. When you outlaw liquor, only outlaws have booze. Some of those new entrepreneurs have a real aptitude for it, too; considering there is no academy to train in or associations to network with. It is learning on the job, with little, if any, tolerance for failure.

Speakeasies, blind pigs, and gin joints are the watering holes where thirsty Philadelphians gather. The bootleggers and rumrunners supply all the forbidden hooch. In the early days it was smuggled, and when supplies were short, they watered it down. As the good imported stuff got harder to find and more expensive, the moonshiners stepped in to meet the need.

In Peggy's world, even on Peggy's street, moonshiners continue to have a brisk business distilling spirits that a thirsty population demands.

It hasn't taken long for the warehouse, Mickey's place of business, to get back to normal after the raid. Not a shard of glass or a stray bullet in sight. He likes a tidy operation.

A couple of men fill bottles and attach labels that have been printed with forged permit stamps. With the stamps, the liquor will be sold with the appearance of legitimacy to hospitals, pharmacies and religious organizations. Taking care of body and soul with a nice tidy profit all round. Quickly, and with precision, the bottles are stacked into crates, readied for delivery. A few more men unload heavy barrels from the back of the truck to replace those that were smashed during the raid. Yup, its business as usual.

Another half-dozen characters are gathered around a table in the center of the warehouse. They sport fedoras and wear natty suits. Mohair topcoats are slung over the backs of the chairs. Most have a gun and holster slung over their shoulder, some have one on each. From the confident swaggers to the braggadocio boasts, these are men at the top of their game.

Gamblers, risk-takers, law-breakers—the new elite. Playing cards are face up—a game interrupted or complete. Half-finished beer has lost its taste; ashtrays are filled with cigarette butts.

In another part of the warehouse there's a guy working under a car, his two-tone brogues flashy for a mechanic. Occasionally he demands a tool from another fellow who leans on the car, smoking. They manage to have a conversation, despite not being face to face. The helper talks nonstop about last year's baseball series, next week's boxing match, his luck at the track, a dame at the club.

After the war, the men had come home and tried to pick up their former lives. It was tough to act like those flying bullets had never happened. There were some men who still woke screaming; memories in dreams of being buried in mud and blood. Tough going back to being a baker or a delivery man after that. Conditions were perfect for 'new' careers.

There were others who had seemed to thrive on survival and the adrenaline rushes of making it through one more day, of being the hunter instead of the hunted. This was also difficult to lay aside when they came home. They needed a way to put new skills to use, and find a way to channel that new attitude about the world.

For a lot of Mickey's crew, the federal government's Volstead Act that established Prohibition in 1920 destroyed their livelihoods. Bootlegging, in a city where most folks didn't have a problem with drinking illegally, was a sure way of putting groceries back on the table. It restored pride and even gave an outlaw hero's shine to the men. They'd hung up their waiters' aprons, farmers' overalls, and rail workers' coveralls, and strapped on shoulder holsters. Because of the war, the guns had a familiar, comfortable weight. But even soldiers, even bootleggers are still family men, worried about their children's grades and obsessed with the latest baseball scores. Maybe it's because they are soldiers that bootleggers need that tether to find their way home.

All the relaxed banter in the warehouse comes to a halt when, outside, a stack of crates tips. "Go check it out, Fingers," says one of the men. Fingers, a stocky man, missing the last two fingers on his left hand, gets up.

He returns moments later. "Nuthin but damn kids. I chased 'em off."

A guy at the table drains his glass. Weapons are reholstered.

"Geeze Louise. What are we? A nursery? What's with all the kids all of a sudden?" says Fingers.

Mickey Duffy sits quietly at one end of the table. A modern-day Napoleon. He has ears that stick out like an elephant, but nobody ever mentions that. He demands and gets the respect of his crew. His fedora hangs on the back of the chair, and his camelhair top coat and expensive suit jacket are draped over an empty one nearby.

At the table are the men he trusts to run his business, to have his back. "So, give it to me straight. How bad is it?" His words slide past the cigar that's tucked into the side of his mouth.

No one wants to speak. Everyone at the table knows the news is bad, despite the money in their pockets. None of the men want to tell Mickey. 'Don't shoot the messenger' goes beyond being cliché in the Duffy gang, especially with Mickey's hair-trigger temper.

Mickey's bookkeeper, Eugene Smith, who is making one of his rare appearances at the warehouse, pulls a ledger from the briefcase at his feet. "It's been a one-two punch to the business, Boss. Revenues are down over last month because of all the raids. Expenses are going up, what with replacing inventory and more cops on the payroll. It's been an expensive month."

Mickey leans back, chewing the cigar in his mouth. "Those cops are an investment, Eugene. Same as the lawyers and judges. We're paying good money for blind eyes, for them to look after our interests and ensure that our businesses run smooth. But like any good investment, we need to see a return. There are too many raids. What are we paying these guys for?"

Fingers leans in. "That last one was more a timing issue, Boss. They was supposed to wait until all the booze was loaded, but something set 'em off. That's when the shooting started. We was still loading booze on the truck when the cops came in early. If they'd been half an hour later, there'd have been nuthin for them to smash."

Under Mickey's hard gaze, Fingers begins to pick at the label on his beer bottle. Mickey turns his attention back to Eugene. "Where are we short on dough?" Mickey asks.

"Well, we have lots of product right now. The shipments from the Flynn boys out in Pennypack are top quality, so we'll be able to charge premium prices. We'll even water it a bit to stretch it further. That'll help with cash flow. The moonshine from the stills in Yorkshire and Morgan are crap. We'll have to doctor it a lot," says Eugene.

58

Somebody from the edge of the room mutters, "Stupid pig farmers. Can't get nuthin' right."

"We've had a few screw-ups with transfers from the Camden breweries, but nothing we can't handle. Max Hassel has really come through for us." Eugene points at the new barrels being unloaded.

"The problem is moving the product. Ever since Butler showed up, police have shut down over half the speakeasies and blind pigs in the city. Most of those joints are open again, but it throws a wrench into delivery and, of course, their original inventory is either poured out or confiscated."

"Eugene's right. They've closed the Cadix seven times." The latest detail is supplied by a man with a large scar over his eye. He sits at the other end of the table from Mickey. "The staff are getting a bit testy, missing their tips."

Mickey draws on his cigar. "Shit, Henry, it's always about the money. What do we know about Butler?"

Henry Mercer is Mickey's top lieutenant. They'd been at Eastern State Pen together; Mickey trusts him like a brother. The crew like to tell the story that Henry and Mickey had been back-to-back in a knife fight when Henry had his face slashed.

"Despite the screw-up on the timing the last time the cops were here, we've got pretty good information about where and when the raids are going to happen. We've been able to get our people out, and inventory secured. The real problem is this new head copper and the number of raids," Henry says.

"Like I asked, what do we know about Butler?"

"One of Butler's cops is living at my boarding house," says Eugene.

All the men at the table look at him.

"Living with a cop? Better watch yourself, Eugene. You'll get arrested for snoring," taunts Gus.

Loud guffaws from the fellows around the table attract the attention of the others working in the warehouse.

Mickey puts his elbows on the table and the group falls silent again. "Good. Eugene, stick to him like glue, and keep your ears open."

"Butler's cops are trouble, Mickey. The owners aren't happy with all the raids. Even though they can be open for business the next day, they're complaining sales are tanking. And legal expenses are going through the roof. They're feeling the pinch, and when they're not making money, we're not making money," says Henry.

"And that's a big problem," Mickey says.

Porter, another man at the table, joins in. "And there's loads of cops out there looking for this missing kid, Mickey. One of them coppers remembers seeing some kids here at the warehouse last Tuesday, so they're looking at us and casing the joints we run."

"Kids. Here. Today. Last week. The week before. What's that all about?" Mickey asks.

"They see their big brothers and they have big dreams. I'll talk to the men," Henry Mercer says. "We need to keep the kids away from the business until they're old enough, Mickey. It's not safe to have them around."

Mickey nods, "And for *chrissakes*, tell the men not to go bragging. It just encourages trouble."

They've all heard about the missing kid. Mickey knows it is on their minds. Bad enough a child is missing, but even worse when it's connected to one of their own.

"Hey Al, isn't the missing kid one of your sister's?" Mickey asks.

Al, a big, bald man who's been labeling bottles, shrugs. "Nephew. Oskar's my wife's sister's kid. You remember Stan Leszek? He's in stir right now at Allegheny."

"Pretty cushy. How'd he arrange that?" asks Porter.

"Mickey's mouthpiece couldn't get him off completely, but they did manage to score a reduced sentence, and off he goes to the workhouse instead of the joint," Al says. "Stan was a farmer in Poland, so he's pretty happy there, what with the orchards and animals and all."

"I remember now. He was sent over for a three spot? About two years ago?" Mickey says.

"Yeah, he'll be out next year," Al says.

"Leszek's a good man. Don't we have one of his other kids working for us? Running numbers?" asks Mickey.

Al nods his head. "Yeah, Ernie."

"Anybody that wants to help hunt for Leszek's kid should go do that. Stan may be away, but we look after our own." Mickey moves his chair back. "Look, I still don't get it. I thought we had all the arrangements for that last raid sewed up. How'd we get caught out?"

"That would be me and Gus," says Fingers, stepping forward. "Me and Gus Toland were on watch that night."

"So, where's Toland at? Why's he not here?" asks Mickey. "Get him in. You and him come see me tomorrow. Mercer, you come too." He takes another draw on the cigar and the men in the room tense. Mickey blows smoke at the ceiling. "You guys did a crappy job and now it's costing me money and business."

Shoes suddenly become really interesting.

"Anything else?" Mickey asks. He leans over to the spare chair for his coat. "Then I gotta scram. I've got a date with a dame."

"Sorry Boss. But there is another thing." Henry unconsciously rubs his scar. "The attention on our business because of the botched raid and looking for the kid are causing other problems. Some of the joints are moving their business over to Boo-Boo Hoff. With all the cops right now, they say we're too hot."

"*Sukinsyn*!" Mickey shouts. "What the hell! After all the money we've made those *sukinsyn* bastards, and they're buying from that scumbag now?" Mickey glares at each one of his men in turn. "What, nobody's come up with a solution to persuade these turncoats? Huh, nobody?"

None of the men around the table have the nerve to look him in the eyes. A nervous cough is the only thing that breaks the silence.

"I'll look after it, Boss," Fingers says, leaning forward. "Me and Gus will go have a little chat with them and convince them that sticking with us is the better business decision." Mickey looks Fingers up and down. There won't be any arguing with Fingers. The man looks like he could take more pain than all the trouble Philly had to give. A bull.

Mickey nods. "And Mercer, go talk to the police about wrapping up their search for the kid. Let's get some of the heat off our backs. Tell 'em that he ran away to join the circus, or maybe left town to visit his old man. It don't matter what you tell 'em. I mean, you boys can keep an eye out for him. But take the heat off; whatever it takes to get 'em to stop looking around. We don't need them meddling in our business," Mickey says.

Porter scoops Mickey's hat off the dirt floor and brushes it off for him.

"Anyone else have any more *gówno* they want to share tonight? Or are we done here?" Mickey says.

The choir responds: a mix of nothing else, all done, and 'night Boss.

Chapter 9

Saturday morning. What a week it's been. With Tommy already out the door to play with a friend and her lodgers all scattered, Peggy packs another box of food for the searchers. Putting on her coat, hat, and gloves, Peggy smiles to herself. *A lady would never leave the house without her hat and gloves—one of Mother's rules.* She puts the box of food in the wagon and heads to Alicja Leszek's.

Peggy stops in front of Oskar's house. Tommy's mentioned a few times they've passed that his friend lives here. It's strange to think that he's been in that house to play, probably knows it well, and she's never set foot inside. It's nice enough, she supposes; a rowhouse much like hers, some kind of shrub near the front step. It could use a coat of paint on the front porch.

Peggy heads knocks at the front door. The knock echoes. *Perhaps Mrs. Leszek is out? At the police station? At church? With other family?* Frustrated, and put out with the inconvenience, Peggy looks up and down the street. *I can't leave the food on the front door step, it might get stolen. What a bother. Well, they're probably backdoor people, anyway.*

She steps off the veranda, grabs the handle of the wagon and heads around the corner of the house to the back door.

There's laundry on the line. *On a Saturday!* Mrs. Leszek's sitting on the back stoop, laundry basket at her feet, sobbing into a small boy's school shirt. Painful, heart-wrenching sobs.

Peggy hurries over and begins patting the woman's shoulder. She looks around, hoping that someone will rescue her and deal with the overwrought woman. Mrs. Leszek continues to sob. Peggy sits beside her and puts her arm around her. "There, there. It will be all right. Come on now, no more tears."

Mrs. Leszek lifts her head from the shirt. Her hair has come unpinned and strands hang around her face. She lifts the shirt, offering a view to Peggy. "Oskar his shirt," Mrs. Leszek says, choking on her tears. "My boy's."

Peggy gives Mrs. Leszek's shoulder a squeeze. "Poor Oskar. You've not had news, have you?"

Mrs. Leszek shakes her head, clutching the shirt close. "No, nothing. *Nic.* No news."

"I'm sure that something will turn up soon."

Peggy sits on the step, her arm around Mrs. Leszek. She's unsure what to say. Comforting a stranger is not something she has much familiarity with. *How long should I stay? It's cool out. If I have to stay long, I'm glad I have my coat.*

"You know, our boys have played together for years, but I don't know Oskar very well. What's he like, your boy?"

Mrs. Leszek regards the shirt, and then shrugs. "Oskar good boy. He in middle, older brothers, younger brother, he never any trouble. Always listen good."

"You have a big family."

"Not so big. Only six. Four boys and two girls."

"Oh, my goodness, Mrs. Leszek. That's a handful."

Mrs. Leszek gives her a small smile. "Alicja, Missus Barnes. My name Alicja."

"Then, you must call me Peggy."

"Oskar, he no good at school. But that no big deal. He go work with his father when he older."

"With Mickey's gang?"

"No. No. Stan, he drive truck. When Prohibition stop, Stan drive truck again."

"He's not home right now? Stan?"

"No. He in Allegheny. One year more."

"I imagine it's hard. Being on your own with the children, I mean."

"They need father home. Nobody to keep older boys in line. Tommy's father gone, too. Yes?"

"Yes. He passed four years ago. We've been on our own since then."

"Alone no good. No family? No mother or father to help?"

"No. We're all on our own. My mother comes by sometimes, but I don't see my father. And Jack's parents—Jack was my husband—are older and don't live near here, so we don't see them very often. It would be nice if they could be closer. Do you have family here? To help you with all this?"

"Stan's brother and family here. They big help. My sister and brother, too. Everybody always look for Oskar. Father and mother in Poland." Alicja heaves a wet sigh. "Oh, Missus, I wish my mother here." A tear rolls down Alicja's cheek again. "I miss her. She know how to make this better."

Peggy gives Alicja's shoulder another squeeze. "Brrr, are you cold, Alicja? Would you like to go inside?" Alicja sits and stares at the shirt. *I can't just leave her out here. Not like this.* Peggy tries again. "Does Oskar want to work with his father?"

"Oh sure. Money good. He like cars and trucks. Good with hands. He fix old bicycle, you know. Put new chain on. New wheel. Just like new." For the first time since she sat, Peggy sees a small smile on Alicja's face.

"Ah, so he's a clever boy, then."

66

"Yes, he very smart boy. Not like older brothers. They always trouble, let me tell you. Bad friends. Not like Tommy. He good boy."

"Thank you. Yes, Tommy is a good boy. He likes school. And he likes to read."

"Oskar not read much. Always outside."

"Six children. I don't know how you do it. Dinner time must be hectic."

"Stan and I have lots of brothers and sisters. Big families. My mother, she show me. Always cooking. Always laundry." Alicja nudges the laundry basket with her foot; another small smile.

"Even with one child, it seems like it's always laundry," says Peggy. "You know, it's the worry that gets me. At night. I worry about Tommy and his future. I worry about money. With Stan gone, it must be hard. How do you manage?"

"Stan's boss, Mr. Duffy. He look after us while Stan gone. He make sure we have money. And Stan's brother, he help, too. We make do until Stan home."

"That's the tough part, isn't it? Keeping a roof over your head and food on the table. And I only have Tommy. No family. No Mr. Duffy."

"Mr. Duffy, he good man."

"Well, Alicja, the rest of this laundry won't hang itself, now. How about I give you a hand and we can get it done lickety-split."

"Lickety-split?"

"It means quick. Come on. I'll pass and you peg."

"First, we put food in kitchen. Thank you, Peggy. You kind. You help. Thank you." Alicja taps her heart. "It good to talk. Thank you."

"Don't mention it, Alicja. That's what neighbors do."

Chapter 10

On Saturday, Peggy's kitchen is crowded and noisy. The chatter of the women is a new sound compared to the reserved silence usually found in her home. It reminds Peggy of her days working with Jack at the labor rallies. You get a group of people together and there are always sandwiches to be made, coffee to be poured, and gossip to be shared.

Earlier in the morning, a group of ladies, some from the neighborhood, some from the Polish Catholic Church, as well as some of the Leszek women, had appeared at Peggy's back door. There will be a big search party heading out later this morning and everyone wants to lend a hand. Some are hopeful that Oskar will be found. Sad as it is, others are here for the excitement and break in the daily routine.

Peggy's getting more comfortable with the different ways of her neighbors. Her Northern Liberties neighborhood is a blend of primarily Polish and other eastern-European immigrants with a few Irish families thrown in. She wishes she had taken the opportunity to sit on the back step with Jack when he was getting to know the folks in the neighborhood. Aloofness has kept her from these generous and kind people.

In the short time of helping out—even though it is over a devastating situation; the disappearance of Oskar—Peggy is picking up a few phrases and has even had a pickle with a glass of vodka. She is beginning to see why Jack admired these people; beginning to understand how big their dreams must be to pull them across the ocean. Or, thinking of it another way, how huge the terrors at home must be to have pushed them all the way to a strange, new land. The community has always been tight-knit as any group of outsiders are, and she is grateful that they have loosened the borders a bit to let her slip in.

To the extent that she can, amongst the tears and the worry of it all, she is finding purpose and connection again, and enjoys it. Conversation in the kitchen swings widely from tales of woe with spouses or children to gasps of shock over juicy bits of gossip. Peggy moves from group to group, passing wax paper, getting the salt and pepper, and pouring endless cups of coffee and tea. She eavesdrops on one particularly raucous story of someone's younger sister and an extra beau at a party; finds herself laughing.

One of the ladies, Magda, asks after Tommy. Magda is trying to get her own son into Boys' Central High School. "Is a good school. School is important. Maybe my boy be doctor or lawyer, or maybe businessman. He smart, my boy," she says with pride.

Another neighbor, Berta, has a tip on meat from a butcher's shop that Peggy has never gone to—she hadn't understood the signs in the window, so had always hurried past. "You go and tell Henrik that Berta send you. He treat you right. Much cheaper than Johnson's. Better meat, too." She jabs her finger at Peggy.

"So what's your story, Mrs. Barnes? You lost your husband in the strike, yeah?"

Peggy pauses, her hands full of bread. She thinks the woman is Mrs. Barry, another neighbor; short, busty, red arms, red face, red hair.

"Yes," replies Peggy, not wanting to share, but also not wanting to interrupt the easy camaraderie in the kitchen. "He was one of the organizers, and got caught in a riot when the mounted police charged."

"Dark times indeed," says an aproned woman, shaking her head. Other women echo how lives have been affected by the Great Steel

Strike in 1919. A lot of men in the neighborhood had been, like Jack, laid off after Hog Island Shipyards closed after the war.

"You can't put thirty thousand men out on the street and expect them to go quietly," says Mrs. Barry.

She steps close to Peggy, chin thrust forward. "Mrs. Barnes, is it true that your own Da' worked for American International, them that owned the Shipyard? He was one of them swells that locked our men out?" There is a definite challenge to Mrs. Barry's question, and a sudden chill in the room.

Peggy is cautious. Four-and-a-half years have passed since the layoffs, but feelings run deep. Jack's reputation and sacrifice give her some protection, but her father is seen as the enemy by the women in this room, a sentiment she doesn't disagree with. "We haven't spoken since the strike. Jack was a good man. He's Tommy's father. But, yes, my father worked in the Accounting Office. He was the one that called in the police to break the strike, and that was the day my dear Jack was killed."

"Well, that must have been a difficult funeral," says a woman who lives beside Mrs. Barry.

There is a collective gasp.

"Not really," says Peggy. "My father is dead to me. I told my family that I didn't want them at Jack's funeral. Lines were drawn when we got married, and the trench has been dug deeper with each year. My family, my real family, was with my husband—our son Tommy, and Jack's parents."

While there are a few lingering looks, the women perceive the drama is over and resume their tasks and their chatter.

70

Suddenly, Peggy's back door swings open. Alicja Leszek is almost doubled over, weeping. A small child at her knees tries to hold the adult upright.

Peggy rushes over to lend support. "Alicja, come, let me help." She guides her to a chair. "Please, take your time. What's happened?"

In a flood of Polish, Mrs. Leszek pours out the horrific news. Those who understand the language look on in shock.

"The police are calling off the search for Oskar," someone translates.

"They say he's run away. Maybe even joined the circus," says another.

"Damn them, *cholera policja.*"

"*Sukinsyn!*"

"Trust them to turn their backs on us."

"Well, I never." says Peggy. *The circus? Not a chance. Tommy would have said something about a circus. Had one even been through the city?*

The women try and adapt to the news. "What will happen now?"

"The men have to go back to work on Monday."

"They can't take any more time off to look."

"We've already looked everywhere."

"If the police aren't going to help, we'll need more than eyes and legs. We'll need someone who knows what they're doing."

"Those *policja* have it out for us."

"Always give trouble, never help."

"Because we can't pay the bribes."

Alicja Leszek has remained silent since her outburst, tears streaming.

"But who will look for Oskar?" asks Peggy. "They can't get away this." Peggy wraps her arms around Alicja. "There, there. Don't worry. We'll keep looking. We won't give up. We'll bring Oskar home."

Chapter 11

The street lights begin to flicker in the gathering dusk. A cup of coffee balances on the front railing, and Peggy, bundled in her winter coat, sits in a tattered wicker chair on the veranda. She needed to get out of the house, away from people. The walls were closing in on her.

Peggy's home has been a hive of activity and tension, what with the women in the morning and Alicja Leszek's visit. It is as if the very house absorbed Alicja's news about the police calling off the search for her son, Oskar. That news, and the wails of the mothers, are now part of the plaster and lath. It had taken several hours before Alicja could be persuaded to return home. The rest of the women had also lingered, wanting solidarity in numbers against a decision they didn't understand.

Emotions have been high. By the time Peggy prepared the evening meal for her lodgers, Tommy, and herself, she was emotionally spent.

At dinner, Tommy had poked at his food. He said that everyone had abandoned his friend. Peggy wondered if he wasn't feeling that he had too; she tried to reassure him that there was nothing more he could do.

Guilt doesn't sit easily on his narrow, young shoulders. His small lie lives in his chest, pressing down and making it hard to breathe sometimes. It has him firmly now, and is growing. The way to get back to telling the truth about that night at the warehouse is getting harder to find.

As a member of the police, poor Constable Kelly was given a rough ride over dinner. Eugene Smith had been particularly nasty in his comments, to the point of blaming the police for allowing harm to come to the boy. Peggy silently agreed with the man. The police have shirked their duty, and now the safety of a young boy, a friend of Tommy's, is at risk. She wouldn't say anything aloud, but her pinched lips gave her away. Tommy hadn't even waited for his pudding; he'd stormed upstairs, loudly slamming his door. Peggy envied him that release. Adding to the evening's upsets, Constable Kelly had been called away before he got to finish his dinner. Peggy couldn't help but think that the bitterness at dinner was the perfect topper for a really horrible day.

The end result of the police's verdict to suspend the search had spurred the organization of another large search party later that evening; a last heroic effort. If the police wouldn't help, ordinary people would try to find the lad. Various church congregations, folks from all over the south end of the city, workers from the mills and other businesses; together they were combing the area again. Peggy can hear Oskar's name being shouted from blocks away.

Alone on the veranda, Peggy has time to reflect. She knows the police are generally seen as a corrupt lot, and held in low regard in Philadelphia. She reaches for her coffee. *Poor Constable Kelly, he is so committed. It's not his fault the search was called off.* As far as her neighbors are concerned, it is just another case of foreigners' children not being important. Some had said it was about the police looking out for themselves first. *Looking out for themselves, why? For what? Had they been asked to look the other way? If so, who would ask such a thing? Who would pay them off? And, more importantly, why? Don't let it be true that little boys don't matter in the grand scheme of payoffs and corruption. Little boys do matter. Oskar is lost and he'll be found.*

The fresh air is invigorating; Peggy's neck and shoulders begin to unknot. She spots a stocky, older gentleman walking slowly, swinging his walking stick. His clothes are old-fashioned; the heavy wool suit, a shirt with a high collar, and a bowler hat securely on his head. Her grandfather wore such a hat, and had the same generous mustache and beard.

There've been a lot of strangers in the neighborhood, helping with the search. He must be someone's older relative making his way home.

With all the tragedy surrounding Oskar's disappearance, Peggy is comforted by the generous show of support. Everyone has been united in their concern about a missing boy. It appears that not all of Philadelphia has abandoned civility and decency.

The old gentleman nears. *Poor fellow. He looks preoccupied. I guess the search didn't go well.*

A rush of gratitude for the stranger; a solitary, weary, old man. Kindness overcomes her.

"Good evening. You look like you've had a long day. Have you been out searching?"

The man turns as if Peggy is speaking to someone behind him. Then he stares directly at her.

"Good evening, sir. A long day?" Peggy raises her voice.

The old man continues to stare.

"Sir, any news on young Oskar?" Peggy shouts. *Perhaps he is hard of hearing? Or maybe he doesn't understand English?* Peggy leans over the veranda railing and speaks louder and slower.

"I said, any news on the boy?"

"Um, are you addressing me, madam?"

Daft, as well as deaf. Peggy regrets extending her newly discovered neighborliness. Tonight is not the night for anything difficult.

The man rests against his walking stick. "Yes. I was out searching. Alas, no luck. It appears the boy has vanished."

"You heard that the police have called off the search?"

"But justice will prevail, madam, it always does."

"I wish I had your certainty. It looks pretty bleak right now."

"Fear not, my dear. It's too early to give up hope. I was just contemplating the similarities between this case and one I worked on years ago. We were victorious then, and will be again. Back then, a girl and her two brothers went missing. They'd been abducted. It was over a year before the villain was brought to justice. 'Victory belongs to the most persevering', you know."

"Ah, so you're a policeman?"

He tips his hat in Peggy's direction. "Inspector Frank Geyer with the Philadelphia Police. Although I admit to being retired for some time now." He rubs his chin. "It seems, however, that I've been called back into active service."

"And thank goodness you have been. Now that the regular force has walked away, we're going to need your seniority and experience," says Peggy.

Inspector Geyer doffs his hat again. "Excuse me madam, but I'm afraid I may have to temper your expectations. I'm at a bit of a disadvantage in this case. Usually, I would interview the family and others that may have known the boy, but I have been unable to do so. Do you happen to know him? Would you mind if I spoke to you about this?"

"Well, you'd better come in then. My boy, Tommy, is a good friend of Oskar's, and I know the Leszek family well," she says. *A stretch, but I am part of the neighborhood now.*

Peggy settles the Inspector in the living room, and tells him she'll check if the coffee from supper is still warm.

"Milk and sugar?" She places the cup on the side table beside Inspector Geyer. He looks ill at ease. *Surely, before retirement, he'd been in people's homes for interviews? Maybe a jealous wife at home? Nervous around women?*

Before she sits, she extends her hand. "I'm sorry, I didn't introduce myself. I'm Mrs. Barnes." The gentleman shrinks back against the cushions of the chair, away from her hand. Peggy doesn't know what to do with her empty, outstretched hand, so she pats her hair. *What an odd duck. Maybe I was too forward. In his generation, were handshakes only between men?*

"Charmed, madam. As I mentioned outside, I'm Inspector Geyer. Frank Geyer." He pauses as if awaiting recognition. "Retired from the Philadelphia police."

"So you said. It's a pleasure to meet you. It's good to know that the police have not totally abandoned the search for Oskar. I must admit that I'm quite put out with the police right now. It could have been my son that went missing; and to think that they give up so easily. It doesn't fill one with confidence."

"A missing child leaves a hole in the community, does it not? I too am mystified by the announcement. In my day, we wouldn't have abandoned the case so quickly. In truth, in the past I have been relentless in police efforts to return lost innocents to their families. I have something of a reputation for it."

"I am relieved to hear that, Inspector Geyer. It goes a way to restoring my faith in the police to think that they have brought you in."

"I am glad to be of service on this matter, madam. As I mentioned, I've been retired for some time. Perhaps the rationale for my involvement now stems from my reputation for pursuing criminals that harm children. I expect to be able to use my expertise in this case."

"Goodness then, do you think Oskar's been taken? Harmed?"

"I think that the police are misguided in their belief that Oskar has run off. And I'm mystified as to why they would have leapt to that conclusion, especially without a thorough investigation. In my experience, the number of young boys who run away to join the circus is seriously exaggerated. No, I'm inclined to believe that something sinister may have happened to Oskar. If injured, he would have been found by now."

"Though I don't want it to be true, I must admit I am actually relieved to hear you say that, because that's what I've been thinking. But when I tried to talk to Constable Kelly about it, he brushed away my concerns as those of an emotional mother."

"Constable Kelly?"

"One of my lodgers. He's also a policeman. He should be home shortly."

"Oh, excuse me. You run a boarding house?" the Inspector says, looking around the room more closely.

"Certainly not. I take in lodgers. They're all good gentlemen. Quiet and well mannered."

"You're not concerned with how it might look? A young woman with a houseful of men?" he asks, with a slight frown. "This is very different than in my day. I mean my own wife was a widow when she opened... I mean, in my day women were much older when they opened boarding houses."

"Well, times are changing Inspector, and we have to change with them. These are the twenties, after all. There are many young women who earn their own keep. They, I mean we, are an independent bunch, making our own decisions and managing our own lives."

I shouldn't be so sensitive, but he shouldn't be so judgemental. He sounds like Mother. After the day I've had, I should never have invited him in. Except it was to help Oskar, of course. It's too late to ask him to leave. And rude. I can be polite, but that doesn't mean I have to be welcoming.

"Of course," says the Inspector. "Forgive me. I forget these are different times."

"Perhaps you could share some of the case details, Inspector. I'm afraid that the police haven't told Mrs. Leszek much."

"From what I can fathom, Mrs. Barnes, young Oskar went out after supper last Tuesday, allegedly to study for a math test with friends, and never returned. So it's been over a week. No one has seen or heard from him since. Which isn't possible. People, especially small boys, don't disappear into thin air. Certainly, someone knows something. They just aren't saying anything. Their silence could be attributed to any number of reasons. What puzzles me is the shoddiness of the police search efforts. I haven't seen the police even circulate a photograph. We've just been looking for a young, fair-haired boy. And there are a large number of those in Philadelphia."

"I knew the police weren't making an effort," Peggy says. "What should they be doing, Inspector?"

"I would have expected them to confirm his activities the night he disappeared, canvassed his friends and family, circulated a picture, and put the photograph in the newspapers. Perhaps even contacted other communities' police forces. Police work involves pursuing many lines of inquiry to find the one thread that leads you to a successful resolution."

"I knew it. They have totally dropped the ball. And it's poor Oskar that pays the price."

"I agree. It appears they have been negligent, although I wouldn't want to pass judgement on an active police investigation."

"Not that active, apparently."

"Sometimes, these matters take a long time to resolve. On a similar case, the one I had mentioned earlier, the children had been abducted for nefarious purposes. Mr. Holms, their kidnapper, took them from Philadelphia. They traveled through Chicago, and all the way to Toronto in Canada, before he was apprehended. Unfortunately, by the time we found him he had murdered the children."

"Oh, how dreadful. Surely you don't suspect something like that has happened to Oskar?"

"I sincerely hope not. Mr. Holms was a very disturbed individual. He enjoyed outsmarting the police. The alienist, the doctor that dealt in psychiatric disorders that examined him, described him as a psychopath. I, on the other hand, tended to agree with the newspapers' description and just thought of him as a monster. I was dogged in my determination to bring him to justice. I didn't abandon the case, even though initially we had very few leads." Inspector Geyer relaxes into the chair, folds his hands over his vest—a portrait of satisfaction at being able to recount his tale—just as Joe Kelly pops his head around the doorway.

"Good evening Mrs. Barnes. My apologies for once again missing dinner."

"That's all right, Constable. I've put your supper on a plate in the stove to keep warm."

"I hope you weren't waiting up for me, Mrs. Barnes."

"Not at all, Constable. I've been talking with Inspector Geyer about Oskar, and his efforts to continue the search." She looks expectantly at the old man who sits very still in the chair. He has a hopeful, eager look as he stares intently at the young policeman.

Joe follows her eyes and spies the cup of coffee on the table. "Oh lovely, a cup of coffee. Have you poured it for me, Mrs. Barnes? Do you mind if I carry it into the kitchen while I eat my supper? It's been a long day and I'm famished." He grabs the drink and heads toward the kitchen.

Inspector Geyer stares after Joe, a deflated expression on his face.

Peggy's mouth falls open. "I'm so sorry, Inspector. I'm not sure what's got into him. Constable Kelly is never rude like that. Please, let me get you another cup."

In the kitchen, Peggy advances upon the unsuspecting and hungry police officer. "Constable Kelly, just now you were unbelievably rude to my guest, who is also a fellow officer."

"Excuse me, Mrs. Barnes. I'm not sure I follow."

"In the living room. You took his coffee."

"I'm so sorry Mrs. Barnes. I'll go and apologize immediately. I'm not sure how I missed him, although it's been a long day and I'm quite exhausted."

By the time Peggy has poured another cup of coffee for the Inspector, Joe returns to the kitchen. "I'm sorry Mrs. Barnes, but your guest seems to have left. I hope it wasn't on account of me. Can you give me his address? I'll go after him."

"I don't know his address. I just met him. He was telling me the most interesting things about a case he had worked on, and what he thinks may have happened to Oskar. No matter, you might as well have this last cup. I'll go and clean up."

In the living room, Inspector Geyer still occupies the chair. "Inspector, my goodness, you startled me. Constable Kelly had said that you left."

"My apologies again, Mrs. Barnes. Perhaps Constable Kelly failed to see me sitting here."

"Yes, I suppose that's it. He did mention that he is exhausted. Let me go and figure out your coffee."

"No need, Mrs. Barnes. I'm just fine without."

"You were telling me about your efforts to locate Oskar."

"Yes, I've been attempting to canvas various hotels, train stations, and real estate offices. The man who abducted the children in my former case checked into numerous hotels and leased accommodations to cover his trail. He claimed to be the children's uncle. It was the way he was able to hide in plain sight, so to speak."

"That's fascinating and horrifying. Any leads with Oskar's case?"

"None, I'm afraid. I'm having rather a difficult time of it. I'm finding it challenging to converse with the proprietors."

Joe Kelly pokes his head around the corner again. "Um, excuse me Mrs. Barnes, I'll go upstairs now. Thank you for a delicious dinner, and for keeping it warm for me. And, I did want to check, *um*... Is everything all right, ma'am? I heard you speaking. Were you talking to me?"

"No, I was talking with the Inspector."

Joe looks around the living room, confused. "Oh, right then. It's been a stressful time. Perhaps you should get some rest as well," says Joe.

"Constable Kelly, really, this is just beyond the pale. My apologies again, Inspector, but the Constable's exhaustion is no excuse for rude behavior. Perhaps you should take yourself upstairs if you are too tired for good manners, Constable Kelly."

"*Um*, yes. Yes, Mrs. Barnes. Perhaps that's best. Good night."

"How very strange. I really don't know what's gotten into the young man."

"No apologies necessary, madam. No one knows better than I how mentally fatiguing police work can be." The Inspector rises, picks up his hat and walking stick, and offers a small bow. "With your permission, I too will depart. I have enjoyed our conversation and your kindness at letting an old man ramble. Perhaps we could resume our conversation tomorrow, and I could follow up with you regarding young Oskar?"

"Certainly, Inspector," says Peggy, walking him to the door. "Anything I can do to help. I'll see you tomorrow. Good night."

Chapter 12

Peggy can see the uneasiness in Joe as he stands by the sink with his coat on, quickly gulping his morning coffee. He's shouldering some of the blame for the search cancellation, even though he's equally confused by the investigation being closed.

Finding out yesterday that the police were going to stop their search for Oskar had been rough. The official decision hung over the neighborhood and over the Barnes' household like a shroud. Oskar was being abandoned.

"Joe, do you have a moment? I met the most interesting man last night. The fellow I had mentioned to you? A retired police Inspector. He's been brought in to assist with Oskar's disappearance."

"No, I don't think so, Mrs. Barnes. We don't use those retired war horses that way. Once they're out to pasture, they stay out. He may be bored and wanting to be back in the traces, but certainly he's not acting in an official capacity," Joe says.

"Isn't that curious. I could swear he told me otherwise. He's coming back 'round later today to discuss the case with me. Is there anything wrong with that?"

"I don't see any harm. As long as you realize that the official investigation has been closed."

"Yes, how could I forget? You police are all so busy with the bootleggers, you've no time for little boys."

"Mrs. Barnes, wait." Joe speaks to Peggy's rigid back as she leaves the room.

Tommy remains sullen at lunchtime. Not even a door slam on the way out. Normally, Peggy would have been pleased by the restraint, but today with everyone so upset, it reinforces her own tension.

Looking for something to occupy her until the Inspector arrives, she starts in on the ironing. One scorched shirt later, she puts everything away in disgust.

She exercises her agitation by pacing back and forth to the window. All afternoon, she keeps watch for the mysterious policeman. She was concerned when Joe said that he was acting without proper authority. It has added to her sense that there's something about the Inspector that's just not quite right. Jack was always teasing her how she never let down her guard, and now when she has just started to accept people as they are, she's conflicted. She wants Oskar found. Inspector Geyer, however odd, might be the key.

And she's intrigued. She's even intrigued that she's intrigued. It's been forever since she's been so engaged in something besides Tommy or the finances. But still, there's a twitch between her shoulder blades every time she thinks she sees him coming along the street. Her front veranda stays empty of callers.

At dinner, the tension around the table is thick. The day's newspaper headlines have shouted accusations and spun horrific tales of lost children. Every coffee shop and lunch counter patron had a theory to share, or a finger to point at the police. Last night's arguments and complaints linger, fed by the city's reaction to the search being called off. There's none of the usual banter and casual chatter. Tonight, the household at the table just want to get through dinner and escape.

It is into this silence that Archie Mansfield, in good professorial fashion, clears his throat. "I think that the police have been quite negligent in their duties." The blunt statement lays there in the middle of the table. He frowns at Joe with the disapproving look of a math teacher marking a paper that will fail.

"You shouldn't have closed the books on the boy, Constable. I'm disappointed in you and in the police. You gave up too soon. Perhaps he has run off, but don't you think you should confirm that? Contact police in other cities and towns nearby? Don't you think you owe it to his poor mother to give her some peace?"

Joe squirms and keeps his head down. Adjusts his chair. Picks at his food. Guilt-ridden.

The math teacher shifts his attention to Tommy, then Peggy. "I know from my own classroom experience how rebellious young men can be. They have a wild, independent streak that is often allowed to flourish in the families of the foreigners. There isn't the same kind of discipline you'd find in other homes." Archie pats his mouth with his napkin.

"Are you saying that poor Alicja is to blame for Oskar's disappearance?" Peggy asks. Tommy recognizes the signs of a coming storm and eats faster, anxious to be finished and away. "I've gotten to know the family quite well recently, and I can assure you that Alicja is a loving and devoted mother."

"Mrs. Barnes, are you aware that her husband is in jail? The family is without a strong male influence to guide the young boys, who run wild." Constable Kelly and Mr. Smith focus on their plates.

"Mr. Mansfield, you are treading on thin ice. This household is also without a strong, male influence and has been for several years. Tommy and I are managing just fine, unless you think otherwise?" Peggy folds her napkin in a controlled manner, placing it on the table. She rises to clear those plates that are empty, the back of her neck flushed with anger. Those still eating finish quickly.

"Mrs. Barnes, my apologies, but... oh, I am sorry. You misunderstand my intent," Archie says, but she is already in the kitchen.

After dinner, dishes are cleared and the household safely disperses to private tasks behind closed doors. Peggy resumes her vigil in front of the living room window. She's left her drapes open to the evening so as to see the street. Her arms are crossed and one foot taps impatiently. *The nerve of Archie Mansfield. What an unpleasant man. They always blame the mother. Tommy and I are doing just fine. I hope this interview with the Inspector doesn't take too long. I am ready for bed. If it weren't for Tommy and Oskar--*

Her heart skips a beat when Inspector Geyer approaches her front step.

Peggy opens the door before the Inspector can knock. "Good evening, Inspector Geyer. Please, come in."

"Good evening, Mrs. Barnes," he says, doffing his hat.

Peggy closes the drapes, fusses a bit too much in getting the old Inspector comfortable, compensating for her crankiness and determined to be a gracious hostess.

"Has something happened? You seem preoccupied."

"No, and my apologies, Inspector. It's been a rather long day and everyone here is testy. There were words spoken at dinner and now everyone is hiding in their rooms," Peggy says.

They sit awkwardly in silence, the mantle clock counting off the seconds that seem like minutes. "Mrs. Barnes... " Frank begins.

"You have news about Oskar, Inspector?"

"No, not at the moment. However, I have another matter to discuss with you. Something of a personal nature," Inspector Geyer says.

Oh-oh, here it comes. I knew I should have turned off the lights and gone to bed. We're not even going to talk about the case. And he's such a weird duck. Joe says that he isn't officially on the case.

He clears his throat and begins again. "Mrs. Barnes, yesterday when I was here, you apologized on several occasions for the Constable's behavior."

"Yes, he was quite rude."

"Mrs. Barnes. I feel that it is I who should apologize to you."

Peggy looks at him with a puzzled, but expectant half smile. "I'm sorry, Inspector, but I don't follow. What have you done that requires an apology?"

"I have thought about little else but this conversation since yesterday, madam. I would like to share something with you. It may cause you some unease. However, I assure you my intentions are all good."

What's he going on about? Am I safe? Inviting him back wasn't a good idea.

"Inspector, when I told you I was a widow yesterday, you may have misunderstood," Peggy says.

Inspector Geyer looks at her, alarmed. "Oh no, my intentions are honorable. I just need to be able to explain—"

"Inspector Geyer, I really don't have the energy for more drama tonight. Why don't you just get to the point?"

The Inspector gives his head a small shake as if to clear his vision, and takes a deep breath. "I'm not sure how to begin. Or what to say."

Can I ask him to leave? Maybe I could say I need to check on Tommy?

Peggy stands. "I'm sorry Inspector, but it's been an exhausting day. I'm not sure where you're going with this, but Constable Kelly is just upstairs. Perhaps it would be better for you to leave, or do I need to call him?"

Inspector Geyer holds his hand as if stopping traffic. "Please madam, let me continue. Please be seated. I really do not wish to cause you any distress. This is quite difficult for me. If you could give me but a few moments?"

There is something about the man. Curiosity, compassion, and a lifetime of good manners oblige her to sit, albeit perched on the edge of the chair. "Two minutes, Inspector. And then my patience is done."

"You should not find fault with Constable Kelly. He was not rude last evening. Rather, he could not see me sitting here. He thought you were talking to yourself."

"Inspector, I still don't understand what you are trying to tell me." *What if he's not right in the head? It sometimes happens to older people.*

"Mrs. Barnes, Constable Kelly couldn't see me last evening. He couldn't see me because..."

Peggy frowns. "Oh Inspector, please do just come out with it. Constable Kelly couldn't see you because..."

"Mrs. Barnes, please don't be alarmed, but you're talking to a spirit. A ghost."

All right, that's it then. I'm going to get Joe. This is some kind of a hoax. But to what end?

Peggy rises, but something in the Inspector's searching look causes her to pause. She studies him carefully; keeps coming back to his eyes, which are regarding her in a thoughtful, kind, but determined manner. He reminds her of her grandfather.

She sits, closes her eyes, and takes a deep breath. *Maybe I'm imaging all of this? Am I working too hard? And it has been stressful lately. He's just a sick, old man. Be kind.*

When she opens them, Inspector Geyer is still in his chair. "But Inspector, I can see you. Sitting right here in front of me. My apologies, sir, I don't want to be unkind, but perhaps you aren't well? Maybe it would be better if you were to leave."

"Please, madam, I will leave at your next request, but please hear me out. I beg you. Yes, you can see me, although I'm not sure why. No one ever has before."

"Are you sure you're a ghost, Inspector? You're not perhaps a lunatic are you?" *A lunatic wouldn't know that he was crazy. And if he's not, then maybe I am? Oh God, what if I'm the one that's sick in the head?*

"Not a lunatic, no. Constable Kelly couldn't see me sitting here, or hear me talking to you. But I can see you're not convinced. Perhaps you could ask Constable Kelly to come to confirm it?"

"Yes, that's an excellent idea." *And he can help me get this madman out of my living room.*

As Peggy waits for Joe, she gives her head a shake. *It's too bad, really. He seems so harmless. Quite a courtly gentleman. I feel badly asking him to leave. He's obviously just a dotty old man, but I can't have him here with Tommy in the house.*

When he arrives in the living room, Peggy links her arm through Joe's. "Constable Kelly, do you see a man sitting in the chair, over there by the table?"

"No ma'am. Is this a game like charades? Am I supposed to guess?"

Peggy strides over to the chair that the Inspector is sitting in. "This chair, Constable Kelly. Is there a man sitting in this chair?"

"No, ma'am. Still no man. Are you sure you're all right? Perhaps you should go upstairs so that you can rest. I'll lock up and turn out the lights."

Peggy grabs the back of the chair by its corner. "In this chair. An older man, with a large mustache. A beard. Holding a bowler hat. Surely, you see him?"

"I knew this yesterday. I am not visible to the young Constable," the Inspector says, shaking his head. "He can't hear me, either."

"Okay, Mrs. Barnes," says Joe. "Please, let's just go upstairs and you can have a nice lie-down. This has been an upsetting day and you're not yourself." He attempts to take her arm.

Peggy shakes him off. "Oh, Constable Kelly—Joe—I am sorry. It's been a long day and I must have dozed off while reading. It was Mary Shelley's novel about Frankenstein. I think I've given myself the willies. Too many monsters before bed. Of course, there's no one there. Silly me, you head off now, and don't worry. I'll put the book away and not read it again."

"Well, as long as you're all right. Goodnight, then," Joe says.

Peggy waits until she hears Joe's bedroom door close. She whispers to the Inspector. "Please leave, Inspector Geyer. I'm not sure what is happening, but I must insist that you go. This is all too much for me tonight." *The chances are more in favor of me being crazy than being visited by a ghost. A police ghost, at that.*

"Of course, Mrs. Barnes. I am so ashamed to have caused you this deep distress. I apologize most profoundly. I should not have said anything. Please excuse me."

Out of habit, Peggy stands and follows her guest to the door. "Thank you for coming, Inspector. I hope you're successful in your efforts to find Oskar. Obviously, we're both a bit bonkers tonight, but it has been an interesting experience to meet you."

She pauses by the door and gives a shaky laugh. "And Inspector, I'd really appreciate it if you don't dissolve through the door. I'm not sure I could handle it."

"Thank you for your kindness, Mrs. Barnes. And again, please accept my apologies. May I beg another indulgence from you? May I call 'round again tomorrow? Perhaps in the afternoon, when the others are out? I know that it is asking a lot, but this is such an exceptional experience for me, and I would hate to curtail it."

Peggy pauses, her head tipped to one side, regarding the man. "Oh, it is exceptional for me as well, Inspector. Tomorrow afternoon, then." She opens the door. "Good night, Inspector."

I must be crazy. Just bonkers. Mad as a hatter. Who will take care of Tommy when they take me away? Peggy closes the door and locks it.

Chapter 13

Peggy tosses and turns all night, worrying about her state of mind, trying to decide if the Inspector is the crazy one. The sheets twist, wrapping her tightly. At one point, she gets out of bed and goes downstairs to check the lock at the front door.

As the sun rises, Peggy gives up trying to sleep and starts her day. The lodgers head off to work. Tommy goes off to school. She clings to the comfort of routine. Peggy does not want to be crazy. She does not want there to be a ghost. Which would be the lesser of two evils? She tunes in to the radio for company and for distraction; keeps herself busy through the day, indulging Tommy with a heartier lunch than usual.

She has almost dismissed the bizarre events from the previous evening until she sees Inspector Geyer on the sidewalk in front of her house. It is a perfectly normal, sunny afternoon. He looks as real as anyone.

Peggy hurries to the front door, unsure of whom she'll be inviting in: a lunatic, a senile old man, a con artist, a ghost, a figment of her own imagination? She takes a deep breath and opens the door.

Inspector Geyer slowly climbs the steps to the veranda, leaning heavily on his walking stick. "I wasn't sure if I should come. I feel that I'm being selfish, imposing myself on you again."

"Nonsense, Inspector. I spent all night thinking of our conversation and look forward to continuing it in the bright light of day. I would like to make some sense of it. And of course, I also appreciate your insight into Oskar's disappearance. As to the other? Well, I guess I'll wait and see. Neither one of us was at our best last night."

"Yes, quite," Frank says with a smile.

Forcing the guise of normalcy over the visit, Peggy comments on the weather as they settle into their chairs with coffee. She shares how worried Tommy is. It has tugged at her heart to see her son's distress. She leaves space for the Inspector to explain the unexplainable.

"I don't know how I can describe it, Mrs. Barnes. Ten years ago, I died in my own bed. I believed in heaven, in God, in an afterlife. But this," he opens his arms wide, "is not that."

The clock ticks. Peggy knows time is passing. There is relief that she is not imagining him. No figment of imagination could be so convincing, with such a kind face. The dialect and his clothing reflect another era. He wears his police authority as comfortably as his jacket.

"Since that time I continue to see, to reason, to contemplate. To be. I am a man as I have always been, with one notable exception. I have no physical form. I am just..." He shrugs again, his arms still open wide. "I am just here."

The Inspector stares at his hands. "I'm a policeman, Mrs. Barnes, not a theologian. I've never been anything else but a policeman. I like facts. I like puzzles that I can solve. I like things to be black and white, concrete. I don't like this. I don't understand this."

The old man's abstract musings swirl around the room. Slowly, one of his statements settles into Peggy's consciousness. "You died in your bed? Ten years ago?"

"Yes, of old age apparently. Much older than I appear now." He smiles, and pats his stomach.

"How can you be younger than when you died? And why are you here in my living room?"

"Beyond vanity? Perhaps my purpose requires me to be more in my prime and not at the age I was when I died. After much thought, I'm convinced that I am meant to find out what happened to Oskar. Like an old dog, I've caught the scent. Despite hoping to the contrary, I'm sure that his disappearance is nefarious, and I believe I am supposed to bring the criminals to justice."

"But how will you do that, being a ghost, and invisible?" Peggy asks. With every creak and groan of the settling house, Peggy glances around; should anyone see her now, they would think she was crazy, chatting away in an empty room.

"It has been a challenge," says the Inspector. "I had never fully appreciated the advantages of the physical form, and I envy you. You can talk to another person, you can lift a piece of paper or turn a page, you can knock on a door, you can hold a child's hand." He sighs. "I miss being able to touch." He extends his hand out then lets it fall into his lap.

"But you hold your cigar, you touch your walking stick. Why can you do that and not be able to knock on my door?"

"I think it's because those items are my personal possessions. Like my jacket and my hat. They're not real to others; however they are real to me. It's always the same cigar, freshly clipped, never more and never less. I can smoke it or put it in my pocket, but I can't leave it behind."

"And doorways?" Peggy's curiosity of the unknown is stronger than her fear. "Do you walk through walls?"

"I prefer to cling to the conventions of normalcy and use doorways. I was raised in a different era, Mrs. Barnes, and I still appreciate good manners such as last night and this morning when you held the door for me. It's a comfort but not a requirement. And I think you may be more comfortable with me entering a room rather than suddenly appearing in it."

"Boo?" Peggy jests and then regrets it when she sees the reaction on the Inspector's face. This is no joking matter to him. *How would I deal with this spectral existence? How strange to incorporate the extraordinary into day to day practice.*

Their conversation has been punctuated with silences, the radio, turned low, providing cover for their soft voices.

Peggy speaks more with it than over it. "Have you ever thought that maybe it's like radio waves? I can't see a frequency. I don't understand the science, but I can enjoy listening to the music. As the bard said, 'There are more things in heaven and earth, Horatio, than are dreamt of in your philosophy.' Maybe we don't need to understand everything to know that it exists?"

"You have a very open mind. A characteristic that I admire, and could perhaps benefit from. You are close to the missing boy's family, and your son is distraught over his disappearance. Would you consider assisting me? In the investigation?"

"Oh no, Inspector. I'm not sure what is happening with all of this." She waves her hand through the air. "Maybe this whole experience is a very realistic dream, and I'm actually snuggled in my bed upstairs, asleep. But I do know that not even in my dreams would I ever contemplate helping a phantom Inspector with a police investigation."

"But Mrs. Barnes, if you don't help, who will? We need to find Oskar and return him to his family. The police will do nothing more. Are we going to turn our backs on a little boy who is counting on the adults to look after him?"

"Inspector, the police themselves could produce no leads. For goodness sakes, I'm a widow and a homemaker. I have no investigative skills or experience. You must realize that it is beyond my capacity to assist you."

"You underestimate yourself and what you could bring to an investigation. A very great man once said *'there is no strength without justice.'* I believe that, Mrs. Barnes. And I also believe that there can be no justice without strength. There is no justice for Oskar or his mother if we abandon them. I believe that you have the inner strength and fortitude to be of great assistance in this case."

"Inspector, let's be honest with each other. You need me because you have no other options. Under normal circumstances, we would not be having this conversation."

"It's not useful to deal with what might have been or should have been. As abnormal as it is, and for reasons beyond our understanding, we are sitting here together, having a conversation, considering the options. There is a reason for it. I believe we need to accept the situation and take advantage of it. We have been called to a higher purpose," Frank says with force and conviction.

Peggy regards the Inspector thoughtfully. He leans forward and rests his elbows on his knees. "I need someone to be my voice, Mrs. Barnes. I can guide you through the investigative process. I assure you that you will be utterly safe. I won't ask you to take on any aspect of the investigation that you are uncomfortable with. Please consider it, won't you?"

"Oh Inspector, I just can't. A woman, especially one who is a mother, can't traipse around town, going into hotels and accosting desk clerks about missing boys. What would people say?"

"But why not? You could pretend to be Oskar's mother. There would be nothing more natural than a mother searching for her son. Nothing more compelling. And I know you're not concerned about what others may say. You told me yourself that you're an independent woman, one of the new generation who makes her own decisions and manages her own life," says the Inspector.

Peggy sits quietly a few moments, lost in her thoughts. "Inspector, I need a minute or two to think. Excuse me while I go make another pot of coffee."

Peggy leans against the sink, looking out the window at a perfectly normal day. Behind her in her living room, a ghost has just proposed a crime-solving partnership. She grips the edge of the sink.

Perhaps being Inspector Geyer's assistant could work. I made a promise to Alicja to keep looking for Oskar. Certainly, the police have made their position clear. Tommy would be so proud of me. The people in the neighborhood would admire me, too. We'd all be safe because a threat has been removed. I can see it now: 'widowed mother brings criminal to justice, young boy safely returned to his family's warm embrace'.

Turning to face the direction of the living room, Peggy takes a deep breath. *Ghost or not, crazy or not, he is an experienced policeman, and we need that. I was reckless once and ran off with Jack and, as difficult as it is some days, it was one of the best decisions I ever made. Am I still that girl who takes risks? Is she in here somewhere?*

Peggy carries the coffee pot back into the living room.

"All right, I'll assist you, Inspector. But I have conditions," she says. "Firstly, if I am uncomfortable in any way, I will stop."

"Certainly, I wouldn't go forward without such an understanding."

"Secondly, any information that we discover, we turn over to the police. They may have suspended their investigations into Oskar's disappearance, but they are still responsible for the safety and well-being of this community."

"Of course. I am still a policeman, madam, and an officer of the court. The criminals must be brought to justice, but I'm certain that won't happen if we do not augment police resources with our own efforts."

Peggy squares her shoulders and takes a deep breath to steady herself. "And finally, we must have a clear understanding. I am not an assistant, to fetch and carry. Nor am I a ventriloquist's doll. I expect to be treated as a legitimate and full partner. If I have ideas about what might have happened to Oskar, I want you to consider them equally in our investigation."

"An equal partner? Mrs. Barnes, this may be the 1920s, but women do not serve on the police force. You're a woman. Investigations are cold and clinical, no place for a woman's tender heart. And you have no experience. You don't know the first thing about investigations or police procedure."

"Which you said you'd teach me, Inspector. Now, you're arguing against your own case. These are the very objections that I raised earlier and which you said were surmountable."

Peggy smiles, recognizing the gumption she'd thought she'd lost forever. *Yup, that girl Jack fell in love with is still here. I can be a detective.* "Of course you'll have senior rank, Inspector, and will be leading the investigation. Surely you can compromise on some authority in order to acquire a voice and physical presence, can't you?"

I can do this. After Jack's death I held on to this house, and I continued to raise Tommy. I've started a rooming-house business. I'm no silent helpmate, only capable of transcription. I have a voice of my own and the strength to use it. Oh, please agree to this, Inspector Geyer.

It is now Frank's turn to sit silently while Peggy leans forward. "I realize that it is unorthodox. But here we sit, a woman and a ghost and, if I join the investigation, I don't know which of us would shock people more. Surely you see that the whole situation is very unorthodox," Peggy says.

"Unorthodox, indeed. You drive a hard bargain, Mrs. Barnes, but I think that I can live with this."

"Very good, Inspector. Although 'live' with it may be a bit ironic, don't you think? Shall we shake on it?" She extends her hand. Forgetting himself, Inspector Geyer reaches for it, to confirm their new partnership.

"Oh dear," says Peggy, as his hand passes right through hers.

"We'll start training right away," says Frank.

Chapter 14

The cutlery scrapes and clinks as everyone eats. Frank leans against the dining room archway.

Earlier, Frank had suggested to Peggy that she try out some questioning techniques over dinner. Initially, she had been reluctant to appear rude or nosy. It required several attempts at coaching before she picked up some confidence to break a lifetime of her mother's conditioning regarding good manners.

"Tell me, Constable Kelly, how was your day?" she asks.

Joe has become the most popular raconteur around the table. His stories of gangsters and crooked politicians are vastly entertaining for a housewife, a clerk, a math teacher, and a seven-year-old boy.

Joe looks up from his stew. "It was busy, Mrs. Barnes. Our squad led raids today on a couple of cover-up houses."

"Cover what?" Peggy asks.

"Cover-up houses. Those are places, like barbershops and beauty salons that have licenses for products with alcohol. Bootleggers use these businesses as a place to sell booze disguised as hair tonic and perfume."

Peggy is fascinated. She has no idea that ordinary, legitimate businesses could be part of bootlegging. *I take Tommy to a barbershop.*

"But surely you can't sell too much out of a barbershop? The hair tonic bottles are rather small and there is only so much hair tonic a man can use," Archie Mansfield says.

"Oh, you'd be surprised, Mr. Mansfield. There's a small village of about fifty people outside of Philadelphia that has gone through 500 gallons of hair tonic in the last twelve months," Joe says, chuckling.

Peggy laughs with him. "That's a very busy barbershop."

"There's a serious side to it as well, ma'am. Sometimes, the denatured industrial alcohol in the tonic is improperly distilled. Customers who drink the stuff get very sick. I overheard a doctor talking with Colonel Butler, and he said that Philadelphia has ten to twelve deaths from alcohol poisoning every day," Joe says. "And that doesn't count the blindness that can sometimes happen."

"Billy says his pa—" Tommy catches his mother's frown. "Sorry, Mother. Billy says his father was blind drunk on the weekend. Did that mean he was drinking hair tonic, do you think?"

"That's dreadful, Tommy," Peggy says. "It's appalling how this language around Prohibition is becoming part of our children's lives."

Archie Mansfield nods in agreement. "You know, Constable, the public doesn't like Prohibition, and hasn't stopped drinking despite the efforts of the police, and of the 'Drys' who are leading the charge on Prohibition. Philadelphia is sopping wet, ma'am," Archie says. "And there are more speakeasies than statues of Ben Franklin. Up and down Broad Street, along Market, and just around the corner: thirst-relief stations."

Joe snorts at the term.

Archie continues: "Yes, thirst-relief stations: people selling booze on street corners. They're stacked one on top of the other. There might be a quarter mile between nightclubs and speakeasies, but there's always a drink within a funnel's throw where someone can fill his hip flask for the trip." Archie waves his butter knife around like he would use chalk on a blackboard, underscoring his point. "They have women on the streets, canisters of alcohol with a funnel or a cup under their coat, selling the stuff one drink at a time."

Peggy notices that there is still chalk dust on the sleeves of Mr. Mansfield's jacket. *Perhaps I should include laundry services for an additional charge? That bit of extra money would be handy. I'll ask them tomorrow.*

"It sounds like you might be speaking from personal experience, Mr. Mansfield," Joe says.

"Of course not. But I'm not as blind as some police are."

With the tension rising, Peggy speaks. "And how was your day, Mr. Smith?"

"Nothing nearly so interesting as Constable Kelly's. Just adding columns of numbers, writing balances, sending out reports. Just me and some dusty old ledgers. I'd much rather hear more about what Constable Kelly's been up to than talk about my boring, uneventful day. Do you have any raids planned for tomorrow, Constable?" He butters his bread.

"I mustn't say, Mr. Smith. Everything is hush hush. There's a big problem with leaks right now. Saloons and moonshine still operators are getting the heads up before we even get there. Colonel Butler is really cracking down," says Joe.

Peggy hears the Inspector groan. He's mentioned his contempt over the current level of police corruption to her many times. She watches him walk away, and knows he's gone to find a comfortable spot in the living room.

"That's good," says Eugene. "We wouldn't want information falling into the wrong hands. What are you doing about it? The leaks, I mean."

"Well," says Joe around another mouthful of stew, "One of the things we're doing is we've got ginks; you know, undercover cops, watching other cops."

"In my day, you didn't need coppers to watch coppers." Frank's statement reaches Peggy.

"Really?" says Eugene. "That sounds like a poor use of manpower. Surely the problem isn't all that bad?"

Everyone at the table stops eating and stares at Eugene. Even Tommy's mouth falls open. It's an astounding bit of naivety from someone who lives in a city where it's common knowledge that most cops pad their salaries with kickbacks and bribes.

"I'd like to hear more about the barbershops," interrupts Tommy. "I get my haircut at Tony's. Do you think that he's selling alky hair tonic?"

"I really can't say, Tommy. But Eddie's Barbershop on Bainbridge was raided late this afternoon. It'll be in the papers tomorrow, so I guess I can tell you about that."

"Are you all right, Mr. Smith?" asks Peggy. He has started to choke.

"Yes, ma'am. A bit of beef just went down the wrong pipe," answers a shaken Eugene.

Joe resumes his tale. "Anyway, we confiscated boxes of that coffin varnish. Eddie's Barbershop has been a cover-up house for Mickey Duffy for a couple of years. We arrested the barber and two other people. And they're just the tip of the iceberg. We've got long lists of known cover-up houses that we'll be checking out."

104

"I wish you'd tell us about whether Tony's was safe. Tommy's got to get his hair cut next week and I'd hate to think that we'd be in the middle of a raid," Peggy says.

"Tell you what, Mrs. Barnes. I'll check into it and see if it'll be okay to take Tommy to Tony's Barbershop. You know, Tommy is looking a bit woolly, now that you mention it."

Tommy sticks his tongue out at Joe, earning another frown from his mother.

Frank watches it all from his vantage point, sitting on the sofa in the living room. Peggy checks, from time to time, looking for his approval at her questioning technique, trying to see what he sees. He seems to be observing Eugene quite closely.

"My, you are certainly curious about all this criminal activity, Mrs. Barnes," Eugene says. "Perhaps you should read one of those lurid police detective novels that they sell in drugstores. Constable Kelly has barely had a chance to eat his dinner with all the chatter. I, for one, have had a long day and would like to retire. With your permission, Mrs. Barnes?"

"Oh. Uh, why yes, of course," says Peggy, flustered. His footsteps heading to his room off the kitchen drive a wedge into the conversation.

"My apologies, Constable. Has your dinner gone cold? Can I get you another plate?"

"No, I'm fine ma'am. And dinner is delicious."

Peggy looks questioningly at the Inspector. He nods in the direction of the kitchen. She gathers a few plates as an excuse to leave the room, and he follows her through.

Even though she checks to make sure Eugene's door off the kitchen is closed, she speaks quietly. "I'm not sure I'm going to be any good at this interrogation thing. I certainly can't be chasing lodgers from my table or serving them cold stew, Inspector. That was a disaster, and we didn't learn anything at all."

"You're questioning was good, but your listening skills need some work, Mrs. Barnes. On the contrary, tonight we learned that Enforcement Unit Number One is going to be very busy over the next few days. And more importantly, we also learned that the recruitment practices at the police department are questionable. In my day, we didn't hire untrustworthy men to be police officers. Imagine, needing ginks?"

Eugene opens his door and grabs his coat and hat off the rack. "Excuse me, Mrs. Barnes, but I think that I'll go out for a bit of a stroll. Stretch my legs after dinner."

"Oh, of course, Mr. Smith." She and Frank wait for him to close the back door. "How very curious."

"Indeed," says Frank. "He looks familiar, but I just can't place him. Curious, indeed."

Chapter 15

Peggy stands outside Green's Hotel on Chestnut Street. The strap of the handbag she carries is indented from her grip. She and Frank decided that today was the day she'd begin questioning hotel clerks about Oskar.

The street is busy, a symbol of Philadelphia's transition from yesterday to tomorrow. It's full of motor cars and wagons. The electric trolleys rattle along. Shoppers dart past, in a hurry to be somewhere. There are women in long skirts, their hair piled under large, brimmed hats. In contrast, other women dash about dressed in mid-calf-length skirts with short, bobbed hair under tight-fitting cloche hats. The energy from this crossroads of time is palpable, and Philadelphia thrives on it.

Green's Hotel fills almost the whole block, the building complete with turrets at its corners. Peggy sizes up the doorman standing in front of the ornate double doors. *Now or never*. She climbs the steps and allows him to direct her inside.

The lobby is dark, despite the efforts of numerous crystal chandeliers dripping from the ceiling. Groupings of men in leather armchairs are buried behind the latest editions of the Philadelphia Inquirer. Others sit talking, their heads bent close. Large potted palms and ferns create small islands of privacy. Off to one side is the elegant dining room that Peggy has heard about, but never visited. Muted laughter and the music of the lunchtime orchestra floats through its doorway.

Several gentlemen, glancing at her over the tops of their newspapers, wear the look of disapproval. The only women Peggy can see are wrapped in furs; ornaments dangling on the arms of their gentlemen escorts. Those women appear to be on the move, either heading out the hotel's front door or into the restaurant.

"Oh my, I don't think anyone who abducted Oskar would be in a place like this," she whispers to the Inspector, who stands beside her. "I don't think I should be in a place like this."

"You never know, Mrs. Barnes. We have to start somewhere. Go on now, you can do this. Remember what we talked about."

Peggy smooths the front of her worn, cloth coat before approaching the front desk. The clerk is bent over the register, his posture accentuating the careful part down the middle of his well-oiled hair. He looks up, allowing her a glimpse of a fussy little mustache as he gives Peggy the once-over above his spectacles. He returns to his paperwork. "Yes, madam? How may I help you?"

"Excuse me," Peggy says hesitantly, clutching her handbag in front of her like a shield. "I'm looking for my son? He is seven years old, and is about this high?" she adds, holding her hand waist high, "and he may be traveling with an older gentleman?"

The front desk clerk looks up to take in the 'this high'. "Have you lost him?" he says, peering around the lobby.

"Yes, but not here. I'm afraid he may have run off. With my brother." Peggy is frantically creating the story while Frank supplies her with additional details. "My brother has a ranch, in Texas. Oskar, that's my son, is caught up in the adventure of horses and Indians and riding the range. He wasn't in his bed this morning, and my brother left last night."

"If your son had followed your brother, wouldn't he have returned the boy?" the clerk asks reasonably.

"*Um*, I'm afraid Oskar may have told his uncle that he had my permission to accompany him back to Texas." Peggy's cheeks glow a bright pink.

The clerk's eyebrows climb. "If they are traveling together, couldn't you just wire your brother and ask him to put your son on the train home?" He taps his pencil against the register.

"Ah yes, that is what I should do. Of course. Thank you for your time." Peggy nods all the way out of the hotel, trying her best not to look like she's fleeing.

Frank begins his evaluation as soon as they reach the sidewalk. "I think we have a problem, Mrs. Barnes. Something that I'd failed to consider. Without the authority of either gender or a badge, it's going to be difficult to get the cooperation of your interviewees. Perhaps you shouldn't engage the clerk in so much conversation; the best lie is a simple one. Rather, you should play up the distraught mother with more effect, don't you think? Don't be so mousy. You're a distressed mother looking for her son. You're frantic with worry. I think we had better work on a better cover story about young Oskar's disappearance."

"Oh, you think?" Peggy whirls around to face him, fists clenched white-knuckled around the strap of her handbag. "That was horrible, Inspector. I have never been a liar. And now I find out that is a good thing, because I'm a terrible liar. That clerk thinks I am just a foolish woman. And to top it off, he also believes I'm a bad mother."

"Now, now, Mrs. Barnes. Don't overreact. Don't think of it as lying. Think of it as acting. We'll do better next time," says Frank, his hands patting at the air between them.

"Next time? There won't be a next time, Inspector." Peggy shouts.

Passersby stare at the wild woman who is gesturing wildly and talking animatedly into thin air. They give her a wide berth. Peggy glares at her reflection in the shop window, then clamps her jaw shut.

She takes two deep breaths. "This is impossible. I don't think I can do this, Inspector. You need someone like Constable Kelly for help. Someone who has more authority and experience."

"But there's the rub, Missus Barnes. I can't speak to Constable Kelly. You know he can't see me. For better or worse, you have been given to me to solve this case, and together we will. Oskar is depending on us."

Frank stands behind her, but Peggy cannot see his reflection. "Remember Mrs. Barnes, 'in the time of revolution, with perseverance and courage, a soldier should think nothing is impossible'. It's just a matter of trying again and not giving up."

"Of course, you and General Bonaparte are right, Inspector. You always are, it seems. I will try harder." Peggy turns to face Frank. "You said you had some ideas about our cover story?"

As Peggy and Frank walk to the next hotel, he makes suggestions, and Peggy builds on them. By the time they reach their destination, she has regained her confidence.

The hotel clerk looks around the lobby worriedly as Peggy sobs loudly into her handkerchief. "There was a man, a stranger near our house. And now my son is gone," she wails. "Oh please help me, I've been searching and searching for my dear little Oskar. No one has been able to help me. Has a man with a boy checked into the hotel, probably two Wednesdays ago?" Peggy peeks out anxiously from under the brim of her hat at the embarrassed clerk.

"Wednesday?" he says, consulting the register, anxious to have the noisy, emotional woman out of his lobby.

As they leave the hotel and step outside, Frank is encouraging. "Much more successful, although I think you should ask Oskar's mother for a photograph. It would be helpful to be able to show them a picture of him," Frank says. Peggy glows from the praise. *I may not be a good liar, but I'm not a bad actress. Maybe I can do this.*

The rest of Peggy's day is spent interrogating desk clerks about her missing son, Oskar. She adds chambermaids to the list of interviewees; women may be more helpful to a worried mother. While almost everyone is sympathetic, she and the Inspector cannot find anyone remembering a boy and a man traveling together.

In the lobby of the last hotel, Peggy sits to give her tired feet a rest. *People are going to think that I'm a working girl. What did Joe call them? Pro skirts. I'd better get home and get dinner started. I hope Tommy found the note and ate his sandwich I left for his lunch. Now, that is something my mother would never have done. Mother was home for my lunch every single day.*

Peggy pulls herself onto the next trolley and finds two empty seats. She collapses wearily into one and Frank takes the other. She stares out the window as she half-listens to Frank discuss the case.

I hope the inquiries wrap up quickly for dear little Oskar's sake. Plus, I can't be leaving Tommy alone every day. What will the neighbors think?

"You see, your young Constable Kelly and the police never considered a kidnapping. If they were still pursuing Oskar's disappearance, his theory would be focused on gangsters and bootleggers. Now, what would a gangster want with a small boy? No, I don't think there's evidence to support that. We're better off to be focusing our efforts on abduction. We'll do train stations next. Maybe Oskar and his abductor are no longer in Philadelphia. You'll get that photo I asked for, Mrs. Barnes? Mrs. Barnes?"

With the trolley window as her headrest, a closed-eyed Peggy mumbles enough of a response to keep Frank going.

"We'll need a photograph to show around the ticket windows, and maybe we should chat with some of the train crews. Find out who would have been working the night that Oskar disappeared. Maybe the next day's shift as well. I say, Mrs. Barnes, isn't this your stop?"

"Goodness, I must have nodded off." She leaps from her seat and rushes down the trolley steps. "Inspector, are you coming?" she asks over her shoulder. She turns. Frank is gone.

I'll stop in for a quick visit with Alicja on her way home and ask her for a photograph of Oskar. I'll say it's for Tommy.

Chapter 16

Peggy understands, from Frank's criminal psychology lessons, that crises in communities follow similar patterns. Oskar's disappearance is no exception. First had been the delay, while everyone denied that something could be wrong. 'Oskar will be home in the morning.'

Next, there was the building flurry of activity, sometimes organized and sometimes frantic. Often a bit of both. Searching for Oskar. Newspaper reporters hanging around looking for tears or drama. People talking about it in the coffee shops, and around their own kitchen tables. Everyone wanting the latest updates, or to propose theories. Some volunteer to help, wanting to be directly involved with the spectacle.

Eventually, and sadly, interest wanes and people slowly disengage and move on to follow another story. That has to be the toughest part for the families. With the spotlight gone, they're left alone with a bit of clothing or a beloved toy. In Oskar's case, a school shirt to clutch close to his mother's heart on laundry day.

Three weeks. The story is no longer front page news. It doesn't even merit the back page anymore. Friends and family helps out when they can, but most folks have moved on with their lives.

Peggy hasn't given up. She drops by to visit with Alicja every few days. She sits in Alicja's kitchen, patting her hand, telling her that 'a policeman' is still looking for her son, and not to give up hope. It's easy to see that hope is the last thing that Alicja will give up. A mother is always sure that her child is out there somewhere, wanting to get home.

Peggy juggles her household duties with her newfound responsibilities as an investigator. Sometimes a few balls are dropped, but her passion for the pursuit drives her forward. The lodgers are too new to know that it's not Peggy's usual routine to be out and about every day. Ever business-minded, she's added laundry to her landlady services and is bringing in a little more money from that. The lodgers have clean laundry every week and a good supper on the table every night. Peggy is learning that there are many advantages to being taken for granted; it almost makes one invisible.

Tommy notices her change in routine, yet between school, his friends, and being preoccupied with thoughts of Oskar, he doesn't dwell on it. There is one thing that does puzzle him. In an effort to solve it, he crouches beside the living room doorway. He tucks himself behind the coats hanging in the front hall—he's only partially hidden.

One of the finely-honed instincts of a policeman is to be curious, even when he's off duty and heading to the kitchen for coffee.

"What are you doing, Tommy?" Joe asks, quietly.

Startled, Tommy retreats into the coats.

"Nuthin. I'm not doing nuthin."

"Sure you are," Joe says in a low voice. "Is that your mother in the living room? Who's she talking to?" Joe crouches beside Tommy, hands on his knees. "You know it's rude to listen to other people's conversations?"

Tommy shakes his head. "But she's not talking to anybody. She's sitting in there alone. She's been doing that a lot. I just want to hear what she's talking about."

Joe and Tommy crouch in silence.

114

Peggy speaks. "Once I got used to it, it wasn't as hard as I'd thought... I think I made good headway today, even if we didn't find any evidence."

Tick. Tick. Tick. The seconds hand on the mantle clock audible.

"What did you think of that clerk at the Seventh Ward Hotel? Something's going on there... I think he's hiding something. He didn't even check the register."

And the ticking of the clock.

"What was going on in the back room?"

Tick. Tick. Tick.

"I missed that," says Peggy. "Interesting."

Tommy and Joe share a look and a shrug.

"No way. You think they were bootleggers?" she says. "I hope that we don't run into any trouble... We're not having much luck with the hotels or train stations."

Tick. Tick. Tick.

"Maybe we should turn our attention away from them and meet with real estate agents about rental properties? Didn't you say that was a fruitful line of inquiry in your last case?"

Joe whispers to Tommy, "Hey, didn't Mr. Smith suggest she start reading mysteries? It sounds like a plot for a book. Maybe she's writing one? I'm glad your mother has found something to keep her busy. Let's not disturb her or do anymore eavesdropping." Joe stands.

"A book? Like she's going to be a writer or something?" Tommy asks, also standing.

"Gotta be. Maybe she's got a character in her head and he's speaking when she takes those breaks in her sentences. Let's leave her to her thoughts. Let's go eat the last of that cake from dinner."

Joe leads the way. "Besides, it's a stressful time for your mother; tough on all the ladies, what with Oskar missing."

Tommy drags his feet. His shoulders are hunched and he slumps into a chair. Joe puts two plates of cake on the table and pours two glasses of milk. Tommy just stares at the cake.

"*Mmmm*, this is good. Eat up, Tommy, or I'll eat it for you." Joe attempts to stab Tommy's cake with his fork. Tommy shields it with his arm and starts eating. "I was thinking, it can't be easy with a bunch of lodgers in your house."

"Right," says Tommy.

"You had promised to tell me all about the neighborhood, Tommy. Is this a dangerous place to live, do you think? I hear that some of your pals from around here like to hang out at the warehouses by the train tracks. You wouldn't know anything about that, would you?" Joe asks.

Tommy pushes the cake around the plate with his fork, shaking his head. He doesn't look at Joe. "Yes, sir. I mean no sir. I don't know anything about that."

"Look Tommy, man to man here. I know about the other night at the warehouse. Police on the scene report seeing three boys there. One of those boys sounds a lot like you. Was it you? Were you there?"

116

Tommy puts down his fork and slumps in his chair. He crosses his arms and refuses to meet Joe's eyes. "Come on Tommy, talk to me. Was Oskar there too? Did you see anything?"

"I wasn't in any warehouse. I don't know what happened, Constable Kelly. It must have been somebody else. I don't know anything about it." Tommy kicks at the table leg.

"I'm trying to help Oskar, Tommy. If you know anything, you should tell me. To help Oskar."

Tommy sits straighter. Joe waits while Tommy looks at his plate and then at Joe. "I heard that there were some boys at the warehouse. But it wasn't me or my pals who were there," Tommy says, narrowing his eyes, daring Joe to call him a liar.

Joe looks hard at Tommy, weighing what the young boy has said. "Well, it's a good thing it wasn't you that night. And I hope that you know better than to be hanging around bootleggers. Those are dangerous fellas."

Joe pats Tommy's shoulder. "Look, Tommy, we may have to accept that Oskar has run off and left home. It wouldn't be the first time a boy did that. I don't think he's hurt. We checked the hospitals when Oskar first went missing and nothing turned up."

"You don't think he's hurt. You checked the hospitals. So that's good, right? He's coming home, right?"

"I sure hope so. Well, kiddo, I bet you have homework to do. Better get to it, eh? I'll wash these plates. And, Tommy, don't go adding to your mother's worries, lad. Warehouses are not good places for young boys to be."

Peggy's murmuring continues against the backdrop of the music on the radio. Joe's curiosity raised, he takes a cup of coffee into the living room.

"I'm hoping I'm not intruding, Mrs. Barnes. May I join you?" Joe asks. Without waiting for an invitation, he plants himself on the couch across from Peggy. "So you're a fan of Wendell Hall and the Eveready Hour? Me mam loves that program." Joe nods in the direction of the radio.

"*Um*, yes, it's a favorite of mine, too. I try and listen to it every night." She looks over at Frank sitting in the chair beside her. He's staring fixedly at Joe. "May I help you, Constable? Is there something you need?"

"Everything is fine, Ma'am. I was just checking to see if there was anything you need. I know that there have been lots of changes: new lodgers, the neighborhood upset, you're helping out at the Leszeks', and before, with the search parties and all. Tommy and I were just heading into the kitchen for a late snack and we couldn't help overhearing you talking to yourself. I just wanted to make sure everything was okay."

Peggy glances nervously around the room. She spies one of Tommy's school scribblers on the edge of the desk. "Oh, that. I was just getting ready to write in my journal." Getting up, she goes and sits in front of the desk. "I like to sit here every night and record my thoughts. I must have been composing aloud. Ha-ha, silly me."

"Ah, I see," says Joe.

"Mr. Smith's comments about being interested in solving crime got me thinking about writing a mystery like the Sherlock Holmes kind. What do you think of that idea, Constable? Do you think that I could solve a mystery?" she asks.

Peggy doesn't know whether to be amused or annoyed when Frank chuckles.

"Mysteries and crime are such unpleasant topics for a woman, Ma'am. Why don't you write a good romance? Now, me sister loves to read those serials when they come out in the ladies' magazines."

"Perhaps you're right, Constable." Peggy turns back to the desk. "Although I do like a good mystery. Maybe you could give me a few pointers? For my novel?" Peggy says, taking a bit of smug satisfaction from Frank's glower.

Joe smiles. "I'm flattered, Mrs. Barnes. I'm just new to policing."

"*Harrumpf*. You can say that again," Frank says.

"But I'll help if I can. What were you wanting to know?" Joe asks.

"Oh, maybe how the police would gather evidence, maybe look for clues? How do you solve a crime, Constable?"

Frank stands and starts pacing, his hands behind his back.

"That's quite complicated, Mrs. Barnes, but I'll do the best I can."

Joe goes on for some time about modern police methods. Frank punctuates Joe's points with eye rolls and sarcastic comments. Peggy jots notes in Tommy's scribbler.

"Thank you, Constable. This has all been quite fascinating." Peggy waves the small notebook in the air. "Now, I must get back to my book. The muse calls."

"Of course, good night then," Joe says.

"Really, Inspector." Peggy says, indulging in a bit of eye rolling herself. "The young man has enthusiasm. You can't fault that."

Chapter 17

Peggy is grimy and frustrated from more fruitless trudging. When she had first started out, after the first-day jitters, it was exciting and challenging, a real adventure. She loved investigating at all the hotels and train stations; grilling the staff. She felt like she was doing something important to bring Oskar home.

Two long weeks of hitting the streets of Philadelphia has worn away the shine. *We're doing the same thing every day. Learning nothing new, accomplishing nothing. This is just a waste of time, running in circles. I should think of a new approach. And while I'm at it, I should be home doing laundry. Tommy won't have a clean shirt tomorrow for school. And him having his lunch alone at the kitchen table three days in a row this week; what would Mother say?*

Yesterday's visits with the real estate agents had been unproductive. Most were disappointed when her interest turned out to be tracking her missing son rather than renting property. One had even offered to come by and do an appraisal on her house.

Today, Peggy is back bothering hotel clerks. Frank has disappeared, off to follow another line of inquiry. It is the first time she's alone. She misses his company and advice. She's also a bit nervous on her own, especially travelling between spring Garden and Vine—the Tenderloin; silly, given the Inspector is a ghost that no one can see, and who couldn't help her anyway.

Peggy's seeing bootlegging activity everywhere. How had she missed it before? The ladies with their heavy coats weighted by bottles sewn into the lining. The doormen outside the hotels seem to have a steady flow of out-of-towners looking to buy liquor. And perhaps the most distressing evidence is the display of public drunkenness, even during the day. Peggy can't remember seeing men staggering down the street before Prohibition. While she admits that she didn't get out much then, she knows her mother would have mentioned it if it had been a real problem. *Perhaps there's something to be said for quality control. All this homemade hooch and moonshine sometimes carries more of a kick than intended.*

A hair tonic advertisement in a barbershop window reminds Peggy that she needs to take Tommy to Tony's after school. While she does the trims at home, she takes him to a real barber every few months.

Peggy's aching feet and empty stomach remind her that she should head home soon. It's been another long day. One more hotel and then a quick stop at the grocer. Going to Howard's is a much more pleasant experience, now that her account is up to date. She is aware he still seems to be carrying a torch for her, despite her numerous dismissals of his advances. *His tomatoes aren't the only thing fresh in that store.*

Peggy approaches the Merchants' Hotel. It could be one of any number of seedy joints along
Callowhill or Vine, an area popular with swindlers, scoundrels, and gamblers. Not the place for a
gal on her own, not looking for a good time.

Merchants' has a look of neglect: windows that need washing, a front door crying out for paint, a torn awning. It looks as tired and run down as Peggy feels right now.

It takes a few moments for her eyes to adjust to the dark lobby and her nose to get used to the smell of stale beer, spoiled food, and cigarette smoke. A couple of men lean against the counter, their hands wrapped around heavy pottery mugs. Peggy sniffs disapprovingly. *Idle at this time of day, and I bet that it's not tea in those mugs. Say, did I go through the wrong door and wind up in the saloon instead of the hotel?* As she turns to make a hasty retreat, she is grabbed from behind.

"Whoa, there sweetheart. Don't run off so fast. Stay and have a drink with us." It's a raspy voice. Too close. Wet breath in her ear. Stubbly whiskers scratching her cheek. His arms wrap her tightly. Peggy struggles to free herself.

"Hey! Let go of me." Peggy tugs at the arms, looking around for help.

"Oh, aren't you the feisty one. Come 'ere, sweetie, and give old Bill a kiss." The boozy-smelling man tightens his arms around her waist and puckers up, lips smacking, spittle flying.

"Get your hands off me. Let go of me, now." Twisting and turning, trying to evade the groping hands, she spies a man standing behind the counter, polishing a glass. He's watching it all with an amused grin. "Hey mister, how about a little help here?" she says loudly.

"Oh, I don't think Bill needs any help. He seems to be managing all right on his own." His comment brings guffaws from the other men at the counter. Peggy tries to push the boozy man away, but he's all hands.

A short man appears at her side. "Come on now Bill, let go of the lady. This dame's got way too much class for the likes of you."

Bill looks blearily at the new participant in the drama. "Oh, Mickey. Sorry, Mr. Duffy. I didn't see you. Yes, sir. Sorry, ma'am." Letting her go, Bill slinks back to the counter and his stool.

"This dump's no place for you, doll. Let's get you back outside," says her rescuer.

"Thank you, sir." *Oh gosh, it's Mickey Duffy.*

123

Mickey reaches for her elbow to steady her as she stumbles. "A bit of fresh air is what you need."

Out on the street, Mickey holds her by the shoulders, peering closely into her face. "Are you sure you're all right, doll? You look white as a sheet. You want me to find somebody to take you home?"

Peggy stands there, shaken. She's relieved when she sees a uniformed policeman on the beat. The officer tips his hat. "Afternoon, Mr. Duffy. Ma'am," and saunters on by. Now Peggy is doubly shocked. She shakes her head, trying to regain her composure. She isn't sure which rattles her more: the scene in the hotel, the policeman so deferential to a bootlegger, or standing on the sidewalk with the notorious Mickey Duffy.

"Thank you, but I can manage, Mr. Duffy." Peggy adjusts her hat, tugs at her gloves.

"Well, if you're sure you're okay, I'll scram. I have business in that joint," he says, indicating the Merchants' Hotel with his thumb. Mickey tips his hat and disappears inside.

Peggy hurries home, away from the perils of amateur detective work. She aches for the safety of her house and family. *The Inspector is not going to believe this.*

Chapter 18

Peggy taps the end of her pencil against her teeth. She's been working on her 'Things-to-Do' list that might help with Oskar's disappearance. Interviewing Oskar's friends is at the top of the list, but for the life of her she can't figure out how she'll manage it. The boys may recognize her as Tommy's mother. And even if they don't, they'll know she's someone's mother. And mothers rarely get easy answers out of little boys. What she needs is a man the boys wouldn't recognize. But who?

Peggy has been pacing for the better part of an hour. Waiting. As soon as Archie Mansfield comes in, she pounces. "Mr. Mansfield, I have a bizarre favor to ask you."

Archie flinches in surprise. "Mrs. Barnes? Whatever is the matter?"

Peggy takes his arm and leads him into the living room, settling him on the couch. She looks around, and is relieved to see that she is alone.

"Mr. Mansfield. I would like to tap into some of your expertise with school-age boys."

"Oh, are you having problems with Tommy? I was going to mention that I could be an ear..."

Peggy waves that away. "No, Tommy is fine. What I was wondering if you'd help me with an inquiry I'd like to make."

Archie leans forward. A natural gossip, he's intrigued. "Really. An inquiry? That sounds official. What would you need me to do?"

"As you know, Tommy is upset about the disappearance of his friend Oskar Leszek. As you've pointed out, on several occasions, the police did a terrible job trying to find him. There's a whole list of things they should have done, but didn't, including they never interviewed any of Oskar Leszek's friends. It's a travesty. Those friends might know something about his disappearance. It just seemed to me that they should be questioned, and if the police aren't interested, perhaps we could do it. They'd never open up to me because I'm Tommy's mother, but I bet they'd talk to you. You have such a good way with children, given you're a teacher." She finishes in a rush. What had seemed like a perfectly reasonable approach now seems like a crazy, harebrained idea.

Archie preens at the compliment. "I am a very popular teacher at school. So, a bit of amateur sleuthing, eh? I've always fancied myself a bit of a detective. Read all of Doyle, you know."

Maggie resists rolling her eyes. *This idea better work. I have a feeling I'll never hear the end of it, from either the Inspector or Archie.*

"Or maybe it's not a good idea after all. I know how frustrated you are with Constable Kelly's inaction on this case, but now that I think on it further, maybe we shouldn't do it. It could upset him, having you uncover a piece of information rather than the police."

Archie chuckles. "You're right, that would tweak his nose, wouldn't it? No, I think it's important to follow through, Mrs. Barnes. Of course, I'd be willing to help. Just tell me what you need me to do."

"Well, they have a drama department at Boys' Central, right?"

* * * *

Peggy laughs when she sees Archie the next day. He's changed out of his usual suit and tie and is wearing an old sweater and pair of dungarees. He's glued a mustache under his nose, and added whiskers on his chin. He's carrying an old sea captain's greatcoat and hat, borrowed from the school's wardrobe department.

"Oh, excellent." Peggy claps her hands.

"Not bad for a math teacher, if I do say so myself. Have I told you I was in the major production of my college? I got great reviews. The idea for the disguise started with the moustache and kind of went from there. I thought about a peg-leg but couldn't quite figure out how to do it. You don't think it's too much, do you?" Archie says, peering into the mirror.

"Oh no, it's perfect."

"So, you say that Jimmy and some other boys will be at their school?" Archie asks, pulling on the great coat.

"Yes. At their school grounds. They have baseball practice this afternoon. I've told Tommy he has to come straight home. Your disguise is excellent, but I don't know whether it will fool him. Up close, I mean."

"True. True. He'd probably recognize my voice. I'll wait for him to head home and then I'll go have a chat with his friends. And I'm asking them about the night that Oskar disappeared, right?"

"Yes. We're trying to establish a timeline."

"Anything else?"

"Just follow their lead. Take note if something sounds useful."

Archie settles the hat. "All right then. I'm off."

"Oh, and Archie? Mum's the word, especially to Constable Kelly. Let's just keep this between ourselves until we know more. Okay?"

Archie pantomimes zipping his mouth and locking it. He winks and heads out the door.

* * * *

Captain Archie loiters beside the fence, watching the school baseball team break up. Along the way, he'd spied a prop; a scruffy lab. A piece of rope attached to the mutt completes the look. The confused, but obedient dog sits by Archie.

Archie spots Tommy talking with a few other boys. Tommy slaps one on the back and then heads home. The other boys break open a bag of marbles and start a game.

Archie and the dog saunter past the schoolyard. He whistles a tune, hoping it's a sea shanty. As he closes in on the boys, he releases the rope. The dog looks at him, then bolts toward the boys.

"Rex! Rex, you bad dog. Come here." Archie lunges after the dog, who has burst in on the marble game.

"Hey! Watch it."

"Grab him," Archie shouts.

A boy grabs the rope and waits for Archie. "Here's your dog, sir," A blonde boy of about eight hands the rope to the sea captain.

"Thanks, young fella. Rex, you are a bad dog." Archie sits on the ground. "Say, that dash tuckered me out."

The boys look at each other and at the odd sea captain who has just plopped down beside them.

"You okay, Mister?" asked one of the boys, his hands buried deeply in the ruff of 'Rex'. Rex's tail thumps.

"Oh sure. Just need to catch my breath. Rex and I will just sit a spell, if that's okay with you. You youngsters go on with your game."

The circle of boys look at one another. "Okay, but we're not gonna be here long." The cautious comment delivered in a nervous tone came from a taller boy.

"Yeah, cuz you were winning all the marbles. I want a chance to get some back," says a large boy.

The smaller boy shrugs, and the game resumes.

"I'm surprised you kids are out here at all. I would have thought your mamas would be telling you to come straight home. What with that young boy that went missing. Oskar something? Sad. Sad." Archie shakes his head. "Do you know him?"

"Yeah, we know Oskar."

"I heard he ran off and joined the circus. That true?"

"Naw," scoffs one of the boys. "Ain't no circus in town. That's just some story the police made up."

"So, what really happened then? He jump a train?"

"Why would he do that?"

"I don't know. Just something else I heard."

"Well, my Pa says that he's probably running with one of the bootlegger gangs. His brother is part of one, you know."

Another boy cuts in. "That's crazy. Tommy says that he went over to Oskar's house and Oskar's brother didn't know where he was."

"Maybe he was playing by the river and fell in?" Archie asks, an innocent look on his face.

The boys look to each other, and shrug. One of the boys, a taller one, has not said a word since he first spoke when Archie sat down.

"What about you, young fella. You have any theories?" Archie asks.

"No. I gotta go. Now," he says.

"Hey, Jimmy. I thought you wanted to win your marbles back from the last game. What's your hurry?"

"I gotta go is all. See ya tomorrow." Jimmy pockets his remaining marbles and jogs off. The dog whines, eager to chase.

"Sorry about that. I seem to have upset him."

"Don't mind him, Mister. Jimmy and Oskar are best pals. He's been weird since Oskar disappeared."

* * * *

"I don't believe it. You asked Mr. Mansfield to do what?" Frank says.

"Well, Oskar's friends were never questioned. The police didn't do it. I couldn't do it. You certainly couldn't do it. So, I asked Mr. Mansfield." Peggy and the Inspector are in their usual chairs after dinner.

Archie had worn a smug smile on his face all through dinner, and Peggy was sure he was going to spill the beans. Maybe asking him to help hadn't been such a good idea; not that she'd admit that to the Inspector now.

"Did he learn anything?" asks Frank.

"Not much. Although Oskar's best friend, Jimmy, seems to know something. But he's not saying anything. And neither is Tommy, by the way. I asked him about it again, while I was getting supper ready."

"Following the procedure is important. Not every lead pans out, but it's important to follow up. A lot of police work is tedious, although Archie Mansfield posing as a sea captain wouldn't have been dull by a long shot."

Frank takes a puff on his cigar and considers the glowing tip. Some of his most insightful observations seem to reside there. "Well, I must say that it is a bit unorthodox. But you have good instincts. And interviewing the boys should have been a priority for the police. I'm glad we've been able to eliminate it from our list. However, perhaps next time you come up with an idea for our inquiry, you could run it past me first?"

"Certainly, Inspector. As long as you don't say no." Peggy says. Her eyes twinkle. She feels it. And she knows Frank does too. "Oh, you should have seen him, Inspector. He looked like Captain Bligh," Peggy says, giggling.

"Indeed," Frank says. "Oh, Lordy, indeed."

Chapter 19

"But Mother, I don't need a haircut." Tommy's hands are deep in his pockets as he marches along the sidewalk.

"You most certainly do, young man. And don't dawdle. We have to stop by the grocer as well. I wasn't able to get there yesterday. We're almost out of potatoes and carrots." Tommy takes two steps to every one of Peggy's, and still scrambles to catch up. Peggy can see the red, white, and blue striped pole across the street in the next block.

They're almost there. Tommy slows, then stops, causing Peggy to backtrack. "You don't have to come with me, Mother. I can go on my own, you know."

BOOM!

The explosion knocks them to the sidewalk. Peggy covers Tommy, shielding him with her body. The sounds of destruction around them. Debris is flung everywhere. Panicked people shout, some calling for help. Frightened horses rear, crying out in terror. Clouds of smoke billow onto the street.

"Oh, my goodness." Peggy holds Tommy tighter. "Are you all right, sweetheart? Are you hurt?"

They lie on the sidewalk, waiting, listening. Sensing the threat is over, she stands. Tommy scrambles up and stands close beside her. The smoke clears. The front window of the barbershop is gone, the street is littered with glass, broken bricks, and twisted bits of metal. A car parked in front of the barbershop has Tony's door on its front seat. The striped barber pole dangles loosely from the side of the building. Peggy and

Tommy watch it crash to the ground. Somewhere inside the destruction, a woman is shrieking.

People on both sides of the street stare at the devastation. Huddled together in groups, they quiz each other about what was seen or remembered.

"What's happened, Mother?"

"I don't know, Tommy, but I think we'd better go." Peggy brushes at her coat. She gathers Tommy into a tight hug. *Our world could have been over two minutes ago. It was that close.* Fire engines and police sirens ring out in the distance. "It's not safe out on the street like this. Let's go home."

* * *

At dinner, Joe confirms that Tony's Barbershop had been bombed. Peggy is sick thinking about the close call. She pushes food around the plate with trembling hands, trying to focus and be calm—to be braver than she feels.

Tommy vibrates with excitement.

Joe gives them a report. "Witnesses say that a young man on a bicycle tossed the bomb through the front window. It was a bottle of alcohol with a rag stuffed into its neck, but it caused a much bigger explosion because of all the flammable products inside the barbershop. Tony is badly injured, and his wife, who was in the apartment upstairs, has also been hurt."

Peggy's cutlery falls to her plate. "Tommy could have been in the barber's chair when it happened." She chokes back a sob.

133

Eugene Smith appears equally shaken. "You should have told me you were taking Tommy for a haircut today, Mrs. Barnes."

Tommy leans forward, waving his fork in the air. "There was a loud bang and then lots of smashing glass and smoke. *Boom,*" he roars, throwing his arms in the air, potatoes flying. Peggy barely notices.

"How old was the boy on the bicycle? Do you know who did it? Who was the lady that was screaming? How bad is Tony? How hurt is Mrs. Tony? Was anyone killed?" Tommy peppers Joe.

"It looks like it had something to do with bootlegging. Maybe a turf war, or customer dispute. Just like we thought, the barbershop was a cover-up house, one of thousands in the city," Joe says.

Peggy jerks her head up, glaring at Joe. "Constable, you said that you were going to check to see if Tony's was safe. You gave me your word," Peggy says accusingly. Tears threaten to spill as she shakes her head. "Tommy and I could have been killed."

"I had checked, Ma'am. But, obviously, this place has been under the radar. Nobody had it on their list."

Frank, on sentry duty in his chair in the living room, gives his customary *harrumph*. "And why would that be, I wonder." His words are for Peggy's ears alone.

"Apparently, Tony recently changed suppliers; the bomb was a message about loyalty. You know, to warn other barbershops about switching," Joe says.

"It's crazy how dangerous Philadelphia is getting," says Archie Mansfield. "There have been instances close to the school, and the headlines in the papers are full of shootings, violence, and raids."

"There are always turf war battles going on, as rival gangs fight for territory. Now that gambling is in the mix, it's even worse," Joe says.

Eugene eats his dinner, head down, ears open.

"What happens next, Constable? More raids?" Archie asks.

"We're pretty sure the Duffy gang is behind the bombing at Tony's. So we'll start there and see what we can find."

"Mickey Duffy?" Peggy asks. The name has caught her attention, pulling her from her dark thoughts. Eugene also looks up.

"One and the same, Ma'am. He and Boo-Boo Hoff have been battling it out on the streets for the past month. They've always been feuding over the beer and whiskey sales, but things have taken a nasty turn lately," Joe says.

"Isn't Boo-Boo the man that manages the boxers, who does the prize fights?" Tommy asks.

"He manages lots of boxers, but that's just his sideline. His real business is bootlegging. He's the Bootleg King here in Philadelphia," Joe says.

"Ha," Eugene sneers. "The Bootleg King. That's rich. Well, I hear King Boo-Boo has lots of cops on the payroll," Eugene glares at Joe aggressively. "He hands out lots of dough, and turkeys at Christmas, too. I hear that he pays five hundred bucks a month to some of the cops in Enforcement Unit Number One, just to be in the know about what's going on."

"Where did you hear that, Mr. Smith?" Joe sits tall in his chair and returns Eugene's scowl.

Eugene grins at Joe and shrugs. "I'm not sure. Just heard it around." Eugene gets up as Peggy rises. "Here, let me help you with those dishes." He knocks Joe's chair as he passes.

"I'll just get these washed up and then I think I'll write for a bit. The day has been quite traumatic," Peggy says.

"That book of yours must be really coming along, Mrs. Barnes," Eugene says as he stacks the last dishes.

Everyone is getting used to her writing every night. She has her own scribbler. They're her case notes, just like a real detective. She's told Tommy they contain notes for a book she wants to write.

Washing dishes calms Peggy a bit. She's somewhat more settled when she sits in front of the desk, the radio playing softly. As is his habit, Frank takes the armchair next to the desk, his cane leaning against the upholstery, his hat resting on the table next to him. For him, the evening ritual is reminiscent of attending 'report' at the end of every shift.

Taking two matches from the box in his vest pocket, he holds them up with his unlit cigar. "Do you mind, Mrs. Barnes?"

"No, of course not. That cigar of yours is a ghostly as you are. I never smell a thing."

She waits while he strikes the double matches, twirling the end of the cigar to ensure that the burning is even. He lifts it to his lips and puffs. She gets up and leaves an ashtray beside him. A habit as she's never seen an ash remain behind after the Inspector leaves.

"Inspector, I have concerns. I'm not sure I'm comfortable continuing. The other day I was groped, today was the bombing. This is all getting too close to home, and too violent. If we were making progress, I might reconsider, but as it is we've had no luck so far. I've talked with lots of the hotel clerks and a few real estate agents. I've checked the train station twice. We've interviewed Oskar's friends. No one has seen Oskar, either alone or in the company of a man. It doesn't make any sense to me. This can't be a kidnapping. What would be the point? Alicja Leszek doesn't have any money for ransom. If someone did take Oskar, why would they stay in Philadelphia? How did they get out of town without being seen?"

"I agree. As much as I hate to set aside that line of inquiry, a kidnapping or abduction is appearing to be unlikely. But every crime needs a motive. Someone wanted the boy for something."

"Inspector, I don't think that is what happened to Oskar. I know you said that there were similarities between this case and your older one, but I think you're wrong. Somehow Oskar got caught up in all the bootlegging business, that's what I think happened. Something like what happened today. At the barbershop bombing. I mean, Tommy and I were almost at the wrong place at the wrong time."

"Bootleggers appear to be Constable Kelly's theory, as well." Frank raises an eyebrow. "Right now, he's preoccupied with bootleggers, so every crime must be related. But there is no evidence, Mrs. Barnes. I can't believe that a man, even a gangster, would gun down a little boy. Therefore, something else has happened. We just need to keep on the case, and we'll find the lead."

"Who said anything about gunned down? Wrong place at the wrong time. He's disappeared, but not dead, surely. There's a lot of focus on bootleggers, and so there should be. The barbershop was bombed. The city is in trouble, but to mention guns and little boys in the same sentence, Inspector, well that goes beyond troubling. You said you can't believe a gangster would do that. Does that mean you're thinking it could be possible?"

Peggy taps her pencil against on the desk. "Perhaps Oskar's working for one of the other bootleggers. His brother works for Mickey and would know if he was there. But, maybe he's with another group? I don't know how you can presume to know either the motive or the alibi, without a theory of who the perpetrator is. Shouldn't we be following the facts?"

Frank shakes his head, rises, and begins pacing in front of the fireplace, cigar grasped firmly behind his back. A trail of smoke following him like a tail.

"Back in your day, Philadelphia was a different city." Peggy jabs her pencil in Frank's direction. "Today, bad things regularly happen to innocent people. There's criminals on every corner, right out in the open. Look what happened to us today. These days, everything in Philadelphia relates to bootleggers."

"All these ideas have strong potential, Mrs. Barnes, and I concede your point about the bootleggers. I'm also relieved to see that you're thinking about the case again, instead of giving up. Remember that *'victory belongs to the most persevering'*. You've got to stay the course. Keep interviewing. Eventually, we'll find a clue," Frank says.

"You know, your constant quotations of General Bonaparte can be really irritating, Inspector."

Frank is wrapped up in his own thoughts. "We must refocus our efforts. Perhaps I made an error in judgement allowing you to work alone. Maybe you're not ready yet, despite the initiative you've shown. Maybe you're not asking the right questions, or not trying hard enough? There has to be an answer out there somewhere."

"Not trying hard enough? I'll have you know—"

Tommy pokes his head around the corner of the doorway from the hallway. "Is everything all right, Mother?" He's dressed in his nightshirt, and his hair is tussled from sleeping.

"I'm sorry, sweetheart. Did I wake you? Is the radio too loud?" Peggy says, casting an accusing look at the Inspector. "I'll be quieter." She holds out her arms to Tommy.

Tommy gives his mother a quick hug. "That's okay. Something just woke me up is all," Tommy yawns. "As long as you're okay."

"Probably a noise coming from outside," says Peggy.

Tommy yawns again.

"Off you go to bed, sweetheart."

"Night, Mother," Tommy says and heads back upstairs.

"Well, I'm sorry that you don't think that I'm doing a good job, Inspector. It's not easy for me you know, going into all these hotels and talking with desk clerks. If women were meant to do this job, there would be female police officers. Maybe I'm not good enough, but I'm trying. And I will try harder, but I don't think it's going to make any difference."

Peggy's pencil is keeping a staccato beat, and her right foot taps as well. "When we started this venture, Inspector, it was to be an equal partnership. I'll stick with your strategy for a few more days, but then I think we need to try something else," Peggy says. Pencil and toe are still as she delivers her ultimatum.

She gets up, turns out the desk lamp, abandoning Frank to near darkness. "I think that I'm going to turn in and go upstairs. You can show yourself out, I'm sure. It's been a very long day. I'm exhausted."

"I'm sorry for pushing you so hard, Mrs. Barnes-- Peggy, but there is a little boy out there that needs our help." Frank's voice reaches her as she mounts the first stair.

She steps back. "That last comment is undeserved, Inspector. I know Oskar and am as worried as the next person. Now, I really must go upstairs," *before I say something I regret.*

But she turns on the second stair. "I agree there is merit in the statement about victory going to the most persevering, but at what point do we open other lines of investigation? I know that you've had great success with this approach in the past, but those were different times. You need to let go of the idea, broaden your approach. We need to adapt to modern times and look at the circumstances we live in today. These bootleggers and mobsters have taken control. Anything's possible."

The realization of what she is stating so passionately hits Peggy. She grips the stair rail tightly. "Yes, anything's possible. You say you can't believe that a man, even a gangster, would shoot a little boy. Oh my heavens, Inspector, I'm afraid I can."

"Wrong place, wrong time," whispers the Inspector.

"You don't think..."

"It could have been you, today, my dear. And Tommy. Wrong place, wrong time. The question is, was it young Oskar's fate as well?"

The Inspector waits by the front door. Peggy sighs and returns to the front hall. *It's only good manners. I'm still right.* She opens the door, locking it behind him.

Chapter 20

The moment Peggy has been dreading has arrived. She stands facing the open front door as her mother, Cordelia Gifford, storms past, dressed for battle in a fur stole and covered in an ankle-length dress, under which she is tightly corseted. Her large hat is pinned securely into the mass of hair on her head, the extravagant adornments a rooster in his prime has sacrificed his tail feathers for. She is ready to take on all comers, including her daughter.

Cordelia is a force, striding over to the table, yanking off her gloves and slapping them against the hall stand. She reaches into her handbag and pulls out a folded newspaper and a series of pamphlets.

"Margaret! What do you make of this?" Cordelia glares at Peggy.

"Hello, Mother, it's lovely to see you, too. My day? Well, I have a lot of things on the go."

"Don't be impertinent, Margaret. Look at these headlines. 'Flippant Flapper a Real Peril, Says Labor Secretary', and this one, 'Is the Younger Generation in Jeopardy?' She enunciates each word.

"I like this one," says Peggy. " 'Mother Not to Blame for Flapper's Flapping' ". That must be a comfort?"

"My dear, do not adopt that tone with me. This is real. We had a man in to speak to the Garden Club. He's a physician. An expert. He talked about young women these days smoking and drinking in public." Cordelia dabs her neck with her handkerchief and sits. "And it's not just newspaper headlines. It's right on our own doorsteps. Mrs. Tate, you remember Mrs. Tate? Her daughter was seen cavorting with a young man and no chaperone. Imagine."

Peggy coughs quietly into her hand. "Excuse me a moment, Mother. I'll just get the coffee." She barely makes it through into the kitchen before doubling over in laughter. *That old relic. Stuck in the good old days. You can't keep young girls at home and in the kitchen anymore. Well, she never could.* Peggy smirks, thinking of her own escape.

"Margaret? Can you hear what I'm saying? I said that this article says that women are working in offices and factories, earning the salary a family man would need."

Peggy returns with the coffee tray. "It was all right when ladies worked in factories during the war. Why should they give up their jobs just because the men are home?"

"That's just ridiculous. Men need those jobs. And each woman needs to find a man with a job to support them. So they can stay at home with their children. I mean really, Margaret. It's always been that way. Something perhaps you could aspire to."

No, it hasn't always been that way. "Yes, Mother."

"And the clothes young girls are wearing. Scandalous. You can see their knees. And short hair. I am so glad you've kept yours long, Margaret. A woman's hair is her crowning glory."

Maybe I should cut my hair? Give it one of those sassy bobs? So much handier, a quick flip and you're out the door instead of hours of braiding and piling and pinning. "Yes, Mother," Peggy replies.

"Since women got the vote, the whole country has fallen apart, let me tell you, Margaret."

Women have been fighting for the vote since Mother was a girl. Pushing for change it seems like forever, and now, almost overnight, change is pulling us along so fast we can hardly keep up.

"Margaret. You aren't paying attention. I was saying…"

When is she going to realize that the soft, demure Gibson Girl is gone; replaced with a sharp-edged, sassy flapper? All those rules for women? Well, rules are made to be broken, and then some.

"Women don't even sound like they used to. I can't understand a thing they say. Bee's knees. What does that even mean? It's ridiculous. All this independence. Young women are not shy to give their opinions anymore, Margaret. I fear for you, getting all caught up in this modern age."

That's true. All this change happening around me, but where do I fit in?

The mink's head on her mother's stole clutches its tail in its teeth. Above it, Peggy watches her mother warily. She waits for the next eruption.

"You don't want people thinking you're a flapper, do you? My dear Margaret, I really must insist again that you come home."

Well, that didn't take long. "Mother, I keep telling you that I left home to be with Jack, to start a new life. We've had this conversation many times: we're living in a new age, and I am a new woman."

"I see nothing new about a widow struggling to raise her son, Margaret. There have been women left alone since there were families. Look at your Aunt Elizabeth, who lived with Grand-mamma when dear Uncle Charles fell in the Boer War."

Peggy grimaces. Mother produces these martyrs effortlessly, as if they are out of her handbag like a grocery list.

"Yes, dear Uncle Charles. Now he was a real soldier. A hero. Unlike some, he fought and died honorably" Cordelia says.

Peggy will have none of it. She's convinced that her mother wishes Jack's death had been on the front lines in battle rather than on a picket line. *That would have made it more honorable for Mother. She doesn't understand that for him, that picket line was about the honor protecting his comrades and their families.* There is a way her mother's mouth curls when she talks about Jack's work with the labor movement, as if she's chewed a bit of spoiled food.

"Jack fought for what he believed in as well, Mother. And died for it."

Cordelia frowns at Peggy. "That was a shame, and selfish of him, leaving you and Tommy alone. Aunt Elizabeth would never have been able to manage on her own, without her family to stand by her. By new age, do you mean that you should turn your back on your family, my dear? Well then, I want nothing to do with this *'new'*." Cordelia moves into her favorite line of attack. "And you know, Tommy would be much better growing up in a secure home, with all the advantages you had."

"I know no such thing, Mother. You forget that I chose to leave all those so-called advantages behind to have a life with Jack, a life that includes Tommy. We're doing just fine on our own." Peggy lowers her teacup to the table, afraid she'll snap the handle.

"Well, if you're not going to think of what's best for Tommy, then think about us, Margaret. You used to care about what people thought. You have no idea what I've had to endure since you left. It's still the main topic of conversation at the Club."

"Yes, I'm sure it's been difficult for you, Mother. I, on the other hand, have enjoyed nothing but the life of Riley since I left. Nothing but good times for me."

Cordelia huffs and puffs at the accusation.

"I have to think about what's best for my family, Mother. And my family is Tommy. I've told you before, it's best that he and I remain in Philadelphia. There are opportunities here, and good schools."

"Opportunities?" Peggy now has her mother's close attention. "Does that mean you are you seeing someone, Margaret?"

"Not those kinds of opportunities, Mother. Economic opportunities."

There's a commotion in the front hall. Joe and a young woman are standing in the entry to the living room. She is a tiny thing, done up in the latest fashion; her skirt ends mid-calf, her hair is a short, neat bob. The flappers' typical bee-stung mouth pouts prettily as she peers out from behind long bangs. A little cloche cap sits snug on her head.

"Excuse me, ma'am. Oh, I'm sorry, you already have a visitor. I wanted you to meet a family friend from my hometown. Mrs. Barnes, let me introduce Fanny Carmichael. Fanny, this is my landlady, Mrs. Barnes," Joe says.

Peggy rises to greet her new guests. "It's a pleasure to meet you, Miss Carmichael. And this is my mother, Mrs. Gifford," Peggy says.

"Ah yes, the young boarder. Good afternoon, Constable Kelly," Cordelia says. "And charming to make your acquaintance, Miss Carmichael."

Peggy notices that Joe has his arm around Fanny. *Family friend? Sure.*

"We were just having coffee. Would you and Miss Carmichael like to join us?" Peggy says. Joe and Fanny may be the cavalry that she's been hoping for in the ongoing skirmish with her mother.

As the young couple settles on the couch and Peggy pours them coffee, she admires the neat T-strapped heels that Fanny is wearing. *What I wouldn't give for a pair of those. Like anyone would see them under my long skirts. I look more like Mother than Fanny.*

"So, Miss Carmichael, you must be from Ardmore, like the Constable here. Margaret has mentioned that your family are in coal, Constable Kelly. And Miss Carmichael, are you enjoying your visit to Philadelphia, my dear?" Mrs. Gifford asks. She leans back to better peer down her nose at Fanny.

"Nope, I don't live in Ardmore anymore. I'm a Philly gal, now. Moved here six weeks ago. And it's the cat's pajamas, I tell ya." Fanny tosses her head as she speaks; her earrings twinkle in the light.

"Oh, I'm sorry to hear that, my dear. I understand then that your parents have passed. Was it an accident?"

"Mother," Peggy warns.

"Oh no, they're still alive and kicking. I just decided I needed a change of scene and thought I'd give Philly a try." Fanny says, with a gay little smile.

Peggy smiles at Fanny, admiring her pluck.

"Excuse me, but surely your parents did not give you permission to move to Philadelphia? Are they not concerned? A young woman, on her own, in a big city?" Mrs. Gifford tries gamely to re-establish her footing.

"Oh, they were put out, all right. We had a huge row before I left. They really didn't approve. But I just felt that I could do better on my own. I found a good job as a telephone operator at Atlantic Refining."

"Ah, so you're one of those modern women I hear so much about from Margaret." Mrs. Gifford frowns at Peggy. "Well, I certainly don't approve of young, single women leaving home. Margaret was bad enough, and she left to be married. There is far too much selfish thinking these days, and not enough respect for traditions and family."

Peggy watches the volley pass between Fanny and her mother. She would intervene but is enjoying the rare opportunity to spectate rather than participate.

"Oh la, Mrs. Gifford, you slay me." Fanny giggles, gazing around the room, humming, her toe tapping. "You know this song, don'tcha? It's the bee's-knees." Fanny leaps up and shimmies around the living room. "You have to move with the times, right Mrs. Barnes? Like I told my own ma." She belts out in her best Tin Pan Alley style:
"Every morning, every evening
Ain't we got fun?
Not much money, oh but honey
Ain't we got fun?"

Peggy's delighted to be included 'with the times'. She taps her foot in time to the song. At the end of the tune, Fanny collapses on the couch in Joe's lap. Joe is in awe.

"Well, I have never heard such poppycock. Nor seen such behavior. Young lady, I'll have you know that in MY day..."

"Mother, perhaps we could finish this visit another time? I'm sure that Constable Kelly and Miss Carmichael have things they'd rather be doing than sitting here, being lectured to? And I'm sure that you have other errands in the city as well?"

Peggy's mother stares at her stonily. "Are you asking me to leave, Margaret?"

Peggy stands, then heads for the front door. "Yes Mother, I guess I am. I look forward to visiting with you another time."

Cordelia Gifford rises slowly and casts a disparaging glance around the small living room. Her gaze settles on the young flapper, who has moved off of Joe's lap and is once again perched on the edge of the sofa beside him, still humming, still tapping.

Cordelia turns to Peggy. "As I said, my dear, there is a distinct lack of respect these days." And in a parting shot at Fanny, declares, "Young ladies who run wild come to no good end, as my daughter knows only too well." She sweeps out of the room, and out the front door.

"My apologies for my mother's very rude behavior, Miss Carmichael. She can be a stubborn and opinionated old woman at times. Well, actually, all the time."

"Oh heck, Missus B., don't give it a mind. I got one of those at home, too. Your ma's a real Mrs. Grundy," Fanny says. She giggles, snuggling closer to Joe. "Hey Joe, didn't you say you needed to get something from your room? Before we head out tonight?" Fanny gives him a push. "Go on, ya' big palooka. Missus B and I are just going to sit here and have a bit of a chinwag. You go do what you need to do." Joe pats her hand then heads upstairs.

As Joe climbs the stairs, Fanny turns to Peggy. "I hope you don't mind me barging over like this, Missus B., but Joe talks about you all the time and I just had to meet you."

"I'm glad you came over, Fanny. I've been wondering where Joe has been off to these past few weeks. He's never home."

Peggy, still rattled by her mother's parting jab, smiles at Fanny perched beside her. "It must be quite the adventure to be living on your own. When I left home with Jack, it caused a major scandal up and down the Main Line, as you can imagine. It was seven years ago and, back then, that kind of thing just wasn't done. It was years before my parents would speak with me. Even after Tommy was born."

"Oh, I'm not on my own, not really. Me and a couple of gals share an apartment downtown. It's the only way I can afford to live here. Even with a regular paycheck, I never seem to have any dough," Fanny says. "Being on your own, with a baby and all, now that would have been hard, but you've done okay. It's swell that you have this house and have folks like Joe to live here. Joe says that you got hitched real young. He died, didn't he? Your husband, I mean, not Joe..." Fanny says, giggling again. "You're swell. Not like those old gals."

This girl admires me?

"Yes, my Jack was killed in the Great Steel Strike four years ago. It's been a struggle, as there wasn't much money to begin with. His pals from the union helped out, and his parents as well, when they could. And I took in mending and some sewing. It's been hard, but we're managing."

"Jeepers, Missus B. Can I call you Missus B?" Fanny says, taking both of Peggy's hands in her own. "I just knew it. You and me, both on our own in the big city. Our folks steamin'. It's like we're sisters or something." Fanny leans in with a hug. Peggy pats Fanny's back. *My, but she's a peppy thing.*

"I mean, you and me, we got tons in common, it feels like. And I think that you're just awesome," Fanny gushes. "When I left home, I felt that I was the only girl ever to do that, you know what I mean? Nobody in my family got it. Lots of frowny faces, I can tell you. Then finding a place, and then figuring out how I was going to find the clams to stay here. I gotta tell you, Missus B, walking into the Atlantic was the hardest thing I ever had to do. They're in one of those twenty-story skyscrapers, you know, downtown? I rode an elevator, first time ever. And then had to talk my way into trying out for the job. But I got it."

"I bet you did." *It's exhausting, keeping up with her.*

"And then I couldn't believe it when Joe tells me that you did the same thing. Leaving home. Your folks put out. And I have it easy compared to you. I mean, a little boy, all on your own. Your husband gone." Fanny's wide eyes fill with tears. "Losing your one true love. I mean, that's all pretty rough, ain't it?"

Peggy pats Fanny's hand. She's flustered and proud at the same time. She's never thought of herself as a role model. Or been praised for doing what needs to be done. *This young girl is looking up to me. Me. Maybe Tommy and I can make it on our own after all.*

Joe bounds down the stairs wearing a different jacket.

"Don't you look spiffy," says Fanny. She hops up to greet him. "Bye, Missus B. We got to vamoose. Big plans tonight." With a wave of her fingers and a twinkle of her earrings she is gone, Joe in her wake.

Chapter 21

Peggy gathers the coffee cups and heads into the kitchen. *What a breath of fresh air Fanny is. The perfect antidote to Mother. Gosh, I hope I never become as rigid as that old battle ax.* Peggy turns the tap. Nothing. "Nerts!" she stamps her foot.

Broken again. That plumber sure did a crappy job. And this is crappy plumbing. In a crappy house. And I have a crappy, crappy life. How will I make breakfast in the morning? How will the lodgers wash up? Oh no, I'll lose the lodgers. They won't stay in a house without water. Without the lodgers, I'll have to marry Howard. Or worse, move back in with my parents. All because of these stupid, crappy taps.

"Why don't you just fix them yourself?" Frank asks.

"You. Your sudden appearances throw me for a loop, Inspector." She paces in front of the sink and tries the taps again.

"Fix them myself? Yes, why don't I just. And shingle the roof while I'm at it." She places her hands on her hips. "It doesn't seem to matter what I do, I just can't get ahead." She smacks at the taps.

"You know, Constable Kelly brought a young woman around this afternoon, and she thought I was the cat's pajamas for what I've accomplished on my own. She loves my independence. Ha! She should see the real consequences of foolish decisions. No water, a stack of bills, a dead husband, raising a child alone, no one to talk to, except for an old codger who's been dead for a dozen years. Sometimes, Inspector, I think it's just all too much."

Frank is pushed back by the ferociousness of her remarks.

Peggy collapses into a chair, leans her elbows on the table, and cups her forehead in her hands. "I gave up my home, my family, my security. For what? A twinkling eye and a warm kiss?" She fights off tears by breathing deeply.

"Do you know that I even gave up my name? Names are important, you know. They're a label. I was christened Margaret. Mother stills calls me Margaret, even though I've asked her not to. Jack always called me Peggy. I think he called me that because Margaret was too fine for him. He said Margaret was a name for an old person. And Peggy was young and full of dreams. I wanted to leave my old life behind, to start a brand new life. By marrying Jack, I'd have a new last name and, golly, I got a new first name, too."

Peggy checks to see if Frank is still there.

"Peggy suited me then, but it doesn't suit me now. Peggy's are young and vivacious, without a care. I guess I'm back to being a Margaret again. Stiff and straight. Old and corseted. A version of Mother."

Frank is now on the floor, peering under the sink.

"Enough of that, Peggy. There's no sense moaning. It won't fix your plumbing." He scrabbles his old bones off the floor and plants his feet firmly apart, one hand on his hip and one hand upstretched, his head raised. "Sometimes 'a single battle decides everything and, sometimes too, the slightest circumstance decides the issue of a battle. There is a moment in every battle at which the least maneuver is decisive and gives superiority, just as one drop of water causes overflow'."

Peggy stares open-mouthed at the theatrics. Frank bows. "Or in this case, the lack of one drop of water. If you have the tools, we can win this particular battle. I can walk you through fixing the plumbing. You still have your husband's tools, don't you?" Frank removes his jacket, hangs it on the back of a kitchen chair, and then rolls up his shirt sleeves.

Peggy hesitates. Looking after chores like the plumbing was always Jack's job, something she's always hired a man for. "On the back porch. I'll get them."

After turning off the water supply and fetching the tools, Peggy pushes back the gingham skirt around the sink, then sits on the floor "It's all a mystery to me. What do I do first?"

"Take the wrench and loosen the valve on the supply."

Peggy looks into the box of tools beside her. *Which one is a wrench?* Her hand hovers over the tools.

"For goodness sake, the metal one with the crescent end. You twist the screw in the middle to make it get bigger and smaller," he says.

Slowly and methodically, Frank walks her through the repair. There's a piece that blocks the water flow; the plumber should have removed it instead of letting it keep sliding—damming the pipe. At one point Peggy has her foot braced against the leg of the sink, using the force to turn the wrench.

Peggy makes a final, satisfied twist of the wrench and puts it back in the toolbox. Wiping her hands on a towel, she rises with a great sense of accomplishment.

"Well?" asks Frank. "Shall we see whether it works?"

Peggy turns the tap and water gushes out. "I did it! I did it!"

Delighted, Peggy claps her hands and then raises them in a boxer's victory salute. With sparkling eyes and a grin, she opens her arms wide and steps toward the Inspector to give him a hug. He raises his arms and steps back. He celebrates instead with a grin.

"Yes, you did," he says proudly. "I couldn't have done it better myself." Frank unrolls his sleeves and puts his jacket on. He waits at the table while Peggy puts the tools away.

"You know, Peggy, watching you work, I've realized that Jack was right. You're definitely not a Margaret. A Margaret wouldn't have crawled under the sink. And a Margaret certainly wouldn't have used that language when the wrench slipped."

Peggy blushes.

"But, I don't think a Peggy would have done it, either. A Peggy would have waited until her young man could look after it. She would have wrung her hands and moaned about not being able to wash her hair or some such thing." Peggy snaps her dish towel at him. "And a Peggy certainly wouldn't have done that."

Grinning, she snaps it again.

"No," Frank continues, "I think that a modern, independent woman who fixes her own plumbing, looks after her son and a house full of lodgers, pays her bills, and still has time to glance in the mirror to fix her hair is definitely a…"

The towel dangles between the two of them.

"…definitely a Maggie."

"Maggie?" She tries out the new name. "Maggie. I like it." The towel becomes a flag; she waves it in the air. "Well, since I'm changing my life, maybe it's time I changed my name again. Maggie Barnes, landlady."

"In a Maggie, there's a Margaret's spine and a Peggy's bounce. Yes, you're definitely a Maggie."

"A new name for my new life. Not Father's daughter or Jack's wife. A person in my own right, steering my own course." Maggie laughs delightedly. "Maggie Barnes. I think I'll keep it!"

Chapter 22

Maggie had made the big announcement of the name over dinner the night before, still flush with excitement over her achievement of fixing the tap. Though she was Mrs. Barnes to her lodgers, and Mother to Tommy, she had felt they all needed to know, and once they knew, and smiled about it, she extended an invitation to call her Maggie.

Joe announced that if she was going to get a new name, then she would have to drop the formality and start calling him Joe all the time, not just sometimes. Archie and Eugene insisted on being on a first name basis as well. Of course, the new familiarity in the house didn't extend down the ranks to Tommy. The barrier between adult and child was still firmly in place.

With the start of a new day, and with renewed determination, the newly christened Maggie hits the streets as soon as Tommy leaves for school. *I have a few more hotels on my list and will visit them, stop by the grocery store, and then be home in time to fix Tommy some lunch. A productive day starts as an organized day.*

She likes the change. Maggie Barnes, formerly Peggy Barnes, formerly Margaret Gifford, smiles with satisfaction as she walks along Dock Street, the heart of the wholesale district.

Wagons line the streets. The neighborhood is full of greengrocers with their crates of vegetables and bags of potatoes. Butchers are busy directing workmen with heavy meat carcasses slung over their backs. The chickens squawking in their crates almost drown out the shouts and car horns.

The Alexander Inn is a little off the beaten track, certainly not one of the posh hotels in Philadelphia. Used mainly by out-of-town patrons of the markets, it is definitely a working-class hotel. *No fancy pillars or doormen here.*

She pushes open the front door. Inside, there is a small vestibule with a caged counter window off to one side. There, a small, squat man in a tattered bowler sits behind the counter. His mustache bristles when he sees Maggie alone; he gives her a long, slow once-over.

"Sorry darlin', no pro skirts allowed in here." Maggie takes a step back. *Well, that's the limit. To be mistaken for a prostitute. That's just too much.* Despite her annoyance, Maggie continues with her task.

"Can you help me, please?" she says coolly. "My brother is traveling with my son, and I need to get in touch with them urgently." Realizing she doesn't sound like the worried mother she's pretending to be, she puts a quaver in her voice and tries again. "Would you check your register, please? To see if a man and young boy, about seven, checked in during the past month?" Maggie gives a small sniffle and dabs at her eyes with a handkerchief. She fishes out the photo of Oskar that Alicja had given her from her purse and slides it across the counter. Maggie gives him what she hopes is a worried mother's smile.

The man briefly glances at the photo, and then looks her over. He gives Maggie a slow leer. "Well now, I may have seen a young boy like that... How tall is he?"

Maggie is thrilled. This could be the lead that they've been searching for. She grips the front of the counter. "About this high," indicating about four feet, "with blond hair and blue eyes."

"*Hmm*, why don't you come back behind the counter so we can look through the register together? I'm sure I saw a boy like that." The man opens a door leading to the area. Once behind the counter, Maggie

157

realizes what a small, tight space it is. They are very close together. Her intuition is firing on all cylinders, but she dismisses it as adrenaline from the possibility that she has discovered a lead to Oskar's whereabouts.

The man reaches, his arms on either side of her, and takes a journal off the shelf. He's awfully close. She shrinks into the counter. He places the register near him and asks, "*Hmm*, could this be your brother?"

As Maggie leans in to look at the name he's pointing to, he slides his arm around her waist. She shakes him off impatiently and looks again at the list of names.

"Now, darling, is that any way to treat somebody trying to help? Why don't you give me a little incentive to keep looking through this big, heavy ledger?" He leers and grabs her waist again.

"Back off!" Maggie pushes him so hard that he bangs against the wall. Glaring, she takes a step forward and slaps him hard across the face. She stands there for a moment, stunned by what she's done.

"*Ooff*," he gasps, rubbing at his red cheek. "Now darling, there's no need to be hasty. I was just trying to help."

"You haven't seen Oskar. And the bank's closed, you creep. Keep your mitts to yourself." She sweeps haughtily out the door. *Peggy may have needed rescuing, but Maggie doesn't.*

Back on the street, Maggie brushes her hands and pats her hair. *And that's how it's done*, she smiles. There's a confident swagger to her step as Maggie the detective walks the several blocks to the next hotel.

She gazes at the ornate façade. *This is a bit of an improvement over the Octopus Hotel.* The doorman holds the door open for her as she steps inside. Maggie looks around and gazes longingly at the café off the lobby, wishing she had both the time and the money to stop for one of the delicious cream cakes on display. *Maybe I'll bring Tommy here if he does well on his exams. He'll love all that frosting.*

As she crosses the lobby, she sees Fanny.

Fanny, dressed to the nines in a slinky purple dress and fetching beaded hat, clutches the arm of a mysterious gentleman. She leans in, giggling at something he has just said. *My, but they certainly look cozy.*

When Fanny sees Maggie, she stiffens and pulls her arm away. The color drains from her rouged cheeks. She looks at Maggie nervously, and then turns to the man, patting his arm. "Can you wait just a minute, hon? I see someone I know that I should say hello to."

Maggie narrows her eyes. "Fanny, what a surprise to run into you. Are you on a break and here for an early lunch? With?" Maggie raises her eyebrow and looks at the man, now standing by the counter. He is glancing at his watch.

"Oh Missus B, please don't tell anyone you saw me, especially Joe," Fanny searches Maggie's face. "Georgie wanted to take me for a special Valentine's lunch and he's promised to buy me the most beautiful dress. I need some new glad rags. I want something special to wear the next time Joe takes me dancing."

"Fanny, do you mean to tell me that you're with that man over there because he buys you things? Oh, Fanny, that's just wrong. Does Joe know that you're seeing other people?"

"Oh, no. Joe'd never go for that. But you, more than anybody, knows how hard it is for a girl to make ends meet. Even with roommates, a girl just can't get ahead, Missus B."

Fanny looks back at George, who is tapping his foot impatiently. She flutters her fingers at him and flashes a smile. Turning back to Maggie, she says, "I'm not like you. If some guy wants to buy me nice things, what's wrong with that? It doesn't mean anything, just a bit of fun." Fanny raises her chin defiantly.

Fun for who? "Well I won't say anything Fanny, but you're going to have to tell Joe. He's head over heels for you. You need to come clean. And if you don't say something, then I'm going to have to mention it. Joe Kelly is a good man. I won't have him hurt, or lied to."

"Oh, thanks, Missus B. That's real swell of you." Fanny grabs hold of Maggie's hands, nodding. "And I will talk to him. I'm sure he'll understand. It's not like we're serious or anything."

I wouldn't be too sure about that. Maggie leans over and, right after she gives Fanny a quick peck on the cheek, she whispers, "Just make sure that you do."

Chapter 23

Like much of society, the humble corner grocery store is also in the throes of major change. The local neighborhood anchor, front windows piled high with cans and produce, is being threatened by the larger, self-serve phenomenon that is springing up in larger cities. Traditionalists are reluctant to move away from the single counter and personal service of the grocer who would fetch the items you asked for, while modern folks in a hurry like to be able to wander past shelves filled with a much broader selection of goods, fill their baskets themselves, go through the check-out, and be amazed by the memories of the clerks who have memorized the price of every item.

Even with her new persona, Maggie remains a traditionalist when it comes to her grocery store. She's been a loyal customer of Howard Lawson's store since she and Jack moved into the neighborhood. She likes the smells, the dark wood, the familiarity of the products. Why decide what brand of peas to buy? A pea is a pea. Howard's prices are fair, and Lordy knows he's carried her through some dark times financially. Half the families in the neighborhood will be listed in the little black "On Account" ledger he keeps under the counter.

But today, with her foot tapping impatiently, she would appreciate the speed and convenience of the new 'super markets'. Mrs. Neufeld is ahead of her at the counter. And that woman does go on: lumbago, rheumatism, Dr. Quincy's Miracle Cure, what her daughter's family is excelling at. *Some of us have things to do, Mrs. Neufeld. Wrap it up and move along.*

Unfortunately, Mrs. Neufeld's daughter appears to be very fruitful, and she's launching into a new story of yet another perfect grandchild.

Maggie glances idly around the store displays. Behind her she can hear the chatter of a group of small boys, eagerly pursuing the latest edition of Boys Own magazine. Tommy loves that magazine. *Maybe I should buy a copy for him? I can hold it out as a bribe to study hard on the next test.* She's mulling it over and casually listening in on their conversation.

"Did you hear about Patterson's warehouse? Gerald and Curly were there on Saturday. They found a case of beer, just left behind it was."

"What? No way. Nobody leaves a case of beer."

"Well, maybe it was just a bottle. But we should still go over there and check it out."

"Why go there? They already cleaned it out. We should go to a different warehouse. Maybe we'll get lucky, too."

"Like where?"

"How about that old Ostermeier one? We haven't been there in a while."

"Isn't that the place that Shorty twisted his ankle? Jumping off the loading dock?"

"Yeah, he's such a girl. Come on. It'll be fun. And after, we can go over to the tracks and see if there are any hobos."

Maggie listens closely. The warehouses. She turns to look at the boys. They are younger than Tommy. And in need of a good scrub. She reaches past them and selects a magazine.

"Do you boys play at the warehouses a lot?"

"No, ma'am. We don't play there." The boys stare at their shoes.

"But I just heard you talking about it."

The boys grab each other's sleeves and high-tail it out of the store.

Maggie smiles. She has another idea. And it doesn't involve Archie Mansfield.

* * * *

Her errands today also included calling by Alicja's; there'd been a group of women keeping her company. She'd made her inquiries and dropped off a bag of candies for the children to share. Though many of the women still called her Mrs. Barnes, she mentioned her first name was Maggie. If any of them had known her as Peggy, it wasn't mentioned. Of course, they were all in a fog. Oskar was still missing.

After the supper dishes are cleared away and the kitchen tidy, Maggie lays out the maps she's checked out from the Public Library, as well as several books on city architecture.

Tommy is sprawled on the floor in the living room, listening to the latest detective serial on the radio. "Tommy, can I borrow one of your colored pencils?"

Tommy comes over to the table and hands her a red and a blue one. "What are you doing, Mother? Is that a map of Philadelphia?"

Maggie takes a pencil and starts making small Xs in red. "*Hmm.* What was that, sweetheart?"

"I asked what you're doing. What are those Xs for?"

"Oh, I'm just helping a friend with a project." She makes a few more Xs.

"What kind of project?" Tommy leans over the map, curious.

"She's taking photographs." Playing up her role, Maggie puts down her pencil with an exaggerated sigh. "Here, I'll show you." She opens one of the books to a section of photographs of the warehouse district along the river. "See here, these photographs are of Philadelphia. Some of the buildings are from the Revolutionary War and Ben Franklin's time. And some just look like interesting places."

Tommy looks at the pictures in the book. "But what's the map for?"

"Well, she wants to take pictures of warehouses. Not ones being used a lot, ones that are kind of empty. So I'm looking at the map and marking the ones that she might want to check out."

Maggie leans over and frowns, then makes another X.

"Oh, that one is too busy, Mother. The ones down by the markets are used all the time."

"Oh? Well, right you are. I remember that now. Which ones would you think would work better? For my friend."

Tommy climbs on the dining room chair so he can lean closely over the map. "I'd tell her to go here," Maggie makes a blue X, "and here", and another X, "and here." Tommy looks over his shoulder at her and smiles, delighted to be helping.

Frank has also wandered over and peers at the map. "What are you doing, Maggie?"

"That's wonderful, Tommy. I never would have thought of those. Just excellent. She'll be so pleased. Do you know any bootlegger warehouses? Maybe she'd like to take pictures of those, too."

Tommy leans over the map. "Try this one, and that one there," he says, pointing to the locations. "And maybe that one."

"Really?"

Tommy catches himself. "My friends say that's where they are."

Maggie looks at the Inspector and winks over Tommy's head. Frank's eyes widen. "Excellent idea, Maggie. Ask Tommy why there are no exes further along the river."

Maggie pauses, considering the top of Tommy's head as he looks over the map. "Tommy, how much money do you have in your pocket right now?"

Puzzled, Tommy reaches in and pulls out some string, a dog-eared baseball card, and five cents. "A nickel, Mother."

"And how much is in your tobacco tin upstairs?"

Tommy thinks, head tipped to one side. "I think there might be more than a dollar. Want me to check?"

"No that's all right. Say, if you wanted to go somewhere further along the river, maybe out near the stockyards or maybe even Hog Island, how would you get there?"

"By myself?"

"Well, you and your friends."

"We'd walk, I guess. I don't know. I've never thought about it."

"But it would take hours. Why not take a trolley?"

Tommy laughed at his mother's joke. "We don't have money for trolley rides. If I had that kind of money, I'd be buying candy at the store."

"Well, I have a treat for you." Maggie walks over to her desk and opens the top drawer, pulling out the copy of Boys Own she'd bought earlier.

"Oh, wow. This is the new one. Thanks, Mother."

"And thanks for your help here, Tommy. Now, why don't you head upstairs and get ready for bed. You can read until I come to tuck you in."

Tommy needs no further coaxing, but rushes up the stairs to his room, clutching the prized magazine.

"That was an interesting exercise, Maggie."

Maggie smiles a self-satisfied smile. "Yes, that went better than I thought."

"But why the subterfuge? Why not just ask Tommy?"

"Oh, Inspector. Little boys never tell their mothers anything directly. If I'd asked, he would have clammed up."

"Interesting. I must admit, my interrogation skills on children are somewhat rusty. So, what's the point of all this?" Frank asks, gesturing to the map on the table.

166

"I got thinking today that we've been approaching this the wrong way. We're trying to think like a criminal, an adult. Maybe we should be thinking about it like a little boy?"

Frank nods, his forehead creased in concentration. "Yes, I see what you mean."

"Exactly. Where would Oskar go? To know that, you need to think like a seven-year-old. Fortunately, I have one of those right here."

"So, we should look at the warehouses where the blue Xs are?"

"The boys are told not to play there, that it's dangerous. So naturally, that's where they'll play. Tommy has told us where the likely ones are in the area. The lure of the bootleggers' operations are a magnet for small boys."

"And the money in his pocket? What was that about?"

"The boys all play together, but have to be home for supper. So the distance they could go would be limited. I needed to know how likely it would be for them to jump on a trolley and travel further. I'm glad to hear that Tommy isn't doing that. And a smaller search radius will make our work easier."

Frank beams at Maggie. "Listen to you. Search radius. Well done, my dear. I like your reasoning. You have the makings of a fine detective. We'll start searching the warehouse areas on Sunday, when there's less likely to be workers about. I recognize a couple of them myself."

Chapter 24

At dinner, Maggie thinks about warehouses while Joe regales everyone with tales of the new 'Soup and Fish Squad' set up within the Enforcement Unit. "A bunch of the lads, all dressed in tux and tails, sit in swank restaurants and try and get the waiters to serve them drinks, all on the Department's tab. And some of the guys take their girlfriends or wives along."

"Are you going to sign up, Constable Kelly?" Tommy asks between mouthfuls.

Maggie shoots her son a disapproving look. He chews, swallows, and then grins at her. *I'm never going to be able to teach that boy table manners.*

"I don't think so, Tommy," says Joe. "Me manners aren't near as fine as they need to be, and I don't have one of them penguin suits to wear, either. Although I know that Fanny would love to go. It might be the only chance I get to take her someplace swell like that. Maybe I should borrow a tux and join up for the night?"

Everyone is laughing as Joe mimics the over-the-top table manners he would use in a fancy restaurant, when there is a pounding at the back door. Maggie hurries from the room, and opens the door to her next door neighbor, Clara Fitzgerald. Clara is sobbing, and clutches at Maggie. "Oh Lord, it's awful. They've found poor Oskar. He's dead."

Maggie puts her fist to her mouth to hold in her own startled sob. "Clara, no. Where? What happened? Come in, come in. Oh, poor, poor Alicja."

Maggie settles Clara at the kitchen table. Coffee is poured in seconds. "Just a moment, Clara, I'll be right back."

Though she intends to tell everyone to keep eating, emotions get the best of her; she blurts out who the visitor is and Clara's news. The men follow her into the kitchen with Tommy trailing behind. Joe kneels before Clara and takes her hand gently. "I am so very sorry to hear about Oskar, Mrs. Fitzgerald. Can you tell us what you know?"

Slowly, the story comes out. Oskar's body has been found floating in the Delaware River, near the construction of the new bridge. It appeared he had floated quite a ways downriver, eventually getting tangled in debris around the footings they were pouring for the new bridge. Even though the body was badly decomposed from a month in the water, the police could see that he had been shot.

At that news, Maggie looks at Tommy's white face. She goes to her son, gives him a powerful hug and leads him from the room. She catches Archie's eye on the way out of the kitchen. "Why don't you go and wait with Mr. Mansfield? As soon as we learn more, I'll come and tell you."

Maggie turns to Joe and Eugene. "I don't think that Clara has any more information. Why don't you two go back into the dining room and finish your supper? And Joe, could you make sure that Tommy is all right? I don't want to leave Clara, and this news has shaken him badly."

"You bet, Mrs. Barnes... Maggie. But as soon as I've checked on Tommy, I think I'll head down to the precinct to see if they know anything." Joe pulls his coat off the hook by the door.

Eugene is also reaching for his own coat. "I think I'll head out as well, Mrs. Barnes. I'll be back in a bit," he says.

Maggie hugs her neighbor, then sits beside her at the table. "Poor Oskar. Clara, this is just terrible."

* * * *

Later that night, Maggie looks in on Tommy to tuck him in for the night. His small face is the color of the pillow case, and his eyes are red from crying. She scoops him into her arms. "Oh Tommy, I'm so sorry about your friend. Oskar was a good lad. I know that the two of you were close, sweetheart, and you'll miss him."

"Oh, Mother," Tommy wails into her shoulder. "How'd it happen? When did it happen? Who would shoot Oskar? He's just a kid like me." Tommy shudders against his mother. "Poor guy. Floating down the river. He can't even swim."

"Look, son." Maggie holds Tommy by the shoulders. "There are evil people in the world. Oskar was obviously in the wrong place at the wrong time. You need to be safe, Tommy. I don't want whatever happened to Oskar to happen to you."

Tommy starts crying again, and Maggie holds him tight. "They better catch who did this. They should pay for hurting Oskar," he says, choking on his tears.

"I hope so, Tommy. I know Constable Kelly will work very hard to find out who did this, and then arrest them. But Philadelphia is a strange place these days, sweetheart. Not all the bad men get caught and go to jail."

Tommy snuggles under the covers, in close to Maggie where he feels safe. She strokes his hair.

"What are you thinking, Tommy?" Maggie asks quietly.

"I think he was still okay the night he didn't come home. I think he got hurt after."

"After what?" Maggie asks. She's puzzled by what Tommy has said but lets it lie. He's upset and not making much sense. It's too much for a small boy to take in. Heck, too much for her to take in. She keeps stroking his hair.

"It's like he's still here, Mother. I keep trying to think about him being dead, but it's like he's just away."

Maggie kisses the top of his head. "I think I know how you feel, Tommy. When your father died, I kept listening for him to come through the front door. Or I'd forget that he wasn't just at work, and go ahead and set the table for all three of us."

Maggie keeps her arm around Tommy. She rests her cheek against his hair, breathing in the smell of him. "Saying goodbye is hard, Tommy. Especially when we don't know what happened, or understand why."

"Oh, Ma." whispers Tommy. "Why would somebody hurt Oskar? He never did nothing wrong."

Nothing wrong. Wrong time and wrong place.

"We don't know yet, but we will. And when we do, it will be easier to say goodbye. If you want, you can come with me to his funeral. There will be lots of your friends and his family there as well. It might help to be with them. What do you think of that idea?"

"Would I have to see him put in the ground?" Tommy asks quietly.

"No sweetheart. We don't have to see that." Maggie kisses the top of his head.

171

"Although it's hard right now to see beyond how sad you feel, Tommy, you have wonderful memories of all your times with Oskar. Those will help get you through tomorrow, and the next day, and the next."

Wrong time and wrong place.

She shifts a bit so that she can look him in the eye again. "Right now we must focus on Oskar's mother and his family. His brothers and sisters will be grieving. We can let Constable Kelly look after finding the bad men, and making sure they can't hurt anyone else."

Maggie waits until Tommy has drifted off. Then she heads downstairs to her desk and picks up her journal, her fingers clenched around its cover. "Inspector Geyer... Frank, are you there? Have you heard?"

Frank answers from behind, "Yes, it's a terrible thing."

Maggie whirls on him, eyes blazing, and hisses, "I'll tell you what's a terrible thing, Inspector Frank Geyer; that we've been wasting all our time looking at hotels and rental properties when Oskar had already been shot. We were looking in the wrong place. We didn't start thinking about warehouses soon enough. I told you it had to be bootleggers, Inspector. They did this evil thing. It wasn't just Oskar in the wrong time and place. So were we. We were in the wrong place, Inspector."

"I know Maggie, I know," says Frank. "Since I heard, I've been thinking of nothing else: what I could have done differently, clues that I missed. I'm ashamed to admit that I was probably at Mickey's warehouse the night that Oskar disappeared."

Maggie looks at him, stunned.

"There was a raid. Bullets were flying. I saw three boys there, but that wasn't unheard of. It was dark and I didn't really look at them closely. They were with a policeman. I was watching the bootleggers and Philadelphia's finest battle it out."

Maggie gasps. "Oh no, Frank."

"When I heard that a young boy had gone missing, I didn't put two and two together. Me, the supposedly trained police inspector. I was too wrapped up in my own thoughts, I guess. It has only just occurred to me that young Oskar could have been one of those boys."

"You left them there? In the middle of a gun fight? What were you thinking?" Maggie says, raging.

"Maggie, no one hears me or sees me, except you. And there was a policeman there with them when I left."

Frank hangs his head, his shoulders bowed with guilt.

"Well, it should have occurred to you. It's a good thing that Tommy wasn't there that night."

Maggie is furious: at Frank, at the police, at the bootleggers, at a random criminal if it wasn't the bootleggers, and at herself. A friend of her son, a young innocent boy, has died horribly, and she has been spending valuable time traipsing around to hotels playing at being a detective. She slams her journal on the desk.

"Maggie," Frank speaks softly, slowly sitting down in a chair close by. "Maggie, I am so sorry. I am an old man. I have not been a policeman for a very long time. You are right, this is my fault. If I hadn't been so obstinate, I would have been listening more to what Joe Kelly was saying. I let my ego lead me into thinking I was the better policeman. I shouldn't have been blind to what others were saying about the bootleggers. It probably was them. You're right, this isn't the city I lived in. I know that now. "

Maggie sits silently, hearing Frank's remorse, thinking her own dark thoughts.

"I'm an old fossil, Maggie. And a young boy died because of it."

Maggie looks at him, a defeated old gentleman, sitting slumped in the chair. A gentle man. She takes a deep breath and raises her chin. "So, what are we going to do now? Let the police stumble through a sham of an investigation?"

He lifts his head.

"And even if they manage to find out who did this, crooked lawyers and a crooked judge will make sure that the guilty get off. I had to tell my son tonight that there is no justice in Philadelphia. Little boys can be killed and dumped into the river, and nobody will do anything. Nobody cares."

Frank shakes his head. "Well, I care," Frank says, forcefully. "And so do you."

"And if we do nothing? What does that get us, Inspector? Except for a guilty conscience and lost hope?"

"I'll tell you what it gets. It gets us looking in a different direction, maybe this time the right direction. We know where we need to start over." Frank leans forward and clasps his hands together. "Maggie, together we can find out who did this to Oskar. And we can make sure that Constable Kelly brings them to justice. We must have faith, Maggie. We must make it right."

"You say faith, Inspector. Well, I need to have faith that the police, for once, will do their job. I have to have faith in the rule of law. I have to have faith in justice. I'm no vigilante, taking the law into my own hands."

"All right, but if not us, then who?" Frank says. "This is our city. It could have been your son, young Tommy, in harm's way. You mustn't surrender and let evil triumph." He grabs the arms of the chair. "I guess I AM asking you to be a vigilante. I want to take justice out of the greedy, corrupt hands of judges, lawyers, and police, and put it into your hands, Maggie. A mother's hands."

His grip continues, and his stare is penetrating. "It's a matter of faith," Frank says. " 'We are afflicted in every way, but not crushed; perplexed but not driven to despair; persecuted, but not forsaken; struck down, but not destroyed.' "

Maggie lets the words hang in the air. She manages a smile. "Are those more of your wise words from General Bonaparte?"

"No, Maggie. A much higher authority than even Napoleon. Its 2 Corinthians 4:8-9. We can't give up, Maggie, we have to have faith," Frank says gently.

"I don't know Inspector. Maybe the best way for me to keep Tommy safe is to move home and live with my parents."

"That sounds like Peggy. Worse, it sounds like Margaret. Come on, Maggie. Maggie would never give in to the rule of gangsters. Too many people have just been sitting back, waiting for Prohibition to be repealed. They're waiting for other people to make their homes and neighborhoods safe again."

"You're asking me to go chasing after men so evil that they shoot innocent children? You're saying that you and I, a ghost and a woman, can do what Colonel Butler and the rest of the Philadelphia police have been unable or unwilling to do?"

"Sometimes it's not the size of the choir that matters. 'Ten people who speak make more noise than ten thousand who are silent.' "

"Now, that must be your Napoleon. And that's exactly what I'm afraid of. To be a noisy person. Fate has a way of shutting noisy people up. And when I say fate, I mean Mickey Duffy and his ilk, the corrupt police, and all the forces of greed and self-interest that would be organized against us. We are a weak team, Inspector: a woman and a ghost. Not exactly the thing that would strike fear into our enemies' hearts."

Maggie looks at Frank, and then at the floor. She too feels remorse for her part of their investigation. She wants to make things right, for her own sake as well as Oskar's. And for Tommy, especially Tommy. It is a hard decision she must make. There will be no turning back once the journey has started.

Maggie imagines Alicja's grief. She feels Tommy's helplessness and confusion. She feels the Inspector's guilt.

"You're asking a lot, Inspector. Let me sleep on this. My first responsibility is to Tommy. I'm afraid. I can't risk losing him, or him losing me. But one thing I'm sure of: you didn't cause Oskar's death. You didn't. Those children couldn't see or hear you. Please don't blame yourself. Wrong place, wrong time."

Chapter 25

Maggie checks on Tommy several times during the night. She has no idea what time Eugene comes in, nor Joe, even though she has been awake much of the time.

After breakfast, she corners Joe in the hallway by the front door before he leaves for the police station. She glances toward the kitchen, where Tommy is eating his breakfast and speaks softly. "What have you heard, Joe? What did you learn last night? Is there any news about what happened to Oskar?"

"It's not for me to say, Maggie," Joe whispers. "If anyone saw anything, they're not telling us. There are a lot of warehouses upstream from where they found him. Many of them are used by bootleggers like Boo-Boo Hoff, the Lanzettas, Mickey Duffy. It could have been any one of them that shot the boy. More likely bootleggers than some random criminal looking to kill a kid."

Maggie flinches at the harsh tone. She's not the only one upset. "What would Oskar be doing at a bootlegger's warehouse? When you said he'd been shot, I was thinking he was out on a street somewhere, another innocent bystander caught in the crossfire, shot by accident."

"That may be true, but most bodies don't end up in the river when that happens. We'll keep looking. But there's also a good chance he was with the bootleggers. His older brother works for Duffy. Oskar was too young to be part of the crew, but he may have been at the warehouse. There are always young boys hanging around, hoping for a bit of work, fascinated by the glamour and excitement of the life. If Oskar had been hanging around, he may have been involved in something. You know, in the wrong place at the wrong time."

Joe places his hand on Maggie's shoulder. "We're doing the best we can to find out who did this. What you want to do is talk to Tommy about how dangerous those warehouses are, and both of you stay away from bootleggers."

Tommy is still eating his oatmeal. Maggie takes a pie out of the oven that she has baked for the Leszek family.

"You look half asleep, Tommy," she says.

"I'm still tired. Something kept waking me up last night."

"Did you have bad dreams? That's understandable with everything that happened yesterday."

"No, it wasn't dreams. It was like it was windy in my room. Or something like that. But my window was closed, and the curtains weren't moving." Tommy shrugs and continues to eat his breakfast. He yawns. "Weird, huh?"

Maggie studies her son. *Tommy's a sweet boy. This is hard on him, harder than I thought. Maybe I'll ask Joe to have a quiet chat with him. Maybe he needs a man to talk to?*

"Are you sure you want to go to school this morning? I can let them know you're not up to it, if you like."

Tommy shrugs. "Jimmy will be there. And some of the other guys."

"Well, if you're sure. It will help to be with your friends." She pats his arm. "Finish your breakfast, son. If you're going, it's best not to be late."

Maggie sees him to the door, then spies an envelope on the hallway floor. She picks it up and kisses Tommy goodbye.

178

Once he's out the door, she checks the envelope and rolls her eyes. *From Mother. A card? Condolences already?* Inside, a kitten in a basket offers birthday greetings. *My birthday. Between the investigation, Oskar's death, worry over Tommy, I've completely forgotten. I don't think there'll be much celebrating this year.* She carries it upstairs, setting it on her bedside table. *Another year older. But not wiser, that's for sure. Next year, I'll celebrate. Today I'll just put an extra spoonful of sugar in my coffee.*

Not long after Tommy leaves for school, Maggie's finds herself in Alicja's kitchen. The sorrow in the room is overwhelming. She adds her pie to the rows of casseroles and baking that are accumulating on the counter.

The kitchen is full of women, and Maggie is surprised she knows most of them. The women she has been working with for the past weeks are as devastated as she is. Together, they had stood shoulder to shoulder; making sandwiches for the searchers, making meals for Alicja and her family while they waited for news. Where once they had been united in hope, they are now united in grief.

They are all fearing the worst; that the violence that is commonplace in Philadelphia will now somehow find a path to their door. The compassion they feel for Alicja and her loss is mixed with personal anxiety for the safety of their own sons, husbands, and brothers.

Alicja is upstairs, resting. Oskar's brothers have gone to the mortuary to collect the body and deliver it to the church. There will be a funeral service on Saturday. Oskar's father is still in prison and will not be there. The women in the kitchen say that he went wild when he heard, believing it to be related to bootleggers, and calling out for revenge.

"Do you think that one of the bootlegger gangs did it? Could it have involved Mickey Duffy?" Maggie quietly asks Clara. They two of them are standing in the corner by the counter, unpacking yet another box of food. "Or someone who has it in for him?"

"*Shh*, don't be saying that. Half the families in this room, including Alicja's own, have boys and men working for Mickey. There will be trouble, no doubt about it. Mickey's men will go after Boo-Boo. That's who my Bert says is to blame. They've been at each other's throats over territory for the past month or so. Since Christmas. That's when Butler shut down all the speaks and blind pigs. The police are useless, but our men—Mickey's men—will hunt down the bastard that did this and make it right."

Berta, another neighbor, drifts over and chimes in. "There be more guns and there be more trouble. And at end of the day, more men be killed. More families crying. Is that how you think to solve this?" Berta shakes her head sadly. "You crazy if you think revenge is answer. What about your boy, Mrs. Barnes? More shooting keep him safe? What about your own man, Clara. What you do if he die?"

"We can run and hide, Berta, or we can stand up," Maggie says through gritted teeth. She knows what Jack would do.

Berta shakes her head and scowls at Maggie. "That's easy for you to say. You not know. You not part of this. You sit in nice, safe kitchen, away from guns, late nights, and booze. You no worry if there knock at door, or lie awake wait for husband to get home. Hope he does get home. This not your life."

Maggie is taken aback by Berta's intensity. "But it is my life, Berta. That worry was my life once before when Jack was alive, and it could easily be my son's life now. It's already claimed his friend. It's happening just outside my front door and, like you, I hope to heaven that it doesn't cross the threshold. But it could."

Maggie turns to Clara, who has been standing silently beside her. "Tony and his wife, at the barbershop, got hurt. Tommy and I were almost there when it happened. We would have been had it not been for Tommy's dawdling. And what about those people who were shot on Market. They were just out shopping. Oh, Clara, this is happening everywhere, and no one is safe."

Clara shakes her head and turns away to talk with someone else.

What are we going to do about it? And what am I going to do about it?

* * * *

Tommy sits on the edge of his bed, waiting for Constable Kelly to get home for supper. He needs to talk to him about something. Something private. When the front door opens and closes, and he hears his mother and Constable Kelly talking in the kitchen, Tommy knows it won't be long before Joe comes upstairs to change out of his uniform.

As the stairs creak, Tommy goes to Joe's bedroom door. "Constable Kelly? Can I ask you something?"

"Sure, Tommy. What's up?"

"And you won't tell Mother?"

"Well, that depends, lad. Why don't you tell me and then we can decide if she needs to know?"

"Constable Kelly, do you believe in ghosts?"

Joe sits on the bed. He studies his hands and then pats the bed beside him, inviting Tommy to sit. "That's a strange question, Tommy. Where did that come from? Is it Oskar?"

181

"Well, weird stuff has been happening around here. Sometimes I get this feeling. Like I'm not alone. And sometimes there's this wind in my room, for no reason." He studies his shoes, an embarrassed grin on his face. "It's silly, isn't it? There's no such things as ghosts. I know that."

"There are lots of things in the world that we can't explain, Tommy. That's what me gran says. When I was a wee lad, I worried about stuff like that, too. Things that go bump in the night. Weird happenings. But, usually there's a reason if you think about it hard enough. Maybe the window in the room across the hall was open. Maybe you're worried about something else and that's what you're feeling. I know that it's been hard on you to learn about what happened to your friend. You've got a good imagination. Maybe too good."

"But have you ever seen a ghost, Constable Kelly?"

"No, Tommy. I've seen a lot of strange things but I've never seen a ghost. I don't believe in ghosts, and I don't think you need to worry about it. Okay?"

Tommy nods, looking relieved.

"Right then. Let me get changed and we'll go down for supper. And no more talk of ghosts, okay?"

Chapter 26

Saturday, the day of the funeral, is a cold, grim day.

Tommy has been anxious and withdrawn since he heard of his friend's death. Maggie decided they'll skip the church service and cemetery because the intensity of the Polish Catholic service would be more than Tommy could bear.

Now, bundled in coats and mittens, the pair walk over to Oskar's house where his family, friends, and neighbors have gathered following the service.

Maggie hovers in the doorway of Alicja's kitchen. For the past month, she has been here often, stopping in on her way home from sleuthing, to check in on Alicja.

Maggie remembers how reluctant she had been to become involved. Her friendship with Alicja had started when she had helped with the lunches for the searchers, and grown as she and Alicja sat together at the kitchen table over a cup of coffee. Now that kitchen is full of strangers; women with heavily accented English or speaking Polish. The ladies from Alicja's church, her family, and almost everyone in the Polish community, Maggie guesses, are squeezed into the tiny house.

The men hold court in Alicja's front room. It isn't coffee in the mugs they're holding. There's frequent digging into the pockets of nearby overcoats, and subsequent 'clinks' from flasks. Mickey Duffy sits in the best chair. Gathered around him are men from his crew and the men in Oskar's family. In Oskar's father absence, they have all taken on the role of head of the family, at least for the afternoon.

Also part of that group is Eugene Smith. Surprised, Maggie nods in his direction when their eyes meet, but continues her vigilance from the kitchen doorway.

"*Skurwysyn. Skurwysyn.* I'll kill them with my own bare hands," seethes one of the men. Maggie has come to learn *Skurwysyn* is Polish for bastard. There are general murmurings of agreement.

"Mickey, whaddya say we take a little jaunt over to Boo-Boo's place and give them some *what-for*?" A man slaps his own fist into his own palm. The comment generates nodding heads and low murmurings.

Violence brews in the room. The afternoon is full of hard feelings and braggadocio, with many mugs of liquor stoking the fire.

From Maggie's vantage point in the doorway, she can see out the front window where the children are gathered. They are a somber tribe. The boys are huddled together around Oskar's brothers, the neighborhood girls and cousins forming a similar protective circle around his sisters.

It saddens her to see the light dimmed in these normally bright, mischievous faces. Today, there are no skipping songs. No games of tag. No filling of pockets with string and marbles and other treasures. Just shoulders hunched against a cool wind and a harsh reality. The girls are red-eyed from weeping, but the boys don't have that option in front of their friends. No, they gotta be tough; boys don't cry, although there are a few sniffles with the excuse 'I gotta cold' coming from the group.

Maggie returns her gaze to the men in the living room. Heavy, ill-fitting suit jackets are off, and shirt sleeves are rolled up. Everyone seems to be smoking heavily, drinking steadily, and the moody nastiness continues to grow.

184

From the hubbub in the kitchen, one of her neighbors hands her a tray of sandwiches, giving a quick nod in the direction of the living room. "See if you can get them to eat some of these. Maybe it will help soak up the booze and, hopefully, settle things down in there."

She passes the plate to Eugene, who grabs a sandwich. He raises his coffee mug in thanks.

"Such a sad day, Mr. Smith," Maggie says.

Eugene nods solemnly. "Yes, indeed, Mrs. Barnes. I know the Leszeks through work. Stan, mostly. But I thought I'd come today, you know, to make sure Mrs. Leszek or them kids don't need anything."

"Very kind, and I know Alicja appreciates it. Tommy's real shook by it all. I'll see you at supper?"

"Not sure, Mrs. Barnes. I may have to go back to the office after this."

Maggie nods and offers the plate again. "Then you'd better have another sandwich."

She moves along among the men and stops in front of the small, dapper man sitting in the chair, and offers him the now half-full plate. "Something to eat, Mr. Duffy?"

Mickey's eyes never stop scanning the room. He is vigilant, on the lookout for trouble. "Nah, thanks though," he says, waving her away. Maggie moves on to the next man, strangely disappointed, yet somewhat relieved, he hasn't recognized her from the hotel.

Maggie looks at the remaining sandwiches and then glances out the window to the children clustered on the sidewalk. With the plate, she goes over to the front door, and opens it. "Come inside children, and get something to eat." She shows them the food. The small cluster of girls immediately troops inside, their sad faces making a mockery of the bouncing Sunday-best hair bows.

The boys haven't heard, and seem deep in conversation. *Planning something.* Mothers' intuition leads her to investigate. One of the boys notices her coming and nudges Tommy. The boys stop talking and stand silently, nervously. *What are they up to?* "Why don't you boys come inside and have something to eat. There are sandwiches, and pies, and all kinds of sweet things."

The tallest boy, Jimmy, says, "Um, thanks, but we'll stay outside here."

"No, I think that you should come in."

Jimmy juts out his chin and sneers back, "No, we wanna stay outside."

Maggie grits her teeth, growing more frustrated and concerned. She looks at Tommy, who is looking at Jimmy.

"Maybe we can have our sandwiches out here, Mother? The house is crowded, and me and the fellas are just hanging out."

Maggie thrusts the plate at Tommy. "Here then. Make sure to bring the plate back inside."

Once in the house, she feels Mickey's eyes follow her progress across the room. She turns to him. "Are you sure I can't get you anything, Mr. Duffy?"

He gives her an amused smile and shakes his head. "I'm good, thanks, doll." Maggie is certain he's seen the showdown on the

186

sidewalk. *Grown men in saloons and little boys on sidewalks, they all seem to get the better of me when he's around.*

Maggie resumes her position, standing rigidly in the doorway between the two rooms, well within sight of Tommy and his friends outside.

"He's just upset, you know," says a well-dressed woman next to her. Maggie looks at her, confused. *Is she referring to Tommy or that other boy?*

"The boy's death has hit him hard. It bothers him when one of his men's children get caught up in any trouble," the woman says.

"I'm sure it does. It bothers us all," says Maggie.

"Excuse me, Mrs. Duffy," says Clara, as she passes by Maggie and the well-dressed woman.

"Mrs. Duffy?"

"Please, call me Edith, hon. How's Alicja coping? With all those kids, and her own man away. Talk about rough," says Edith Duffy.

"We're here for her," Maggie says quietly, looking back into the kitchen. "There but for the grace of God go any one of us."

Edith looks at Maggie more closely. "Are you a neighbor? Does your husband work for Mickey?"

"I'm Maggie Barnes, a neighbor. Oskar was a good friend of my son's."

"Poor kid. And how is he feeling about all this? Your son, I mean. It can't be easy to explain something like this to a boy that age."

"I'll say. I'm finding it hard trying to explain it to myself," Maggie says. "It is so senseless."

Edith and Maggie stand together on an island between two storms. The men in the living room, and the women in the kitchen; each group dealing with grief in their own way.

An easy intimacy grows. It surprises Maggie. "This has been hard on Tommy, but I'm hoping he will be fine in a few days. I try and keep him safe and, since it happened, I hold him tighter than I used to. Before all this." Maggie gestures to the room in front of them. "It's terrifying to have something like this happen to someone you know, especially a little boy. And it's so random. So frightening."

Edith stares into the room, her eyes settling on Mickey. "Hon, it's something you never get used to. Doesn't matter who it is."

Maggie studies Edith and then Mickey. "How do you cope?" Maggie asks her. "I'd be scared to death worrying about him all the time. I read the papers, and guns seem to be part of the life when you're in that kind of business."

"It's not like we have a choice, doll. It's the same for soldiers' wives, and the gals married to cops, I guess. You cope because you have to. I go to too many funerals, that's for sure. And spend too much time consoling widows. And then there's the wives left behind when their men get put away. Mickey's men are our family. He helps them out with cash, and he leaves it to me to dish out some comfort."

The emotionally charged afternoon seems to invite confidences. Maggie draws closer to Edith. She's fascinated by the woman standing next to her. "What kind of business was Mickey in, I mean, before Prohibition? Did he run a saloon?" Maggie knows bar owners had been quick to seize the opportunity to keep their bars open and increase their profits when Prohibition started.

"Oh Lordy, no, Mickey was a mechanic back then. He had dirt under his nails and talked non-stop about maybe owning his own garage someday. He's always been a whiz with the cars. And he loves business."

More people are arriving at both the front and back doors. Edith and Maggie move into the hall, out of the traffic, looking to find a space a bit quieter.

"Prohibition was an opportunity, really, for a self-starter like Mickey," says Edith. "He saw a need and figured a way to meet it. And he's good at it. As the business grew, he got more men working. Running the booze put money in their pockets and food back on their families' tables. They'd follow him anywhere now."

From where she's standing, Maggie can just see Mickey sitting in the chair. There is a circle of men around him, but they're at a slight distance. She can't tell whether the barrier is created by friendship or respect. *Or maybe fear?*

"He just wants to be successful," Edith continues. "It's important to him. To have Philadelphia look up to him. It's a long way from the days of being a grubby mechanic."

"But what of the risks?" Maggie asks. She's beginning to warm to this petite woman.

Edith smiles. "I guess the rewards are worth it, but I'd rather have Mickey safe than a giant house, or a closet full of shoes."

"I've met him, you know. Your husband, Mickey." Maggie notices the eyebrow arch on Edith's suddenly still face. Maggie hurries to finish her story before Edith can misunderstand the nature of the meeting. "I was someplace I shouldn't have been, and there was a man—"

Edith laughs. "Ah, there's always a man, doll. There's always a man."

During their conversation, the talk in the front room has grown noticeably louder and more forceful. With every shout, the men shift to look at Mickey, to gauge his reaction. He seems content to let the situation develop.

"I hear Stan, the kid's pop, went nuts when he heard about it. It took more than a couple of the screws in the joint to hold him down. Raving, he was," a man says.

"I say we go now." Ernie, Oskar's oldest brother shouts. "We can't let them get away with this. Come on, let's take a ride and show 'em they can't go around shootin' little boys."

Maggie has been trained well by the Inspector. She takes in Mickey's nuanced look at Ernie, then glances at two of the men who had been standing quietly against the wall. One of the men has an ugly scar running along his forehead. Something passes between them, and Mickey gives a slight nod of his head to acknowledge it.

He stands and the room falls silent. "I think that there's been enough sadness for one day." He looks around the room. "Ah, Edith, there you are," he says, locating his wife in the doorway where she and Maggie had been listening. "Come, let's pay our respects to Alicja, before we head home."

Alone, Maggie watches the two men who have been standing by the front door quietly turn and leave. Several men who have been sitting in the living room, including Oskar's brother, file out after them. From her vantage point, Maggie can see Tommy and his friends, who have been standing on the sidewalk, also watch the older men climb into a couple of cars and head off.

I bet there's trouble somewhere in town tonight.

Chapter 27

"I think we need for the boys to let off a bit of steam," Mickey says to Henry Mercer. The two are seated in the warehouse. Night has fallen and, for once, the place is quiet. "So, Henry, ya think Boo-Boo's good for it? The murder thing, I mean. They're looking to make things square for Stan, the kid's old man, and it would be handy for us to have Boo-Boo lined up."

Mickey pours each of them a glass of the premium Canadian whiskey he keeps on hand. "You're even quieter than usual," says Mickey. He clinks Henry's static glass with his own. "Drink up. Come on. It's Canadian." Mickey pushes the glass closer to Henry.

Henry shakes his head, but can't look Mickey in the eye. "It's bad, Mickey, really bad. I shoulda told ya sooner, but I just couldn't, ya know?" Henry says, talking to his untouched glass of whiskey more than Mickey.

"Look. It was me. I'm the one that found the kid." Henry's head hangs low, his hands rest on the table on either side of his glass.

"What do you mean, Henry? The cops fished him out of the river."

"Yeah, and I put him there. After the raid. I came back, ya know? To check on the booze. And I found him."

"Henry. No way. Was it the cops that shot him?"

"Who knows? He caught a stray bullet. Someone fired it." Henry shrugs. "The kid was just in the wrong place at the wrong time. Nobody's said they saw what happened. Nobody's said they saw who done it. It coulda been one of them cops who done it." Henry lowers his

192

head. "Or it coulda been one of us. Coulda been me. No one else in the group's come forward to say he did it, or came back to move a body they knew was there. That's why it really coulda been me. Oh, God forgive me, it was probably me."

"That's just crazy talk, Henry. You can't know. And it's not like it happened on purpose, for God's sake. From the sounds of it, there was lots of bullets flying that night. It was just a shame that the kid walked in front of one of them." Mickey takes another sip, considering. "Look, if none of the boys don't know it happened here, we should keep it that way, Henry."

Henry sits motionless in front of his untouched glass of whiskey.

"Come on. Pal. We've been in tough spots before. We've stolen apples to cars, Henry. Always together. We can't let it fall apart now. You remember that time that you and me had to have a chat with a couple of the Eye-talians? It was a good thing you had my back then." Mickey looks over at Henry, who is motionless, lost in the bottom of his glass. "Maybe a run over to Boo-Boo's isn't such a bad idea. We can knock a few heads. Just like old times. What do you think?"

"I think I shouldn't have dumped him, Mickey. I mean jeeze, he was just a little kid. Coming back into the warehouse after the cops had left. Seeing the crates and barrels destroyed, a week's worth of inventory smashed and spilled on the ground. I was pissed off when I saw it, but it's just stuff, ya' know? I called the boys in to clean up the mess later but, before I did, I found him. That small crumpled body face down in the dirt, in the middle of all the broken boards and glass. A kid, Mickey. A little kid."

Mickey downs his glass, pours another one. "Yeah, that was tough, but you did good. I mean, what do you think would have happened if the cops had found him here? It was a lucky thing you came back, pal."

193

"His body all limp, arms and legs dangling. It was like putting a baby in the backseat of the car. I never wiped a child's face before, Mickey, but I had to. I cleaned dirt off the poor boy's face."

"Henry. Don't let your mind go there. Drink up."

"That face. Sweet, innocent, sleeping. Mickey, I swear to you it was the loneliest sound in the world when he splashed into the water. "

"Henry, ya gotta stop this. I hear what you're saying. It was bad. But it's not the end of the world. He shouldn't have been here. His bad luck. But it's done. Drink up. Please, Henry. Drink up."

Henry is immobile, lost in a dark place.

"Henry. We faced worse in the joint. Remember that ape that came at me with the knife. You stepped right in. Gave him what was comin' to him. Nobody sweated it."

Henry looks for answers in his untouched whiskey.

"Now, don't you be getting soft on me, Mercer. For God's sake, it was an accident. You did what you had to do."

"It coulda been me. My gun. My bullet. I did a lot of shooting over that way. The cops started too early. Something tipped them off. Probably the kid. A little boy."

"Pull yourself together, Mercer. Come on, Henry. Drink. You don't know it was you. As for the other, you were only doing what you had to do."

"You're right. We've been through a lot."

Mickey nods, "And we can't have dead kids turning up on our doorstep. It would be bad for business. You know what I'm sayin'? It was an accident, and you moved him. There's no harm in that. Self-preservation. The boy was already gone."

"Already dead. Right. Gone when I moved him."

"We're all stressed," says Mickey. "Organize the boys and blame it on Boo-Boo. The boys need something else to think about. And so do you."

Henry looks up at Mickey.

"Go find some of Boo-Boo Hoff's boys for some target practice. And then haul the fellas over to Freddie's to celebrate. It'll make you feel better." Mickey drains his glass.

"Okay, we'll get something organized for Tuesday. Something fast, in and out. They won't know what hit 'em." Henry says. He looks over Mickey's shoulder. "And then we'll all feel better."

"Stop staring at that spot," says Mickey.

"I can't help it. That's where he was."

As Mickey drives out of the warehouse, he looks in the rear view mirror. Henry is framed in a weak cone of light from an overhead bulb, the rest of the garage in darkness. He remains clutching his untouched glass of whiskey, staring at a spot in the distance.

Chapter 28

Supper in the Barnes' household following the funeral is a somber affair. Afterwards, Maggie takes comfort in tidying up her kitchen. So different than the kitchen down the street with its sadness and the press of people. There's relief to be away from it and regret for feeling that way.

Standing next to her at the sink, Joe is wrapped in an apron with his shirt sleeves rolled up. He has a dish towel in hand, drying the dishes Maggie passes to him.

"Growing up in a houseful of sisters, I'd have thought that you'd be the last person to tie on an apron and help in the kitchen, Joe," Maggie says.

"Me Mam was a trailblazer," Joe says with a grin. "An equal opportunity chore assigner. But you know, doing dishes was always my favorite part of the day. It gave me a chance to talk with her about whatever was on my mind."

Maggie smiles at him. "So then, is there something on your mind?"

Joe chuckles. "No, nothing in particular. Although, I'm worried about Tommy. He's a great kid, but all this has been hard on him."

"I know. I've seen it, too. He was so quiet at dinner tonight. He didn't eat a thing."

"And for a chow hound like Tommy, that's always a sign that something's on his mind. I think you're right. Just give him time."

"I suppose. And you, Joe? How goes the battle? Is our side winning?"

"I wish I had more to report, Mrs. Barnes—Maggie. We just get one joint closed down and padlocked, and the court throws out the warrant on a technicality. Before you know it, they're back open for business. Half the cops on the force have their hand in a bootlegger's pocket. The crews know about our raids before we even leave the precinct. It'd be a heck a lot easier to do my job if I could figure out whose side everybody's on."

"That's got to be frustrating."

"Colonel Butler calls Philadelphia a cesspool, which doesn't go down well with Mayor Kendrick. He told the newspaper that trying to enforce the law here was worse than any battle he was ever in".

"What do you think of Mickey Duffy? He was at Alicja's house this afternoon. I heard that Oskar's father and his oldest brother are part of Mickey's crew."

"He's a slick, dangerous criminal. Stay clear of him. He's been in and out of courtrooms a bunch of times, but his lawyer is always too slippery and he gets off. I heard Duffy gunned down one of the liquor inspectors while the guy was out walking with his wife and family. Shot him right there in front of them."

"That's awful. Although that doesn't sound like the man I met. He didn't seem the cold-blooded killer type."

"Make no mistake, Maggie. He may have a nice wrapper, and lots of charm, but at his core he's as rotten as they come. You don't get to be one of the most powerful bootleggers in Philadelphia by being a nice guy. If you'd seen the things I've seen, you wouldn't be so taken by that snake. The guy's nothing but a ruthless thug."

"I'm sure you're right. You know, I've had my quota of gloom today. How about a sunnier subject, then. Have you seen much of Fanny these days?"

"What a gal. But no, I've been busy at work and she's been busy with family things I guess. We are going out on Saturday. I have someplace special in mind." Joe pauses and then adds shyly, "I think that I might ask her to marry me."

"Oh Joe, that seems a bit sudden."

Joe looks at Maggie, puzzled. He hands a plate back to her. "You missed a spot."

Maggie immerses the plate into the sink, suds spilling on the counter, and over-scrubs it. "What do you really know about Fanny?"

"I don't get it. I thought you two gals liked each other, and now it sounds like you think maybe I'm making a mistake. I've known her and her family my whole life. We grew up together in Ardmore. Sure, she's a bit of a wild thing and has some of these foolish flapper notions in her head, but really, once you get to know her better, you'll see she's a great gal," Joe says.

Maggie drains the water from the sink and dries her hands on the dish towel Joe is holding. "Marriage is a big step, Joe. Take it from someone who rushed headfirst into romance. Fanny may not be ready to settle down. Take your time to make sure."

"Understood, Mrs. Barnes."

"Come on, Joe. Don't be like that. It's Maggie. But, promise me that you'll have a good heart-to-heart with Fanny, to make sure you're both wanting the same things out of life. Policemen don't get paid what they're worth, and I know that Fanny likes her fancy shoes and feather boas."

"Those are just passing fads, Maggie. Fanny grew up with nothing. She'll get it out of her system once we're married."

Maggie hangs her apron on the hook by the stove and pours herself a cup of coffee. "Well, I think that I'll take this into the front room and just jot down a few thoughts before I turn in. Thanks for your help tonight. Dinner was a bit of a rushed affair, with the funeral and all."

"No problem. I'm always glad to help out." He hangs the dish towel to dry.

* * * *

Joe climbs the stairs slower than usual, still trying to figure out what Maggie was on about. That wasn't the reaction he was expecting with his big announcement. He thought all dames were ga-ga over weddings.

Tommy waits by Joe's door.

"Well, hello there. What's up? Looking for me, Tommy?"

"Can I talk to you some more, Constable Kelly?"

"Oh. Sure thing, laddie. Why don't you come inside and we can have a bit of privacy."

They head into the bedroom. Joe quickly retrieves his service revolver from the top of his dresser and puts it in a box, sliding it under the bed. Tommy sits on the edge of the bed, picking at the edge of the bedspread.

"What can I do for you, son. Still worried about ghosts? Is it the funeral?" Joe plants a chair across from Tommy.

Tommy shakes his head, but becomes mute; searching for his courage by his feet.

"You won't find your voice on the floor, pal," says Joe. "Okay, let's start with how's school?"

"It's all right." Tommy reports the status to Joe's shoes.

"But there's something on your mind, right?"

"I know who killed Oskar," he whispers, speaking to Joe's knees.

"What's that? Tommy, if you have something to say, you'd best just get it out. What do you know about what happened to Oskar?"

"I know who killed him." For the whole five words, Tommy stares directly into Joe's eyes. Then hangs his head. "Well, not exactly who, but how and why."

After another moment, Joe reaches out and puts a hand on Tommy's shoulder. "Trust me lad, you'll feel better getting it off your chest."

"It's not like I told you before. It wasn't somebody else at that warehouse. It was me and Jimmy and Oskar. Me and my pals. We were the ones at Mickey's warehouse that night. Oh, please don't let on to Jimmy that it was me that told you. Please don't let anyone know I told, especially Mother."

Joe leans toward him. "Not a chance, Tommy. This is just between you and me. Scout's honor."

Tommy takes a deep breath and lets it out. "Sometimes we go to the warehouse. You know which one?"

Joe nods.

"We were spying on the crew that night because we thought Oskar's brother would be there. And we hoped we'd see Mickey. We were hiding behind some boxes. Nobody saw us. We were careful. And then there was police, and shooting, and we ran. Constable Kelly, Oskar was right there with me and Jimmy. We thought everyone had got away, but Oskar... but Oskar..."

Tommy face is tear-stained. "I guess Oskar didn't. He didn't make it home. But he was right there," he whispered. Tommy looks at Joe with searching eyes. "I thought he got out ahead of us. That he ran faster and got away. I wouldn't have left him, Constable Kelly. You gotta believe me."

"You did the right thing, telling me this, Tommy. You surely did."

"But that's not all Constable Kelly. It's my pals. Jimmy told some of the other guys what happened and now they want to go after Mickey, because Jimmy knows Oskar was there and on account of Oskar not coming home. They were talking about it at Oskar's house today. Constable Kelly, they'll skin me if they find out I told."

Joe takes a breath. The patting on the shoulder seems to settle Tommy. "No one will know, Tommy. You understand, don't you, that Mickey Duffy and his gang are really dangerous? Did they see you that night, at the warehouse?"

"I'm pretty sure that the trucks had driven off. Just a cop saw us. He told us to get outta there."

Joe holds Tommy's shoulders, and has a face-to-face. "You and your friends need to stay away from them. Lots of people get hurt. Like Oskar did." Joe shakes Tommy. "Promise me, Tommy. Promise me you'll stay clear away from Duffy and any bootleggers."

"Okay, Constable Kelly. What about my pals?"

"Don't you worry, kiddo. I'll make sure none of your pals goes after Duffy." Nodding his agreement, Tommy rises.

"Thanks. Really, thanks. My head doesn't hurt as much now," says Tommy.

Chapter 29

While Tommy's been upstairs, unburdening himself with Joe, Maggie is downstairs performing a similar ritual with the Inspector. She's sipping her coffee in the living room, having given up her usual spot at the desk in return for a comfortable chair next to Frank.

"You look tired, Maggie. It has been a rough few days," he says.

"I am tired," Maggie admits. "Oskar's death, Tommy's moodiness, the gathering after the funeral today, Joe getting serious about Fanny. All of it is weighing on my mind." She closes her eyes and leans back into the chair. "And our last conversation, of course, Inspector. That's been on my mind, too."

"Have you come to any conclusions, then?" Frank asks. "Are we going to keep going, as partners?"

"Oh Inspector, I don't know. Part of me wants to say 'yes'. But part of me wants to hide out here and pretend that what's happening in Philadelphia won't touch me."

"Even after today?"

"Especially after today. The men at the funeral. Those are hard men, Inspector. I don't want to be mixed up in anything they're involved with."

Frank takes a deep breath. "I need you, Maggie. And you have good skills that should be put to use. I know you're worried about Tommy and whether he'll be safe. After what happened to Oskar, who wouldn't be? But pretending that everything is fine won't protect him either. Fantasy is no shield against real evil, my dear."

"Enough, Inspector. Just stop pushing me. Every point you make is another straw on the camel's back. It's just too much right now, especially after the funeral. That poor boy. And Alicja. There's been so much violence and so much grief. Too much. I know you want to keep investigating, but what about the risks? I'm not sure I want to take that on anymore."

Maggie looks around the room, at the life she's built. She thinks of Tommy upstairs. "I don't know what I'm going to do. I'll make a decision, but in my time, not yours. I'm really very tired, Inspector. I'm not up for any more badgering tonight. Perhaps you should go."

Frank lifts his hat from the table next to his chair, preparing to leave, but remains seated.

Maggie sighs. "Let's face it, there's isn't any urgency. Poor Oskar is dead. His killer feels safe and isn't going anywhere. If I need to take a few days to think this through, and all that it means for me and my family, then I'll take a few days."

Rising, Maggie starts turning off the lights. "Good night, Inspector. I presume you know your way out." *Good manners be darned.*

Maggie's shoulders are bowed with the weight of the decision as she climbs the stairs to her room. *Yes or no? Forward or back? Can I go back to regular life, knowing what I know?* She pauses and peeks into Tommy's room to check on him.

"Ma?"

"Tommy, can't sleep, love?"

"Mother, I told Constable Kelly that I know where Oskar was the night he disappeared."

The story of the night at the warehouse tumbles out again, although Tommy leaves out the part that his friends are planning to go after Mickey. Maggie listens to his tale with growing alarm.

"Tommy, you must stay away from those gangsters. They're dangerous, and wouldn't hesitate to hurt you if they think that you saw something."

Maggie smooths the covers around Tommy, tucking him in. "I'm glad that you talked to Constable Kelly, Tommy. Now that he knows that you and Oskar were at the warehouse that night, he and the colonel will be able to get to the bottom of things. There will be justice because Oskar was..." Maggie searches for a soft word.

"Killed," says Tommy.

"Oh, Tommy. If Oskar's death involves Mickey Duffy or his gang, then they will go to jail. You did the right thing by telling."

"Mother, do you think that they'll ever find out who killed Oskar?"

"I know they will, sweetie. I'm sure of it." Maggie feels the resonance of those words. *A pledge to my son.*

"I hope so. I wouldn't want that happening to another kid. And it makes me mad to think that somebody would get away with doing something bad like that."

Maggie brushes away a stray lock of hair on his forehead. "Me too, sweetie. How about I read you one more chapter of *The Three Musketeers*?"

"Great. Do you think that D'Artagnon will save the day?"

"Undoubtedly. Now hush, and I'll start. 'My son, be worthy of your noble name, worthily borne by your ancestors for over five hundred years. Remember it's by courage, and courage alone, that a nobleman makes his way nowadays. Don't be afraid of opportunities, and seek out adventures. My son, all I have to give you is fifteen ecus, my horse, and the advice you've just heard. Make the most of these gifts, and have a long, happy life.' "

Maggie glances up from the book, surprised to see Tommy asleep already. *Mr. Dumas could be talking about Jack. He was such a champion of the underdog. What would he think about this situation? He always did what was right, regardless of the consequences. I know if it were him acting alone, he'd be like Joe and charge full tilt toward the threat. And what if it were Tommy or I that were threatened? There's no question, he'd fight.*

Maggie turns off Tommy's lamp and pulls his door almost shut. "Good night, sweetheart," she whispers and turns in herself.

Maggie lies awake in her own bed. *Tommy is in real danger if Mickey finds out that he'd seen the shootout and could tell others that Oskar was there. He might hurt Tommy. Or worse. There is no way I can ignore what I know about Duffy and let him go free. It would be wrong. By courage alone, Dumas said. Maybe Frank's right and the best defense is a good offense. Or maybe Clara's right and I shouldn't bring trouble to my door?*

Maggie punches the pillow into a more comfortable shape.

I need to talk to the Inspector.

Despite best intentions to sleep, Maggie tosses, and turns. At one point, she goes downstairs to make sure the front and back doors are locked. She peers into the living room, in case the Inspector is still sitting there.

Back in bed, she pulls the covers tight to her chin. *Proving it's the bootleggers and bringing down Mickey Duffy won't be easy. We're going to need to have a very good plan, because we're probably only going to get one chance at this. I need to talk to the Inspector so that we can figure this out.*

Chapter 30

Maggie is invigorated. A new day and a solid direction. A decision made. A renewed sense of purpose. Courage over fear. All that energy needs an outlet, so she puts a pie together and takes it, and last night's leftover casserole, to Alicja's house.

Alicja looks as if she hasn't slept in days. The funeral was less than twenty-four hours ago.

"How this happen, Maggie?" Alicja slumps in the kitchen chair. She shreds a sodden handkerchief. The counters are filled with food from the funeral, Maggie's pie and her chicken casserole part of the spread. "Four years ago, Stanislaw drive delivery truck for brewery. We not have much money, but more than when we live in Poland. Children are healthy, boys doing good in school. We even manage to put a little away for trip. Life good and we happy."

Alicja suddenly pounds the table with her fist. "Then *sukinsyn* politicians bring in Prohibition and it all goes *gówno*. You know *gówno*? Shit, crap, poo poo. Now Stanislaw in jail, Ernie part of Duffy gang, no money, and my baby, he dead." Tears are rolling down Alicja's face. Maggie pats her hand, letting her friend try and make sense of it all.

"These bad times for everybody. Like Lena," Alicja peers at Maggie. "You know Lena? Husband work for Duffy. Start out fine. Drive some trucks, lift some barrels, get paid lots of money. They buy car, she get refrigerator in her kitchen, all is good, no? Then guns. Her man shot. He get better and go back. But Lena worry all time that he get shot again. Maybe killed. Then what she do?" Alicja shrugs. "He quit, but no other jobs pay good. So he go back and work with Mickey. Poor Lena, she worry all the time, all the time."

Maggie begins to clean the breakfast dishes in the sink.

"And Ula Dorn, she live on this street for long time. Husband gone. She have nice little place around corner; sell some beer, some good sausage. But police close her down. *Swinia*. Pigs. Now Ula run same thing out of her house. At night she puts radio on and pours vodka. People come over and drink in her front room. Sometimes there are fights, sometimes there are police. Her kids cry. Ula cry. Maybe go to jail. That just wrong Maggie. Not good. Bar is bar. Living room is living room."

Alicja looks at Maggie. Pushing herself away from the table, she sighs and nudges Maggie out of the way and takes the dishrag from her hand. Maggie reaches for a dish towel to start drying.

The stories surprise Maggie. *A bar on my street? Is anything the way it was before?*

* * * *

A few days pass. Maggie is weighing various angles to the way she'll get information about Oskar's murder. She's adamant that if she is to keep going, and Frank is involved, that their next step be in the right direction.

Keeping her hands busy so that her mind can wander, she's sweeping off the front veranda when a police paddy wagon pulls in front of a house a few doors away. They knock on the front door of Ula Dorn's house. At first, Maggie is puzzled, and then it falls into place.

After her conversation with Alicja, curiosity had prompted Maggie to ask Joe about beer flats in the neighborhood. *How could I have been so naive? I shouldn't have been specific about who it was. That was an error in judgement that Mrs. Dorn is now paying dearly for.*

209

Two police officers pull a struggling Mrs. Dorn down her front steps. There's an apron over her house dress and she's wearing slippers. A trio of small children cling to her, crying. Mrs. Dorn is yelling and trying to hit the police.

Maggie stands watching on the veranda, arms crossed and cheeks burning. *I'm a stoolie. I'm to blame here. Poor Mrs. Dorn. Those sukinsyn policja.*

Another neighbor hurries over, pulling the children away from their mother. She wraps her arms around them. "Don't worry Ula, I'll look after them. They can stay with me until this gets sorted."

Ula continues to struggle to get away from the policemen and back to her children. Finally, she is shoved into the back of the paddy wagon and driven off. One slipper left on the sidewalk. The neighbor picks it up and leads the crying children away.

Maggie grips the broom handle so tightly her knuckles turn white. *Those policemen are probably on somebody's payroll, yet it's poor Mrs. Dorn that is hauled away for breaking the law. Where's the justice in that? And with all the trouble right now in Philadelphia, including the murder of an innocent, wee boy, arresting a single mother for pouring a few drinks in her living room is their biggest priority? This is the grand plan to keep us safe from gangsters? Protect us from mothers and old women? What is this world coming to?*

Maggie tries to calm herself. *If I hadn't said anything to Joe, Mrs. Dorn would be getting lunch ready for her children. No man at home. What happens to those children if she goes to jail? All she wanted to do was put food on the table for her family. Those poor children.*

Maggie throws the broom down the hall.

"This isn't your fault." Frank's in 'his' chair next to Maggie's desk. "You couldn't have known what would happen."

Maggie stomps over to the couch. The couch rocks with the force of her throwing herself into it.

"There are plenty of victims, Maggie. Folks get backed into corners. You can't blame yourself," Frank says.

"Blame?" she throws her hands in the air. "I'm not sure whom I'm angrier at, Inspector: me for saying something to Joe, Joe for saying something to his captain, a bunch of cops who are profiting from the illegal booze business arresting a desperate woman with hungry mouths to feed, or the police for having time for this and not for finding out who murdered Oskar. Oh, there's a lot of blame to go around," Maggie punches a cushion.

"Well, keep spreading that blame around, my dear. Some of it belongs at the door of the politicians who brought in Prohibition in the first place. But that doesn't help Mrs. Dorn."

"What will happen to her, Inspector?"

"Judges are usually pretty lenient on women, especially mothers. She might get a warning. What she does after that is anyone's guess. She'll still need to feed those children."

Maggie smooths the injured cushion. "Life's not very fair," says Maggie.

The clock ticks and ticks and ticks. "No, Maggie, life is not fair."

"All right then, what do we do next?"

"Next?" he asks.

"Yes, next. Obviously, the police are too busy or too dishonest to look into real crime. If we're going to get to the bottom of Oskar's murder, and that involves bringing Mickey Duffy to justice, we're going to have to have a plan. We've been doing a lot of talking, but now I think it's time to move forward. We need a plan, Inspector. And the first part of the plan is going to have to be to keep Joe Kelly out of it. I can't have any more struggling mothers on my conscience."

Frank looks at Maggie, a slow smile peeking out from beneath his walrus mustache. "That's excellent news, Maggie. Just excellent."

"How certain are we that Oskar was killed at the warehouse and then put into the river? And how certain are we that the place is Mickey Duffy's warehouse?" Maggie asks.

"Pretty certain, on the first. And absolutely certain, on the second," Frank says, nodding.

"All right, then here's what I think we should do..." The two heads bend together, generals plotting the next advance on the battlefield.

Chapter 31

Spirits are higher that night at dinner; a special guest adds to the energy. On his way home from work, Joe had picked up Fanny so she could join them for dinner. Joe is flush from a triumphant day for Enforcement Unit Number One. He is regaling all with tales from the five raids that day, one of which was Mrs. Dorn.

Everyone has something to share, something that adds to the celebration. Tommy bounces in his chair, peppering Joe with questions and acting out the exciting parts of Joe's day. Archie's baseball team, the Phillies, is just starting spring training and there is a pitcher on the team that shows early promise. Eugene's fighter is in line for a title fight, having just won a major bout the night before.

While the rest of the table jabbers and laughs, Maggie continues to fume. She bangs down the bowl of potatoes, and puts the gravy jug on the table with such force it slops over the side. She snaps open her napkin and gives everyone at the table a look, daring them to say something. Napkin on lap, Maggie squeezes her hands into tight fists under the table. She can't get the image out of her mind: Ula Dorn, in her apron, being dragged down the steps. *Broken people just trying to hold the pieces together.* She stabs at her meat. *Corrupt, corpulent cops!*

Several times, Maggie opens her mouth to comment on what Joe is saying, but then clamps it shut, biting her tongue. Eventually, she pushes back her chair and stomps to the kitchen to get more bread. When she gets back to the table, he's just finishing his tale. "Yes, it was a grand day! A dozen arrests and an impressive haul of illegal booze. Colonel Butler was pleased. And there may even be a promotion in it for me." He winks at Fanny.

"Oh, a promotion. That's wonderful, Joe," Fanny squeals, clapping her hands with delight.

"A Sergeant Kelly can certainly afford to look after a wife," he says to a blushing Fanny across the table.

Archie raises his glass. "To the future Sergeant Kelly."

Amidst the verbal backslapping and cheers, Maggie raises an eyebrow to Fanny. Fanny shakes her head. *Fanny needs to get this over with before things go any further.*

"Why don't you take Fanny into the front room, Joe? Tommy can help me clean up tonight." Joe leaps up and pulls out Fanny's chair. "Yes, and thanks, ma'am."

"Mother?" Tommy asks while they are cleaning the kitchen.

"I'm sorry, Tommy. I missed that. What did you say, love?"

"I asked if Jimmy can come over for supper tomorrow. We're working on a project for school."

"Yes, I suppose that would be all right." *He's the taller, outspoken boy, out front of the Leszeks' after the funeral. Not someone I'd pick for Tommy, but I guess he deserves a second chance.*

Maggie keeps Tommy out of the living room with a promise of another piece of cake and glass of milk to eat in his room while he does his homework. She wants to give the couple as much privacy as possible in a house full of people.

Joe and Fanny are still talking in the living room when Maggie goes to bed.

* * * *

"Good morning, Maggie." Joe is already in the kitchen when Maggie comes downstairs. Her nose tells her the coffee is almost ready.

"Good morning, Joe. You're up early. Everything go okay last night with Fanny?"

"Ah Maggie, I don't know." Joe rubs his hand through his hair, sitting at the kitchen table. "Fanny and I had a long talk. She came clean about a lot of stuff. And I'm glad she told me because I don't want any secrets. Which is easy for me to say, I guess. Not having any."

"And how do you feel about it, Joe?" Maggie puts a coffee in front of him.

"Of course I'm put out. Who wouldn't be? But Fanny says that she won't do it again. That it didn't mean anything, and I believe her. I guess."

Maggie busies herself at the counter. *Give him some space. Don't be like Mother.*

"I've known Fanny my whole life, Maggie. That's not the girl she is. She'd never betray a friend. I love her, and she says she loves me, too."

"You know, Joe. You and Fanny are just starting out and have lots of time. It's tough, being a young girl in a big city. You see all the pretty things, temptation dangling in every store window. It's easy to lose yourself in sequins and feathers and fancy T-strap shoes, especially when you have money in your handbag for the first time ever."

"I want to be able to give her all those things. When we're married, I'll look after her. Maybe we'll even move back to Ardmore. Settle

215

down, raise some kids. They have police in Ardmore. Maybe I'd even be chief someday."

"That's a rosy picture you paint, Joe Kelly. I hope it all comes true." Maggie gives him a hug. "I wish you and Fanny all the happiness in the world."

Chapter 32

Maggie sinks into the chair beside the Inspector. "There are days when I would love to have the house to myself. It would be wonderful not have to pretend to write in a journal, Inspector."

"You're a busy woman, Maggie, with a busy household. When the case is over, you'll be able to enjoy having some peaceful time to yourself," says Frank.

"Until then, if there ever is a 'then', where shall we start?"

"We need some evidence we can turn over to the police. Something that puts Duffy squarely in the center of the crime."

"Because we're confident it has to do with Mickey?" Maggie asks.

"We are. For a couple of reasons: Oskar was last seen in Mickey's warehouse. We know that for certain. The boy was there, and never seen again. Importantly, who else has the power to interfere in an investigation? We can also surmise Mickey's involved because of police behavior: a bribe or a word in the right ear and suddenly they're conducting a shoddy investigation and calling off the search prematurely."

"How will we find anything to do with Oskar's murder at this late date? The trail's gone cold, and certainly no witnesses will be prepared to come forward and testify against Mickey."

"And there's the rub, Maggie. I've also learned that Mickey wasn't in Philadelphia the night Oskar was killed. So it wasn't him that actually pulled the trigger. He was responsible, of that I have no doubt, but he's not actually the shooter."

"Oh, this is hopeless. Oskar's killer will never have to pay for his crime. What a giant waste of time this has been."

"Victory is not winning the battle, my dear, but rising every time you fall. Don't lose hope yet, Maggie. Here's my thinking on the matter, and I admit, it's a bit unorthodox, so hear me out. We should consider the question of why I'm still here. Oskar's been found, but I remain here with you. Therefore, I believe that my purpose remains, as of yet, unfulfilled."

"Your purpose? Unfulfilled?" says Maggie.

"Yes. My purpose. The reason why I'm here with you and not in heaven with my dear wife. I have to believe that it's not random, or God being capricious."

"I think I understand. So what do you think your purpose is?"

"Here's my reasoning so far. Your being able to see me gave us the opportunity to investigate Oskar's death, which I initially thought was the reason I was here. But with his death sounding more and more like misadventure, I'm not so sure that finding justice for Oskar was, indeed, my purpose."

"I'm both puzzled and fascinated," says Maggie.

"There's more. You've read the headlines. You see what's happening in our city. The barber, those innocent people caught in the crossfire last week, Mrs. Dorn's children. They are all trapped in the middle of this lawlessness. There's so much corruption amongst the police. There is considerable suffering because of the anarchy. Philadelphia herself may have been mortally wounded by the venal actions of the bootleggers and the corruption they grow fat on."

Maggie sits straighter. "An eloquent speech. And I say this with no disrespect intended, Inspector, but so what?"

"Maggie, you're an intelligent woman. Think this through. We can continue to flail away at symptoms, at branches, if you will, but until we attack the root, the tree will continue to grow."

"We should be gardeners? I'm sorry, Inspector, I'm not following. How does trimming branches relate to discovering your purpose?"

"We need to go to the source of this evil. We need to take out the bootleggers. I think that's the reason why I'm still here. I had surmised, originally, that it was to protect one small boy. But now, I think it is to protect the entire city. Maggie, I confused the battle for the war."

"Goodness, I see where you're going with this. We may not ever discover who shot Oskar, but by taking down the entire lot of them, we can make sure no one else is harmed. But Inspector, how does a woman and a ghost take on the entire network of bootleggers and gangsters? That's just crazy."

"No, it's not. We can do it by going after the head. The organization. The drive. The brains. We need to go to the source, Mickey Duffy. And then Boo-Boo Hoff. Then the Lanzettas. All of them."

"You're talking crusade. There are bootleggers in every corner of the country. There's no way we can get rid of them all. Someone else will just move in."

"So we shouldn't try? Remember what Napoleon had said about rising every time you fall. Every war is just a series of battles, Maggie. We'll take on one battle at a time. Pick one adversary."

"Mickey Duffy. You're saying we should try and take down Mickey Duffy first? After he's already gotten away with murder?"

"He is the one we know the most about. The one we're closest to. The one with the close connection to Oskar. We need a plan, of course. But I know we can do this, Maggie." Frank punches his fist into his open palm. "And even more importantly, I know we need to do this."

Hands behind his back, Frank begins pacing in front of the fireplace. His focus reminds Maggie that he must have been a formidable police officer in his day.

"Mickey Duffy is the head of a violent gang that causes a lot of harm in Philadelphia. He's virtually unchallenged and is growing bolder and stronger. He's at the center of all this, I'm certain. I suggest we focus on getting Mickey off the streets and behind bars. To do that, we might have to delay our quest into finding Oskar's actual murderer."

"I don't know, Inspector. I think about poor Alicja and her family, and Tommy, and I just get angry. I don't want to leave off looking for Oskar's killer. I agree that Mickey should be behind bars, as should the rest of the bootleggers in the city, but that little boy needs some justice, too."

Frank strokes his beard. "It's likely that getting the information we need to bring Mickey down will uncover who killed Oskar. We've got enough circumstantial evidence to see a clear connection. Perhaps we can pursue parallel lines of inquiry here. We'll keep turning over rocks. Oskar's killer will be under one of them, and evidence against Mickey will be under another. They've taken the bullet from Oskar's body, but the police have only just started doing interesting things with ballistic forensics. I don't even know if it would stand up in court. And that's if someone doesn't try to get rid of it first."

"What if it's a police bullet? Or maybe a ricochet?"

"What if it is? We still need to know." says Frank. "Although, I believe at the end of the day, it's the kind of world we live in now that ultimately killed Oskar. The crossfire of lawlessness, bootleggers, police raids, random violence. We can't recover what has been lost, Maggie, but we can create a new future. One of civility and justice."

Maggie snorts. "Enough of your fine talk, Inspector. It wasn't injustice that pulled the trigger that killed Oskar. It was a flesh and blood man."

"As you say. Which is why, at the end of the day, we will need to rid ourselves of these bootleggers, and we do that one battle at a time. It would serve us well to find out information about Mickey's bootlegging business. Something the police can use in court to send him away."

"What about his office or headquarters? I could search there," Maggie says.

"Most of his business is staged out of that warehouse where the boys were. Near the tracks. There's always somebody around in the evening. That's when most of the work is done. Why don't I find out when the warehouse is usually empty. Then we'll know the best time for you to go in and look around. And while I'm staking out the warehouse, I can eavesdrop on Mickey and his men. Hopefully, I'll find something we can take advantage of."

"While you're doing that, I need something to do, too. You know, Inspector, maybe I can get to know Edith Duffy better. I met her at the gathering they had after Oskar's funeral. She seems to know a lot about Mickey's business."

"That's an interesting idea. She's not likely to suspect you," Frank says. "Yes, let's see what she knows."

Chapter 33

Frank takes a seat in the corner of Mickey's warehouse. It's just after sunset, and the place is busy with Mickey's crew getting ready for a delivery run.

He's been surveying the warehouse at various times throughout the day for the past week, trying to determine a pattern to the gang's movements.

The place is relatively quiet until noon. That might be a good time for Maggie to get in and look around. The earlier the better.

Frank has begun to recognize a routine in the gang's activities. Tonight, like most weeknights, a pair of men head off in specially outfitted cars and trucks to collect the illegal alcohol from the moonshiners and breweries in the countryside. They usually complete the run by the wee hours of the morning, bringing it back to the warehouse before heading home. During the day, the hard alcohol is watered down and repackaged into bottles labeled with fake authorization stamps.

With the many hours that the Inspector has been spending casing the warehouse, he's gotten to know Mickey's crew. Out of all of the bootleggers, he's formed a grudging respect for Alfred, the crew's mechanic. Alfred and Mickey spend a lot of time discussing the vehicles, debating modifications, sourcing parts, and kicking tires. Maggie had told Frank that Mickey had been a mechanic and it's obviously still a passion of his.

Frank is particularly intrigued with the cars and trucks. Despite Alfred and his mechanical genius being on the wrong side of the law, Frank would love to have a discussion about motor vehicles with him—the man's created the finest hooch haulers in all of Philly.

There have been dramatic improvements since Frank was a young man. Back then, cars were just horseless carriages, temperamental to start and unreliable to drive. Most folks were still using horse and carriages. Cars were considered a dangerous novelty, not a mode of transportation. Even at top speed, it was easy to outwalk them.

That's a far cry from Mickey's crew, and other bootleggers, who rely on their vehicles for business and status. They have very specific criteria, with the most desirable cars designed to be both fast and to carry large payloads. Of the various cars and trucks, the two Packards, affectionately known as Whiskey Sixes because of their purpose and size of the engines, are the crew's pride and joy.

Mickey and Alfred have made extensive modifications to them to haul the illegal gin, vodka, and whiskey from the moonshine stills out in the country.

Alfred's altered two vehicles in particular, removing the back seat of each to create more cargo space. False floorboards hide some of the booze, and there's even more storage areas under the cars for more bottles. No space is wasted; the stuffing and spiral springs have been removed from the cars' seatbacks, making room for tin containers.

Because of the added weight when fully loaded, Alfred has changed the suspension to a degree that, when running empty, unless they weight it with bricks or jugs of water, the rear end will ride high and have a distinctive bounce. Alfred laughs when he sees them running without the ballast, calling them 'cats in heat'.

The current trend of dividing the gas tank so that one side can hold alcohol has been rejected by Alfred. So many of their moonshine runs are out to the isolated countryside, he's made sure Mickey's cars have two gas tanks for distance, and he's armor plated them.

Anticipating the inevitable chases with Prohbies and hijackers, Alfred has taken out the windows, loaded the front passenger floor with chains and cans of nails, and mounted spotlights on the rear of each car. These can be turned on to blind pursuers. He has also drilled holes through the floorboards so that the man riding shotgun can pour oil onto the hot muffler to create a smokescreen.

His main challenge is to keep tires on the two Packards. It is a tough job, with gravel roads, dirt tracks, open fields, and reckless speeds putting severe strain on the rubber. Alfred knows of one crew that had seven blowouts running from Spokane, Washington up to Fernie, British Columbia. Everyone in the crew has a story of someone who is sitting in jail because his tires had failed at some critical moment.

Sometimes the whiskey six runs are long and the men won't return until just before dawn. Frank has seen them leave the loads in place while they head home to sleep. Other times the men pick up orders off a train car that is conveniently stopped on the railway siding next to the warehouse.

Liquor is usually delivered early in the week. By midweek, all bottles are ready to go back out for the busy weekend business. Mickey never keeps a large inventory of alcohol onsite; does his best to move it in and out quickly. The opportunity for theft or seizure is high. As well, given the quality of some of the hooch, Frank also assumes Mickey must be concerned about explosions.

Off in the corner, within eyesight of the door, is a long table and chairs. Here the men gather to get their assignments, play cards, and, of course, sample the product. Quality control.

In another corner, at the top of a short flight of stairs, is a small office with glass windows overlooking the floor of the warehouse. Frank has rarely seen anyone go into the office except to use the phone. When the orders or messages come in, they are written out and given to Mickey or Harry Mercer during the gang's evening meeting.

What Frank hasn't seen in the warehouse office are ledgers. Somewhere there has to be a list of who the suppliers are, who the customers are, who has paid, which cops and judges are on the take and for how much, and, importantly, how much each man in the gang is owed from each job. He'd been hopeful when he first saw the small office that it might be a good source of information, but he has since learned that Mickey's bookkeeper's office is somewhere else in the city.

The cash-only nature of the bootlegging business means keeping a sharp eye out for theft and 'breakage'. There aren't a lot of invoices given out. Mickey runs a tight ship, making sure that personal greed is never the primary motivation for his crew, because he'll never be able to control it.

The more Frank thinks about it, the more convinced he is that it will be the paperwork that will do Mickey in.

Frank isn't sure how to deal with Maggie's curiosity about the warehouse operations. She keeps insisting that she wants to be part of a stakeout. She wants to see for herself the comings and goings and get a sense of Mickey's business. Frank hasn't yet found a place where she might hide and spy, and he isn't going to put her in harm's way or risk her discovery.

* * * *

While Frank stakes out the warehouse, Maggie has her own surveillance assignment. Each day, after getting Tommy off to school, and her lodgers off to work, she catches the trolley and gets off on North Broad Street.

The street is lined with grand homes, in all kinds of architectural styles, set close to the sidewalks. Further along Broad are theatres, restaurants, and hotels. The Duffy mansion is a Romanesque red brick and stone three-story home with towering chimneys and turrets. Maggie is intrigued with the small, curved balcony on the second floor, wondering what lies behind its Palladian windows.

The various housekeepers and other household staff have already arrived by the time Maggie is in place. Sometimes she's in a park across the street if the weather is decent. She takes shelter in an alleyway if the wind is too chilly.

Most days, Edith is at home until eleven. After that, Maggie sees her being driven off. Maggie presumes she's going to luncheons downtown or to various clubs or private homes. There is always a steady stream of deliveries to the house from various boutiques and shops from downtown Philadelphia known as Center City. Maggie takes note of the box labels so she can 'bump into' Edith at one of the stores she frequents.

Mickey leaves before Edith--around ten. He rarely returns before dinner, which, Maggie has learned from chatting with the staff, is served around seven. Several times a week, there are guests for dinner.

More often as not, Mickey and Edith head out to the clubs in the evening. Maggie has heard tell of the fancy clothes from the staff, but she is usually back home sitting at her own dining room table when the Duffys go out, so has yet to see for herself.

Today, reading through the society pages in the café close to the Duffys', Maggie notes that a club that Edith belongs to will be meeting at Green's Hotel next Tuesday for lunch. *How exciting. Finally, I'll get to do a bit of inside work. Maybe I'll even get to tail her.*

Chapter 34

Maggie dresses with care, disguising herself as best she can as a well-heeled matron. There isn't much in her wardrobe that would meet Vogue's standards but, with a bit of creative flair, she might be able to pull off the bit of sleuthing she has on today's calendar.

A different set of decisions, years ago, and I may have become this woman in the mirror. She is the woman Mother wanted me to be before I fell for Jack. If I'd chosen the easy path, I'd probably have less gray in my hair, and certainly fewer frown lines on my forehead. But no Tommy, so no chance. But when did I give up caring about how I looked? After Jack died? These have been hard years, raising Tommy. Looking good takes a back seat when money is short.

Maggie dabs on a bit of lip color and rouge, then winks at herself. Putting her hair up, rather than just twisting it into a bun at the back, adds style. She turns her head from side to side, debating the merits of bobbing it. The dress is a bit too long, but will have to do. A string of pearls, a gift from her parents on her sixteenth birthday, completes the ensemble. She hasn't yet got hungry enough or desperate enough to pawn those pearls, and if the boarding house continues to prosper, she never will. Maggie imagines a matching set of pearl earrings, and laughs. *A washing machine and new refrigerator first. I'll have to wait for a man in my life if I'm going to own pearl earrings.*

As the finishing touch, she fixes a new cloche hat firmly on her head. It was the hat's feather Maggie had fallen in love with.

Full of resolve and last minute advice from the Inspector, Maggie sets out to get to know Edith Duffy better. She's convinced that Edith holds some of the answers to build the case against Mickey Duffy.

The Zonta Club is holding its monthly luncheon at Green's Hotel, the first hotel Maggie had approached after she and the Inspector had started their investigation. She remembers the fussy desk clerk, and grimaces.

Maggie finds a bench across the street from Green's. She eats her sandwich brought from home while she passes the time from Edith's arrival. Closer to two o'clock, she moves into the lobby, knowing that it will soon be filled with exiting Zonta Club members who have lunched on delicacies much finer than her sandwich. One more woman in a hat, even a hat with such an elegant feather, will not be noticed.

The Grand Ballroom doors open and the first women begin to trickle out. They are a parade of women's fashion. Maggie is distracted from checking faces as she checks out hemlines, waists, and the new spring colors. She watches as they head to the coat check to collect their warm, fur-collared coats. Looking at her galoshes, she sighs. No fancy, delicate shoes for her. Without a driver to ferry her from place to place, she has to walk through slush to catch the trolley.

Edith walks out of the ballroom with another woman. Maggie hopes the two of them aren't going shopping together. They stop to peck each other on the cheek, then Edith's companion heads to the powder room. Edith collects her wrap at the coat check. Maggie swings in behind, keeping other people between herself and her quarry, like the Inspector has taught her.

On Market Street, Edith pauses to glance in several of the store windows. It looks like hemlines are going up again this season. Maggie concentrates on Edith and tries not to get distracted in her own enjoyment of window shopping. Edith admires Strawbridge's large window, and its display of European hats—a rainbow of colors. Edith enters. Maggie follows.

They wander through the racks of beautiful silk scarves, past the counters of jewelry and perfume, and arrive at the hat department. Women's hats of every description adorn mannequins' heads. Wooley roll-brim hats and lovely embroidered tam o'shanters suitable for winter are on sale to make way for some of the prettiest spring straw hats Maggie has seen. There is a fetching purple hat whose black band has fanciful silk flowers along the front.

Edith moves between the displays, Maggie admires a tri-corner musketeer hat in luscious blue velvet. The front brim is smocked and holds a large peacock-blue satin bow on one side.

"Good afternoon, Madame. May I be of assistance?" The fashionably dressed young woman cuts a fine balance between officious disdain toward any customer not worthy to shop in Strawbridge's and helpful assistance, as she works on commission.

"I'm wanting something new for spring. Maybe in blue?" Maggie declares with false confidence. She is 'undercover'; wants to play her role.

As the sales clerk gathers a few blue items, Maggie drifts over to Edith, who is looking at a toque hat that a saleswoman is holding. Its tall, stiff emerald-green panels are sewn with beads and sequins. Edith initially centers it on top of her head, which is where the ladies from her club would normally wear it. But, glancing around, she tilts it rakishly forward over her forehead and grins, adopting a mischievous flapper pose.

"Oh Mrs. Duffy, that looks lovely on you. It is so your color."

Edith turns and looks at Maggie, a puzzled smile on her face. She is trying to place her.

"I'm Mrs. Maggie Barnes. We met at Alicja Leszek's. At the funeral reception for her son, Oskar."

Edith's brow smooths. "Now I remember. Wasn't that just the saddest day? It's great seeing you again, Mrs. Barnes." Edith turns back to consider the hat, tilting her head from one side to the other. "You don't think that it's too... flashy? I need a new hat for church and club meetings and I don't want those old dames' chins to start wagging."

Maggie also considers the hat, which definitely has style. "It's maybe a bit too much for Sundays, but you look great in it. Maybe you could wear it to lunch? Or to the movies?"

"Oh, yes." Edith puckers up and blows herself a kiss in the mirror, and turns to face Maggie. "It's been ages since Mickey and I went to the flicks. I'd love to see that new Valentino picture. Have you seen it yet?"

I'm lucky to see the poster let alone sit inside one of those movie palaces. "No, not yet. Maybe this weekend, if it's still playing at The Stanton. I loved him in The Four Horsemen of the Apocalypse. Those eyes." Maggie plays at swooning, and then giggles.

Edith removes the gorgeous hat and hands it to the salesclerk. "I'll take it. Please box it and I'll have my driver fetch it this afternoon."

Edith leans close to Maggie. "I'm so glad you talked me into buying that hat. I love it."

Maggie nods. "It's going to turn a few heads at The Stanton, for sure." She examines one of the blue hats. "I'll have to think on this," she tells the salesclerk.

"How swell that we ran into each other again. Do you have time to join me for tea or coffee before heading off? We could just pop in to the lunchroom?" Edith grabs Maggie's arm. "Oh, I know. Instead, let's go over to Child's for ice cream." She bounces and wiggles like a puppy.

"Ice cream would be lovely, but I don't think I have time for Child's today. I have to be off soon, but I'd love a quick cup of coffee first." Seeing Edith's pout, she pats the hand that is still on her arm. "Tell you what, we'll go to Child's next time, when I have more time. We can share one of their banana splits. How does that sound, Mrs. Duffy?"

"Oh please, call me Edith." She hooks her arm through Maggie's.

"And you must call me Maggie."

Settling into a table in Strawbridge's lunch room, Edith leans forward, inviting a confidence. "And how is Alicja doing? It must be so hard to lose a child, especially under those horrific circumstances."

"She is managing as best she can. With so many other children, she hasn't had time to think about herself too much. Do you have children?"

Edith slowly stirs her cup of coffee. "No, Mickey and I haven't been that lucky."

There is genuine sorrow in Edith's eyes. Maggie reaches over and clasps her hand. "I'm so sorry, Edith. I imagine that it's been tough."

"Not just for me, you know. Mickey would love to be a father. When we first got hitched, we were sure it was just a matter of time. But month after month, nothing, *bupkiss*. There were a couple of times I thought maybe, but it didn't last. You know, it didn't... take."

"Oh Edith, that's so sad. But surely there's lots of time yet?"

232

Edith gives a bitter, little laugh. "Oh yeah, we still have lots of time. And boy, we do like to practice." Edith wiggles her eyebrows.

Maggie's blush makes Edith laugh.

"How did you and Mickey meet?"

"Oh Maggie, it's a wonderful story. I was a sweet, young thing, working at the coat check in a club downtown. Mickey came in one night, full of life and energy and just swept me off my feet. He was a real big-timer. A man with plans, that Mickey. And in a hurry to get where he was sure he was going. We've had such swell times, he and I."

"At the funeral, we talked a little bit about Mickey's work," Maggie says. "It doesn't scare you?"

"Oh honey, I've always been a bit of a wild child. That danger was part of the spark in the first place. But things change. I sure didn't expect to wind up looking for a nice quiet hat for church."

Edith throws her head back and laughs. She raises her arms in the air, keeping time with an invisible bandleader. Customers and wait staff look away.

"Back in those days, it was all about the Charleston, and drinking sidecars, and keeping up with the boys."

"So, what happened?" Maggie asks.

"Well, Mickey grew up around Gray's Ferry. He was a real thug for sure. The toughest tough boy in a tough part of town." Edith leans forward, enjoying telling her tale. She lights a cigarette. "Do you mind? I'm desperate for a ciggy."

Maggie can't get used to a woman smoking in a public place. But, being undercover, she shrugs casually, "Naw, help yourself."

Edith blows smoke out of the corner of her mouth and continues. "He made some bad decisions and got sent up. When we met, he'd just been let out of Eastern State Pen. But he had already seen what a bit of moxie and some luck could do. He was never going to make any real money as a mechanic, so he came up with a different plan. Do you know Henry Mercer? Got a big scar on his face. On account of Mickey. Them two spent time together in the joint. After they got out, he and Mickey joined up to make some clams with all the illegal booze."

I am a mother, I have lodgers, responsibilities, and here I sit, undercover, listening to the wife of a notorious gangster leader speak casually about a whole other world.

Edith takes another puff of her cigarette, knocking the ash into the ashtray in the center of the table. "I remember you saying at Alicja's that you were a widow. That must be rough."

"It's lonely, yes. I miss having someone to talk to about Tommy. That's my son. And I miss having someone look at me in that certain way. You know?" Maggie says, wiggling her eyebrows like Edith had. Both women laugh. "It's tough only being someone's mother. I enjoyed being someone's wife."

"I getcha, doll. I'm alone a lot, too. Mickey's on the road a ton and doesn't take me with him as much as he used to."

"He's working hard?"

"Oh yeah. Who knows when this Prohibition gravy train will stop? Right now we're sitting pretty, raking in the dough. And it keeps me in glad rags and hats." Edith flutters her eyelashes and blows a kiss to Maggie. "But everybody knows it's gotta end sometime."

The Inspector's instruction included not to be too eager. "Oh, gosh, look at the time. I must run. Edith, thank you so much for a wonderful afternoon. Next time it's Child's, okay? And let me know how the new hat works out."

"Ab-so-lute-ly, Maggie. Getting together again will be the bee's-knees." Edith jumps up and gives Maggie a big, noisy kiss on the cheek. She scribbles her telephone number on the back of a napkin. "See you soon, doll."

Chapter 35

Since he's moved to the city, Joe's seen so much. Heard it, too. After all, he is more than a police officer; he's Fanny's fella and there's a lot of razzamatazz in that gal. He thinks jazz is the perfect music for these times. Heck, he wouldn't even be surprised if folks in the future look back and call it The Jazz Age.

Every time has its symbols. For the 1920s, it's the music. Jazz, the voice of freedom and abandon. Get out there and improvise, take chances, break rules. It's the only music where the same note can be played night after night, but sound different each time. There's wildness in jazz, and it flows out of the clubs and speakeasies and onto the streets.

Downtown Philadelphia sparkles at night. The streetlights glow and the electric bulbs in the marquee signs above the clubs and restaurants blaze brightly. Folks dolled up in their glad rags and wrapped in furs head into clubs and speakeasies up and down the strip. Anything can happen on a night like tonight, and usually does.

The strip stands for everything that Colonel Smedley Butler despises about his assignment as the chief law enforcement officer in Philadelphia. It's a wanton flaunting of the law. He's offended by the giddiness people feel at being outlaws. If there was no demand, there'd be no bootleggers or moonshiners, and the city would be a safer place. Joe knows, despite Butler only being on the job a few months, that the colonel's determined to restore dignity and authority to the city.

Joe stands in the squad room with other policemen; they're getting ready for the raid. The officers cluster around the colonel.

"Okay men, we know what we're up against, and we know what we're fighting for. Our wives and children are depending on us to keep the streets safe and to uphold the law." Butler marches back and forth across the front of the room. At every turn, his scarlet cape, his trademark, swirls. "For too long, these criminals have grown fat off the sale of illegal alcohol. Tonight, we'll take another step toward making our city pure again."

Listening to Colonel Butler, Joe feels a swell of pride, mixed in with a healthy dose of adrenaline. He loves going on the raids. Busting speakeasies and gin joints are always chaotic. Lots of people, lots of noise, and maybe a little gunfire.

"Captain Copeland will give you your assignments." Colonel Butler nods to a chubby police officer at his side.

* * * *

As they pull alongside the curb, the officers pile out of the cars and charge into the nightclub, nightsticks raised. Joe is at the end of the pack; he can already hear the men inside shouting and the women shrieking. Joe bursts through the door.

It is a large, elegant room with crystal chandeliers and matching wall sconces. Clustered around the dance floor are small tables, once full of cocktails and bottles of champagne. Where the clientele had been sitting a few moments before, enjoying the music and watching the dancers, now chairs are overturned as men leap to their feet with the arrival of the police. Women are squealing, slapping the policemen with their small evening bags. Police call for order. Waiters scramble over the fallen chairs, heading for the exit door.

On stage, members of a Negro jazz combo lean against the wall or sit on stools, smoking and watching the drama play out on the floor in front of them with bored indifference. They've seen it all before, many times.

In one corner, a portly man in a tuxedo calmly finishes his steak. On the table in front of him is a half-empty bottle of wine. Across the table sits an elegant woman, dressed in feathers and jewels, smoking a cigarette in a long holder. She tilts her head and blows a stream of smoke to the ceiling. One gloved arm is casually hooked across the back of her chair. The pair regard the raid action as if it is part of the floor show.

Captain Copeland walks over to the couple and stands deferentially off to one side, waiting for the gentleman to stop eating. The club patron reaches over and takes a long swallow of wine to wash down the last bite of steak.

Joe is behind the bar, boxing the contraband booze. He watches the curious scene play out between his captain and the two swells. He can't hear what is being said, but the captain pulls out the lady's chair and the gentleman collects his top hat and holds out his arm to her. Instead of leading the pair out the front door to the waiting paddy wagons, Captain Copeland escorts them to the kitchen door. Joe assumes they're going into the back alley.

When the captain re-enters the room he's alone, tucking a wad of bills into his pocket. He isn't the only one making sure some of the patrons find a secure exit from the raid. Throughout the room, lucky customers are being ushered out of another back door exit by the police. City councillors, wealthy businessmen, two judges.

Joe longs to work with honest cops. "Forget about fighting for justice. It seems the real reason we're here is to line our pockets. At this rate, there won't be anyone left to take back to the precinct," he says to no one in particular. He knows the colonel is trying to clean up the force, but it's tough to fight on two fronts, and the bootlegging racket is the priority.

The bartender locks the liquor cabinet and argues with Captain Copeland. The captain moves away and seizes a few open bottles from the tables.

Officers direct a dozen waiters and one cigar girl to the paddy wagon. They join a few patrons who didn't have the pull to escape the consequences of the raid. The officers are in a jubilant mood, slapping each other on the back as they leave the bar.

"A good haul tonight, boyos."
"There will be lots of pay-olla for this job."
"I'm going to put this on one of those Nash Rambler coups. Fast and sweet."
"Ha! Fast and sweet. Just like your wife."

Joe loads the last of the prisoners into the back of the paddy wagon and then looks back at the door of the club where the bartender and captain are talking. He watches the bartender count out a stack of bills into the outstretched hand of Captain Copeland. The bartender then goes back into the building; a tidy up and he'll be ready to open tomorrow. By then, his waiters will be out on bail and the customers will be back, thirsty for more.

Joe sits on the hard bench in the back of the paddy wagon with the luckless lawbreakers they've picked up in the raid. It's dark in the back, and he can barely make out the people sitting across from him.

"I hope this isn't going to take long," a male with a gravelly voice says.

"It shouldn't. Bennie keeps on top of these things pretty good. Lots of palms are greased so it shouldn't take too long," another male answers.

"Have you got plans for tonight?" a female asks. "I was thinking that once we're sprung, we could head over to the Pirates' Den for a drink. They have a great band playing."

"Sure, that would be great. Say, can you do the Lindy Hop?" the gravelly voiced man asks.

"Can I ever." She giggles. This trip to the station is a mere detour between watering holes.

Joe's eyes are shut, his head leans against the side of the paddy wagon. He's jolted with every bump in the road. He's is in a pretty glum mood as they drive back to the station to book their prisoners and put the few cases of confiscated booze into lockup for evidence.

"Not much action?" inquires the desk clerk as the unfortunate few from the speakeasy raid are brought in. "Yeah, it was a dud. The place was half empty, right boys?" Captain Copeland says.

"Yeah, a real bust," says one.

"Not worth our time to go out," says another. Both comments lead to some good-natured backslapping and ribbing.

Joe stands apart. He focuses on filling in the paperwork for the raid led by Philadelphia's finest. Joe knows that corruption is rampant in the force. Officers from the captain down through the ranks to the beat cops are on the take. Over four-hundred officers were implicated in a brewery surveillance operation bust last month, and Colonel Butler is assigning as many police to watch over their fellow officers as he is assigning to watch the criminals. The take from tonight's small raid is merely a drop in the payoff bucket.

There are days when he thinks of quitting, but then who'd be left to keep the streets safe for the likes of Fanny, or Maggie and Tommy? Eventually, Prohibition will be repealed and this madness will be over. He places his hand around his shield: Honor. Integrity. Service.

Chapter 36

Ah, spring. Even though drifts of stubborn snow remain against fences and under porches, buds are starting to appear. Sidewalks are busy with boys on bicycles and girls playing hopscotch. Women sit on verandas and front steps, enjoying the sunshine. Maggie, Joe alongside, nods to them as she pulls her wagon of groceries—some are friends since the early days of Oskar's disappearance.

"Thanks for helping me carry home these groceries, Joe. You're sure those bags aren't too heavy for you? I can put more in the wagon."

"Not a problem, Maggie. I'm glad to do it. That grocer seemed particularly put out to see me, though. He sweet on you?"

"There's been a certain interest on his end for some time, although I can't imagine why. I keep trying to discourage him, but he's persistent. I did notice that he didn't tuck a jar of imported marmalade into the bag like he usually does, so maybe he's got the hint."

"Too bad. That sure is good marmalade. I guess there won't be any more? I was always telling me mam it was magic what she did in the kitchen, and you're a great cook, too, Maggie. When I write home, I tell her about your delicious pies and stews."

"Do you miss home, Joe? Are you enjoying living in the city?"

"I'm glad to be on the police force. I'm really enjoying that. But I do miss my family, especially mam and me sisters. My oldest sister is getting married this summer, so I'll go home for the wedding. Even though Ardmore isn't that far away by train, it's hard to get away. There's always something happening in the First."

"I think Colonel Butler works you all too hard," Maggie says. "You've not had a day off in ages, Joe. Fanny is complaining."

"Well, nobody works harder than Colonel Butler. He had a cot brought into his office so he could sleep there. The first few weeks, we were working round the clock on those raids. It's a bit better now that the number of raids has slowed down."

"I take it progress is being made, then?" Maggie says.

"Ah, I wish. More like the saloon owners are getting wise to how to work the system. Lots of places aren't even looked at anymore because somebody's paying somebody else off."

"How terrible, Joe. Surely it's not as bad as all that?"

"Oh, it's even worse. Colonel Butler's threatening to resign. He and Mayor Kendrick are fighting each other in the newspapers and at rallies all over the city. Kendrick says that if he can't have a man who will cooperate with him, he'll find another man. When he heard that, the colonel called Kendrick disloyal and said that he regretted not pulling his nose." Joe throws back his head and laughs. "I'd like to pull his nose, too."

"He sounds like quite a character, your colonel."

"Ah, he is. I think the hardest thing he's had to figure out is the pay-offs. He's a military man and thought he could run the Public Safety Department like the Marines. But he didn't understand that almost every single position in the city, and probably the state as well, is a patronage position. We have to pay a ward boss to get and keep our jobs. When he took on the job, I don't think he thought he'd be trying to lead a bunch of police who carry their wallets with more enthusiasm than their badges."

"I thought everyone in Philadelphia knew that's how it works."

"That's part of the problem, for sure. It's not a big stretch for everybody that's paying out to start thinking that somebody should pay them under the table, too. It's the way things have always been done in Philadelphia. Imagine there's a long line of city workers: you have your hand in the pocket in front of you and somebody's hand is in your back pocket; the line stretches from here to the state capital."

"A regular chain gang. I've read about it in the newspaper, and the women in the neighborhood seem to think it's perfectly normal. But I gotta say, Joe, it's upsetting to hear you talk about it."

"Oh, I'm not on anybody's payroll. Not to worry. I slip the ward boss a few bucks for the job every month, but I don't take any money for doing the job."

"So, what's Colonel Butler trying to do about all the payoffs?"

"Well, that's going to be the tricky part. It's certainly ruffling a lot of feathers at city hall. He's trying to end the payoffs: the hand in the back pockets, first. He met with all forty-two police districts and said that we had forty-eight hours to end the corruption. He said that he didn't care what had happened yesterday, and we should tell that to the bootleggers and saloon owners who are trying to silence us. He says what's more important is how we conduct ourselves going forward. That it's a new day in Philadelphia policing. He says that we need to earn back the respect of the public."

"And how'd that work out?"

"Pretty much like you'd expect. That was a while ago and nothing's changed, except maybe the lads got smarter at accepting the bribes. The big problem is that everybody is so poorly paid. I figure I make only about twelve hundred dollars a year. You just can't look after a family on what a copper makes."

Joe juggles the bags, shakes his head. "I heard about this one cop in California who was getting a divorce from his wife. He made thirty-five dollars a week. When she demanded her share of the family assets, they found a townhouse, a country house, two cars, a speedboat, and a bunch of bank accounts. The goodies dangled by millionaire bootleggers are pretty tempting for cops making thirty-five a week."

"It sounds pretty bad, all right," Maggie says

Joe and Maggie climb the steps of the back stoop to the kitchen door. "Well, don't quit, Joe. You're good at your job and, from the sounds of it, one of the few honest cops we have. Philadelphia needs you."

"Oh, not to worry, Maggie. It's not just Philly that needs me. Colonel Butler needs me, too."

Chapter 37

"It's swell you're coming for supper, Jimmy. My ma doesn't usually say yes when I ask her about my pals coming over," says Tommy. They round the street corner and pick up the pace to Tommy's house.

"It'll be great. We can figure out what we're going to do about getting even with Duffy. What do you think about the plan?" Jimmy asks.

Tommy shrugs. "I don't know, Jimmy. It seems crazy. Mickey's got guns and stuff."

"Now who's chicken?" Jimmy shoves Tommy into a hedge.

"Ow! Quit that." Tommy brushes off the prickly twigs caught in his jacket. "The other times we was only looking in windows and stuff. This is a whole lot different. What happens if they catch us? Oskar was our best pal, but maybe we should let the police catch the guy that did it, if it happened at the warehouse."

Jimmy bunches his fists and steps toward Tommy. "To do that, them cops would have to know we was there. And that would be telling. You ain't a rat are ya Tommy?"

"No, I'm not a rat." Tommy thrusts his hands in his pockets and turns away. Jimmy catches up.

"We was all at that warehouse. We need revenge, buck-o. Now, let's go see what your ma has cooked for supper. I could eat a horse."

* * * *

Jimmy's elbows are on the table. He chews noisily, opening his mouth to show Tommy the food. He hasn't even swallowed when he gulps a big glass of milk. A second later he leans back in the chair and belches. Tommy's eyes widen as he dares to look at his mother.

Maggie smiles through narrow, tight lips; Tommy knows that means trouble.

"So, youse a cop?" Jimmy asks Joe between mouthfuls.

"Yes Jimmy, I work downtown at Enforcement Unit Number One's headquarters," Joe says.

"That means you go after bootleggers and moonshiners, right?"

"Yup, I make sure people don't break the law. Liquor is illegal."

"Well, me Da' says it's a stupid law. He drinks beer all the time," Jimmy says.

"Jimmy, would you like more potatoes?" asks Maggie.

"Sure, Mrs. Barnes. This all tastes great. You're a swell cook."

"Thank you, Jimmy. What are you boys up to after dinner?"

"*Um*, I think we're going to do some homework. Right, Tommy?"

"Yeah, homework, Mother. We have lots of homework."

"Say, Constable Kelly? Did you ever shoot anybody?" Jimmy asks

Maggie and Archie Mansfield choke on their food. Eugene laughs.

"I'm pretty sure that that's not dinner table conversation, Jimmy," Joe says.

"You got any more pork chops, Mrs. Barnes? They're real good."

"Sorry, we're finished with them. But if you're still hungry, I've got a cake for dessert."

All the boys at the table, big and small, crack wide smiles.

After supper, Tommy and Jimmy head upstairs before the adults. "*Shh*, be quiet!" Jimmy whispers.

"Which is the cop's room?"

Tommy nods to Joe's bedroom door directly ahead.

"You said that you saw where he puts his gun, right?"

Tommy listens. Joe's voice floats from the kitchen; he's doing the dishes with Maggie. Archie Mansfield has retired to his room and closed the door. His humming travels under the door frame and Tommy knows, from experience, it means he's reading. Both boys heard Eugene Smith go out; his room is off the kitchen.

"I don't think we should be doing this, Jimmy."

"Yeah, you said that already. Like a million times. Show me where it is." Jimmy turns the knob to Joe's room.

Tommy scoots under Joe's bed and pulls out a box. Jimmy lifts the lid. The two boys stare at Joe's service revolver inside its holster. Jimmy reaches in and pulls the gun from the holster. "Okay, let's go find Mickey."

"Whoa Jimmy, you never said anything about taking the gun with us. Are you nuts?" He tries to grab the gun from Jimmy, who keeps it out of his reach.

"Chicken. I thought you said you were Oskar's friend? What kind of friend won't stick up for a pal? He got shot down in cold blood. We were there. We gotta go back and make them pay for what they did."

"So, who you gonna shoot, Jimmy? You don't even know who did it."

"I'm gonna shoot Mickey Duffy. He's the boss. And somebody's gotta pay for what they done to Oskar." Jimmy's scowl causes Tommy to shiver.

"Come on, you chicken. Or I'll go me-self, and tell everybody that you were too scared to go." Jimmy leaves the room, tucking the gun into his waistband, under his sweater.

"You always get me in trouble, Jimmy." Tommy follows Jimmy.

"Mrs. Barnes. I forgot some of me books at home and need them for me homework. Is it okay if Tommy comes with me over to my house to finish what we're working on?"

Tommy is anxious, shifting his weight from one foot to the other. His eyes pleading. If ever there was a time for a mother to say no, this would be it. But, Maggie isn't picking up any of his nervous signals.

Joe frowns at Tommy. "Just over to Jimmy's, right? Will you be late, Tommy?" he asks.

Tommy's eyes blink rapidly. His face is pale as if he might throw up. "No. I just have to go over to Jimmy's for a few minutes."

"Don't be too long, Tommy." Maggie brushes the hair off Tommy's forehead. "Are you okay, sweetie?" Tommy shrugs her off. "And thank you for coming, Jimmy. It was nice to meet you." Maggie hangs up the dish towel on the stove handle to dry.

Tommy slowly pulls on his jacket and hat. He trails after Jimmy. The boys head off in the direction of the warehouse.

* * * *

Before Oskar's death had been announced, Tommy and Jimmy had snuck back to the warehouse a couple of times since the night of the police raid. They'd told each other they'd look for clues of his disappearance, but a big part of their reason was that they were generally fascinated by the bootleggers; had even hoped they'd see Oskar working for Mickey. Each time they'd gotten close, they'd been chased off by one of the guys in Mickey's crew.

They hadn't dared go back since Oskar's body had been found.

Tonight, they are extra cautious. Jimmy has moved the heavy gun from his waistband to his pocket. The two boys creep closer.

Jimmy climbs to the top of a crate, and peers in a dirty window. "Whaddya see, Jimmy? Is Mickey there?" Tommy tugs at Jimmy's sock, which is tucked into the bottom of his knickers. Jimmy tries to kick him loose.

"Naw, I don't see Mickey yet. Just a bunch of guys doing bootlegger stuff."

"Maybe we should come back another night? What do you think? Wait until Mickey's there?" Tommy continues to tug at Jimmy's sock.

250

"Let go, you jerk," Jimmy climbs to a better spot. For a moment the space is illuminated; headlights sweeping from a wide turn. *"Shh, someone's coming."*

Car doors slam. The warehouse door opens. "Hey Mickey," says one of the men.

"It's him. He's here." Jimmy fumbles with the gun in his pocket. The barrel keeps getting caught in the fabric.

Suddenly, Tommy is grabbed by the collar from behind and hoisted off the ground. He squawks in surprise, arms and legs flailing. Jimmy turns. The color drains from his face.

"What are you boys doing here?" Joe Kelly whispers. He shakes Tommy. "I thought I told you this is dangerous." Jimmy tries to scramble away, but Joe drops Tommy and catches Jimmy's arm and drags him off the crates. The racket draws the attention of the crew inside. Several of Mickey's men come out with guns drawn.

Joe shoves Tommy and Jimmy behind him. The three of them crouch behind the fallen crates. One of the crew fires off a warning shot. "Hey, who's there?" the bootlegger shouts. "Come out where I can see ya."

Tommy shakes at the sound of the gun. Jimmy starts to tug at Joe's hold on his arm. Another shot rings out. "I said, come outta there." Holding firmly to Jimmy, Joe looks cautiously around the corner of the crates. Tommy peeks around Joe. The bootlegger stands with his back to where they are hiding. They watch the bootlegger holster his gun.

"Cats after rats." He slams the door of the warehouse.

Eventually, Joe nods and the three creep away out of the yard, and down the street to the alley.

When they reach the alley, Joe slams Jimmy against the wall. "What the hell, kid? What did you think you were doing? And where did you get that gun?" he snarls into Jimmy's face, grabbing the gun out of Jimmy's pocket. "Hey, this is my gun. You *idgits*. It's not even loaded. What the heck were you thinking?" Holding Jimmy against the wall, he turns and glowers at Tommy. "I thought you knew better."

Jimmy hangs limply against the wall.

Tommy stares at his shoes; it's becoming a habit.

"If they had caught you, what do you think would have happened? Do you think they would have maybe shot you?" Joe shoves hard at Jimmy to emphasize the word shot. Jimmy whimpers and Tommy's knees weaken. "Do you think they would have dumped your sorry bodies in the river?" Joe gives Jimmy another shake. Jimmy starts blubbering.

"What do you think it feels like to get shot? To be bleeding everywhere? To be stuffed in the trunk of a car? To be thrown into the river? Do you float or do you sink?" With each question, Joe gives Jimmy a little shake and glares at Tommy. Both boys are now blubbering and shaking their heads vigorously.

"We won't do it again." Tommy can't stop shivering.

"I don't wanna float or sink. No, sir. We're done," says Jimmy.

Jimmy slides down the wall into a heap. Joe keeps his voice low. "You boys get home. Now."

The two boys collide with each other, and with a wall, then scramble out of the alley and high tail it for home.

Chapter 38

What with the turn of the century and then the war, it is a time of many advances in America: cars, planes, radios, telephones. Lots of changes, and yet some things are still the same. Monday is still Wash Day and clothes are still scrubbed on a board and wrung out to dry, then pinned on the line. Tuesday is still Ironing Day, with a hot iron from the stove. Wednesday is mending, usually replacing the buttons torn off by the washing machine's mangle. Thursday means cleaning the upstairs. Baking is done on Fridays. Saturday's chores are to clean downstairs. The best day of all is Sunday: a day of rest, church, and visiting.

Now that Maggie's doing the lodgers' wash, her Mondays are longer than ever. She bends over the large galvanized tin washtub on the back porch, and scrubs Tommy's shirt on the washboard. There are two more washtubs next to it on a wooden washstand. A hand-wringer, the infamous mangle, is mounted above the wash tubs. Two wooden rollers and a crank squeeze out the excess dirty water before the shirt is rinsed in the second tub. Her mangle often breaks a few buttons, keeping Maggie busy with repairs for her own household as well as for the public laundry downtown.

Like most of the houses in the neighborhood, the windows at the back of Maggie's house are always steamed on Mondays. Inside the kitchen, a large pot of water is on a slow boil so that the washing water stays hot and the soap is dissolved. Maggie uses a second rinse tub to make sure the harsh Borax soap is rinsed out of the clothes before she hangs them on the line. As the shirt goes through the wringer for the last time, it falls into a wicker laundry basket.

It's a mild March day, and Maggie puts clothes on the line to dry. Even with it being sunnier, after pinning out the clothes this morning, her fingers are blue from the cold. She picks up one of Tommy's school shirts and remembers that day she found Alicja crying. She feels a lump in her throat. It seems a lifetime ago.

Next door, Clara hangs her own wash. Maggie hadn't enjoyed washdays before, but now looks forward to them. It's her way of staying connected to her neighbors now that she's not needed over in the Leszek kitchen.

There's a community conversation going on under the washing lines and over the fences of the houses every Monday.

"So, Joe was telling me about this cop in California who had two houses, a couple of cars, a speedboat, and cash stashed in every bank in town," Maggie says.

Clara mumbles around the wooden peg in her mouth. "I should have married a cop. I'd get me one of those new washing machines."

"And sit and eat bonbons on Mondays, while the rest of us work?" Maggie asks with a chuckle.

"Nah. You can come over and use my machine too, Maggie. I'll let you. But it will have to be a Tuesday, because I'll need it on Mondays."

"Then when would I do my ironing? Wednesday? Clara, that wouldn't work. And I suppose mending day would get pushed to Thursday and before you know it my whole week is turned upside down."

Their laughter is caught by the flapping sheets.

"Yes, but you'd have Mondays free, Maggie. You could eat bonbons with me."

Fanny appears from around the corner of the house. "I thought I'd find you out here, Missus B."

"Fanny, oh, right, Monday is your day off," Maggie says.

Fanny steps around the basket of wet clothes and holds a grease-stained paper bag. "I brought donuts." She takes a seat on the step.

"*Eee-* you great gal, you." Clara shouts from behind a wet sheet being hung on the line. "I hope you brought enough for three."

"I brought one for Joe, too. You can eat his. Just don't tell him."

Fanny sits on the step, enjoying her donut while the two women finish hanging out the wash. The sun shines through the bare branches. The three women gossip about movie stars.

"So, I hear you and Joe are getting married, Fanny," Clara says over her shoulder as she continues to pick from her basket of wet laundry.

"Someday, but not right now. We're going to take it slow for a bit. Joe says it will give us a chance to get to know each other better."

"So, how's work, Fanny? Fanny works downtown at the Atlantic Refining Company as a telephone operator," Maggie explains to Clara as she pins more clothes to the line.

"*Oohh*, very posh. That keeps you in donuts, does it?" Clara asks.

"Not really. I'm always running out of money. Living in the city is so-o-o expensive." Fanny sighs and takes another bite of her donut. Clara hangs her last item, brushes her hands together, and parks herself on Maggie's back steps. Fanny offers her Joe's donut.

Maggie brushes back a stray hair off her face. She grabs a clothespin and jabs it down on the shoulder of Tommy's wet shirt.

"What have you been doing, Maggie," Fanny asks. "Joe says you've been pretty busy lately."

"Oh, out and about. You know…" Maggie says. She ducks behind a pillowcase to avoid looking at Fanny.

"Yes, she's always heading out to lunches and going shopping, so she says. And looking pretty swell too, I must say. I think she has a sugar daddy," says Clara.

Maggie pokes her head around a pair of Tommy's trousers. "I've been seeing a lot of my friends lately."

"Ah, is that a little blush there, toots?" asks Fanny.

"A friend called Howard, perhaps?" asks Clara. Fanny and Clara burst into giggles. Maggie rolls her eyes, grins, and ducks back behind the trousers. *If only they knew what I was up to and the crowd I'm running with. Seeing Howard would be mild compared to my life as a lady detective. And if they knew I'd had a few coffee dates with Edith Duffy? Oh the tongues would wag then. It would surely entertain these two, and it would definitely put Mother and the Garden Club over the edge.*

Chapter 39

Maggie reflects on the last time she went for coffee with Edith. She'd worked carefully to learn more about Mickey, storing away all kinds of tidbits Edith mentioned. And then Edith had invited Maggie to her house for lunch.

Maggie is nervous climbing the stone steps to Edith's front door. She's been watching the outside of the house for so long, and now she'll finally see the inside. The heavy stonework gives the house an intimidating massiveness, as does the front door, a heavy oak one with stained glass. *I bet even Mother would hesitate to knock on this door.*

While Maggie and the Inspector still haven't found anything that could be a smoking gun, they are slowly building a case that shows the size and power of Mickey's empire. The investigation has been almost too enjoyable; she's had to remind herself, at times, to stay on track. Wandering the shops with Edith, stopping for coffee at lovely cafes; it's been years since she's permitted herself these small indulgences. Maggie knows she'll miss this, and she'll miss Edith too.

The Inspector never mentioned how attached you can get to the people you're tailing. I feel like such a rat. It's almost like I'm lying to Edith. But I'm not pretending. I really do like her. A lot. And I feel sorry for her, too. Edith and Mickey are goofy about each other. It's going to shatter poor Edith when he's sent away to prison.

A uniformed housekeeper answers the door. Maggie barely has time to hand off her coat and gather her impressions of the foyer before Edith squeals hello and gathers her up for the customary peck on both cheeks.

"Maggie, don't you look like the bee's-knees. Is that a new dress? And I love your hat." Edith links her arm through Maggie's and leads her through to the living room. Even though it has a large Palladian window facing the street, the room feels dark and oppressive because of the oversized furniture and dark colors. Every piece is fringed or tasseled. Oil paintings in heavy gilt frames hang in front of dark, flocked wallpaper. Even at noon, all the lights are on. Maggie's surprised. This isn't the house she'd pictured Edith living in at all.

"Lunch will be ready in just a shake, so we have time for a couple of gin rickeys, if that's okay?"

Maggie is getting used to a small tipple in the afternoon.

Edith makes the cocktails and delivers one to Maggie. "Edith, your house is lovely."

"Oh, banana oil." Edith says. "I hate this old pile. Mickey lived here before we got hitched. He likes the address, very posh don't ya know, but I hate it. Living here is like living in a mausoleum or a bad hotel.

"I want to move and build something new and modern. Lots of curves and sparkle. And lots and lots of sunlight. You know, art deco, like at the train station." Edith takes a spot beside Maggie and peers over her own shoulder. "And sometimes this old place smells funny," she whispers behind her hand. Maggie giggles.

Flanking the fireplace with a heavily carved mahogany mantle are matching cabinets filled with ornaments. Curious, Maggie walks over for a closer view. "These are beautiful, Edith. Have you been collecting cats long?"

Edith chatters happily about how she acquired each piece. Most are gifts from Mickey. Maggie sees a new side to him, the indulgent husband. One figurine in particular catches her eye—a small crystal feline. The cat's eyes are topaz and the facets that are carved into the crystal catch the light, casting rainbows around the room. Maggie removes it carefully.

Edith joins Maggie, takes it from her, and cradles it delicately in her open palm. "It's one of my faves. Mickey gave it to me after the grand opening of the Cadix. That's one of his nightclubs, the one I love best. They have the best bands there." Edith carefully returns the cat to its spot on the shelf. "Oh Maggie, you must come out dancing with us some night. We'll cut a rug and have a great time."

"That sounds swell, Edith. Except I'll need to find someone to look after Tommy." *And something to wear.*

The Duffys' housekeeper, Hilda, announces lunch is ready.

The dining room is also oppressive. It reminds Maggie of a castle. Her chair is so heavy it takes two hands to slide it back so she can sit.

Over delicious rolled ham sandwiches, celery stuffed with cream cheese and pimentos, and bowls of clam broth, Edith chatters on about her committees, the Philadelphia social scene, and, of course, Mickey. There are many mentions of evenings alone while Mickey is on the road for business, and there are also outrageous stories of glittering evenings out. Edith is just launching into a description of the feathered headpiece Mayor Kendrick's wife wore at Club Cadix when they hear the front door open and close.

Edith's eyes sparkle as she turns to the door.

"Bunny, you're home. Come in and say hello to my friend, Mrs. Barnes."

"Hello, Kitten. I just wanted to pop home and see how you're doing. Having a good day?" Mickey says.

"It's been a great day. Maggie and I are just having lunch. I'll just let Hilda know that you're here and to lay another plate." Edith gives her husband an enthusiastic kiss and hurries off to the kitchen.

Maggie takes a breath and stares at her hands which are clasped tightly on her lap. *Mickey Duffy. Mickey Duffy's house. Frank won't believe it when I tell him tonight. This is a great chance to question him.*

Mickey comes over, takes Maggie's hand, and gives her a warm smile. "Mrs. Barnes, it's great to see you. I remember you from Leszeks'. I had no idea that you and Edith were pals."

Maggie feels trapped by his smile and hands, but manages to return the smile. "Yes, Edith and I got to know each other at the reception for Oskar."

A shadow passes over his face. He looks at her gravely. "Yes, that was so tragic. A young boy in the wrong place at the wrong time, I understand. How is his poor mother, Alicja?"

"She's coping as best she can. With her man away in prison and five other children, there's a lot on her mind."

"You know, I'll have someone look in on her, to see if there is anything I can do. Her husband, Stan, works for me, or will again, when he gets out next year."

"That's very kind, Mr. Duffy. I'm sure that Alicja will appreciate it."

"We look after our own. But enough of this gloomy-gus stuff. Tell me, what have you and Edith been up to?" Mickey settles into his chair at the head of the table. The king in his castle.

"Oh, just visiting. You know, girl talk. I was admiring all the cats and kittens in Edith's collection. She says you gave her most of them."

"Ha, they're silly things, but Edith likes them. Cats remind me of Edith, always landing on her feet. Soft fur, but with sharp claws. I got her the first one the day after we met and it started from there. I always try and pick her up a new one whenever I'm away."

"It's a large collection, Mr. Duffy. You must be away a lot."

"Business takes me out of town."

"And what kind of business are you in, Mr. Duffy? Edith hasn't said." Maggie is curious about how he'll answer.

"Import export, a bit of manufacturing, although I'm branching out into hotels and other properties. Real estate is a great investment these days. But this is boring you, I'm sure. What about yourself? What's your story, Mrs. Barnes?"

Edith floats back into the room. Hilda follows with a plate, soup bowl, and cutlery. "Mickey Bunny, I was just suggesting that Maggie come out with us some night when we're going out to the Cadix. Wouldn't that be swell?"

"It sure would, doll. And it would give me a chance to meet Mr. Barnes." He unfolds his napkin.

"It would just be me. Mr. Barnes passed away. I've been widowed for a few years now."

Mickey places his spoon beside his bowl, then looks at Maggie with soft, kind eyes. "Oh, I am sorry. What a dope I am. Of course, it would be great if you could join us. A pal of Edith's is a pal of mine."

"Thank you very much, both of you, but I really couldn't."

Edith shoots a glance at Mickey.

"Nonsense, Mrs. Barnes. I insist," he says.

Edith gives a small, fluttery clap. "Oh, good. It's settled. Maggie and I will pick a date later. Oh, I know, why don't you spot Maggie and I new dresses, Bunny? We could get matching ones."

"Sure, no problem. Love to." He begins eating.

Edith grins at Maggie. Conversation flows, Edith happily chattering away, although, like a wind-up toy, she seems to be running down. Throughout lunch, Maggie notices Edith has developed a small tremor in her hands. Mickey has seen it, too. Edith reaches for her glass, but knocks it over, spilling water on the table and in her lap.

"Oh, clumsy me. Look what I've done." There are tears in Edith's eyes when she looks up. Mickey hurries over, napkin in hand.

"Kitten, it's all right. It's just water. Hush now." Mickey dabs at the wet spots on Edith's dress. He shakes the bell beside Edith's plate. Immediately, the housekeeper comes.

"Hilda, Mrs. Duffy needs to change her dress. Can you help her upstairs? And then see to this spill. Mrs. Barnes and I will have coffee and dessert in the living room."

Hilda leads Edith away, one hand on her arm and the other loosely around her waist. Edith turns back to Maggie. "I won't be a sec, hon. Just let me get something dry on, and I'll be right back."

Maggie and Mickey settle in the living room. Mickey clips and lights a cigar.

"Poor Edith, I hope that she'll be all right," says Maggie.

"She'll be fine. Just gets tired, is all. She'll be right as rain in a bit."

"Mr. Duffy, why don't I just slip home? Then Edith can rest."

Mickey sighs. "Maybe you're right, Mrs. Barnes. That might be best. I'll get one of the boys to drive you home, and then go tell Edith." Mickey rises. "It was nice meeting you, Mrs. Barnes. Edith doesn't have many gal pals. And we'll see you at the club real soon, okay?"

"I'm looking forward to it. And don't trouble your driver. I can see my own way home."

"Sure thing." Mickey heads for the stairs. Maggie finds her coat on a hall bench, and lets herself out. *Wait 'til I tell the Inspector.*

Chapter 40

"Great dinner last night, Mrs. Barnes," says Archie. "And my mornings would not be as pleasant if it weren't for your coffee."

"Good home cooking. Healthy, man-sized portions, too," says Eugene.

Maggie wipes the stove and counters. "Ah, you two. Well, thanks fellas." *And to think, I almost didn't do this. Now I've a couple of months' worth of rent saved. And I've got decent, long-term lodgers. I'm glad I decided to take the day off from surveillance. I mustn't forget I've a business to run.*

When the house is empty, she strips the beds and gathers the laundry.

Tommy's clothes basket is full. Socks, underwear, shirts. And in those pants and his jackets, always a stone, twig, or some string to pull out.

Joe's basket is much lighter. His uniform is sent out to be cleaned. She adds his socks, undergarments, and a few shirts to the mix. Archie's clothes usually need a good shake; so much chalk dust.

Maggie's next stop is downstairs, in Eugene's small room off the kitchen. He's separated his collars from his shirts and laid them out on top of his dresser. His suit jacket is draped over the back of a chair; the matching pants and vest hang neatly in the wardrobe. As Maggie lifts the jacket to place it on a hanger with the pants, a wad of folded papers falls out of an inside pocket.

As Maggie places the pages on the dresser, they unfold a little. Maggie's familiar with the format of the sheets, as she's seen ledgers before in her father's office. Driven by curiosity and intuition, Maggie steals a peek. *Thanks to the Inspector, I am developing some awfully nosey habits.* The words in the left column mean little to Maggie: men's names, perhaps farm names, a glassware company she knows of. Many of the names have been crossed out. The dollar amounts are startlingly large. *They appear to be a series of payments for shipments. Lots of the figures have been stroked out and revised; such a messy work. The journal entries are for a client who is doing well.*

Eugene's such a precise kinda fella; perhaps he wants to recopy them neatly. He should leave a space near the top, like Father did. And not make his fives look like esses. I'd write it so much more clearly.

Expenses and revenues, Maggie understands. She peeks at the next page in the loose cluster and immediately recognizes the names of local saloons, notorious speakeasies, clubs, and hotels from front page stories in the newspapers. Some of the crossed-out names are places that have been raided and padlocked recently. Arrows darting across the sheets tell a story that shipments have been redirected to other businesses on the list.

What is Eugene doing, bringing confidential papers out of his workplace for? Hang on a sec—these look like liquor sales. Is his firm keeping the books for one of the bootleggers?

About a dozen names of community leaders, judges, and magistrates are listed on another page. *Oh, oh. There is no way that I should be looking at this.* Maggie peers more closely.

"What's this, then?" A male voice behind her.

Maggie drops the pages. "Oh, Inspector. I wish you wouldn't do that. Can't you knock?" She crouches and gathers the papers, trying to put them in the original order.

"No, I can't," he says. "I can whistle, if that would help."

"Hardly. Just don't creep about so much. Look, what do you make of these? They fell out of Eugene's pocket."

Frank scans the papers as she holds them. Suddenly, he looks up. "I knew it. I have seen him before. At the warehouse. Eugene's the bookkeeper. Duffy's bookkeeper."

"What? That can't be right. Eugene's not a gangster. Maybe you're mistaken?"

"Then what are these?"

"But at the warehouse?"

"I'm positive. Just seen him a couple of times. They'd have him do the books at another location. Probably has an office downtown. But he's definitely part of the Duffy crew. My goodness, this is fortuitous," Frank says, beaming.

Maggie arranges the pages on the bed for Frank's further analysis. Maggie explains the meanings of some of the columns.

"You seem to know a lot about accounting."

"My father. We can discuss it another time," says Maggie.

"You know, Maggie, it looks like you might have the ammunition we need to get to Duffy, but we'll have to check these names to confirm a connection."

"Wouldn't that be a lucky accident?"

"As Boney himself used to say, 'there is no such thing as an accident, it is fate misnamed'." Frank is quoting. "And fate has given us this break in the investigation."

"Should we start looking into these names?"

"No, I think that it might be time to bring young Kelly in to our case. I don't want to ignore his capabilities, like I did during Oskar's disappearance. Nor do I want to put you at risk. I think you should give him these papers. He can ask the hard questions of the people on that list. Given the topic, I very much doubt they will appreciate being questioned."

"I'm not sure about that, Inspector. The last time I went to Joe, poor Mrs. Dorn got arrested. Can I trust him with these? What if Eugene or Mickey finds out I've seen them?"

"The only guarantee that no one will find out is to do nothing, and that's just not conceivable at this point. We're not going to investigate it ourselves, so we have to trust young Kelly. Of course, Eugene may notice that the pages have been disturbed and put two and two together himself, which would also be dangerous. So, that brings us back to telling Joe. I don't think we have any other option, Maggie. Whatever we decide, we need to do it soon before Eugene comes looking for these."

"You're right, but I don't want anyone to know that it was me who found them. Let's go see Joe right now, and then I'll get these back into Eugene's pocket before he gets home."

Maggie is thrilled. "Isn't it the strangest thing, Inspector? We've been traipsing all over the city looking for evidence and here's the best thing, right under our noses. The laundry can wait. It appears we either have a break in the case, or maybe even another case."

* * * *

"And you say you found these in Eugene's room while you were cleaning this morning?" Joe and Maggie are in an interview room at the precinct.

"Fell out when I went to hang up his jacket. Are they what I think they are?" Maggie sits forward on the edge of her chair, twisting her purse handle around and around.

"They're payments in and out of a bootlegger's business. Which one? It's too soon to say. I want to copy the information before you put the papers back."

"I don't want someone who's working for a gangster to be living in the house," says Maggie.

"If that's your rule, you'll never find other lodgers. Some days I think the entire city is on the payroll of one gangster or another. Most everyone is tied up in the business in some way. Respectable ladies run blind pigs out of their living rooms. Barbers selling hooch and a haircut for two bits."

Maggie grabs Joe's arm. "Joe, I just realized. Eugene's been paying me with Mickey's money. Dirty money. I'm tied up in it now, too. He has got to go, Joe."

Joe taps Eugene's sheaf of papers. "Let's wait and see what turns up. Look. You think its Duffy, but we need to look into it further. It could be Duffy, or it could be the Lanzetta brothers, Hoff, or one of the other big gangs. The volumes are too big for it to be one of the smaller independents. I recognize many of the names of the purchasers, but the names of the suppliers are new to me. Lots of them are in the small towns outside Philly. And I'm worried about the names of these public figures. Let me write everything out and then you can get them back into Eugene's pocket."

Maggie shakes, hoping that Eugene has not already returned to his room. But, she can't help smiling; proud of being able to bring important evidence to Joe.

"But whatever you do, Maggie, be careful. These men are dangerous and play for keeps." Joe's caution throws cold water on her excitement.

Chapter 41

Colonel Butler's office is small and meticulously organized. Joe stands at attention in a freshly pressed uniform. His shoes have been vigorously buffed. He reads the citations and admires the medals on the wall. He's heard that the colonel is the most decorated Marine in America, and he believes it.

Copeland, Joe's heavy-set Captain, mops his face and the back of his neck frequently with a well-used handkerchief. His uniform is wrinkled, soiled, and one of his brass buttons is missing, forcing him to leave the collar undone.

Joe looks away. *I guess you don't need strong leadership skills when you're under the protection of the mayor.*

Colonel Butler studies the copy of the journal entries. "Constable, you said you got them where?" The desktop contains only a pen set, a photograph of his wife, and a few papers neatly stacked inside an in-basket.

"Sitting on my desk, sir. Possibly someone in the gang dropped it off," Joe says.

"Captain, what do we know about these names? Is this legitimate information?" Looking at his captain, Butler's usual poker face shows a crack of disdain.

Joe remains stiff. *I've seen the colonel stare down some pretty rough customers without a twitch. He must really have it in for Copeland.*

Captain Copeland stares at his shoes and then out the window. The silence grows awkward. Finally, Colonel Butler looks at Joe. "Constable, do you have information?"

"We haven't talked to anyone directly, sir," says Joe. "We didn't want to alert them. But from the information we have, this looks authentic, sir."

"And who's the bootlegger, captain?" barks Colonel Butler.

Captain Copeland flinches. "Um, not sure yet, sir."

"Anything to add, Constable?" he asks.

"No, sir. Nothing more to add right now, sir, but I hope to have something further to report soon. On your direction, we're going to head out and start interviewing the subjects. We expect to have concrete evidence the day after tomorrow, sir. At the latest." Joe's arm desperately wants to salute.

"Good work, Constable Kelly. Go through the list and shake a few trees to see if any apples fall. Dismissed, gentlemen."

Joe stands and gives a smart salute before leaving the room. Colonel Butler automatically returns Joe's salute.

"Watch yourself, Kelly," Copeland says when the two men are safely out of earshot. "Old Gimlet Eye thinks he's leading the charge, but the Mayor and the Machine have other plans. You'd do best to think about sitting this one out, laddie."

"Are you saying not to interview the subjects on the list, Captain?"

"No. I'm saying not to put your back into it. Let's say it might take a bit longer than promised to get the information gathered together.

Locating all these moonshiners out in the sticks might prove to be a problem. I'm just saying."

"Yes, sir." Joe's arm remains at his side.

* * * *

Maggie replaces the notes in Eugene's pocket before she hangs her coat on its hook in the kitchen.

"Good work, Maggie," says Frank.

"Joe's going to start chasing names from the list, but what am I going to do? It's laundry day. Eugene will wonder why his clothes aren't on the line. So will everyone else in the house, and in the neighborhood.

"Stay calm, Maggie. If asked, you can curse the plumbing."

"I'll start it now. I can't afford to get behind. Dinner will have to be thrown together."

Dinner is a quiet affair. Tommy has a report to do for school: transportation. Each lodger gives his opinion of the future of automobiles. Maggie casts furtive glances at Eugene. He appears to be behaving normally, eating quietly, answering questions, but rarely initiating conversation. *He is a quiet one, that's for sure. You'd never know he was a bookkeeper for gangsters from the look of him.*

After dinner, there are a few moments to catch up. Joe has followed Maggie into the kitchen with a stack of plates from the table. "You don't have to do the dishes, Joe. You've got enough on your plate."

"Well, what with your 'laundry problems' I wanted to help," whispers Joe with a significant look toward Eugene's closed bedroom door. Eugene has not yet retired to his room; Archie has him trapped at the dining table in a conversation about the horsepower of future vehicles.

"And when do you think you'll have news on my 'laundry problem'?"

"Well, I'm going to be very busy tomorrow. Lots of 'plumbers' to check into."

Maggie chuckles. "Then you'd better head off to bed, Joe. I'll finish these up. Off you go. Get some rest, and some sleep. I know how important it is to find the guilty plumber." says Maggie.

Chapter 42

Maggie could not remember ever being grateful for laundry. Finishing the pile left undone yesterday helps her pass the time. Joe had left early. The day crept by. She had a brief meeting with Frank. Now, with supper on the table, they wait for Joe. "I'll put a plate on the stove for him. Eat up everyone," she says.

* * * *

Twenty four hours after their conversation, Maggie is nervous. Joe is still not home. She and the Inspector are in the front room. Her journal is open, a prop should anyone look in. But the household is used to her nightly writing habits; she's rarely interrupted.

Both look up when they hear the front door open then shut. Joe comes into the living room. His arm is in a sling and his face is badly scraped. There is a large bandage on his forehead. He carefully lowers himself to the sofa.

"Oh my goodness, Joe. What happened?"

"I got a bit banged up this afternoon. Been at the hospital this whole time." Joe looks around nervously, one eyebrow raised.

"It's okay, Eugene's out," she says.

"We went to one of the farms from the list. From the smell of it, they had an alky cooker running back in the woods behind the barn. They were none too happy to see us. I got winged with a shotgun blast."

He leans forward and whispers, "But your list is pure gold." He winces then settles back. Maggie abandons her desk chair and perches carefully beside Joe. Frank listens closely.

"Everybody is pretty thrilled to be chasing these new leads. We're uncovering some interesting connections. It's pretty powerful stuff." Joe's pale face is flush with excitement.

"We brought a few hoteliers and saloon owners in for questioning. Seems that they all have Mickey Duffy as a supplier. They wouldn't admit it about their own business, but were happy to talk about the competition. We're going to gather more evidence and then see about getting a warrant to bring Duffy in."

"Joe, that's wonderful." He flinches as she leans in to hug him. She settles for patting his good arm. "No one knows where you got the list from, do they?"

"I said that I found the list on my desk. Your secret's safe."

"And what about those other names? The ones from the expense column."

"Mostly moonshiners. A few were breweries, easy to identify. But those moonshiners are way out in the woods. We got lost a couple of times. Nobody would give us directions. Some of these guys have lived in the area since their great-grandparents settled, yet none of the locals knew where to find them."

"And was it way out there you got hurt?" Maggie asks.

"It was. We were driving down a narrow, dirt farm track. We could smell the mash from the woods behind the barn, but couldn't get the car any closer without getting stuck. We got out and were walking in through the trees when they fired the first shot over our heads. I still don't know where they were at," Joe says, shaking his head. "We never did see them. I shouted out that we were from Philadelphia Police, and I yelled to them who we wanted to talk to. That's when they shot at us again."

"Oh, Joe, you could have been killed."

"Nah, they could have killed us easily enough. No, I think they were warning us not to come back. When some of that buckshot hit me, I tripped backwards over a log." Joe grins at Maggie wryly. "I've turned into a city kid."

"And are you going back?"

"Eventually, I guess. Once we've built the case against Duffy. That's definitely who it is, by the way. We've got a few more names to check tomorrow, including those breweries. So far, everyone has been Mickey's supplier or customer."

"And what are you going to do about the other names on the list? The judges and politicians."

"Well, that's the interesting thing. When the captain handed the list over to us this morning, it was a different list than the one I made from the pages you gave me. All we got on the new list are some of the expenses and some of the customers."

"Isn't that just typical." Maggie's teeth are clenched.

Joe shifts on the couch. Maggie turns to him, fussing over his injuries. "Well, you just be careful, Joe Kelly. Running down bootleggers can be a dangerous thing."

Chapter 43

Maggie hasn't been to Child's Place since Jack died. The Victorian-style ice cream parlor had been a favorite spot when they were courting. It still looks the same: small tables along one wall and down the center of the room. Along the other wall, soda jerks in white jackets and black bowties stand behind a long, wooden, marble-topped counter, ready to pull frothy ice cream sodas. Others scoop rainbows of hard ice cream out of big tubs into tulip-shaped glass bowls.

"I'm so glad we finally got a chance to come to Child's," says Maggie. "Isn't it good? I really must bring Tommy here. Maybe if he does well on his exams." She smiles too brightly. Trying to pretend nothing's wrong with Edith's strange behavior.

Edith stirs her ice cream instead of eating it. She's resting her head on one hand, elbow on the table.

"Edith?"

"I'm sorry, Maggie. My mind seems to have wandered." Edith has turned her ice cream into warm soup.

Maggie covers Edith's hand with her own to stop the stirring. "Edith, doll, what's up?"

"Oh, everything's fine."

"Everything is obviously not fine. Edith, please sweetheart, tell me what's wrong."

"Nothing, really. I guess. I haven't been feeling good lately. The doc gave me something and it seems to help."

"What's wrong, Edith? Are you ill?"

"I'm not sure. It's hard to explain. Something's not right. Maybe I should take some of my medicine right now. It always makes me feel better."

Maggie removes her hand so that Edith can rummage in her handbag. She pulls out a small paper packet and waves a waiter over. "Could I have a glass of water, please?"

Maggie watches Edith pour the contents of the packet into the tall glass of water and stir it until it dissolves. She downs it in one long swallow.

"Better?" Maggie asks after a few minutes.

Edith reaches over and pats Maggie's hand. "Now don't you fret, hon. I'll be right as rain in a sec." Settling back into her chair, Edith pushes the bowl away. "So, what were we talking about?"

"About how much I want to bring Tommy here if he does well on his final tests."

"Hey, Bub! My ice cream's melted. Bring me another, will ya?" She is loud. Customers stare. She waves her arm at a waiter. "So, you were saying, again?"

"Tommy. I want to bring Tommy here."

"Oh yeah, this is a great place for a kid. Look at all the ice cream." Edith throws her arms wide. She pushes off and lifts her feet from the floor. The chair spins. "Wheeeee!"

"Edith?" Maggie is alarmed at the two bright pink spots on Edith's cheeks that have little to do with rouge.

Edith leans in close. "You keep asking me if I'm okay, Mags. What if it's you that's not okay?" She lets out a loud cackle.

"Oh for goodness sakes, Edith. Settle down."

Edith sits straighter in her chair, carefully aligning herself with the edge of the table, and then giggles again.

The waiter brings over a bowl of strawberry ice cream and takes away the pink soup.

"I'm sorry, Maggie. I really haven't been myself lately. Mickey's been on the road a lot. Who knows what he gets up to while he's away? Seems he's never home. Some big deal or other in Atlantic City. Have you ever been to Atlantic City? It's so great. The beaches. And there's a boardwalk that runs along in front of the hotels." Edith takes herself for another spin in her chair.

"It sounds swell, Edith. But, you know what? I think I'd better take you home." Maggie reaches for her purse.

"Sorry, sorry," Edith says. "I'm good now. I don't want to go home yet. The house is so big and lonely. Let's stay awhile, okay? You got time to sit for a bit?"

"A bit longer. But only if you tell me what's bothering you. What are Mickey's trips all about?"

"Oh, I don't know. I think he's trying to buy a hotel or something. He doesn't really talk to me about business. I've been sitting at home alone like I'm some kind of widow or something." Edith suddenly sobers. "Jeepers creepers, doll. I didn't mean nothing by that. I'm sorry."

"It's okay, Edith. I've been a widow for a while now. Say, did you know I've been a widow longer than I was a wife? Jack and I had only been married for three years, and he's been gone these last four."

"You must miss him tons. He sounds like he was a special kinda guy."

"Oh, he was. And I do. It hurts me to see Tommy forgetting his father. A little bit less, year after year. He was only a wee boy when Jack died."

"Do you ever regret it? Getting married so young? Life's been rough for you two, I imagine. A woman on her own with a little one to look after."

"I don't regret it for an instant. Not the romance, not the marriage, not the baby. I don't regret a thing. There isn't anything I would change."

Maggie takes a spoonful of her chocolate ice cream. "No, I'm wrong. There is one thing I would change. If I could, I would have stopped him that night. If only I'd known what was going to happen, I would have thrown myself down a flight of stairs to keep him from walking out that door."

Edith strokes her arm for comfort.

"I guess we're both attracted to guys who love taking chances, I mean, if the rewards are big enough. Both are guys who do what it takes to make it better for the folks they're looking out for."

"I don't know how you do it, Edith. The life that Mickey leads, the danger. What it must be like to wait for him to come home."

280

Edith sits quietly. "You know, when he doesn't come home, I never know whether to be angry or afraid. Is he with some dame somewhere, or has he been hurt? I'm usually in such a twist by the time he walks through the door that I could just throw something." Edith chuckles, "Yeah, and sometimes I do, too. Good thing Mickey has good street reflexes or I'd have clipped him by now."

Maggie takes her friend's hand and gives it a squeeze. She's relieved to see that Edith's coloring is returning to normal and the strange behavior is less. Maggie is worried about her friend.

Perhaps it's not surprising that Maggie finds it easy to slip from her disguise as newly found confidante into a more natural role of close friend. Some friendships mature over years and with shared experiences, and for others, like Maggie and Edith, there is an immediate, natural bonding. They recognize kindred spirits in each other, cut from the same cloth. Resilient survivors.

"Well, we can't change fate now, can we?" Edith waves the waiter over. "Hey, how about we order something to take home to Tommy. I'll give you a lift home in the car so it doesn't melt. He'll be home from school soon, right? And what little boy doesn't love ice cream?"

Chapter 44

As Maggie and Edith leave their table at Child's, Mickey's gang is gathered around their own table at the warehouse. Frank leans against the brick wall and takes stock of the grim faces.

"So, where are we at?" barks Mickey. He sits at the head of the table, looking like he is ready to strangle someone.

Henry Mercer absently rubs the scar on his forehead.

"While you've been in Atlanta, we've lost a bunch of dough. About a half dozen of our customers, saloons, and hotels have been raided or closed. Of those, two are still closed," Henry says. "Of the suppliers, all but three of the moonshiners have been raided, their inventory confiscated and their alky cookers and stills destroyed. It doesn't look like we'll make our delivery totals for the rest of the month."

Mickey slams the table. "*Sukinsyn*! So what the hell happened? Who would come at us like this? Is it Boo-Boo? Or the Lanzettas? Somebody from out of town?"

"No, Boss, it looks like Prohbies, the G-Men and the local police. And I checked with some of the other guys; it's only us they're lookin' at. They show up, ask some questions about how much we're buying or selling. They're asking about specific shipment or delivery dates. It's like they know a lot about it already."

The men look at each other and then at Mickey. Stoolies are bad news.

"That's not possible. Nobody would rat me out." He looks each man in the eye. "Nobody."

Mickey repeatedly taps the table with his knuckles while he thinks. "Henry, find out from our friends on the force what the hell is going on and where they are getting their information. Who else might be on the list? I want to know who talked."

"You bet, Boss," he says.

Mickey moves to the next man. "Bricker, find us more inventory. Buy it from out of town or somebody else's suppliers. Pay whatever you need to pay. We can't let this interrupt business, especially with the other gangs getting so aggressive about moving into our territory. All orders will be met." Mickey strikes the table again to underline his point.

"Sure thing. I'm on it," John Bricker says.

"And finally, Gus. You and Fingers talk to the suppliers to find out when they can be up and running again. Lean on them if you have to. We don't want anybody deciding that they want to get out of doing business with us. And while you're at it, see if you can get any more information from them about where the info is coming from. Be as forceful as you need to be."

Gus and Fingers nod in unison. "Yeah, Boss."

"What about the customers, Boss?" John Bricker asks. "They'll have heard that we've been hit."

"Henry, I want you to go grab Eugene at his office and go see everyone. Make sure he brings the list, okay? 'Cause I do mean everyone. See what they know, and reassure them that the deliveries will be the usual amount and at the usual time. There will be no interruptions. Nobody's going to be short. We have a reputation to uphold, gentlemen. I want the word on the street to be that Mickey Duffy and his boys are open for business."

Henry nods. "You bet, Mickey."

"I'm going to talk to Hassel. Maybe we can get some inventory from him. And maybe it's time for a stronger partnership," Mickey says, and leans back in the chair. "Christ, I'm gone for three days and all hell breaks loose. What the hell happened?"

Chapter 45

The Duffy mansion is ablaze with lights. In the dining room, two men's voices boom out ribald stories. Dinner is finished and plates have been pushed aside. Edith yawns, then rings the small china bell to get Hilda to clear.

"Did you see hear that Jack Dempsy won the Gibbons fight?" Mickey leans back in the dining room chair and starts to light his cigar.

Max Hassel fidgets with his own cigar. Mickey passes him his cigar clipper. It's an antique with a crest engraved in the middle. Max admires the tool, and raises an eyebrow in Mickey's direction.

"It's been in the family for years. My grandfather gave it to me. He got it from his pa, I think. Not sure how he came to have it though."

"Interesting crest. I'm sure there's a story there. It's not every bootlegger that can light his cigar thanks to the Philadelphia police." Max clips the end of his own cigar and passes it back to Mickey. The two men companionably go through the ceremony of lighting the cigars: holding matches to start the tightly rolled tobacco leaves. Mickey's habit is to use two. Once established, they draw down on the cigars. As a kid, one of Max's first jobs had been to roll cigars; he appreciates a good smoke.

They are a pair, sitting at Mickey's table and smoking. Where Mickey prefers to lurk in the shadows, Max likes to be the center of attention, and is known for his flashy plaid suits, with rings on most of his fingers. While Mickey strikes first and asks questions later, Max has a reputation for thoughtful consideration. What they have in common is that they are both very dangerous. Mickey is the tiger, stalking in the bushes, and Max is the rattlesnake, basking in the sun.

They both know this: the bootleggers in Philadelphia are a territorial bunch. They've carved out their turf, and defend it vigorously. But they're also businessmen, and sometimes you have to work with the competition. It's always an uneasy truce, but business is business.

"I hear that Kearns got three-hundred thousand for his boy. In cash. The bets on the Dempsy fight bankrupted Shelby, Montana. The whole town." Max's laughter shakes the house.

"Them's a lot of clams for two-thousand folks to come up with. The town will never be the same," Mickey says. "Any chance that Hoff had a piece of that? Boy, that would be swell to see him lose a pile of dough."

"If you gentlemen will excuse me a minute?" Edith says. Mickey nods in her direction, deep into another story about one of the dancers at the Club. When he's finished, Max howls and keeps slamming his hand on the table.

"Let's go sit in the other room, Max. I need to talk to you about something."

Max and Mickey settle into large wingback chairs in front of a blazing fire. There is a contented feel to the room that only prosperous, well-fed men smoking good cigars can produce. Hilda enters with a crystal decanter and two glasses.

Max raises his glass, sniffs, and takes a small sip, rolling the liquid around in his mouth.

"Imported French brandy, Max. Real smooth." Mickey holds his glass to the light. The amber liquid shimmers. He lowers it and takes a sip.

"So Mickey, what do you want to talk to me about?"

"Well, you've heard that we got hit pretty bad with the raids the last week or two. They padlocked a bunch of our clubs and either smashed or seized the booze."

"Word on the street is it's pretty bad," says Max.

"Whatever you heard, it's worse. They've shut down all our suppliers. Al Hendrie's brewery is padlocked and all the barrels smashed. The moonshiners and alky cookers we run out of town are out, too. I've got my guys rounding up new suppliers but, in the short term, I need to lay my hands on a lot of booze."

"How much are we talking about, Mickey?"

"A month's worth. That'll give me time to get my supply line back up and running."

Max whistles. He looks into the fire and then sips his brandy. The end of the cigar glows bright as he sucks in the rich tobacco. "I think I can help you out, Mickey. I've got inventory in a warehouse in Camden that I can get my hands on. Of course, it's good stuff, so it'll cost you a bit more than usual."

"I'd expect nothing less, Max. Business is business. I'll have Henry Mercer call 'round tomorrow to make the arrangements."

"Okay gents, enough of this lounging by the fire. Let's head out and go dancing somewheres. Who wants to cut a rug?" Edith has burst through the door. She twirls around, showing off a red dress covered in bugle beads. She shimmies so that they fly. "It's new," she says. A beaded red headband with two long red ostrich feathers waves gaily as she prances around the room.

Mickey laughs and jumps up, grabbing Edith around the waist and giving her a twirl. "Doll, you are simply irresistible."

Chapter 46

Someone is banging on the front door. Maggie sits up in her bed, alarmed. It is dark. She pulls on her housecoat over her nightgown and steps into the upstairs hallway. Archie's door closes faster than it opens when he sees his landlady is in her nightclothes. In the meantime, Joe has emerged wearing a pair of pants and suspenders over his nightshirt. His hair is disheveled; otherwise he seems alert.

Eugene meets them at the bottom of the stairs. "Who the hell?" he asks Joe.

From the front hall, Maggie peeks around the corner into the living room and is alarmed to see from the clock on the mantle that it's just after three in the morning.

Maggie hangs back at the foot of the stairs as Joe opens the door.

Two large men in topcoats and fedoras stand on the veranda.

Eugene positions himself behind the door in the kitchen, curious about why Gus and Fingers are on the veranda in the middle of the night.

"Can I help you, gentlemen?" Joe asks.

"Mr. Duffy sent us to get Mrs. Barnes," Gus replies.

"What does Mr. Duffy need with Mrs. Barnes at this time of night?"

Maggie hugs her housecoat tight. Her long braid swings behind her as she takes a small step back.

"Mr. Duffy said to get Mrs. Barnes right away," Fingers, the larger of the pair, replies stubbornly.

"Mrs. Barnes isn't going nowhere, bub." Joe moves to block the doorway. "You can tell Mr. Duffy that Constable Kelly said to call around in the morning." Joe begins to shut the front door.

Fingers pushes his heavy, size twelve brogue into the doorway and braces the door open with a large meaty hand.

"Look copper, it's important."

"What can't wait until sunrise?" asks Joe.

"It's Mrs. Duffy. She's poorly and is asking for Mrs. Barnes."

"What's wrong with Edith?" Maggie steps out from behind Joe.

"I don't know, Mrs. Barnes. I was told to come get you. That Mrs. Duffy needed you."

"Okay you two, you can head on home now," Joe says. "Message received, and Mrs. Barnes will call on Mrs. Duffy first thing in the morning."

Maggie reaches out. "Wait, Joe. If Edith is asking for me, it must be urgent. I should go." She meets Finger's eyes. "Wait for me in your car. Let me get dressed. I'll be along shortly."

"You can't go off alone in the middle of the night with two armed men. I should go with you," Joe says.

"Now, wait a sec. The Boss didn't mention nothing about bringing a cop along." Fingers speaks up.

"It's the two of us or no one," Joe says with his arms crossed and his chin out.

"Fine. We'll wait for youse in the car," says Gus.

Joe pushes the door closed, raking his fingers through his hair. "What the hell is going on, Maggie? These goons work for Mickey Duffy. You don't mean to tell me the gal you've been palling around with is Edith Duffy? Whoa, that's not good."

"We don't have time to get into it, Joe. I've got to get dressed. You can come or not, but I'm going."

Joe shakes his head. "Let me wake Mansfield so he knows where we've gone," says Joe. "If we're not back by morning, he can get Tommy his breakfast. And we need someone we trust to know where we're going."

* * * *

Looking up the front sidewalk, Maggie can see Mickey waiting in the open doorway. She does a quick introduction. He looks askance at Joe, but says nothing as he gestures them into the house.

"Thank you for coming Mrs. Barnes," Mickey says. "The doctor has just left. Edith is anxious that you come and sit with her."

Maggie puts her hand on Mickey's arm. "Of course, Mr. Duffy. But what has happened to Edith?"

"I'll explain as we go upstairs. Constable Kelly, would you please wait in the living room. Hilda can bring you some coffee."

Joe looks at Maggie. "I'll be fine, Joe. Just let me find out how Edith is," Maggie says.

290

Mickey takes Maggie's elbow and guides her across the foyer and up the stairs. "She's in there. Her bedroom. And she's having one of her spells. She's had them before. She can be a real piece of work. I let her have her own way when she's in one of those moods. The doctor was here. He's given her something that's supposed to calm her, so she should sleep shortly. I'll owe you one, Mrs. Barnes, if you stay until she falls asleep."

"Did the doctor give any other instructions?" Maggie reaches for the door handle.

A shriek breaks their low tones. "Mickey, you bastard. I hate you." It is followed by a crash of breaking glass against the closed door. Maggie recoils, taking three steps back.

"Please, Mrs. Barnes? She's just not right in the head tonight, but she'll listen to you. Please?"

Nodding, Maggie steps forward. She speaks through the gap between the door and the frame. "Edith, dear. It's Maggie." She grips the handle, turns it, slips inside the bedroom, and gently shuts the door behind her, carefully stepping over and around the shattered glass.

Edith is pacing in front of the window. Her embroidered silk dressing gown has slipped off one shoulder. Her feet are bare, peeking out from beneath her peignoir. "Edith, sweetie, what's wrong? What's happened to put you in such a tizzy?" Maggie asks.

Edith whirls around and strides over to her dressing table, seizes a brush, and vigorously pulls it through her short, bobbed curls.

"That bastard, Mickey. He slept with Trixie, that cheap floozy at the club. She's a bitch, a bloody bitch."

"Slippers, Edith, you're going to cut your feet."

Maggie looks around the room for the bottle of whiskey she is sure is the cause of the outburst. It stands on the table. There are slippers at the edge of the bed. "Edith, sweetheart, please." Maggie holds them up. "Let's keep you safe, okay?"

Edith paces, angrily brandishing the hairbrush. Sometimes shouting, sometimes crying, she tells Maggie about the other women, the long business trips, the perfume and lipstick she finds on Mickey's collars, and the sly glances from the other women when she and Mickey are out on the town. As Edith patrols the corners of the room, Maggie reflects that she has never seen Edith so out of control. The more she repeats the accusations, the more muddled the details become.

Maggie pokes her head out the door. Mickey is leaning against the landing's rail. "Coffee, and maybe some sandwiches." she says.

Maggie adds another chair to a small table and chair in the corner of the room. "Come put on some slippers, Edith. We'll have some coffee. You can tell me all about this Trixie person."

Edith sits and allows Maggie to slide the slippers onto her feet. "Am I getting old, Maggie? Is it my looks?" She swings her head around the room, then rises and rushes over to her dressing table, looking into the mirror.

Maggie follows her friend. "You're a stunner, Edith. And Mickey is a fool if he doesn't see that. Please," she says, putting her arm around Edith, "come and sit. I've asked them to bring you something to eat."

Flappers are typically thin, but it is too easy to feel the bones under Edith's silk dressing gown. Maggie tries to lead her over to the table again, but Edith breaks away. "You don't understand," she wails, clenching her fists. "He did this to me. I used to be the prettiest girl in the club, all the men dangling at the end of my little finger." Her laugh is wild.

"Hush, sweetness. You're still the prettiest girl."

There's a knock at the door. Maggie steps around the glass shards and slips outside. "Thank you, Hilda. I've got it from here. No need to trail though the glass." Maggie takes the tray containing a coffee pot and a plate of sandwiches to the small table.

"Goodness, look at these delicious sandwiches. Come sit with me, Edith."

Edith glides over as if she were crossing a club floor, tall and confident, an easy, sexy sway to her hips. "I felt lousy at supper tonight. And then, poof, all better." She snaps her fingers like a magician.

"Have some coffee," says Maggie. "Please eat. You're probably cranky because you didn't eat supper."

"I'm not cranky 'cause I'm hungry, doll. I'm cranky 'cause Mickey's given me the pox. You know, the Spanish Disease," says Edith.

Maggie looks perplexed.

"You know, syphilis. The Spanish Disease. Although I doubt the Spaniards call it that. Mickey gave it to me. Sort of a wedding anniversary present. Although not a very good one. I wish he'd got me another damn cat, instead," Edith throws her half-eaten sandwich on the table. "And wouldn't you know it, he gives it to me and his dose goes away all by itself. Didn't have to take or shot or nuthin. I ask you, Maggie, how fair is that?"

Maggie swallows Edith's statement. "Oh, Edith, I'm sorry. Does it hurt?"

"Only when I laugh." Edith gives Maggie a maniacal demonstration.

"Seriously, Edith. What do the doctors say?"

"Doctors. A bunch of quacks. They don't know shit." Edith waves her hands through the air. "Wait, I'll get my medicine. The doc said not to take any more tonight. I took a whole bunch before we went out tonight. It did the trick. Maybe I should. Just a little. To feel better." She is a projectile aiming straight for the dresser.

Edith tosses bits of pastel-colored silk from the drawer to the floor. "Ahaa! Here you are." Edith twirls and staggers, passing a small, white pharmacy envelope to Maggie.

"That's the medicine you took at the ice cream parlor, isn't it?"

"It's a mixture of something with just a smidge of cocaine, darling. The latest thing if you have syphilis. Comes with its own doctor's prescription."

Maggie's alarmed. "Cocaine? Isn't that dangerous?"

"Nah, you goose. There isn't much more than in a bottle of Coca-Cola from at the drugstore. Well, maybe a bit more. But not much." Edith giggles again. "Sometimes, it makes me feel so good, I take two."

She raises her arms and dances slowly around the room, humming a jazz tune. "You know, I'd wanted to be a dancer at the club, but they put me in the coat check instead."

"Is that what the doctor gave you tonight, Edith?"

"He gave me a needle. Said it would help me sleep. But I don't feel sleepy." Edith folds herself on the floor beside the bed. She gazes at

Maggie. "I wish I could have a baby. Then Mickey would love me." Tears begin to stream. "Do you think that's why he's sleeping with those other women?"

Maggie crouches, wrapping her arms around her. Edith cries into Maggie's shoulder. Through her tears, Edith confesses how lonely and unhappy she is. Maggie rocks her, murmuring comforting words into the top of her head, just like she used to do when Tommy was younger.

Edith winds down and relaxes. She's feeling the effects of the earlier injection, or Maggie's comforting, or both. She helps Edith into bed and pulls the covers over her shoulders.

"Maggie, don' go, don' leave me. Everybody always leaves me. You're the only fren' I have." Edith grasps at Maggie's hand.

Maggie sits on the side of the bed, one hand holding Edith's hand, the other stroking the bangs away from Edith's fevered forehead. "Don't worry, Edith. I'll sit right here until you fall asleep, and then I'll come in the morning, after I get Tommy off to school."

Less than a half-hour later, Maggie turns her head to the opening door. Mickey pokes his head into the room. He gazes at his sleeping wife, then gestures Maggie to join him in the hallway.

Maggie releases Edith's hand, and snugs the sheet around it.

"Thanks for coming, Mrs. Barnes. And thanks for being such a good pal to Edith." He takes Maggie's hands into his own. "It means a lot to me that you came tonight. It's swell Edith has a friend she can count on. One of my men will take you and the constable home. It's been a heck of a night, for all of us."

Maggie gently withdraws her hands. "Edith's an unhappy woman, Mr. Duffy. Please be kind to her. And remind her that I'll be around in the morning to see how she's feeling."

She notices his reluctance to move; he seems to have forgotten he was going to summon his men. "Don't worry, Mickey, I'm sure that it will all work out. Go sit with her. I'll find the driver," she says, giving his arm a squeeze.

"Thank you for that. Gus and Fingers are waiting downstairs. If you could see yourself out? I want to stay with her for a bit."

Maggie finds Joe sitting on the sofa, an empty coffee cup in front of him, the two meaty bodyguards sitting in chairs watching him. "We can go now, Joe."

They're dropped at the curb of Maggie's house and barely get through the front door when Joe grabs Maggie by the arm.

"Excuse me?" Maggie stares at his hand and then straight into his eyes. Joe drops his hand.

"That was one crazy night. Tell me what's going on. And how did I get to be sitting in Mickey Duffy's living room, drinking coffee?"

"It's been a long night, Joe. Can't it wait until morning?"

"Frankly, no it can't. I spent the night waiting to get shot by a couple of gangsters. You owe me an explanation, Maggie."

"I'd told you before that I met Edith at Oskar's funeral. Since then we've met up a few times for coffee and a bit of shopping. Nothing serious. She's lonely. And so am I. We have a lot of fun together, if you must know. It has nothing to do with Mickey. We're just a couple of gal pals having fun, Joe. Nothing more."

"You know her husband, that man you went upstairs with, is one of Philly's most dangerous criminals. I told you this before. I don't understand why you would get involved."

"Well, you don't need to. I like Edith. I like spending time with her. Now I'm tired and I'm going to bed. Goodnight." Maggie stops halfway up the stairs and looks back at Joe, who is still in the front hallway. Her shoulders relax. "Thanks for coming tonight, Joe. I mean it."

Chapter 47

Joe sits at a conference table with his commanding officer, Captain Copeland, and the District Attorney, Samuel Rotan. At the head of the table, Colonel Butler's hands are steepled. Joe makes eye contact with the colonel, then looks sharply at Captain Copeland. The colonel catches Joe's attention with a cough. Their progress review on the 'Duffy list' is underway.

To date, only one or two of the moonshiners have rolled on Duffy, when presented with dates and payment amounts. Most remain silent, amnesia always being the lesser of two evils when caught between a copper and a vengeful bootlegger. They've had even less success with the hoteliers and saloon owners who see no upside by ratting on one of the more powerful and connected men in Philadelphia. Solidarity amongst thieves.

"Do we have enough to bring him in, Sam?" Colonel Butler asks the District Attorney.

"Frankly, I'm not sure, Smedley. We have some evidence, if it sticks. And if it were anyone but Mickey Duffy, I'd say yes. But you know that he's going to fight this. He has the judge in his pocket, and a team of sharp lawyers working on his behalf."

"Surely you're not afraid of losing, Sam?"

"No, just realistic on our chances. We don't want to be hasty or premature. We'll not have too many opportunities at this. With one shot, I'd like a stronger case."

"Captain Copeland." The colonel's words crack through the captain's reverie. "Is it possible to build a stronger case?"

"No," says the captain. But at the same time Joe answers in the affirmative. Joe bows his head, self-conscious for having spoken out of turn.

"Captain? Which is it? Yes? No?"

"Those moonshiners aren't reliable. They probably sell to a bunch of different bootleggers, for all we know." Captain Copeland rubs his hands together. "For that matter, maybe they're supplying the speaks and blind pigs directly. There isn't anything that directly connects Duffy to the list, or to the stills, or the saloons."

"If we could get someone inside Mickey's gang to come forward?" The District Attorney offers his suggestion.

"Not bloody likely," says Copeland.

"Constable? What do you have to say?" Colonel Butler's right eyebrow is raised.

"Yes, Kelly, what do you have to say?" Captain Copeland's lip curls as he questions Joe.

"Sirs, I think that this is the strongest link we've had yet to Mickey and his gang. The information we've gathered has been good. This could be our best chance to bring him in. Once the operators and owners see we have him behind bars, their memories may improve."

"I appreciate your frankness, Constable," says Butler.

Joe can feel the heat of Captain Copeland's glare.

"Captain, let's bring Mr. Duffy in. Sam, we'll keep investigating and build you a stronger case. I'm loathe to turn this over to the Feds. At this point, there's no evidence that Mickey's transporting alcohol across state lines, so the FBI doesn't have to be involved. The Governor himself has confidence in me and this force to clean up Philadelphia," says Butler. "And we should let those reporters know we have him. I want the good people of Philadelphia to see we're making progress with these criminals."

The captain nods reluctantly.

"And, Captain, when you bring in Mr. Duffy, don't be too hasty to let his lawyers find him. What's the phrase you police use? 'Take him round the horn?'" The District Attorney closes his file folder.

"Thank you, gentlemen," Colonel Butler says. "Constable, walk with me back to the office, as I have another matter to discuss with you."

Captain Copeland's attention is drawn to his junior and senior officers. Joe grimaces at the thought of repercussions.

In the privacy of his office, Colonel Butler takes his place behind his desk. "You have some concerns about the Duffy case, Constable Kelly?"

Joe stands at attention.

"Sir, I believe that everyone here wants to bring the strongest case forward. And the District Attorney is right when he says it will be a difficult charge to make stick, given the circumstances, and...well... Mr. Duffy has a certain, *uhm*, standing in the community at large. The legal community especially."

"You suspect that Duffy has 'special standing' with the officers in this precinct?"

"It's like he's a step or two ahead of us, sir. Like he knows what we're going to do next. Anybody we bring in, his lawyers can spring that same day. The judges won't give us search warrants. He's either got a lot of cops on his payroll, or he's got the luck of the Irish. And we know it's not that. Before he changed his name to Duffy, it was Cusiak." Joe manages a grin.

"Duffy's Polish?"

"He is, sir. So, I think we can eliminate Irish luck."

There is a shared smile.

"Sit down, Constable. We're completely out of view here. It's just us."

Joe follows orders.

"Do you have any thoughts about how we can get someone from inside the Duffy gang to come forward with information we can use in court?" Colonel Butler asks.

Joe clasps his hands tightly in his lap. He weighs how much danger he can put Maggie in, the risk of Eugene in the house, and his desire to please the colonel. "I think I know where the list came from, sir. I might be able to get that person to come forward."

"Good work, son. I knew I could count on you. It would be monumental if we could do more than just bring Duffy in. It would silence the mayor and other critics, and really give Philadelphia a reason to be hopeful. They always say it's darkest before the dawn. Now that we have to the goods on Duffy, maybe this long, dark night is coming to an end."

Joe sits even straighter.

"Constable, I've been impressed with your dedication to duty. I want you to be directly involved in bringing Duffy in, and in his questioning. If you have any concerns that 'his standing in the legal community' is going to get in the way of a conviction, I want you to discuss it with me personally. And keep a sharp eye on Copeland. He may be your superior officer, but I am his. Am I clear, Constable Kelly?"

"Yes, sir."

Once the colonel's door is closed behind him, his shoulders slump. Joe needs to clear his mind. Heading out the front door of the precinct, he walks briskly. With every step he attempts to figure out a way to get all the players to cooperate. And, most importantly, how to keep Maggie safe.

He does a second lap around the station and reaffirms his loyalty to the colonel, and his dedication to serving in his war against the bootleggers. To get caught in the middle of the colonel's other battle with the mayor and the republican political machine is dangerous. He comes face to face with the precinct's entrance, squares his shoulders, and strides with decidedly forceful steps along the hallway.

Chapter 48

Mickey and Eugene had been behind closed doors for most of the morning in the small corner office upstairs, until about half an hour ago when Eugene had left clutching his briefcase and armfuls of papers.

The crew are having a quiet day at the warehouse. There is not as much back and forth to do since their suppliers have dried up. They are stacking crates of liquor from Max Hassel's warehouse that had arrived earlier. They'll deliver them to speakeasies and hotels later.

Alfred's changing the tires on one of the Packards. Next to him, a radio plays. Henry Mercer and John Bricker are deeply immersed in a card game, bottles of beer at their elbows. Fingers is also there, cleaning his gun. Gus leans on the two back legs of his chair, feet on the table. His hat is pushed back, and he chews on a match while he reads the sports section.

And at the head of the table, Mickey sighs at the legal documents that lie in front of him.

"Everything okay, Mick?" Henry puts down his cards.

"It's just this hotel deal." Mickey holds a stack of papers sent over by his lawyer. "Eugene and I were supposed to go to the bank tomorrow, but I'm going to cancel. I hate the thought, but we'll have to put it on the backburner until we get that inventory moved. Until then, cash is gonna be tight."

"We're okay though, right Boss?" asks Porter, one of the bootleggers sorting orders. The guys helping him pause.

"We're fine. This is short term, boys." Mickey addresses the entire workforce. "Only short term changes. Then we climb back aboard the gravy train again."

Porter smiles. *"Toot-toot."*

"Why don't you and me go grab some lunch?" Henry asks. "Give all this hotel stuff a rest."

"Hands up. Stay where you are. " An officer charges through the warehouse door. Joe and a dozen armed police with guns drawn follow him in. Gus tips over in his chair, landing on the dirt floor, newspaper pages fluttering around him. Henry and John stand and reach for their guns.

Captain Copeland moves to the front of the group and barks, "You heard him, hands up, gentlemen. Hands up."

Mickey looks at Copeland calmly. "Good afternoon, Captain Copeland. What brings you to our neck of the woods on this beautiful day?"

Captain Copeland pulls a paper from his pocket. His hands trembled slightly. "Michael Joseph Cusiak, also known as Mickey Duffy, I have a warrant for your arrest for violations to the Volstead Act: the manufacture of illegal alcohol, the sale of illegal alcohol, and the distribution of illegal alcohol." Captain Copeland folds the paper and puts it back into his pocket. "Cuff him, boys. Mr. Duffy, you're coming with us."

"Oh, I don't think so, Captain Copeland." Mickey's smile is almost charming.

"Oh, I do think so." Colonel Butler strides into the warehouse, his scarlet cape swirling. "We're taking you to the precinct for a chat. Right now, Mickey."

Two officers spring forward and pull Mickey from his chair. Henry moves toward him, but Mickey gives him a warning look. "It's okay, Henry. I won't be long. Obviously, a small misunderstanding. While I'm gone, give my attorney, Arthur Werblun, a call. Have him meet me at the station."

"You can tell Mr. Werblun not to hurry. We're going to be taking Mickey around the horn so to speak. It could be a while," Colonel Butler says.

"Sure thing, Mickey. I'll call Art right away," Henry says.

"Oh, and Henry. Call Edith, too. Let her know I might be late for dinner."

* * * *

Maggie has given the bathroom a good scrub. With Tommy and three gentlemen lodgers, it's a regular chore. Her foot is barely on the last stair when Frank is suddenly there.

"Grab your hat and coat, Maggie. Edith needs you," says Frank.

"Inspector? Has she had a relapse? She seemed fine yesterday when I called 'round."

"No, it's not that. The police have just arrested Mickey and taken him in."

"Already? Poor Edith, this will be hard for her to take, maybe even cause a setback." Maggie slips on her coat and settles her hat in place.

"There's more. I saw Eugene earlier this morning. At the warehouse. He's working for Mickey, just like we thought."

"Inspector, no. That's terrible. I was holding out hope that there was a reasonable explanation." Maggie frowns. "I can't have him here. Not with Tommy. A gangster under my roof. No way."

"I agree. But let's make sure Edith's okay first, and then we'll figure out how to deal with Mr. Smith."

* * * *

It's much later when Maggie enjoys an after-dinner cup of coffee in the living room with the Inspector. "It was a very quiet dinner table tonight, Inspector, just Archie, Tommy, and I. At least Joe had the courtesy of letting me know he wouldn't make it, but I've not heard anything from Eugene since he left early this morning."

"I imagine Joe will be busy with questioning Mickey now that he's been arrested. How is Edith?"

"She's stronger than we think. Edith's familiar enough with Mickey's legal troubles, and it's giving her something to focus on. When I left her, she was heading to the precinct with bail money." says Maggie.

"It will be interesting how it plays out. I hope we've got some luck on our side and bail is refused." says Frank.

"Given the amount of bribe money changing hands, luck may have little to do with it. Although, given the notoriety of the case, surely the judges and lawyers will have to at least pay lip service to the law?"

"It's hard to say. Never underestimate the enemy."

"You're right. I guess we'll just have to wait and see. I'm glad that at least our part of it is done and things can get back to normal around here," Maggie says.

"Normal? I'm not so sure," says Frank. "The case against him is not as strong as I'd like. And I have a bad feeling about how confident he is. They may have got Mickey on bootlegging charges, but we still don't know who killed Oskar. There's still more work to do."

"That's true, but it's a huge step in the right direction. And maybe information will come out during his questioning about what happened to that poor boy the night at the warehouse."

"And Eugene? Now we've confirmed he's part of Mickey's payroll, what do you want to do?" Frank asks.

"I meant to tell you. When Joe sent word about dinner he also said that they'd picked up Eugene for questioning. Which must have been before they arrested Mickey? Do you think Eugene told them anything? Maybe the reason he's not here is that Joe has him in jail?"

"It's hard to say. We need more information from Joe," Frank says.

"When he gets home, I'll ask Joe about both Mickey and whether he'll be arresting Eugene. If not, I'm going to talk to Eugene as soon as I see him. Maybe even tomorrow at breakfast. I've never been easy with him here, since the day I found that list. Joe convinced me to let him stay so as not to tip our hand, but now that everything's in motion, he has to go. I don't want him to suspect that I know anything about the list. However, he'll know that Joe knows that he works for Duffy, and may expect that Joe will say something to me."

"Why not do it right away?" Frank asks.

"Eugene's not home and neither is Joe. I'm not comfortable doing it without Joe being here," Maggie says.

"Of course, you're right. Your safety and Tommy's is paramount. You should have Joe in the house when you tell Eugene to leave," says Frank.

"Hopefully, Joe'll be home soon. I heard him come in late last night and leave early this morning."

"I imagine they're keeping him busy. The arrest of the King of the Bootleggers will be quite a feather in the colonel's cap, and I'm sure all the officials on Mickey's payroll are scrambling. It is worrisome about Eugene, though," says Frank.

Maggie glances at the clock on the mantle.

Frank follows her eyes. "With the exception of Eugene, I think we should take a few moments and bask in the satisfaction of a case concluded. You've earned a rest, my dear. It has been rewarding to see it all come together. And I think that young Kelly has done an admirable job."

"I know that you've had your doubts about him, Inspector, but he's just a rookie. He's handled himself well the past few days; you have to give him credit for that."

"Oh, I do. Yes, Constable Kelly has all the markings of becoming a fine policeman. A bit more seasoning and he'll be a credit to the force."

"Given the nature of the force, I'm not sure that's the high praise it used to be."

Chapter 49

The breakfast dishes are stacked to be washed; Maggie has her back to them. Tommy and Archie Mansfield left earlier. It's now been two days since they arrested Mickey and still no sign of Eugene. Looking exhausted, Joe's nursing his coffee.

"You must have gotten home late, Joe. I stayed up late myself, hoping to ask you for help."

"More like 'home' early this morning. I'm sorry you waited up."

"Joe, I'd like to evict Mr. Smith, but I'd like you here when I do it. He's not been home since early yesterday morning, but I'd like to do it as soon as he does come in."

"We had him down at the precinct for questioning yesterday, but had to release him. He's not been home at all?" Joe shakes his head, frowning. "I should have expected that, but with everything going on and my crazy hours the last few days, it completely slipped my mind. When I didn't see him around at breakfast, I just presumed he'd left already."

"He'll have to come back, surely? All his things are here," Maggie says.

"I'm sorry, Maggie. We should have put an officer on him to keep track of him. Since we arrested Mickey yesterday, it's been a madhouse at the station. We've spent hours interviewing Duffy, moving him from precinct to precinct so that his lawyers can't find him and spring him. They're back at it today."

Maggie joins Joe at the table. "Will the charges stick?"

"The DA and the colonel are worried he'll walk. Again. We don't have the original journal entries and Eugene wasn't very forthcoming when we talked to him. He knows we don't have anything concrete, just the list we made based on your original journal pages. And we don't have many confessions from the shiners and speakeasy owners we talked to."

"But he doesn't know that you got the information from me, right?"

"No, we didn't say anything about where it came from." Gripping his coffee tightly, Joe takes a deep breath and looks Maggie in the eye. "Maggie, it's my turn to ask you for help. I know it's asking a lot, but would you come and sign a statement about finding the list? We need to connect that list in Eugene's pocket to Duffy."

The color drains from her face. "You want me to come to the precinct and give a statement? That probably means I'll be obliged to testify at a trial. Joe, I'll not survive. Mickey will make sure of that."

"I wanted to keep your name out of it, Maggie. I really did. But we have to get Eugene to talk. He's the closest link we have to Mickey, however it's doubtful he'll tell us what we need to know unless he's backed into a corner. You're the only person that can at least prove the list came from Eugene, which would give us reason to arrest him and send him away for a very long time. That keeps him from coming back here, which is what you want. And if we can plug a few holes in our case, we can put Mickey away for a long time, too. That's the best way to keep you and Tommy safe."

"Like Mickey wouldn't be able to reach out from prison and tap me behind the ear? I read the newspapers, Joe Kelly. I'm not some naive patsy. I know what you're asking me to do, and what the risks are to me and Tommy. That wasn't the deal, Joe. When I gave you that information, you promised that no one would have to know where it came from."

"Mickey will be focusing on Eugene, who'll hopefully be singing like a canary. Mickey won't care how the list got from Eugene Smith to the police. You just delivered the mail. Nobody holds the postman responsible."

Maggie throws her hands in the air. "Joe, the phrase I'm worried about is 'don't shoot the messenger'. Mickey is going to rain down a torrent of retribution and revenge. There is no way he's going to let anyone come at him without consequences. I won't do it, Joe. I can't."

Wide-eyed, Maggie looks at Frank, who has been standing in the corner of the kitchen, following the conversation. He's none too happy at the turn of events, but nods in agreement with Joe's reasoning. A pair of coppers.

"It's true," says Frank. "Joe's right. They need your testimony. Unfortunately."

Maggie turns and stares out the kitchen window. Her mind is swirling with the implications.

"I don't want Eugene Smith back in this house. I don't want to see his face. I don't even want to clean his room and pack his things."

"No problem. I'll do it," says Joe.

"Joe, that list is a loaded gun. I don't want it pointing at me, okay?"

"Maggie, if we don't tie Eugene to the case against Mickey, then it all falls apart. And we can't get to Eugene without you, because you found the list in Eugene's pocket. If you're serious about putting Mickey away, then you'll have to come forward and testify. I promise you'll have police protection."

Maggie interrupts. "Yeah, right. The police will protect me from Mickey Duffy. What a laugh. Most of them work for him. I don't understand why you don't just raid Eugene's office and take the rest of the ledgers. There should be more than enough evidence there for you to win your case."

"We did that and got mountains of paper. We have the deeds for the warehouses, for hotels, and saloons, but they're all in other people's names, including the name of your pal, Edith Duffy. We need some kind of bargaining chip to force Eugene to roll over on Mickey, and he won't do that unless he knows that we can put the list in his pocket. Come on, Maggie. You gotta do it."

"I don't 'gotta do' anything, Joe Kelly, except put a roof over Tommy's head and protect him as best I can."

"Look, I have to get back to the precinct. Just think about it, okay? I want to find Eugene and pick him up again so that we're ready if you decide to help us. We really need you, Maggie."

* * * *

Maggie leans forward in her chair. After Joe had left, she and the Inspector had moved into the living room to finish the conversation. "What do you think, Inspector?"

"I think it's dangerous, Maggie. I remember we talked about risk when you found the list. And even before that, when we first decided to make Mickey pay for what happened to Oskar. But back then, the risk was abstract. Now it's real. Make no mistake, word will get out about your connection to the list. I'd be surprised if it hasn't already."

Frank looks at Maggie solemnly. "And when Mickey finds out that you found the list, and it will be 'when' not 'if', you're going to be in a very bad spot, my dear. You and Tommy both. Despite what Joe says, Mickey will blame you for all his troubles. So, you have to figure out what to do. And then you'll have to have the courage to act on it."

Maggie opens her mouth, eager to speak.

"Wait," says Frank. "I want you to think on this carefully. I know you always scoff at the comfort and inspiration I find in General Bonaparte's words, but he has been with me through some tough spots. The man had insightful observations about battle and leading men. And it's as if he anticipated our need right now when he said 'Courage isn't having the strength to go on, it's going on when you don't have the strength'."

"Oh, you and General Bonaparte are impossible to argue against." She twists the edge of her skirt. "I'd like to look the other way, Inspector, but I can't unlearn what I know."

Frank nods at her encouragingly.

"Inspector, I'm so tired of living like this; of hearing about good people arrested or killed; of good families left behind to cope; of worrying about walking to the grocery store or taking Tommy to the barber. It's time for me to find the courage to take the next step."

"I admire you, Maggie. You have grown so much. It's a weighty decision for you to make. Heaven knows, I do not have the substance to advise you what to do."

"I haven't noticed it stopping you from giving advice before," Maggie says with a teasing grin. She sits taller. "We've been working to put a case together against Mickey for a while. I'm not sure whether I thought much about what would happen after the case was made, but we're here now."

"We are that," says Frank.

"It will be a good day for this city, a good day for this family when that man is put away."

Frank reaches over to pat her hand, then remembers himself and withdraws the gesture.

"I know, Inspector. I feel the same way. Thank you for everything that you've taught me, for everything that you've done."

The clock ticks. Tommy will not be home until lunchtime. The silence envelops the ghost and Maggie Barnes.

"It's almost comforting," says Maggie. "This sense of calm before the storm."

"While we're talking about the future course of our investigation, there is something that has been weighing on my mind. It worries me, Maggie, to see how immersed you've become in the case."

"I'm sorry, Inspector. I'm not following. I'm committed, but isn't that a good thing?"

"Yes, of course. But when we first met that night, when you were sitting on your veranda, I was so excited to be able to have a conversation with you I got caught up in the potential of what that might mean to me. I got swept away in my zeal to pursue justice, the excitement of being back in harness with an important investigation. Selfishly, I didn't think about the consequences you might have to undergo."

"Do you mean the bombing? I've put that behind me, Inspector. Don't worry."

314

"Yes, that. But it's not just the physical risks. In fact, those are the easiest to guard against. What I'm referring to are the effects of walking in the world of criminals, being part of the violence, seeing firsthand the effects of the lawlessness. It changes a person, Maggie. It's unavoidable."

"And you think it's changing me?"

"I've asked you to take on a role that places you in the center of all this ugliness. With no training, little support or backup. It's not fair to you. It hardens a person. In order to deal with the violence and crime scenes that come with policing, one develops calluses—a tolerance to it. I've noticed how it is affecting you and, importantly, 'not' affecting you. I think Joe's noticed it, too. You're becoming very comfortable moving through the darkness of this new world, more comfortable and familiar than I think is good for you."

"Why is it okay for Joe to be doing this and not me? Is it because I'm a woman and you don't think I can do it?"

"No, no. Not that at all. Joe's had training and he's got an entire police force around him. Men who have walked in his shoes, trodden that path before him. He can talk to them, lean on them if he needs to. You're alone, Maggie."

"But I'm not alone, Inspector. I have you."

"Thank you, my dear. But I am a grizzled old veteran who has forgotten what it's like to see violence for the first time. Those calluses? I have them in spades. I'm not indifferent, but I see things differently at this stage of my career."

"Forewarned is forearmed. I see your point, but I'm not going to let that deter me. We'll keep going forward, together."

The clock counts out ten minutes. Companionable silence fills the room. Dust motes dance in the rays of a sunbeam coming from the window.

"Maggie!"

Maggie startles, clutching at the arms of the chair. "Goodness, Inspector."

"Maggie, I think I know a way where we can get Eugene to talk and you can remain safe," Frank says.

"I'm sorry? You what?"

"It's not the list itself that's crucial, but rather the leverage it provides so that the police can get Eugene to supply eye-witness testimony to Mickey's operations. Joe will have to be the one who came across those papers of Eugene's. It's being caught red-handed that will make Eugene spill the beans about Duffy."

"But why would Joe be in Eugene's room?"

"Because, and this may come as a surprise to some, Constable Kelly has excellent investigative skills. He suspected Eugene Smith was working with the Duffy crew, and he was looking for evidence to prove it." Frank folds his hands over his stomach with a satisfied smile.

"That's brilliant, Inspector. But why wouldn't Joe have thought of that as a way of pressuring Eugene without involving me? It's so obvious."

"Well, there are a couple of reasons. First, no one knows the two of you are friends. He is a lodger in the home of a landlady named Mrs. Barnes. And he happens to suspect a fellow lodger."

316

"That's true," says Maggie. "Next?"

"Joe is an honorable man. He'd never want to take credit for something he didn't do. He is the type of man who wants to earn the honour of putting Mickey Duffy away. This kind of arrest could break the hold of these bootleggers in Philadelphia. It would make Joe's career, but he will have a hard time taking all the glory if he doesn't feel he's earned it. He knows he didn't find the papers. You did. He's not thinking about the whole picture. His subconscious won't take credit for something he didn't do, and his reasoning skills haven't let him see that this may be a solution."

"It'd be so much better for me if he could say it was him suspecting a fellow lodger," says Maggie.

"We need to present that to him. To bring an evil man to justice is every policeman's dream. Joe believes the glory and recognition belong to you because you are the one that discovered the papers. His natural honesty has blurred his vision to see the danger you'll be in."

"Yes, I see that," Maggie says, nodding slowly. She has always admired Joe's integrity.

"And, importantly, if this should go to trial, and Joe is asked on the stand about who found the papers, he'd have to commit perjury. And that will be going against everything that he believes in."

Maggie sits back in her chair, frowning. "Perjury. I hadn't thought of that. Joe will never agree to lie in court."

"Perhaps we can convince him. What we need to do, Maggie, is to get him to believe, as we do, that a justice system controlled by bootleggers and greed is nothing more than a sham. That he would not be lying to Lady Justice herself, because Lady Justice has been kidnapped and held hostage in Philadelphia. In fact, he'd be helping free her. The version of Joe finding the paper will protect you and Tommy. It gets Eugene to testify. And it builds a solid case against Duffy. In this case, lying is the only honorable thing to do."

"I'm convinced, Inspector, but can we convince Joe? Lady Justice may be kidnapped but I don't know that he'd trade her release for perjury. It's a longshot for sure. Let me make a quick sandwich for Tommy's lunch and leave him a note. And then let's go to the precinct and talk to Joe."

Chapter 50

The door of the warehouse bangs hard against the wall. "Where the hell is he?" Mickey's face is mottled red in rage, his hands curled into fists at his side.

Every one of Mickey's men freeze, waiting for a clue about who he is looking for.

"Smith," Mickey barks. "Where the hell is he?"

Some of the men look upward to the stairs and the overhead corner office. Eugene steps out, clutching the doorframe for support.

Gus, who had driven Mickey back from the courthouse, leans in to quietly update Henry Mercer, who is standing next to him. Henry listens intently to the extraordinary circumstances in the courthouse that morning.

"They kept at Mickey the whole night they took him in, all day yesterday, and again all last night, but he told them nuthin'," Gus says. "This morning, they haul him before Judge Winter—"

"He's one of ours, right?" Henry interrupts.

"Yeah. So the prosecutor starts laying out the case and talking about the list. Winter asks to see the list. There's no list to be found. They look high and low. It's gone like it was never there." Gus snaps his fingers. "Poof. Magic. Of course, Copeland had to admit to the judge that nobody on the list had talked either, so they're up a creek. Winter, who had by this time been prepped by Mickey's lawyers, brought the gavel down and threw the case outta court. Mickey was there for less than an hour. Basically in and out. Free to go."

"So, what's all this then?" Mercer says, nodding to Eugene, who is cowering, midway down the stairs.

"Copeland says the list came from Eugene. And because of that list, they was able to shut down our supply of liquor and harass the speakeasys and the rest of the joints selling the stuff. All this trouble we've been having is because of that damn list."

Mickey walks over to where Eugene is standing and shoves him hard against the staircase. Eugene grabs the bannister to keep from falling. Mickey grabs hold of Eugene's tie like a noose and drags him the rest of the way down the stairs.

"What the hell were you thinking? That I wouldn't find out? That you could get away with it?" When he gets Eugene to the bottom step, he flings him to the floor. Eugene curls up on the dirt floor of the garage, whimpering.

Mickey gives him a sharp kick in the stomach and turns away. "Put him in that chair. We're going to have a talk."

Porter and Fingers dump Eugene onto a chair near the head of the table where Mickey usually sits.

Mickey stands over him and lights a cigar. He flings the lit matches at Eugene. Eugene flinches. "So, you rat, why don't you tell me how the City's finest got a hold of my books?"

The men shift shocked faces to Eugene. They form a circle behind Duffy, arms crossed and legs spread. Has he ratted them out, too?

Eugene babbles denials.

Eugene looks at him with pleading eyes. Mickey leans closer and gently brushes the hair from Eugene's forehead.

The punch to Eugene's face contains Mickey's fury of the betrayal and what it may cost him. Blood spurts from Eugene's nose. Mickey pulls a handkerchief from the breast pocket of his suit and wipes his fingers. "Okay, Smith. Think harder. How did the cops get some of my books? Copeland told them they came from you. How did they get those pages, you bastard? *Skurwysyn!*"

Mickey grabs Eugene's lapels, pulling him half out of the chair. He shakes him violently then throws him back in the chair.

"I didn't give them to the cops, Mickey, I swear. Joe Kelly must have got them. Remember, I told you that we rented rooms in the same house?" Eugene is babbling, eyes wild.

"Yeah, and I remember telling you to keep an eye on him." Mickey slaps him again. Blood sprays.

"Please, Mickey. It wasn't me. The police hauled me in the same day they got you, but I didn't tell them nothin'. Nothin'. They let me go and I've been hiding here outta sight ever since. Right boys?"

Eugene looks around the room, eyes wild. No one says anything. "I didn't give them the papers, Mickey. They came from Kelly. Or maybe it was the landlady, Mrs. Barnes. Copeland said she was at the station right before the papers showed up. I don't know how the cops got them, but it wasn't me. You gotta believe me." As Eugene shakes his head in denial, blood flies from his nose. His eye is swelling shut. He slumps in the chair.

"So, the dame finds them in your room and turns them over to the cops. Or maybe the cop finds them in your room. That's a lot of people in and out of your room, Smith. How'd any papers get in your room in the first place? Eh? How'd they wind up there?"

Eugene stares at him like a cornered rat. "I must have put them in my pocket, Mickey. But it wasn't me who turned them into the cops. Not me. That copper must have snooped, or the landlady found them and gave them to him."

Mickey stares at the battered man. "What a sad excuse you are. Hiding behind some dame's skirts. It couldn't be the dame. They were accounting papers. What would she know about accounts and bootlegging? She wouldn't even know what the list meant. She's just a broad. It had to be the cop. Taking stuff out of the office? That's why we have a separate place for you to work. You idiot. *Idiota!*"

Mickey slaps him, first on one side of his head then the other. "You were supposed to be keeping an eye on him. Instead, he was busy watching you. He probably suspected you all along. Because the thing is, I learned last night that the copper's bragging to Copeland that he's the one that found the papers. He's the big hero. What a pile of shit this is." Mickey roars his frustration to the heavens.

Mickey takes a breath and then turns to Henry. "Smith, you are nuthin but a rat. What do we do about rats, Mercer?"

Henry Mercer rubs the scar on his forehead. "We gotta get rid of the rats to keep things nice and tidy."

Mickey turns his back on Eugene and steps away. Mickey doesn't even flinch at the sound of the gunshot. "Rat poison. Works every time," he says to no one in particular.

Mercer walks over to Mickey. "I hear you didn't even get a chance to take your hat off in court."

322

"A piece of cake," Mickey says. "Not much of a case when there ain't any witnesses and the evidence disappears. It's gonna cost a bit more dough for the judge though, greedy bastard."

Mercer shrugs, not surprised by the judge's opportunism.

Mickey jerks his head back toward Eugene's crumpled body. "Take him for a swim and then come back. We've still got loose ends to tie up in his story. And we're going to have to come up with a plan for Copeland. He's just not pulling his weight, Henry."

Chapter 51

Maggie hurries along the sidewalk. The past three days have been frantic. The whole household has been in an uproar ever since Mickey was hauled in. She's been worried about Eugene showing up, although there's still no sign of him. Then there had been the upsetting scene in her kitchen yesterday morning when Joe had asked that she testify. After that, the trip to the police station to talk to Joe about the plan that 'he' claim to have found the list. Joe had taken some convincing but eventually agreed to do it.

And then there was Edith. The longer Mickey stayed in jail, the more overwrought she became. She was spending her days with lawyers at the police station and then stopping by Maggie's on her way home.

Maggie is glad that everything is coming to a head and this will soon be behind her. Joe had left word that Mickey was going to be in court most of the morning today. She was late finishing chores at home and wants to get to the courthouse to see Mickey's initial appearance before the judge.

Joe had explained that it would be some months before the actual trial, but she couldn't resist seeing Mickey in handcuffs. Edith will probably be there as well, finally able to use the bail money she's been carrying around; if the judge allows bail. Maggie has decided that she'll sit with her, despite what others may think. Edith will need a friend.

She's mulling these thoughts, especially how to approach Edith, and doesn't notice a large black sedan beside her. A slamming car door startles her.

Instantly, she is seized by two men. "Let me go. Let. Me. Go." Maggie shouts, trying to gain someone's attention, but a hand covers her mouth. Her head bangs against the doorframe as she's shoved roughly into the back seat of the car.

Maggie goes for the door handle, but the man pushes her back against the seat. "Settle down," he growls.

She recognizes the voices, and then the faces, from the night she was called to Edith's house: Gus and Fingers.

Maggie lurches again for the car door handle. She lets out a blood-curdling scream, hoping that someone nearby will hear.

"Stop the car, Gus, and give me a hand here," Fingers says, as he withdraws a handkerchief from his pocket.

Gus pulls over, leaps out, a gunnysack in his hand. He throws open the back door and Gus holds Maggie's arms tight while Fingers tries to tie the handkerchief around her mouth. Maggie whips her head around and sinks her teeth into Finger's hand. She tries to drive her head against his forehead when he pulls back in surprise.

Fingers lunges at her again. "For Christ's sake, Gus, hold her still. The bitch bit me." Gus grabs Maggie's hair and yanks her head still. Fingers ties the handkerchief, giving it an extra tight tug as he makes the knot.

Gus throws the sack over her head and pushes her to the floor of the car. Maggie's arms are wrenched behind her, and the rough cord bites into her wrists as her hands are tied.

"Holy crap, she's a scrapper." Gus says, pulling away from the curb. Fingers grumbles, then brings his injured hand to his mouth. As she continues to thrash around on the floor of the car, he stomps on her back, leaving a foot firmly on top of her for the rest of the ride. Maggie grunts in pain, riding a wave of nausea.

Mickey has ordered them to grab me, but not kill me. Yet. I have time. He must still be in the courthouse. Maybe they're waiting for him? Won't he be sent to jail until the trial? Joe has told them he found the list. I hope Joe's okay. They're animals. Show no fear.

Lying on the rear floor of the car, Maggie feels it slow and then stop. Gus turns off the motor and gets out. The back car door opens and Fingers lifts his foot off her back. Despite her resolve to show nothing, a small moan escapes from Maggie.

"Okay, we're here. Easy now, no rough stuff."

He pulls her off the floor of the car like a puppet. Maggie hangs in Gus' arms, her legs unable to support her. Still hooded and gagged, she desperately tries to see through the fabric. *Where am I? What are they going to do?*

She's dragged so that her heels dig into the ground. Her back aches. Her body meets the frame of a hard chair. Someone pushes her forward and unties her hands, grabbing her arms tight, then wrenching them behind the chair and retying them.

Maggie shakes her head from side to side. The gag garbles her sound.

"Nice and comfy there, doll?" A man's voice. Others laugh. The voices wander away. *I am either alone or have a quiet guard.*

She smells grease, oil, metal, and dirt. In the distance, she hears men talking in the accents of her neighborhood. When she concentrates, and works to ignore the pain in her back, she pieces together a quilt of voices that talk about Mickey getting off: walking out of the courtroom without a scratch, lost papers, a payoff. No one is speaking about her, her presence, her fate. *Mickey's out. Oh, my God. What does that mean?*

Maggie hears the clinking of glass and, over the metal and oil, smells the sharp tang of alcohol. Occasionally, someone laughs. Another male discusses his son's school grades.

The Inspector has told her about Mickey's warehouse. *The warehouse. It must be. Is that where I am? Maybe the Inspector's here and can help in some way? But if he were here, he'd speak to me.*

"So, Boss, we got your special guest all nice and comfy over here," says a strong male voice just behind her. She flinches, startled at how close he is.

The hood is pulled from Maggie's head. She blinks and squints. Brick. More brick. Warehouse. Mickey's back to her. He's near a table with a group of men. Inspector Geyer is standing beside Mickey. He never takes his eyes off her. She stares back at him. "Be strong," he says. "Be really strong. You're a clever girl. Use your skills. Use your mind."

The man behind her yanks down the gag, leaving the wet cloth around her neck. She jerks her head around, glaring at Fingers.

Mickey pulls a cigar out of his pocket. Striking two matches against the table, he slowly puffs it to life and flicks the matchsticks into the ashtray on the table. Only then does he look in Maggie's direction.

"Mrs. Barnes, Mrs. Barnes." He shakes his head sadly. Looking at him, Maggie can see regret in his eyes. She starts to tremble. *He has made a decision then, and it doesn't look good for me.*

The room falls silent as Mickey's gang forms an audience behind him. They are also watching and waiting. Maggie recognizes a few of the men from her neighborhood. And from Oskar's funeral. Only some of the group will meet her eye. Of those that do, the hard, cold glint does nothing to reassure her. *I'm not going to be able to count on any help from them. Even though some of them know I helped Oskar's mother.*

"Mr. Duffy, please let me go. I'm not sure why I'm here."

"Mrs. Barnes, you're here because I believe you know something you shouldn't. And I aim to find out how you came by that information and how much you know."

He doesn't know that I gave the pages to Joe. Maybe he will let me go after all? Frank holds a finger to his lips and shakes his head. Maggie presses her lips tightly together and looks back at Mickey.

"How did the police get a part of my books? I was talking with our mutual friend, Eugene Smith, who says he didn't give it to them. And I'm inclined to believe a dying man's last words."

Maggie flinches. *Eugene is dead. Mickey killed him to find the leak.*

"A list? I don't understand." Maggie's voice quavers a bit. Her chin comes up. She looks Mickey in the eye.

"I've got people telling me different things, Mrs. Barnes. Nobody seems to know for sure how the police got that list. Was it you? The coppers say Constable Kelly brought it in. The very same man you brought to my house and that was sitting in my own living room."

"Joe's never mentioned a list." Maggie looks to the Inspector for some help or advice but he is gone. *Damn.* She is on her own.

Mickey plants himself on a chair in front of her. "Here's what I know, doll. Smith had the list of some accounting information. He 'lived' at your house. Then the police had the list. Kelly, for now, 'lives' at your house. Your house. You're the piece in the middle, Mrs. Barnes." Mickey leans close. "Now, I gotta plug this leak. A man in my business can't go around with the whole world knowing what he's up to. If it was Eugene, well, that's taken care of. Now we need to find out if it was you. What do you think, Henry?"

"Oh, I don't know, Boss. A dame? Especially when there's a copper living right there in the house?" Henry shakes his head.

"How about you tell me all about Constable Kelly, Mrs. Barnes."

Stall. Appear to cooperate. Inspector? "Joe Kelly, yes," Maggie says, nodding her head. "He's taken a room with me for about four months now." *That much he can easily find out if he doesn't already know. I've got to protect Joe.*

"You and he must be pretty tight if he came with you over to my house the other night. He looks out for you, right? He your boyfriend or something?" Mickey asks.

"Hardly. Joe's like a kid brother. He looks out for me and Tommy." *Oh, no. I just mentioned Tommy.*

"And Constable Kelly works with Colonel Butler, right? He's part of that damn Enforcement Unit One bunch?"

"I'm not sure. Colonel who? Constable Kelly doesn't talk about his work. I don't allow any of that talk in the house." *Eugene better not have said anything about all of Joe's stories at dinner, or I'm sunk. Was he killed here? Today? Will I be killed here? Today? What will they do to Joe? What will happen to Tommy?*

Mickey leans forward and shouts close to her face. "How did Kelly get a hold of my books?"

Maggie cringes. "I don't know, Mr. Duffy. Please. I just don't know." Real tears roll down her cheeks.

"My dilemma, Mrs. Barnes, is this someone has fed important information about my racket to the damn cops. They've closed me down. They've busted up my supply line. That hurts my wallet and my reputation around town."

Maggie blinks to keep the tears flowing.

"Now, we're going to get it up and running again very soon, but I need to make sure that there are no more rats. Stoolies are bad for business. So I need to do it in a way that shows other people that it would be a bad idea to talk to the police, very bad. Provide a bit of motivation to keep their yaps shut. You see my problem? I need to set an example."

It's like he's a regular businessman, not a kidnapper, murderer, and bootlegger. Keep the tears rolling? Play an Edith card? I can do this. I'm not dead yet.

"And I can't let you go. Which is too bad. Really." Mickey shrugs.

Not dead... yet.

"Although Edith'll be cracked up when she hears about your accident. I expect she'll get over it, though. She's a tough cookie, or at least she used to be."

"No, I have a son. Please. Tommy needs me."

"Oh, I'm sure we can find a place for Tommy. A bright lad like him. Say, hows about this? Just so you don't worry, I'll give Tommy to Edith to look after. Edith's crazy about kids. It'd make her happy, and you could go knowing a good friend is looking out for him."

That's just crazy. "Mr. Duffy, I won't say anything. I don't know anything. Why would you want to hurt me? It will only hurt Edith. Why don't you let me go?"

Mickey turns to Henry Mercer, who is standing close by. "Okay, that sounds like a plan. Now, what to do about Kelly?"

Joe's still alive. For now. Mickey can be arrested for my murder. He and Fanny can look after Tommy. Or Mother. She'd step in.

"Look, Mickey," Henry says. "If you really think you need to, poppin' off a dame is one thing. But you can't plug a cop, for God's sake. Sure, we might make a good show of it during those phoney raids, but Mickey, for real? Cop killers attract a lot of attention. And that'll be bad for business. You know what I'm sayin'?"

"So, you're telling me that we're going to bump this skirt off and let the cop, the real rat, walk? That hardly seems fair," Mickey says. "I'm telling you. It's all screwed up. The cop walks and Edith's friend dies."

"I dunno, Mickey. Why waste your time with her? The dame's not a threat. Maybe just slap her around a bit? Kelly's the real problem. Pluggin' her would probably just make sure he came gunning for you," Henry says.

I'm not going to die without a fight.

"Remember that night at the house, Mickey? I was there for Edith. When she needed me. And the next day. And I went over to be with her when you were arrested, so she wouldn't be alone. You can't do this to her. I'm one of the few friends she's got." Maggie pleads with Mickey.

He walks away. Several of his closest follow him up the stairs to the office.

Now what? Oh, where is the Inspector? The gag is yanked back over her mouth.

* * * *

Frank is in the front room of Maggie's house. She's at the warehouse but, in his current form, he can't help her. And he needs to get help to her, fast.

The front door slams and Tommy comes in, "Ma?" He walks past the doorway to the living room and into the kitchen. "Mother?" Frank hears the icebox door open and close. He goes into the kitchen.

Tommy grabs himself a leftover chicken leg.

Frank moves close to Tommy. He pictures Maggie tied to the chair in the warehouse. He focuses on Duffy standing over her shouting. Frank imagines all the things that Mickey and his gang could be doing to Maggie, and gathering all those fears together, he blows in Tommy's face.

Tommy drops the chicken leg and stiffens. The kitchen curtains flutter. The wave of alarm has reached him. "Mother?" he asks hesitantly, looking around the kitchen. "Mother, are you home?"

Frank imagines a cold dark place that could be Maggie's grave, and blows that image at Tommy. He imagines the dampness and the earthy smell. The rough texture of the pine box. Frank is startled, momentarily losing his concentration. It is his own grave he is remembering. That sharpens his dread even more as he sends another blast at Tommy.

The cups on the counter rattle in their saucers. Tommy turns and looks around the kitchen. "Hello, is someone here? Constable Kelly?"

Frank focuses.

332

"Weird." Tommy rubs the back of his head. "No cookies. No note. Maaaa?" Tommy yells.

Frank releases another blast. Pain. Fear. Panic. The cups fall, smashing on the floor.

Tommy races upstairs. "Mother? Constable Kelly? Where are you?" Doors open and slam shut.

Frank sends a bit more terror his way, and Tommy runs out of the house, slamming the front door. He races in the direction of the police station.

Frank, clutching his hat to the top of his head, runs beside him, sending dire thoughts into Tommy. They weave between pedestrians on the sidewalk "Hey." Random people shout. "Look out," voices call. Tommy is oblivious to the horns blaring and fist-shaking wagon drivers.

Tommy runs up the police precinct's front steps and bursts through the door. Frank follows closely.

"Whoa there, young fella," says the uniformed officer that Tommy has just plowed into.

"Sir, I need to speak to Constable Joe Kelly right away. It's a matter of life and death," he gasps.

"Now you just sit here, son, and catch your breath. Then you can tell me all about it."

"There's no time. My mother's in danger. Constable Kelly is my friend and he'll know what to do."

Tommy struggles against the restraining hold of the officer. "Now hang on there, you can't just go barging into the squad room. And I don't even know whether Kelly is at the station. He was downtown at the courthouse all morning. I don't know if he got back yet."

Tommy starts yelling for Joe.

"You calm down right now, hear?" The policeman gives Tommy a shake. "You sit yourself down and I'll see if I can find him."

Joe rounds the corner. "What's all the commotion—Tommy what are you doing here, pal? What's wrong? What's happened?"

"I don't know, but it's Mother. She's not home, and she's always home, or there's a note. And then the cups fell off the counter. I have a really bad feeling, Constable Kelly. I think that something really awful happened to her."

Joe's stomach does a slow roll. Maggie never did show at the courthouse. "Would she be late coming home from some errands?"

"No," Tommy shouts. He shoves Joe. "Something's wrong, you're not listening to me."

"Okay Tommy, be calm, son. We'll find out what's happened. You go back to the house and wait for her there, just in case she's late getting home. Hopefully, she's already back and getting supper started. I'll go check a few places and talk to some people. If she does come home, you run to the grocery store and call the precinct. They'll let me know she's home safe. I'll keep searching until I hear from you, I promise you. I've got this."

Tommy hugs Joe around the waist.

Frank watches Tommy leave the precinct. Joe whips around to a fellow officer, "Hey Bill, do we have any motorbikes in the garage? I need to sign one out for a few hours."

The desk officer grabs a clipboard in his hands. "There are two in the garage. Sign here."

Joe runs over to the garage and jumps on the back of the motorbike. He stands up and kicks down on the pedal. The engine roars to life and he takes off in the direction of the warehouse.

* * * *

Maggie's been dreaming of Tommy and Jack. Sleeping sitting up. Or maybe she has been killed? She's not sure. The metal stairs echo; a procession of men, led by Mickey Duffy, come down the stairs. He nods to the man behind her, who yanks the gag lower. Maggie tries to gather a bit of spit to moisten her mouth and get rid of the rough cotton threads that coat her tongue.

"Change of plan, Mrs. Barnes. You'd better go along with this, 'cause you're out of options. One, you were shopping. Or, two, you decided to go to the pictures. You were any place other than here."

Maggie nods, eyes wide in disbelief.

"And another thing. I want you to keep being friends with Edith. She likes you. But you pretend this never happened; a bad dream, okay. No way Edith should ever find out. It's business, not personal. Understand? If she wants me and her to go out dancing with you, you will go. You will never tell anyone of this afternoon."

Maggie stares at him. *It's like he is dismissing me from a job interview. He's so calm. Reasonable.* "Yes, I understand."

"I'm letting you off so that you can take a message back to that nosey cop. Make sure that Kelly understands that there are no more leaks, you hear?" says Mickey.

He leans in close, "Be real careful how you do that or I'll make sure your next lodger is the kind of guy who really watches over you and your kid."

Maggie gulps, her face pale. Mickey barks behind him to Gus and Fingers. "Take Mrs. Barnes home." He tips his hat to her and walks away.

"You're a lucky broad," Fingers says as he helps her into the back seat of the car. "Yup, one lucky broad."

"The guy's nuts about Edith. Do anything for her," says Gus.

Mickey watches as Maggie is driven away. He turns to Henry, standing behind him. "Never mix broads with business, Mercer. It's a real headache." He sighs, shaking his head.

* * * *

Joe parks the motorbike in the alleyway behind the warehouse and stands on a pile of wooden boxes to peer in a window. The place is deserted. He sees the chair with the dangling ropes, but there is no sign of either Maggie or Duffy. Joe walks around to the front of the building and gives the doors a good tug. They're locked tight. The place is deserted.

Fearing the worst, Joe climbs back on the motorcycle. He'll take a swing past Duffy's house, and then check on Tommy.

Chapter 52

Maggie sees Tommy peering out the front window as she gets out of the car. She hurries up the steps as he barrels out the front door. "Mother," he yells, rushing into her outstretched arms. "I was so scared. Where were you?"

Maggie kisses her son on the top of his head and looks at Frank, who is waiting just inside the door, beaming.

"*Ouch*," she says. "Not too tight, son. I slipped and hurt my back a bit."

"Your face is scratched and red. And your hands," he says.

"I put my hands down when I fell, but not fast enough," she says.

Tommy releases her as Joe's motorcycle screeches to a halt. "Maggie! Thank you Mary, Mother of God. Where have you been?" Joe shouts.

"Oh my goodness, you fellas. Silly me for losing track of the time. I was out running an errand. And when I knew I was going to be late, I hurried and slipped. I'm sorry you were worried, but I'm home safe and sound now."

Maggie leads her little parade into the house. "And goodness, you've missed your supper. You must all be starving. How about I get you something to eat? Are you hungry? Is Mr. Mansfield home from school yet? And Mr. Smith, is he here?" *Oh no, poor Eugene Smith. I think I'm going to be sick.* She staggers slightly, thinking of his murder.

"Are you okay, Mother?"

"Like I said, I slipped and hurt my back. That's why I'm so late. I sat a while at a stranger's house and waited until I felt a bit better."

"They were real nice to bring you home in their car," says Tommy.

"They sure were," says Maggie.

"I'm sorry you were worried today, sweetie. I'll make sure that it won't happen again."

"I'm okay, Mother. When you weren't here, I just got rattled for some reason. It reminded me of when Oskar disappeared, which got me thinking about guns and the river."

"That's some imagination you have, Tommy," she says.

Tommy sits happily at the kitchen table, finishing the piece of fried chicken from earlier. He keeps looking at his mother, reassuring himself that she is there and safe. Joe is also at the table, watching her. Frank leans against the back door and gives Maggie a relieved smile.

Keep it normal for Tommy's sake. Maggie avoids the looks of Frank and Joe, chatting on about a dress pattern she has seen on her imaginary errand. Habit gets her through preparing a quick dinner. Tommy's not long finished his chicken leg, and there's supper on the table.

Tommy's loud burp earns him a disapproving look from his mother and a grin from Joe. "I'm so glad you're home, Mother. I knew you were okay, but Constable Kelly was worried."

Joe laughs and gives him a wink. "You gotta watch out for the ladies when they get shopping, Tommy. It's easy for them to get lost and lose track of time in those big department stores."

Tommy gives his mother another tight hug and heads off into the living room to listen to his favorite radio adventure. Frank takes Tommy's chair, while Joe starts clearing the table. With the sound of the radio drama's intro music swelling, Joe leans in close to Maggie. "So, what really happened? Tommy came tearing into the police station saying that you were in danger. The shops aren't open this late. The truth this time, Maggie."

Maggie starts filling the sink with warm, sudsy water. "I'll tell you everything in a minute. But first, tell me what happened in the courtroom. How'd Mickey get off?"

"Oh, you heard about that, did you? It was a giant farce," Joe says. "There was no sign of Eugene or the list. Both have disappeared."

Maggie chokes back a sob. "Oh Joe, I think he's killed Eugene. Or had him killed."

"What?"

"In a minute. I want to know what happened in court."

Joe gives her a level look, but continues. "It was pretty much what you'd expect. Without any evidence, the DA wasn't able to bring forward a case. The Judge quickly threw everything out the window. Duffy had the gall to tip his hat to me and wink as he walked past me and out of the courtroom. Cheeky bastard."

Joe puts the dishes in the sink, and turns to Maggie. "Your turn. Where were you? What happened? Why do you think Eugene is dead? What did it have to do with Duffy?"

"Mickey Duffy wanted to talk with me, about those pages. He had me grabbed, right off the street."

"Damnit." Joe says. "He hurt you, didn't he?"

"I'm fine, just sore. He really didn't lay a finger on me. But I was tied up. He talked about Eugene like he was dead. He knows you and I are involved in finding those pages. Someone's been talking to him about what happens at the precinct. Joe, he was going to kill me. Then he decided 'dames' aren't that smart and since I was Edith's friend, he let me go. But not before he gave me a warning and a message for you to keep your nose out of his business. And he made it clear that it will be dangerous for Tommy and me if you don't."

Frank glowers at her from the table. "Maggie, no more risks. This time you were lucky, but next time?"

Joe grips the counter. "That bastard. Sorry for the cussing, Maggie, but he hurt you. The man's dangerous. Look, I wouldn't put you or Tommy at risk for the world, you must believe that. But I can't let Mickey get away with everything he's done: the racketeering, the bootlegging, the bombs, the violence. He's bribing cops and judges, threatening witnesses. He probably had Eugene killed. Heck, for all we know, he was the one that tossed wee Oskar in the river."

Joe turns his back on Maggie, his hands curled into fists at his side. "I'm going to have this out with him. He can't threaten you."

"And then what happens to Tommy and me? After you and Mickey have this big showdown?"

Joe turns to the doorway, leaving. "I've gotta go."

Maggie puts a hand gently on Joe's back to stop him. "Joe wait, let's think this through. I'm not frightened, and I'm not going to let him scare me off. But he has managed to get away with everything because he has all of Philadelphia in his pocket."

Maggie can feel the muscles in Joe's back stiffen. "What would happen if you only pretend to look the other way? And we wait for him to make another mistake."

"I'm no coward, Maggie. I don't run from a fight." Joe turns and rests his hands on Maggie's shoulders. He looks at her sternly. "And what's this 'we' business? You're not getting into the middle of this, Maggie Barnes. Me claiming credit for those pages was to keep you and Tommy safe. You can't keep putting yourself in harm's way. One day you'll run out of luck."

"I'm already in the middle of it," says Maggie. "More than you know. But we're smarter than Mickey. He's got a soft spot. And if he thinks he's won and you're cooperating, he'll get sloppy. He's going to make a lot more mistakes as he gets cockier."

Frank has risen and is pacing. He scowls at her. "I need you to be safe," he says. "Convince Joe. Convince him." He walks out of the kitchen.

"Mother, that wind is back. It just blew through the living room this time." Tommy shouts from the living room. Joe leaves the kitchen to check on Tommy and ensure the front door is shut.

Frank returns as soon as Joe leaves the kitchen. "How can you possibly think that you should continue to pursue Mickey Duffy? I saw you in the warehouse. You were hurt. You were almost killed," Frank says. He's standing arms crossed and legs wide.

"This is as much my fight now as anyone's, Inspector. The threats today were real. Tommy could be next."

Joe comes back into the kitchen. "Everything's good. I think he's still a bit rattled from the goings-on today."

Maggie aims her next remarks at Joe and the Inspector, who are the mirror image of each other, standing side-by-side with their arms crossed, scowling at her. "Look, Joe. Tommy and I won't be safe if it doesn't look like you're backing down. Let Mickey think you're playing by his rules now. It's a good strategy. That doesn't mean you actually have to stop investigating. I know you better than that. You swore an oath to protect the city. And Mickey is a threat. He's evil."

Maggie lays her hands flat on the table. "But that doesn't mean that you go charging over there to kick his door in. We tried that last time and look where it got us. Now, hear me out," Maggie says as Joe tries to interrupt her. "We need to take another run at Mickey and his crew. But we need to make sure that it sticks. The best way to do that is to have him let down his guard. To get overconfident. If he's sure of himself, he'll grow reckless and make a mistake, and we'll be ready."

"Good thinking, Maggie. Boney's always said that 'the art of war is to gain time when your strength is inferior'," Frank says, nodding. "Joe's apparent cooperation will give us time to lay a trap."

"Yeah, I get it. It gives us time to set a trap," says Joe.

"You're a remarkable woman, Maggie," Joe says. "I was expecting you to be afraid, and instead you're telling me you want to fight back."

"Darn right, I do. I don't run from a fight." Maggie punches the air with her fist.

Joe laughs. "Okay, slugger, I can pretend to back off, but I want you and Tommy safe. You stay out of it and let me and the police handle the dirty work."

"Yes, of course, Joe. But you know where to find me if you need me."

"And I'll be checking out the next lodger, after I clean out Eugene's gear," says Joe.

* * * *

Maggie sits in the living room and opens her journal. Cab Calloway is quietly crooning on the radio. Leaning her head against the chair back, she closes her eyes, suddenly exhausted.

"Should I go? Would you like to rest, Maggie?" Frank asks from his usual chair.

"I don't need rest, Inspector. I need restitution. I meant what I said in the kitchen, about Mickey and justice. It sounds like you don't think that I can do this. After all we've been through, how can you doubt me? I will do this alone if I have to."

"I've not said anything of the sort. In fact, I haven't had a chance to say anything at all. I know that you're a tiger when your son and home are threatened. Peace, woman."

"Then we're still after Mickey? And we're still partners, right?"

"Maggie, together we are an invincible force. Although I think that we might want to think about expanding our duo to a trio. Young Kelly has the makings of a fine policeman. He's still wet behind the ears, mind you, and will need lots of seasoning to be a great policeman, but he does have potential."

Maggie smiles. *The cranky old dog and the frisky pup working together.*

"You've come a remarkable distance, my dear. From that woman on the veranda, worried about keeping a roof over her head to where you are today, keeping a more dangerous wolf from the door. And you're doing it with skill and cleverness. You remind me of myself, many years ago."

Maggie inclines her head at the compliment. "Thank you, Inspector. It's an honor to work with you. It took a while but I feel confident now, being part of this investigation. Doing right, pursuing justice, protecting my family and community, it's who I am."

* * * *

Maggie climbs the stairs to tuck Tommy into bed. After everything that she's been through today, that cherished routine is a balm to her nerves. He's sound asleep. Pulling the covers up around his chin, she looks down at his freshly scrubbed face, the collar of his pajamas slightly askew, she feels a rush of protectiveness that almost overwhelms her. She will do anything to keep him safe.

Clever and brave. Imagine that. I can't let Tommy down, nor the Inspector. They're both counting on me. I'll need to be clever and brave so I can find a way to give Mickey Duffy what he's got coming to him. It's time to make this neighborhood and this city a safe place for our family.

Maggie's mood is high as she heads back downstairs to turn off the lights and lock up the house. *You know, I'm going to bob my hair. Don't be afraid to start over, my girl. There are seven days in the week, but Someday isn't one of them. I'll call the hairdresser first thing tomorrow.*

And speaking of Somedays, I think the Inspector and I had better start working on that trap.

The End

Wait!! Don't go.

There are two exciting opportunities you might want to check out.

Curious about the day that Edith and Mickey met?
Was it love at first sight or fireworks?
Only Bootlegger Readers Group subscribers get the exclusive novella, Destinations.

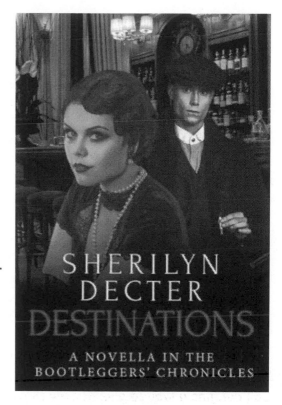

Go to https://sherilyndecter.com/destinations-landing-page and you can start reading today!

Book Two: TASTING THE APPLE
Release date: March 21, 2019

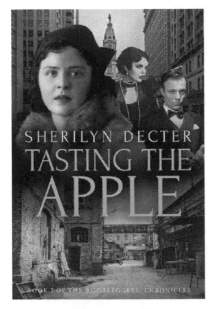

A young widow on the edge. A policeman back from the dead. Together, can they take down the city's most notorious bootlegger?

Philadelphia, 1925. With a son to raise and boarders to feed, Maggie Barnes is at her wit's end. But when a criminal element infiltrates the police force, the single mother puts her cares aside to help. As she tries to dig up dirt on bootlegger mastermind Mickey Duffy, Maggie realizes she can't take on the case alone...

Inspector Frank Geyer used to patrol the streets of Philadelphia a century before Maggie was born. As he attempts to clean up crime from beyond the grave, the spirit uses his Victorian sensibilities to fight back against lawbreakers. But with corruption throughout the police force, can the Inspector save his city and Maggie's livelihood?

With the roof leaking and the lawlessness spiraling, Maggie and Frank have one chance to take down a criminal and prevent the unthinkable...

Tasting the Apple is the second thrilling book in The Bootleggers' Chronicles historical mystery series. If you like strong female characters, stories inspired by actual history, and a touch of the paranormal, then you'll love Sherilyn Decter's tale of temptation and corruption.

Buy Tasting the Apple to experience the dark side of the Roaring Twenties today!

The Bootleggers' Chronicles series:

Innocence Lost (*Book One*)
Tasting the Apple (*Book Two*)
Best Served Cold (*Book Three*)
Watch Your Back (*Book Four*)
Come at the King (*Book Five*)

Coming in 2020
The Rum-Runners' Chronicles series

Author's Notes on the Bootleggers' Chronicles:

There is the romantic image of a writer, toiling alone in a garret, suffering for her muse. Of course, nothing could be further from the truth. I write all my books with a couple of bad dogs curled up at my feet in the comfort of my home, either in Canada or Mexico.

Standing behind me and peering over my shoulder (figuratively, at least) is my editor Marie Beswick-Arthur and her trusty partner in crime, Richard. She's been the most patient of editors and coaches and I certainly couldn't have done it without her. (Although I will keep insisting that draft ninety-seven wasn't necessary- LOL). I was also lucky to work with a great cover designer, Jane Dixon-Smith. She reached into my imagination and brought Maggie, Frank, and all the other rogues and heroes to life.

I also had a great team of beta readers for Innocence Lost: Kate Decter, Rachel Andrews, Jessica Decter, Kim Mitchell, Grant McPhail, Pat Britton, Karen Oliver, Chris Bouchard, Cindy Bouchard, Vickie Brown, Pat Carrabre, JoAnn Engels, Chris Pollard, Sarah Zama, and Nathalie Jottard. They were very kind and gentle in their comments to a first time writer.

Finally, where would I be without my husband Derry? He listened to the subtle difference of phrasing many, many times, provided his medical expertise for several key scenes, and kept me going when I was ready to give up.

Thank you one and all.

* * * *

Historians are vital for those who want to understand our present and get a sense of what the future may hold. They sift through the detritus of people's lives, pulling out facts and patterns and then reweaving them into a whole to provide us mere mortals with a path forward.

As appealing as that is, I am not an historian. I am a story teller. I take those same facts and attempt to reshape them into something that I hope you will find entertaining. My fictional characters get to live with factual characters.

These books are works of fiction and should never be considered anything but. While I've tried to stay true to the grand arch of history, occasionally I've moved an event that happened in one month into another so that it has a better flow through the story.

The Bootleggers' Chronicles series is based in Philadelphia during the 1920s. It is set during the time of Prohibition, an era that reshaped America. Many of the characters found between the pages of the Bootleggers' Chronicles were actual people, walking the streets and living their lives in Philadelphia during this time. I have been inspired by their individual stories, but have reshaped them to fit the plot of my books. Sometimes things happened in real life in a similar fashion to what I have laid out, and sometimes it is a complete fabrication.

In the character listing at the back of each book is a Wikipedia link to many of the real individuals, and I encourage you to do your own research into their fascinating lives. They were compelling characters, both fictional and historical, and it was an honour to get to know them all better.

Cast of Recurring Characters in the Bootleggers' Chronicles:

The Gangsters
Mickey Duffy (https://en.wikipedia.org/wiki/Mickey_Duffy) a fictionalized portrayal of a real bootlegger who was affectionately known as King of the Bootleggers in Philadelphia during the 1920s.

Married to **Edith Duffy**
(http://www.dvrbs.com/people/CamdenPeople-MickeyDuffy.htm)
Duffy crew includes:
Henry Mercer- chief lieutenant
"Fingers" McGee- muscle
Gus Toland- muscle
Porter- muscle
Eugene Smith- accountant, and lodger, Innocence Lost
Mike Malazdrewicz- accountant, and replacement for
Eugene in remaining books.
John Bricker- Mickey's driver and bodyguard
(http://www.dvrbs.com/people/CamdenPeople-
MickeyDuffy.htm)
Arthur Werblun- Mickey's attorney

"Boo-Boo" Max Hoff
(https://en.wikipedia.org/wiki/Max_Hoff_(mobster))
Hated rival of Mickey Duffy, bootlegger and boxing promoter
Crew includes:
Charlie Schwartz- chief lieutenant

Max Hassel
(http://www.berkshistory.org/multimedia/articles/beer-baron-max-
hassel/) Sometime rival, sometime partner of Mickey Duffy

Bailey Gang
Frankie Bailey
(http://philadelphiaencyclopedia.org/archive/bootlegging/)
James Bailey
Petey Ford (Philadelphia: Organized Crime in the 1920s
and 1930s)
Gilbert "Bert" Bailey
George "Skinny" Barrow
Louis "Fats" Barrish
Delores Bailey
Chicago Gangs
Al Capone (The Chicago Outfit)
(https://en.wikipedia.org/wiki/Al_Capone)

Bugs Moran (The North Side Gang)
(https://en.wikipedia.org/wiki/Bugs_Moran)

The Law

Colonel Smedley Butler- Director of Public Safety (aka Chief of Police) (https://en.wikipedia.org/wiki/Smedley_Butler)
Joe Kelly- member of the Philadelphia Police, and lodger
Ralph Copeland- Captain of Special Enforcement Unit Number One
District Attorney Samuel Rotan
Inspector Frank Geyer (https://en.wikipedia.org/wiki/Frank_Geyer as well as <u>Detective in the White City</u>, JD Crighton, 2017, RW Publishing House)

The Politicians

Mayor Freeland Kendrick
(https://en.wikipedia.org/wiki/W._Freeland_Kendrick)
William Vare (https://en.wikipedia.org/wiki/William_Scott_Vare)

The Community

Maggie Barnes (aka Peggy or Margaret)
Tommy Barnes
Archie Mansfield- match teacher, and lodger
Dick Beamish- reporter for the Philadelphia Inquirer, and lodger
Reg Littleton- car salesman, and lodger
Cordelia Gifford- Maggie's Mother
Fanny- Joe's fiancé
Jimmy- Tommy's friend

Made in the USA
Middletown, DE
15 March 2019